The Best of Berry

'Sometimes, at great garden parties, literary luncheons, or in the quiet of an exclusive gunroom, a laugh rings out. The sad, formal faces for a moment relax and a smaller group is formed within the larger. They are admirers of Dornford Yates who have found out each other. We are badly organised, we know little about ourselves and next to nothing about our hero, but we appreciate fine writing when we come across it, and a wit that is ageless united to a courtesy that is extinct.'

Cyril Connolly

JACK ADRIAN has written comic-strip scripts, science fiction, and war, horror and mystery stories under a variety of pseudonyms, and is an authority on popular and genre fiction, especially of the inter-War years. He has edited a number of anthologies and single-author collections over the past five years, of which the most recent are *Sexton Blake Wins* and *Crime At Christmas*, as well as two volumes of previously unpublished ghost stories by A. M. Burrage, *Warning Whispers*, and E. F. Benson, *The Flint-Knife*. He is at present writing a series of action-adventure novels for America, and putting together three anthologies of lost or forgotten weird, mystery and detective stories by major authors of the twentieth century.

THE BEST OF BERRY

Selected Stories of Dornford Yates
edited by Jack Adrian

J. M. Dent & Sons Ltd
London

This selection first published in Great Britain by
J. M. Dent & Sons Ltd, 1989

This book is set in 10/11½pt Linotron Plantin by
Deltatype Ltd, Ellesmere Port, Cheshire
Printed in Great Britain by
The Guernsey Press Co. Ltd,
Guernsey, C. I.
For J. M. Dent & Sons Ltd, 91 Clapham High Street,
London SW4 7TA

British Library Cataloguing in Publication Data

Yates, Dornford, *1885–1960*
The best of Berry: short stories.—
(Classic thrillers).
Rn: Cecil William Mercer I. Title
II. Adrian, Jack, *1945*– III. Series
823′.912[F]

ISBN 0-460-12583-4

CONTENTS

INTRODUCTION

Jack Adrian

Dornford Yates has always been a tough proposition: difficult to admire (or at least difficult to admit an admiration for), difficult to defend.

He was certainly a snob, a bully, hideously class-bound, a vigorous racial élitist; at times sulfurously intolerant. He was also a violent hater with a long memory – in his old age his second wife Elizabeth invariably took new visitors aside and warned them never to mention, in conversation, certain names (George Bernard Shaw, for instance, Aneurin Bevan, Lloyd George, Mrs Pankhurst, Jacob Epstein), unless they wanted to trigger off an eruption of near apoplectic fury. Although for no very good reason that one can see.

But then Yates was irrational about so many things and had a short-fuse temper which sometimes resulted in petty, and on occasion not so petty, violence. A bank clerk was shrieked at for pushing money across the counter 'as if he were shovelling coal', a young servant, Eugène Ascaso, was so brutally beaten for a relatively minor act of negligence that, in the words of another servant (as reported to the novelist Tom Sharpe, like me a confirmed Yates-lover yet at the same time -loather), 'there was blood on the tallboy' – the story goes that Yates was hauled up in court for this but got off on a shell-shock plea, although he'd never been shelled; true or not, he certainly had to dig deep into his wallet to appease the boy's relatives. When it looked as though the attentions of a rich French Jew towards his first wife Bettine were becoming too pressing, Yates horsewhipped him on the steps of the English Club in Pau and possibly (the story is vague on this point) broke the man's arm.

His behaviour in general towards Bettine seems to have been pretty atrocious. She was a chorus girl and *danseuse* in *Chu Chin Chow* when he met her, and while she was by all accounts lively and gregarious, Yates wasn't. Indeed, as he grew older he became more and more reclusive, more and more jealous of his wife's friends. At one stage he was so possessive that he forbade her getting out of the car whenever he visited the English Club so that friends had to come out to talk to her through the half-lowered window. Not content with that, he would shut the drawing-room windows when she sang at the piano so no one but he could hear her voice.

The inevitable divorce was a put-up job in which Yates by turns pressured then wheedled Bettine into not making waves, promising a good settlement of £500 a year if she didn't, then reneging on that promise by cutting the sum by half – and then threatening to stop it altogether if Bettine ever came within a hundred miles of Pau, even after the War when Yates himself was living 4,000 miles away in Rhodesia (Tom Sharpe discovered that when Yates's solicitor, a man who'd been with him at Harrow and Oxford and one of his oldest friends, protested at this Yates broke with him). The thought does occur that the reason he built a precipitous flight of over ninety steps up to the house he erected for himself in the Basses Pyrénées (splendidly fictionalised in *The House That Berry Built*, one of his best and funniest books) was not only to keep possible future pestering suitors away from his beautiful second wife but to keep her immured: she suffered from polio.

In later life his son Richard recalled his father as 'rather aloof and wrathful, smelling of bay rum' and wrote that his days at school in England, 600 miles away from the family home, were the happiest of his life; Yates cut him out of his final will.

'Cutting out', in later years, became something of a ritual; in his novels, too, Yates had a habit of killing off characters for whom he had no more use, more often than not in plane crashes, perfunctorily mentioned in passing. Nor did he mind rewriting history if it exorcised unpleasant or inconvenient shades, and was particularly mean-minded in the matter of his First Edition Dedications, obsessively non-personing all who'd fallen from favour, usually replacing flesh-and-blood with sentimental intangibles.

Not unnaturally, Bettine, to whom most of his early books were dedicated (many effusively), came out of the purging badly: 'To Her . . . My Lady Paramount' (*The Courts of Idleness*, 1920) later became 'To the countryside of England . . .'; 'To the American Girl who did me the honour to become my wife' (*Maiden Stakes*, 1929) became 'To those exquisite Summer evenings . . .'; 'To . . .

the finest lady in the world' (*Blood Royal*, 1929) became 'To Oxford as I remember it . . .'; 'To the portrait of a Lady . . .' (*Safe Custody*, 1932) became 'To the finest city in the world, incomparable London Town'.

All this – and, it has to be said, much more – is the bad side, which often had Yates's biographer A. J. Smithers floundering while trying to present his hero's case in the best possible light;* even Smithers, an arch-apologist, had to admit to the critic Stanley Reynolds that Yates's divorce in particular was 'a black spot' in the record.† But there are too many other black spots. It is hard not to see a strong and in the end emotionally crippling link between Yates's familial past and his own at times ugly temperament.

He was born Cecil William Mercer, in 1885, into a family that was suddenly engulfed in an appalling scandal: his great-uncle George, together with his partner in a firm of highly respected solicitors, had embezzled over £70,000 of their clients' money and, when the truth came out, George Mercer shot himself. George's father had died of 'a deseased brain' and another member of the family perished due to 'sanguineous apoplexy and general paralysis of the insane'. Little wonder that Yates, an only child with an over-protective mother and a father he didn't much care for, spent the rest of his life with a massive inferiority complex, an urge to escape a by no means noble background and a desperate need to be thought highly of (even by association: throughout his life he made much of his cousinly connection with Hector Munro, 'Saki', a writer on a rather higher plane than he; yet the evidence is he only ever met Munro once, when young, and for a few hours only).

The good – the very good – side is to be experienced in his work, most of which is so astonishingly at odds with his public persona that it might have been written by someone else entirely. Although it wasn't: Yates himself ghosted a volume of memoirs but absolutely no one could ghost Dornford Yates.

Seated at his writing desk – a vast baronial appointment, lugged from house to house – Yates threw off unsatisfactory reality and entered another world, a world of fantasy, there to become an altogether more agreeable human being.

***Dornford Yates*, Hodder & Stoughton, 1982.

†'The Gentleman Hero', *Guardian*, 1 March 1982.

As a writer he had two quite distinct and separate personalities. There was the comic novelist who delighted in bathos and all kinds of word-play (especially puns) and could switch with polished ease from sparkling scene-descriptions to high farce at the drop of a colon, and there was the ingenious thriller-merchant who wrote pacey, tight-lipped tales, featuring Richard Chandos and Jonah Mansel, set in south-west France or, more often, the less well-populated tracts of gorge, heath and mountain-meadow in Upper Austria (where, usefully, you could battle it out with a pair of machine-guns all day long and no one would ever hear you).

Invariably, in the thrillers, there was treasure to be found and fought over at the end of those long, dusty, poplar-lined pre-War roads: treasure at the bottom of deep, stone-walled wells; poisoned treasure under castle dungeons and plunging cascades; treasure in the shape of a beautiful girl held hostage as 'perishable goods' as time, and her chances of survival, run out.

Sheer melodrama. Yet for all that, Yates's thrillers (even the rather more subdued post-War performances) were built on strong foundations. His plotting was meticulous, his pacing immaculate; more important to his host of readers, his ability to generate at times an almost unbearable tension was extraordinary (the escape from the Great Well at Wagensburg in *Blind Corner* is truly, as a critic on *The Times* wrote when the book first appeared in 1927, 'story-telling of a high order', as is the beating-off of the attack on Castle Hohenems in *Safe Custody*, as is the finding of the secret chamber in the Great Tower of Brief in *She Painted Her Face*, as is – but we each have our own favourites).

This Yates wrote a kind of Jacobethan prose that relied heavily on the language and rhythms of the law, the Authorised Version, Shakespeare, and the pseudo-Medievalism of the novelist Maurice Hewlett (*Richard Yea-And-Nay*, *The Forest Lovers*, *The Queen's Quair*, etc.), as well as his own personal vision of how things ought to have been. Not only words, but sentences, whole paragraphs, reverberate with the solemn, measured tones of an antique age whose manners and mores never quite existed, except in that best of all places, the writer's own imagination.

It has been said that Yates, while writing an early melodrama *Valerie French* (1923), experienced a curious Road-to-Damascus conversion in the matter of style, suddenly rejecting the light conversational tone of his comedies for the stately, pseudo-archaic prose which was later to be such a feature of the Chandos thrillers. But he was writing in the style that was to make him famous over a decade before he created Richard Chandos (ironically named after his only son, who was to prove such a disappointment in later life).

The autobiography he ghosted – *What I Know* by C. W. Stamper* – is in all ways an illuminating book, exhibiting most of Yates's peculiar stylistic characteristics in full measure. The book contains the memoirs of the motor engineer (*not* chauffeur, as Stamper/Yates is at pains to make clear) to Edward VII. Stamper ran the royal garage and usually accompanied HM on excursions, sitting beside the chauffeur (normally a constable from the Met), ready to leap out when a tyre blew or a big end went to try and sort out the problem.

He was employed by the King from 1905 until the latter's death in 1910, although as intimate social revelation the book is a non-starter, its usefulness gauged by the fact that there is, for instance, one single mention of Mrs Keppel (the King's mistress), and that as a name on a 1909 guest-list. In any case the content of *What I Know* is not important: in the main the anecdotes are of such stunning banality (what happened when they drove through the wrong gate at Buckingham Palace, what HM said when he trod on Stamper's toe, and so on) that the memoirs of a machine-operator in a plastics factory would be more enticing.

Thus it isn't what Stamper tells but how he tells it. How educated he was it's impossible to say (that his brother was an actor is just about the only note of pure autobiography to creep in), and it may well have been that he could pluck an apt quotation from 300 years of English poetry in the twinkling of an eye, and write 120,000 words of Augustan prose to the manner born. But I doubt it.

Yatesian syntax leaps up from almost every page: 'Of me, as his motor expert, he demanded the missing car', 'By my leave he then summoned an ostler', 'Him I told who I was', 'Of tardiness under any circumstances he was impatient'. There are Yatesian ellipses, Yatesian conversation-openers, Yatesian phrases – 'I stepped off the footboard and uncovered' (i.e., took off his hat), 'So soon as we were ready' – that were in later years to do sterling service on

*Mills & Boon, 1913.

countless occasions, and there's a description of a non-stop overnight run from the Belgian coast to the heart of Austria that could only have come from the creator of that matchless driver and champion of the Rolls-Royce Jonah Mansel.

There is, too, more than a hint of things to come in the comedy line: 'He would show his displeasure by assuming an air of the most complete resignation. Instead perhaps of upbraiding me, if I lost the way, he would . . . ascertain what was wrong . . . deplore the way in which Misfortune singled him out for her victim, and then settle himself . . . in his corner, as if resigning himself to his fate. In his countenance there was written . . . a calm expectancy of worse to come.'

Berry to a T, although in this case Edward VII.

Berry was Yates's masterpiece – Bertram Pleydell (accent on the second syllable), clown, wit, sloth, glutton, reviler without peer and letter-writer *extraordinaire*: surely one of the great comic characters of the twentieth century.

In the Berry books Yates put aside for the most part the quaint archaisms and convoluted syntax of the thrillers and settled down to be funny. He succeeded triumphantly. The Yates comedy combined clever word-play and a neat line in grossly absurd exaggeration ('I spent two hours in a gas-mask studying the plan of the drains and calculating whether, if the second manhole was opened and a gorgonzola put down to draw the fire, Jonah could reach the grease-trap before he became unconscious', 'If I massaged a goat in a coal-mine, I couldn't dirty these hands') together with broad, knockabout farce and a heavy dependence upon the humour of bodily functions. Bowels, vomit, slop-pails, cess-pools, slow-bellies (constipation, for those not troubled by it), wind and drains all figure largely in the texts, mainly in bursts of conversational outrage from Berry himself.

Of course, this kind of humour – the humour of insult, the humour of explosive and inflated diatribe – needs an audience; better, a closely-knit group of participants: to revile and be reviled. Instead of a clutch of like-minded but otherwise irrelative friends, Yates cleverly provided a family backdrop against which Berry can strut, and fret, and scold, and slate, and then collapse in undignified confusion as his tribe invariably rise up against him.

Mind you, Berry's nearest and dearest may deride their head, hurl bread-rolls at him, writhe with laughter and resolutely refuse to offer aid as dogs leap into his bath or chase him up walls (and they do, they do), but in the end they will all close ranks at the slightest hint of an outside threat, however great, however small: blood, in an ideal world – or, more precisely, in the author's imagination – will ever triumph over the invader.

It's difficult not to arrive at the conclusion that Berry and Co – the Pleydells and the Mansels – were strong compensation for Yates's own far from satisfactory background. Berry married his cousin Daphne Pleydell and they cohabited with Boy Pleydell, the eponymous hero of Yates's first work of fiction *The Brother of Daphne* (1914), and their cousins Jonah Mansel (who crossed over into Yates's thriller territory) and his sister Jill, who in the end, keeping it all in the family, married Boy. A tightly-knit, self-supportive, carelessly wealthy and problem-free blood-tied group, with a widely scattered circle of friends, in the middle echelons of High Society.

Hopelessly idealised, of course; and yet Berry and Co do come to vigorous life because Yates himself believed in them utterly (to the extent that, after his second marriage, he insisted on calling Elizabeth 'Jill') and for so extended a period of time.

It's generally assumed that after a piece in *Punch* (in May 1910) Yates only started writing seriously a whole year later in 1911, when his first short story, 'Busy Bees', which featured Berry, Daphne and Boy, appeared in the *Windsor Magazine*. It was the author and critic Richard Usborne (who said a great many kind and sensible and even affectionate things about Yates, but who Yates himself regarded, typically, as an enemy – 'Usborne uses such material at his peril' he once cabled thunderously when Usborne wanted to quote a particular passage in his classic critique of the Yates/Buchan/Sapper triumvirate *Clubland Heroes**) who first pointed out that Boy quite clearly marries his cousin (of course) Madrigal Stukeley at the end of 'Busy Bees'. In the book-version, 'The Busy Beers' (much better title and an early Yates pun) this is cut out. Not unnaturally. Boy was an ardent poodlefaker (Edwardian for male flirt) and couldn't be expected to marry every pretty girl who came along, especially as there were so many of them.

*Constable, 1953; revised edition, Barrie & Jenkins, 1974.

Still, even allowing for the curious fantasy-world that was Yates's imagination, it can't be denied that there's a whiff of bigamy about when Boy finally marries Adèle Feste at the end of *Berry And Co* (1921). More than just a whiff, too. Whisper it not in Gath, but the Boy-Madrigal match was actually second time around for the brother of Daphne.

'Busy Bees' was not Yates's first story. It wasn't even the first Berry story. After the *Punch* piece, 'Temporary Insanity' (which was unsigned), Yates sold 'Like A Tale That Is Told', a very peculiar story indeed, to the *Red Magazine* (July 1910), appearing for the first time as 'Dornford Yates' (the name was concocted from Mercer's ancestors). All the Yates idiosyncrasies are there: the use of the colon before speech, the italicised emphases, a hint of the weird (he had a thing about dreams); there's even a servant called Falcon, a favourite name in later books.

At this time the *Red* was printing the early, and throbbing, stories of Ethel M. Dell (there's one in the same issue); perhaps Yates felt uneasy in such company. At any rate he aimed higher and hit the target with *Pearson's Magazine*, a glossy monthly which was probably (apart from Harmsworth's *London Magazine*) the only serious rival to the *Strand*. In the September 1910 issue appeared 'The Babes in the Wood', in which Boy encounters in the New Forest a shoe (a potent symbol for Yates who, on the evidence of his later work, appears to have had something of a foot-fetish), and then its owner, who throughout the story remains nameless – although Boy, in a wince-making moment, christens her 'girl-babe'.

They wander through the woods, bathe (chastely) in a chattering brook, get taken for a married couple by an apple-cheeked old dame, have to bluff it out, and then part. Embarrassing complications ensue some weeks later when they all bump into each other again at the pony fair, much to the amusement of Berry (sardonic) and Daphne (caustic), as well as Jonah (whose role, even then, was to drive the family car) and Jill. But all is resolved and Boy and 'girl-babe' announce their engagement and 'in due course we were married'. Double bigamy, in fact.

Of course, this is taking a writer's fantasies far too seriously – being, in the scolding phrase of Yates's biographer, 'too clever by half'. On the other hand, it's sometimes hard not to treat these figments of his imagination as real people, their experiences and adventures as true – or at least true-ish – for a good deal of what happened to Dornford Yates was later refined into fiction in one way or another. When old, Yates further confused the issue by writing two volumes of memoirs* (both entertaining, although both contain stretches of offensive drivel about modern art, Oscar Wilde, suffragettes, psychology, the French and the Germans, Epstein's Rima, etc.) – not as William Mercer, not even as Dornford Yates (although they were published under that name), but as Boy Pleydell.

Thus, while reminiscing with Berry, Daphne, Jonah and Jill about real experiences (the Crippen trial, the funerals of Victoria and Edward VII, the Suffragette March on Westminster) and real people (Beerbohm Tree, F. E. Smith, the slightly sinister Sir George Lewis), he also talks of fictional things (the Padua pearls, Derry Bagot, Deborah Crane the fortune-teller), at the same time commenting to Berry and the rest on the Berry books and the thrillers in which Jonah appeared as though the events recorded in them are fiction and never happened to the people with whom he's talking, to whom they did.

All very perplexing. Still, what is certain is that Yates, long before he even took up part-time writing (and while still devilling at the Bar), had a clear and concrete vision of the perfect family – the perfect wish-fulfilment – and stuck to it, even down to the names of those involved (although he hadn't quite pulled the relationships together in 1910: Jill is referred to as 'an old friend') and their essential characters, which in each case matured as the years, and the books, progressed and Yates's own confidence as a writer grew.

It may be that there are other forgotten Berry stories hidden away in the dusty pages of old periodicals, although I doubt it. Yates wrote one other piece for *Pearson's Magazine*, 'Rex-v-Blogg', an amusing squib on the law, and then settled for the *Windsor*, whose publisher Ward Lock proved to be a wholly sympathetic firm. Except, that is, in the matter of Yates's suspense novels.

On the grounds that story-cobblers should stick to their lasts (in Yates's case, comedies and tales of romance) Ward Lock refused to

***As Berry And I Were Saying* and *B-Berry And I Look Back*, Ward Lock, 1952, 1958.

publish the Chandos/Mansel thrillers, forecasting disaster, and Yates ruthlessly severed almost all links with the firm for nearly a decade (1927 to 1935), apart from cashing their hefty royalty cheques for past bestsellers twice a year and allowing them to issue a single volume of short stories which turned out to be one of his least popular books. Yates had the last laugh. His thrillers were enormously successful.

Ward Lock finally admitted defeat, offered much better terms and a free hand, and bought the rights to the thrillers, reissuing them themselves – which is probably why Yates conveniently forgot this rift in the lute when he wrote a short but stately preface to Ward Lock's house-history celebrating their centenary in 1954,* making much of his and his publishers' forty-plus years' 'unbroken' association.

In the end Yates was Ward Lock's star author, and over nearly half a century probably contributed far more substantially to their coffers, and with less books, than any score or more of their other writers put together, the money mainly coming from the Berry books – five and a half volumes of short stories (the half is included in *The Courts of Idleness*, the first part of which features other characters), two full-length novels (*Adèle And Co* and *The House That Berry Built*), and the two volumes of Mercer/Yates/Boy memoirs, although Berry and Co also have walk-on parts or mentions in such non-Berry books as *Anthony Lyveden*, *Perishable Goods* and *The Stolen March*, as well as a number of the short stories.

The stories in this volume all come from Berry's, and Yates's, vintage years, the 1920s and 1930s, and are mainly taken from *Berry And Co*, *Jonah And Co* (1922) and *And Berry Came Too* (1936).

All have in them elements, more or less, of mystery, crime, even the mildly supernatural (pre-cognitive dreams, mainly: a useful plot-device which Yates utilised more than once and usually to good effect). The crimes range from confidence trickery through robbery to would-be murder, taking in on the way a car-chase that ought to be standard reading for all tyro suspense writers (with good reason, Ian Fleming was hugely impressed at how Yates

**Adventure In Publishing* by Edward Liveing, Ward Lock, 1954.

could handle a half-dozen pages of hot-pursuit prose) and a perfectly-realised, and perfectly-paced, weird vision where the horror approaches on tip-toe, but is nonetheless unsettling for that.

Of the two stories that aren't from the three Golden Age volumes, one is 'Nemesis', an unusually short tale (1,500 words rather than the normal 7,000–10,000) which has an interesting history. After nearly a decade Yates tried his hand at another *Punch* piece. *Punch* rejected it (in his 'memoirs' Boy records that it was E. V. Lucas, 'Evoe', who turned it down). Yates then pushed it across to Arthur Hutchinson at the *Windsor* who accepted it and printed it in the November 1919 issue. In the original the I-hero is anonymous while the main character is called Jeremy. Yates Berryfied the story but otherwise left it alone: hence its odd length. It appeared in *The Courts of Idleness* (1920).

The other non-series story is the extraordinary 'Letters Patent' which was published in *Maiden Stakes* (1929) and deals with reader reaction to *Perishable Goods*, Yates's conflation of Anthony Hope's *The Prisoner of Zenda* and *Rupert of Hentzau*, in which Boy's wife Adèle is kidnapped by the malevolent Rose Noble who knows that his arch-enemy Jonah Mansel has rather more than a passing, though nobly suppressed, passion for her. *Perishable Goods* is a superb thriller and was hugely successful – no less a writer than Dashiell Hammett, whose own hard-boiled prose (not to mention politics and lifestyle in general) would surely have thrown Yates into a state of near-terminal rage, once recommended it 'without reservation' (but then Yates did have some odd admirers: Cyril Connolly was another). Yet Yates went out of his way to poke inordinate fun at the book and, by extension, himself.

This is all part of the monumental paradox of the man. As Cecil William Mercer he could at times be violent, spiteful, cruel, implacably vindictive. He had few close friends (at one point Smithers, in his biography, has to summon up a nonagenarian colonel who 'was kind enough to tell me that he liked the man' – a phrase which, in its very pathos, almost wrings the heart), and you will find not a mention of him in any of the standard biographies of his writing peers or even their own reminiscences. He was obsessively jealous, ordering in his will that a valuable antique picture-clock, to which he used to talk at great length when in his study, should be taken to a jeweller who 'shall remove the clock from the picture, sever the gongs, dismantle the clock and destroy the parts'. Presumably so that no one else should ever talk to it: a chilling codicil.

And then there is the Curious Case of the Clerihew. In one of his volumes of memoirs Yates takes up a good deal of space fulminating against Clerihews, calling them 'arrant rubbish' and pointing out triumphantly that *they don't scan*: thereby profoundly – even spectacularly – missing the point. Clearly, this man had no sense of humour.

Yet this is manifestly not so. He could, and often did, guy himself and his work. He could, and often did, write gloriously funny prose that can still, even after thirty years, have me guffawing out loud – while, it has to be admitted, at the same time gritting my teeth (if the image can be borne) at his dark side: the snobbery, the ugly values, the egregious opinions that pepper his books.

Yates once made a significant point about Kipling: 'I believe [he] went on writing after he should have stopped, because writing was his great resource: because, once in his study, he could forget an unkind world and live in one of his own.' I'm not at all sure that the world ever treated Kipling badly, but I strongly suspect that Dornford Yates himself thought that the world hadn't been all that sympathetic towards Dornford Yates.

Writing was certainly his great resource: it transformed him into an entirely different person. The man who lived and had his being outside those study doors is undeniably an uneasy companion; yet he's been dust for nearly thirty years, his obituary written, his memory fading. If we make allowances of an other-times-other-mores nature it is the man who sat at the great oaken desk, the man who lived more and more in a world of his own imagination – a carefree world where great cars fled between woodland banks and stately homes echoed to the sound of joyous laughter – the man, in short, who created Berry who will surely survive.

JA
October, 1988

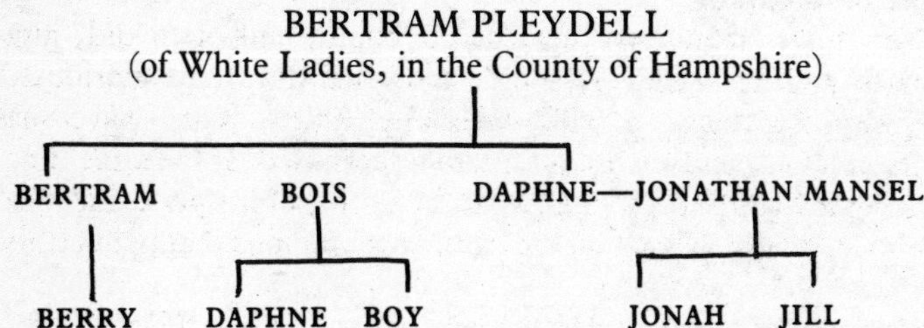

These are the principal players:

Bertram Pleydell – Berry to all – is the head of the house, the master of White Ladies in Hampshire, hereditary squire, Justice of the Peace, murderer of Shakespeare and the Authorised Version. He married Daphne Pleydell, his cousin – 'a famous beauty . . . gentle in fair weather, gallant in foul'. Her brother is Boy – not Bois, who was their father, erstwhile MP for Shrewsbury – barrister, chronicler, dedicated philanderer. Boy later – twenty years later – married his cousin, the elfin Jill, whose brother is Jonathan Mansel – Jonah to all – sportsman, keen driver, nimble with his wit, his fists and, on occasion, an automatic pistol.

This, collectively, is Berry and Co.

It is 1919. After four years of war the Courts of Idleness have reopened their doors. But the ranks of those that once thronged its pleasant thoroughfares have thinned . . .

Boy and Jonah have emerged from the Great War honourably. Boy with an MC, Jonah with a DSO, a slight limp ('a present from Cambrai'), and a good deal of experience in the more shadowy regions of the conflict. Both have the rank of Captain. Berry landed a job at GHQ in Cairo, rank of Major, and beavered away there under Allenby until demobilisation, Daphne and Jill with him.

Boy and Jonah were lucky; both were freed from the military early and joined the rest in Egypt, where Boy met the charming American Adèle Feste. When she returns to the States, Boy experiences more than a pang. It looks very much as though his career as dedicated poodle-faker is drawing to its close, although by no means swiftly.

Once Berry gains his release, the company heads back to England, via Rome. In London, they open up their house in Cholmondeley Street.

NEMESIS

The gates, which it was obviously impossible to shut, were dragged to, those of my organs which had been displaced sank back into position, four bells rang, and the train plunged forward. There was just enough play between my face and a smart little velvet hat for the two to collide violently.

'Ow!' said the owner.

'That was my nose,' I said. 'I hope it won't bleed.'

'So do I,' said the man immediately northwest of me.

Fifteen seconds later, without any warning, the train came to an abrupt stop.

'I'm sure it will bleed now,' said I. 'Nothing can stop it.'

There was an uncomfortable silence. Then: 'I don't wish to jump to any hasty conclusion,' said Berry, 'but I think I saw a notice to the effect that there was more room in the rear of the train.'

'You did,' said I.

'Well, if that's true,' said Berry, 'they must be very crowded in front. You know,' he added, 'this is very nearly as bad as the Victory Ball.'

'At least there was variety about that function,' said the major half-left of my breastbone. 'People removed their feet from your insteps every now and then. I don't mean to say they didn't put them back, but it gave the circulation a chance.'

'Force of will,' said Berry, 'can do anything. Let's all pretend we're waiting to see Wilson.'

The velvet hat shook slightly.

'As a matter of fact,' said I, 'it reminds me irresistibly of Earl's Court.'

The allusion proved unfortunate, and it took us all several seconds to convince a lady with four parcels, whose hat appeared to have been caught in the gates, that the train was in fact going to Warwick Avenue.

When the excitement had subsided:

'Why Earl's Court?' said the man immediately north-west of me.

'Because this is the sort of thing you used to pay for,' said I. 'If you remember, you could ruin a dress-suit there for sixpence, while with eighteenpence and a little judgment you could become a confirmed invalid. Of course,' I added, 'you can't expect so much for twopence halfpenny.'

With a frightful jerk the train resumed its career.

The rearrangement consequent upon its arrival at Oxford Circus partook of the nature of a violent struggle for existence.

Under cover of the confusion I sought to recover a package which I had dropped at Piccadilly. My fingers encountered its surface, but when I tried to pick it up, it appeared to be attached to the floor. While I was digesting this phenomenon:

'Somebody appears to be trying to lift me into the air,' said the major. 'I may as well say at once that, in the circumstances, I believe such a feat to be beyond their strength.'

Guiltily I wriggled the string of my package clear of his right spur.

Amid the frenzied bellowing of officials the train proceeded on its way. Two hundred yards further on it came to a dead stop.

Berry cleared his throat.

'It cannot be too widely known,' he said, 'that I propose to emerge at Regent's Park. The funny-looking man on my left front will accompany me.'

The ripple of amusement that greeted this remark was rudely terminated by a coarse laugh from the conductor.

'You'll 'ave to look sharp about it,' he said. 'We don't stop there.'

There was a roar of merriment.

I addressed myself to the major.

'A walk,' I said, 'will do that vulgar fat man good. If he had walked more in the past, we should not now be suffering quite so much inconvenience.'

'Before we break up,' said Berry, 'I should like to say how much I've enjoyed this. I've been assaulted more times than I can remember, my ticket has been knocked out of my hand, and I've lost my gent's umbrella. It only remains for me to be robbed.'

'All right as long as you don't carry anything in your hip-pocket,' I murmured thoughtlessly.

The effect of my words was electrical. Simultaneously every man within earshot sought to assure himself that his hip-pocket was inviolate. The fact that everyone was wearing an overcoat further complicated a gesture which demands more than ordinary elbow-room, and in a moment the utmost confusion prevailed.

Berry braced himself against the gate.

'May I suggest,' he said, 'that everybody feels in the hip-pocket of the neighbour immediately in front of him? In this way the investigation now afoot will be greatly simplified, and by an exchange of confidences . . .'

Somebody laughed hysterically. There were unmistakable signs of panic.

'The first 'and as feels in my 'ip-pocket'll get wot for,' said an explosive voice.

The threat was launched inside the coach, and I felt glad we were on the platform.

Happily the train chose this moment to resume its journey.

The sudden burst of apologies, which succeeded its impulse, suggested that several hands which should have been straphanging were otherwise engaged.

The major spoke into my ear.

'I'm not a lawyer,' he said, 'but I should say that your friend has been guilty of a summary offence. Conduct more calculated to lead to a breach of the peace I never witnessed.'

I screwed my head round.

'If I give you his address,' I shouted, 'will you promise to summon him?'

The major blenched.

'God forbid!' he said. 'I'd rather go back to France.'

As we were walking down Marylebone Road, Berry demanded a cigarette. Before proceeding to unbutton my overcoat, I eyed him suspiciously.

'Where are your own?' said I.

'Probably still in my case,' he said gloomily.

'Well, why – '

'And that,' said Berry, 'was in my hip-pocket.'

It is early Summer, 1919. Berry and Co have at last returned to their stately home, White Ladies in the County of Hampshire.

All is as once it was . . .

A BLUE-LETTER DAY

'Who's going to church?' said Daphne, consulting her wristwatch.

There was a profound silence.

My sister turned to Jill.

'Are you coming?' she said. 'Berry and I are.'

'I beg your pardon,' said her husband.

'Of course you're coming,' said Daphne.

'Not in these trousers. This is the first time I've worn them, and I'm not going to kneel in them for anyone.'

'Then you'll change,' said his wife. 'You've plenty of time.'

Berry groaned.

'This is sheer Bolshevism,' he said. 'Is not my soul my own?'

'We shall start,' said Daphne, 'in twenty minutes.'

It was nearly half-past ten in the morning of a beautiful summer day, and we were all taking our ease in the sunshine upon the terrace. It was the first Sunday which we had spent all together at White Ladies for nearly five years.

So far as the eye could see, nothing had changed.

At the foot of the steps the great smooth lawn stretched like a fine green carpet, its shadowed patches yet bright with dew. There were the tall elms and the copper beech and all the proud company of spreading giants – what were five years to them? There was the clump of rhododendrons, a ragged blotch of crimson, seemingly spilled upon the green turf, and there the close box hedge that walled away the rose-garden. Beyond the sunk fence a gap showed an acre or so of Bull's Mead – a great deep meadow, and in it two horses beneath a chestnut tree, their long tails a-swish, sleepily nosing each other to rout the flies; while in the distance the haze of heat hung like a film over the rolling hills. Close at hand echoed the soft impertinence of a cuckoo, and two fat wood-pigeons waddled about the lawn, picking and stealing as they went. The sky was cloudless, and there was not a breath of wind.

The stable clock chimed the half-hour.

My sister returned to the attack.

'Are you coming, Boy?'

'Yes,' said I. 'I am.'

Berry sat up and stared at me.

'Don't be silly,' he said. 'There's a service this morning. Besides, they've changed the lock of the poor-box.'

'I want to watch the Vicar's face when he sees you,' said I.

'It will be a bit of a shock,' said Jonah, looking up from the paper. 'Is his heart all right?'

'Rotten,' said Daphne. 'But that doesn't matter. I sent him a note to warn him yesterday.'

'What did you say?' demanded her husband.

'I said, *"We're back at last, and – don't faint – we're all coming to church tomorrow, and you've got to come back to lunch."* And now, for goodness' sake, go and change.'

'But we shall perspire,' said Berry. 'Profusely. To walk half a mile in this sun is simply asking for it. Besides – '

'What's the car done?' said Jonah. 'I'm going, and I can't hurry with this.' He tapped his short leg affectionately. 'We needn't take Fitch. Boy or I can drive.'

'Right oh,' said my sister, rising. 'Is ten-minutes-to early enough?'

Jonah nodded.

'This,' said Berry, 'is a conspiracy for which you will all pay. Literally. I shall take the plate round, and from you four I shall accept nothing but paper. Possibly I shall – '

Here the girls fell upon him and bore him protesting into the house and out of earshot.

'Who's going to look after the car while we're in church?' said I.

'There's sure to be somebody ready to earn a couple of bob,' said Jonah. 'Besides, we can always disconnect the north-east trunnion, or jack her up and put the wheels in the vestry or something.'

'All right. Only we don't want her pinched.' With a yawn I rose to my feet. 'And now I suppose I'd better go and turn her out.'

'Right oh,' said Jonah, picking up his paper again.

I strolled into the house.

We were proud of the car. She was a 1914 Rolls, and we had bought her at a long price less than a week ago. Fresh from the coach-builder's, her touring body was painted silver-grey, while her bonnet was of polished aluminium. Fitted with every conceivable accessory, she was very good-looking, charming alike to ride or drive, and she went like the wind. In a word, she did as handsome as she was.

It was eight minutes to eleven as we slid past the lodge and on to the Bilberry road.

Before we had covered two furlongs, we swung round a corner to see a smart two-seater at rest by the dusty hedgerow, and a slight dark girl in fresh blue and white standing with one foot on the step, wiping her dainty fingers on a handful of cottonwaste.

'Agatha!' cried Daphne and Jill. 'Stop, Boy, stop!'

Obediently I slowed to a standstill, as my lady came running after us.

'You might have told me,' she panted. 'I never knew you were back. And I am so glad.'

'We only arrived on Friday, dear,' said Daphne, and introduced Berry and me. Jonah, it appeared, had met Miss Deriot at tennis in 1914.

'But you had your hair down then,' he said gravely.

'It's a wonder I haven't got it down now,' said Miss Deriot. 'Why didn't you come along ten minutes earlier? Then you could have changed my tyre.'

'And why are you driving away from church?' said Jill.

'One of the colts has sprained his shoulder, and we're out of embrocation, so I'm going to get some from Brooch.'

'I'll come with you,' said Berry eagerly, preparing to leave the car. 'I don't like to think of you – '

'Nonsense,' said Daphne, detaining him.

'But supposing she has another puncture?'

'Yes, I can see you mending it on a day like this.'

'It's very kind of you,' said Miss Deriot, with a puzzled smile.

'Don't thank the fool,' said my sister. 'If I thought he'd be the slightest use to you, I'd send him; but he only wants an excuse to get out of going to church.'

'Poor jade,' said her husband. 'I am a knight, a simple starlit knight, a Quixote of today. Your brutish instincts – '

'Carry on, Boy,' said Daphne. I let in the clutch. 'And come over this afternoon, Agatha, and we'll tell you all about everything.'

'Yes, do,' cried Jill.

'All right,' said Miss Deriot. 'So long.'

Three minutes later I was berthing the car close to the lich-gate in the shade of sweet-smelling limes, that made a trembling screen of foliage within the churchyard wall.

As luck would have it, Will Noggin, once a groom in our service and now a trooper of the Dragoon Guards, was leaning lazily against the grey wall, taking his ease. As we drew abreast of him, he stood to attention and saluted, a pleased grin of recognition lighting his healthy face. We greeted him gladly.

'Glad to see you're all right, Will,' said Jill.

'Thank you, miss.'

'Aren't you going to church?' said Daphne.

'Not today, m'm. I'm on leave, and I've 'ad my share o' church parades i' the last four years, m'm.'

We all laughed.

'Well, if you're not going,' said I, 'we want someone to keep an eye on the car.'

'I'll do it gladly, sir.'

'Right oh! She's a pretty piece of goods, isn't she?'

'She is that, sir,' said Will, visibly impressed.

As I followed the others into the porch, I glanced back to see our sentinel walking about his charge, bending an appreciative gaze upon her points.

They were singing the *Venite*.

On the ledge of our old pew lay a note addressed to 'Major

Pleydell' in the Vicar's handwriting. When Berry had read it, he passed it to Daphne, and I was able to read it over her shoulder.

Dear Major,

Sometimes in the old days you used to read the Lessons. I think we should all like it if you would do so today; but don't, if you don't want to. Yours very sincerely,

John Bagot.

In a postscript the writer named the appointed passages of Holy Writ.

So soon as the first Psalm had started, Berry stepped to the lectern, found his places and cast his eye over the text. Before the second Psalm was finished, he was once more in his place.

Doors and windows were open as wide as they could be set, and the little church was flooded with light and fresh warm air, that coaxed the edge from the chill of thick stone walls and pillars, and made the frozen pavements cool and refreshing. Mustiness was clean gone, swept from her frequent haunts by the sweet breath of Nature. The 'dim, religious light' of Milton's ordering was this day displaced by Summer's honest smile, simpler maybe, but no less reverent. And, when the singing was stilled, you overheard the ceaseless sleepy murmur of that country choir of birds and beasts and insects that keeps its rare contented symphony for summer days in which you can find no fault.

My impious eye wandered affectionately over familiar friends – the old oak pews, almost chin-high, the Spanish organ, the reluctant gift of a proud galleon wrecked on the snarling coast ten miles away, the old 'three-decker' with its dull crimson cushions and the fringed cloths that hung so stiffly. A shaft of sunlight beat full on an old black hatchment, making known the faded quarterings, while, underneath, a slender panel of brass but two years old showed that the teaching of its grim forbear had not been vain.

For so fair a morning, Bilberry village had done well. The church was two-thirds full, and, though there were many strange faces, it was pleasant here and there to recognise one we had known in the old days, and to learn from an involuntary smile that we had not been forgotten.

It was just after the beginning of the Second Lesson that a faint familiar sound fell of a sudden upon our ears. There was no mistaking the purr of our Rolls-Royce. For a second the girls and Jonah and I stared at one another, panic-stricken. Then with one impulse we all started instinctively to our feet. As I left the pew, I heard Daphne whisper, 'H'sh! We can't all – ,' and she and Jonah and Jill sank back twittering. Berry's eyes met mine for an instant as I stepped into the aisle. They spoke volumes, but to his eternal credit his voice never faltered.

I almost ran to the porch, and I reached the lich-gate to see our beautiful car, piloted by a man in a grey hat, scudding up the straight white road, while in her wake tore a gesticulating trooper, shouting impotently, ridiculously outdistanced. Even as I watched, the car flashed round a bend and disappeared.

For a moment I stood still in the middle of the road, stupefied. Then I heard a horn sounded behind me, and I mechanically stepped to one side. Fifty yards away was the two-seater we had encountered on our way to church.

Frantically I signalled to the girl at the wheel. As I did so, a burst of music signified that the Second Lesson had come to an end.

'Whatever's the matter?' cried Miss Deriot, as she pulled up.

'Somebody's pinched the Rolls. Will you – '

'Of course. Get in. Which way did they go?'

'Straight ahead,' said I, opening the door.

We were well under way before I had taken my seat. As we came to the bend I threw a glance over my shoulder, to see four figures that I knew standing without the lich-gate. They appeared to be arguing. As we turned the corner a stentorian voice yelled –

'The Bloodstock road, sir! I can see their blinkin' dust.'

Perched on one of the lower branches of a wayside oak, Will Noggin was pointing a shaking finger in the direction he named.

We were less than three miles from Bloodstock when the off hind tyre burst. Miss Deriot brought the car to the side of the road and stopped in the shadow of an old barn.

'That,' she said, 'has just done it.'

I opened the door and stepped down into the road.

'It means a delay when we least want it,' said I ruefully.

'Worse. I've had one burst already, and I only brought one spare wheel.'

I whistled.

'Then we are indeed done,' said I. 'I'm awfully sorry. Heaven knows how far you are from your home. This comes of helping a comparative stranger. Let it be a lesson to you.'

My companion smiled.

'I don't mind for myself,' she said, 'But what about your car?'

I spread out my hands.

'Reason dictates that I should foot-slog it to Bloodstock and try and get the police moving; but I can't leave you here.'

'You can easily, but you're not going to. I don't want to sit here for the rest of the day.' She pointed to the barn. 'Help me to get her in here, and then we'll push off to Bloodstock together.'

A hurried reconnaissance led to the discovery of a little farmhouse, and two minutes later I was making urgent representations to the owner of the barn. To our relief the latter proved sympathetic and obliging, and before we again took to the road the two-seater was safely under lock and key.

'And now,' said Miss Deriot, 'how did it happen?'

'The theft? I can't imagine. We left that fool who yelled at us in charge. I suppose he left her to get a drink or something. This is only the fourth time we've had her out,' I added gloomily.

'Oh, I say! Never mind. You're bound to get her again. Look at that meadow-sweet. Isn't it lovely? I wish I could paint. Can you?'

'I painted a key-cupboard once. It was hung, too. Outside the stillroom.'

'Pity you didn't keep it up,' said Miss Deriot. 'It's a shame to waste talent like that. Isn't it just broiling? I should love a bathe now.'

'I hope you don't wear stockings in the water,' said I.

Miss Deriot glanced at her white ankles.

'Is that a reflection?' she demanded.

I shook my head.

'By no manner of means. But there's a place for everything, isn't there? I mean – '

We both laughed.

'That's better,' said my companion. 'I couldn't bear to see you so worried this beautiful morning.'

'My dear,' said I, 'you've a nice kind heart, and I thank you.'

'Don't mention it,' said Miss Deriot.

From the crown of her broad-brimmed hat to the soles of her buckskin shoes she was the pink of daintiness. Health was springing in her fresh cheeks, eagerness danced in her eyes, energy leapt from her carriage. Had she been haughty, you would have labelled her 'Diana', and have done with it; but her eyes were gentle, and there was a tenderness about her small mouth that must have pardoned Actæon. A plain gold wrist-watch on a black silk strap was all her jewellery.

'We'd better strike across the next field,' said Miss Deriot. 'There's a path that'll bring us out opposite "The Thatcher". It'll save us about five minutes.'

'You might have been born here,' said I.

'I was,' said Agatha. She nodded towards a beech wood that stood a furlong away. 'The trees hide the house. But we left when I was seven, and only came back to the county five years ago. And here's our field.'

The five-barred gate was padlocked. I looked at my companion.

'Shall I get over, advance ten paces, and gaze into the middle distance? Or aren't you that sort?'

Miss Deriot flung back her head and laughed.

'I'd rather you gave me a leg up,' she said.

With a hand on my shoulder and a foot in my hand, she was up and over in an instant. I vaulted after her.

'You know,' I said, 'we ought to perform you and I. With a painter's ladder, a slack wire, and a little practice, we should do wonders. On non-matinée days I might even lift you with my teeth. That always goes well, and no one would know you were as light as a rose-leaf.'

'Seven stone three in the bathroom,' said Agatha. 'Without stockings. Some rose-leaf.'

We were going uphill. The meadow through which we were passing sloped to an oaken fence, stoutly constructed to save the cattle from a perilous fall. For on its farther side the ground fell away sheer, so that at this point a bluff formed one high wall of the sunken road for which we were making. 'The Thatcher', I remembered, stood immediately opposite to the rough grass-grown steps, hewn years ago for the convenience of such passengers as we. There was a stile set in the fence, and as I swung myself over I glanced down past the edge of the bluff and into the road below.

In the little curved space that fronted the inn the Rolls was standing silent and unoccupied.

I must have exclaimed, for Agatha was over the stile in an instant, and asking me what was the matter. Then she saw, and the words died on her lips. Together we stood spellbound.

The door of the inn was shut, and there was no one in sight.

My first impulse was to dart down the steps, beat upon the door of the tavern, and confront the thief. But valour yielded to discretion. The great thing was to recover the car. I had but a slip of a girl with me, the spot was a lonely one, and it was more than likely that the highwayman was not working alone. Besides, Agatha must not be involved in any violence.

I turned to my lady.

'You stay here. I'm going to take her and drive straight to the police station. I'll pick up some police and come back just as quickly as ever I can.'

Miss Deriot shook her pretty head.

'I'm coming with you,' she said. 'Carry on.'

'But, my dear – '

'I often wish I wasn't so obstinate.' She spoke meditatively. 'But we're all like that. Mules aren't in it with the Deriots,' she added, with a dazzling smile.

'Neither, apparently, are cucumbers,' said I, and with that I began to descend the rough stairs, stepping as delicately as I could.

Halfway down I turned to look at my companion, and at that moment the step upon which I was standing gave way. The scrambling sounds which proclaimed my fall were followed by the rasping protest of yielding cloth, and I came to rest six feet from the road at the expense of a pre-War coat, which had caught the corner of one of the unplaned risers. All had been so still, that in that hollow place the noise could not have failed to attract the attention of anyone who was within earshot, and I lay for a moment where I had fallen, straining my ears for the sound of footsteps or voices.

'Are you all right?' whispered a soft voice above me.

I turned my head and nodded. Miss Deriot, standing with clasped hands, heaved a sigh of relief and prepared to continue her descent.

Gingerly I stepped down into the sandy road and started to cross it a-tiptoe.

Facing towards Bloodstock, the car presented her off-side to us.

With the utmost caution I proceeded to negotiate the two spare wheels and clamber into the driver's seat. As I sat down, Miss Deriot slipped in front of the bonnet and round to the near side. She was opening the high side-door and my foot was on the self-starter, when I heard the murmur of voices.

We were not a second too soon.

The moment I had started the engine, there was a cry, followed by the clattering of heavy shoes upon cobbles, and as the car slid into the road, a man in a grey hat came tearing out of the inn's courtyard, waving his arms and yelling like one possessed. Hard on his heels came pounding his supporters, three of them, all bellowing like bulls.

So much I saw for myself. Agatha, kneeling on the seat by my side, kept me informed of their movements till we swept out of sight.

'He's simply dancing. The one in the grey hat, I mean. Now he's shaking his fist at us. Oh, he's mad. He's thrown his hat on the ground. O-o-oh, Boy, he's trying to kick one of the others. Oh, I wish you could see . . .' The merry voice dissolved into peals of laughter.

Then the road curled, and Agatha turned left about and settled herself by my side.

'How did you know my Christian name?' I demanded.

'Your sister used it this morning. You see, I've forgotten your other, and I can't keep on saying "you". But I won't do it again.'

'Please, Agatha.'

'Deriot. One "r". I say, you've torn your coat properly.'

'It feels as if it was in two pieces,' said I.

'If it wasn't for the collar, it would be,' said Agatha. 'Never mind. Bare backs are still fashionable. And what's a torn coat when you've got the car again?'

'You're right,' I agreed. 'You'd hardly believe it,' I added, 'but I can tell from the feel of her that some stranger's been driving.'

'I can believe it. After all, a car's just like a horse.'

As she spoke, we sped into the market square of Bloodstock. The police station stood in Love Lane, a couple of streets away.

Here a disappointment was in store. The sole representative of the Law was a station sergeant in his shirt-sleeves and a state of profuse perspiration. Between his lips was a penholder, and he held a telephone receiver to his left ear. In an adjoining room the bell of another telephone was ringing violently in long regular spasms, while, somewhere quite close, a dog was giving ceaseless vent to those short sharp barks which denote impatience of detention.

A sudden elevation of the sergeant's eyebrows invited me to state my business, but before I had spoken two sentences he shifted the penholder from his mouth and shook his head.

''Fraid I can't 'elp you at the moment, sir. That's the third car what's been stole in this distric' this mornin'. There's a 'ole gang of 'em about. Everyone excep' me's out after 'em now. 'Eaven knows when they'll come in. An' there's that other telephone goin' like mad, an' the Chief Constable's lef' his bull-dawg tied up there, an' 'e won't let me within six foot of it.' He turned to blare into the mouthpiece. ''Ullo! 'Oo *are* you? 'Oo *are* you? Wot! Oh, I can't bear it. 'Ere, for 'Eaven's sake, 'old the line.' He set down the receiver, shook the sweat out of his eyes, and sank on to a stool. 'Another blinkin' car gone,' he said hoarsely. 'I dunno wot's the matter with the world. I wish I was back in France.'

Love Lane was a narrow street, so I did not attempt to turn the car, but drove on and presently out of the town by back streets on to the Bilberry road.

It would have been better if I had telephoned to White Ladies before leaving Bloodstock, to announce my recovery of the car, but I was expecting to be back there so soon that it seemed unnecessary.

Indeed, it was only when we were once more under way that I thought of the colt and the embrocation, to say nothing of my lady's two-seater, now standing helpless in the gloom of the wayside barn.

'I tell you what,' said I. 'We'll drive to the barn and pick up the lotion, and then I'll take you home. Then I can run your chauffeur back to the barn with a spare cover, drop him there, and push off to White Ladies.'

'I can improve on that,' said Agatha, with a glance at her wrist. 'It'll be past one by the time we get home, so you must stay to lunch. You can telephone to White Ladies from there. And afterwards I'll go back with you – I was to come over this afternoon, wasn't I – and we can drop the chauffeur at the barn on the way. And he can come for me in the evening.'

Agatha was living at Broadacre, a fine old place on the edge of the forest itself, and thither we came without incident, just as an old-fashioned gong was summoning the household to meat.

Admiral and Mrs Deriot were kindness itself. First I was given a long, cold, grateful drink. Then the old sailor led me to his own chamber and ministered personally to my wants. My coat was given to a maid to be roughly stitched, and when I appeared at luncheon it was in a jacket belonging to my host. Our story was told and retold, the lawlessness of the year of Grace 1919 was bewailed, and a violent denunciation of motor-thieves was succeeded by a bitter proscription of the County Police.

In the midst of my entertainment I remembered that I had not telephoned to White Ladies but the servant sent to make the connection was informed by the Exchange that the line was out of order.

'I expect it's fused,' said I. 'With Berry at one end and that station sergeant at the other, the strain must have been fearful.'

It was half-past two before we were once more in the car. On the back seat sat the Deriots' chauffeur, holding a spare wheel between his knees.

It did not take us long to reach the barn, and, so soon as we had once more unearthed the farmer, authorised him to suffer the chauffeur to remove the two-seater, and discharged our debt for 'accommodation', I turned the Rolls round and headed for White Ladies.

'She's certainly a beautiful car,' said Agatha, as the Rolls sailed up a treacherously steep gradient on top. 'It's like being in a lift.'

'And, but for you, we might never have seen her again. Shall I give you a stamp album, or would you like to drive?'

'D'you really mean that?' said Miss Deriot.

I shot her a glance. There was no mistaking the eagerness of her parted lips and the sparkle of her gay brown eyes. By way of replying I brought the car to a standstill. A moment later we had changed places.

'It's awfully kind of you,' said Agatha delightedly, as she let in the clutch. 'I've always wanted to drive a Rolls. I hope I shan't hurt her.'

'You'll do her good,' said I. 'I watched you in the two-seater. You've got beautiful hands.'

'Thank you, Boy.'

'Now you shall have a stamp album as well. Go carefully here. There used to be a wasps' nest in that bank, but it's closed now, same as the German banks. What a war!'

'But I don't collect stamps.'

'Then she shall have a dog. What about a Sealyham to sleep on your bed and bite the postman?'

'I'd love one,' said Agatha.

'And you'll sit up in bed in the morning, with your hair all about your eyes and smile at him, and he'll growl back at you – I can just see you.'

'Thanks awfully. But you're wrong about my hair.'

'Is it never unruly?'

'Only by day. I wish to goodness I could wear it down.'

'So do I. Then we could all sit on it when the grass was wet. At the moment there's a particularly beautiful tress caressing your left shoulder. And I think you ought to know that the wind is kissing it quite openly. It's all very embarrassing. I hope I shan't catch it,' I added cheerfully.

Miss Deriot made a supreme effort to look severe.

'If you do,' she said uncertainly, 'I shall drive straight into the horse-pond.'

'Sh!' said I reprovingly. 'You oughtn't to jest about such things. You might catch it yourself. Easily.' Here we passed the horse-pond. 'You know you'll never be able to look fierce so long as you have that dimple. You'll have to fill it up or something. I suppose it's full of dew every morning now.'

Without a word Agatha slowed down, turned up a by-road and stopped. Then she proceeded to back the car.

'What on earth is she doing?' said I.

She turned a glowing face to mine.

'Going back to the horse-pond,' she flashed.

I laid a hand on her arm and she stopped.

'My dear, if you must have a bath, you shall have one directly you get to White Ladies. I'll turn on the water for you. But let me beg of you – '

'If I go on, will you promise to behave?'

'Faithfully.'

'And fold your arms and sit like a groom all the way?'

'I suppose you couldn't make it a footman. Then I could stand on the petrol tank. However, as it's your birthday – '

I folded my arms with a sigh. Instantly Agatha leaned towards me with a dazzling smile.

'Good Boy,' she said in a caressing tone. 'Now he shall have a stamp album.'

'But I don't collect stamps.'

The smile deepened. But for her red mouth, her little white teeth would have been the prettiest things in the world.

'Well, I'd thought of a stamp album,' she said slowly. 'However, as it's your birthday – '

A minute later we were back in the main road.

By my direction Miss Deriot drove straight to the stables, and we left the car standing in the middle of the yard.

As we walked round to the front of the house, 'We won't tell the others that we've found her just yet,' said I. 'We'll hear what they've got to say first.'

'Perhaps they're all out looking for her,' said Agatha.

'Not all. Daphne's sure to be here somewhere.'

As I spoke we rounded a clump of laurels to see the lady in question comfortably ensconced in a deck chair upon the lawn. By her side was Jill, seated upon a cushion, one little foot tucked under her, nursing the other's instep with her slim brown hand. On a rug at her feet lay Jonah, his chin propped between his two palms and a pipe in his mouth.

All three were gazing contentedly across the grass to where the drive swept wide to the foot of the broad grey steps. *There stood a handsome Rolls-Royce, the facsimile of the one from which we had just alighted.*

With a great gasp Agatha stopped dead and I recoiled as from a spectre. Instinctively we clasped one another.

'It's all right,' I whispered. 'I've seen it too. It'll go away in a moment. Shows what imagination will do.'

'But – but it's real!' cried Agatha.

'Real enough, my lady,' said Jonah's voice. He seemed to be speaking from a great distance. 'And I'll bet you never expected to see her again so soon,' he added, looking at me with a smile.

'To tell you the truth,' said I, 'we didn't.'

As in a dream I watched a dazed and stammering Agatha made welcome and set in a chair by my sister's side. Somebody – Jill, I fancy – led me to the rug and persuaded me to sit down. Mechanically I started to fumble for a cigarette. Then I heard Jonah talking, and I came to my senses.

'We thought you'd be surprised,' he was saying, 'but I didn't think it'd take you like this. After all, there's nothing uncanny about it.'

'But I don't understand – '

'Listen. Will Noggin was sitting in the car when he heard a crash, and there was a fellow lying in the middle of the road, about fifty yards away, with a push-bike beside him. Naturally Will jumped out and ran to his help. The man seemed to be having a fit, and Will was just loosening his collar, when he heard the engine start and saw the Rolls moving. He left the chap in the road and ran like mad, but he was too late. Nobody ever saw the fellow with the push-bike again. Of course he was one of the gang, and his fall was a put-up job to get Will out of the way. Pretty smart – what?

'Well, you hadn't been gone five minutes when Fitch arrived on his motor-bike. He'd come to bring us a can of petrol, for after we'd left he remembered the tank was almost empty.

'That gave me a bit of hope. If they stuck to the main road, you were pretty well bound to catch them, for Fitch swore they'd never get five miles. But of course they might turn off. So I thought the rest of us had better follow and search the by-roads for all we were worth. So I sat on Fitch's carrier with the can under one arm, and Daphne commandeered the curate's push-bike and sent Berry after us.'

'Isn't he back yet?' said I, looking round.

'Not yet,' said Jonah, with a grin.

'And doesn't he know she's found?'

'That pleasure is still awaiting him. Well, Fitch was right. We left the Bloodstock road for the second time at Dew Thicket, and at the foot of the hill there she was, dry as a bone, but as right as rain.'

'Abandoned?'

'Apparently. Anyway, there was no one in sight. I sent Fitch after you and drove her home. Fitch had a burst directly he'd left me, and had to walk back to Bilberry.'

'Is that all?' said I.

'Well, it's enough, isn't it?'

'Not nearly,' said I, rising to my feet. 'Kindly accompany me to the stables.'

'What d'you mean, Boy?' cried Jill.

'Sh!' said I. 'Come and see.'

In silence I led the way, Agatha treading solemnly by my side. As we turned under the archway that led to the stable-yard –

'You see,' I said carelessly, 'we, too, have met with some success.'

The Rolls was standing where I had left her, waiting to be backed into the garage.

My sister gave a cry and caught at Jonah's arm. Jonah started violently and smothered an exclamation. Jill put one hand to her eyes, as if to brush away a vision.

There was a long silence.

At length I turned to Jonah.

'I fear that you were hasty, brother. A moment's reflection will show you that you and Fitch have spoiled some poor car owner's day. Let me suggest that you return your ill-gotten gains to the foot of the hill beyond Dew Thicket without delay. As a matter of fact, I know the police are very concerned about this theft. It was the fourth in this district this morning.'

Fitch came forward, touching his hat.

'It's a mistake anybody might make, sir. They're as like as two pins.' He pointed to the car. 'She's the spit of ours, she is.'

'Don't be silly,' said I. 'I admit they're exactly alike, but that's ours.'

Fitch shook his head.

'Different chassis number, sir, to say nothing of the number-plates.'

I stared at him. Then –

'Nonsense,' I said sturdily.

'It's a fact, sir. The one in the front's ours. I'm afraid you've stole somebody else's car.'

★

We had returned to the front of the house and were wondering what to do, when our attention was attracted by a sudden outburst of cries and the noise of a car's tyres tearing at the road. This lay but a hundred odd yards away on the farther side of the brown stream by which the lawn was edged. For the length of a cricket pitch the hedgerow bounding the highway was visible from where we stood, and as this was not more than four feet high, we were able to observe the scene which was clearly but the prologue to a drama in which we were presently to appear.

Under the explosive directions of a man in a grey hat, who was standing upright and holding on to the windscreen, frantic efforts were being made to turn what seemed to be a small touring car. Even as we looked, a savage gesture in our direction suggested that our friend was identifying the Rolls by our side as stolen property for the benefit of four individuals who crouched timorously behind him. To my consternation I observed that these were no less than an inspector and three constables of the County Police.

The next minute the car had been turned round and was being driven rapidly back to our lodge-gates.

'Leave them to me,' said Jonah quietly. 'Go and sit down on the lawn, all of you. I'll fix them.'

'That's the fellow,' said Grey Hat, in a shaking voice, 'and that's his accomplice.' He pointed a fat hand at myself and Agatha in turn.

'I beg your pardon,' said Jonah. Grey Hat turned and looked him up and down. 'Were you wanting anything? I mean, I live here.'

'I don't know who you are,' came the reply. 'But that's my car, and those are the people who stole it.'

'One thing at a time. My name's Mansel.'

'I'm the Chief Constable of the county.'

'Good. Now, about the car. I was under the impression that it was mine.'

'Don't try and bluff me, sir,' roared the other. 'You know perfectly well that that car was stolen from the outskirts of Bloodstock only a few hours ago. You're a receiver, sir, a common – ' He checked himself with an effort. 'Inspector!' The officer addressed came forward and saluted. 'Caution the three of them.'

'Hadn't you better identify your property first?' said Jonah. 'I mean, I don't want to interfere, but if it's a question of our arrest – '

The inspector hesitated, and the Chief Constable's face took on a darker shade of red. He was a coarse-looking man, generously designed and expensively over-dressed. For a moment I thought he was going to strike Jonah. Then he caught a heavy underlip in his teeth, turned on his heel, and strode to the Rolls-Royce.

He cast a proprietor's eye over her points. Then he stepped behind her as though to come to her other side. The next second he was back and shaking his fist in Jonah's face.

'So you've had the infernal audacity to alter the number-plates, have you?' he yelled. 'Thought to bluff me, I suppose. You impudent – '

'One moment,' said Jonah steadily. 'Without looking at the dash, tell me your chassis number. Your chauffeur should know it.'

'One double seven eight,' came parrotwise from the lips of the gentleman referred to.

'Thank you,' said Jonah.

Grey Hat almost ran to the Rolls, tore open the bonnet, and stared at the dash – stared. . . .

We waited in a silence so charged with expectancy as to be almost unbearable.

At last the Chief Constable straightened his back. His eyes were bulging and his face redder than ever. Twice he essayed to speak without success. Then –

'I said it was my car,' said Jonah placidly.

For a moment Grey Hat stood glaring at him. Then, muttering something about 'a mistake', he started to lurch towards the police car. As the officers turned shamefacedly to follow their chief, Jonah's parade voice rang out.

'Stop!' At the word of command, master and men alike stood still where they were. 'My friends and I have been openly accused of felony and threatened with arrest.'

The Chief Constable swallowed before replying.

'I was mistaken,' he said thickly. 'I – I apologise.'

'You mean to say you believed that to be your car?'

'I did.'

'Why?'

'It's exactly like it.'

'There must be some difference.'

'There's no difference at all. If mine were here, I'd defy you to tell them apart.'

'Do you seriously suggest that I shouldn't know my own car?'

'I do.'

'And that such a mistake on my part would be excusable?'

'Certainly.'

'Thank you,' said Jonah. 'That excusable mistake was made this morning. My car was stolen and sought for. Your car was found. If you will accompany me to the stables, I shall be happy to restore it to you at once.'

Grey Hat started forward, his face transfigured with excitement and relief.

'You mean to say – ' he began.

'Come, sir,' said Jonah icily. 'I feel sure that the ladies will excuse your withdrawal.'

It was half an hour later, just when we were finishing tea, that a cry from Jill made us all turn to follow her gaze down the curling drive.

Twenty paces away was Berry, plodding slowly in our direction, wheeling a tired-looking bicycle. His clothes were thick with dust, his collar was like a piece of wet rag, and on his face there was a look of utter and profound resignation.

As we started to our feet –

'Don't touch me,' he said. 'I'm leading in the Marathon race. The conditions are fearful. Competitors are required not only to walk, but at the same time to propel a bicycle, the hind tyre of which must be deflated. You're only allowed five falls, and I've used four of them.' With a final effort he reached the edge of the lawn and laid the bicycle gently on its side. ' "How we brought the good news from Aix to Ghent," ' he continued. 'Yes, I see the car, but I'm not interested. During the last five hours my life has been so crowded with incident that there is no room for anything else. Isn't there a cycling club about here I can join? I've always fancied a grey sweater.'

'Did I hear you say that you had fallen, brother?' said I.

'You did. Four times were these noble limbs prostrated in the dust. The first time was when the handle-bars came off. Oh, it's a beautiful machine.' Solemnly he waited for the laughter to subside. 'But she doesn't turn easily. If my blood counts, there are at least three corners in the county that are for ever England. And now will somebody fetch the Vicar? I shan't last long. And some drinks.' He stretched himself upon the grass. 'Several drinks. All together in a large vessel.'

Jill fled, weak with laughter, to execute his commands. Berry proceeded to remove his collar and tie.

'I can't think,' he said suddenly, 'why they call them safety bicycles. I suppose it's because they strike only on the box.' He turned to Daphne. 'Since I left you this morning, woman, I have walked with Death. Oh, more than once. Of course I've walked without him, too. Miles and miles.' He groaned. 'I never knew there was so much road.'

'Didn't you do any riding?' said Jonah. 'I know they're called push-bikes, but that's misleading. Lots of people ride them. That's what the saddle's for.'

'Foul drain,' said my brother-in-law. 'Your venomous bile pollutes the crystal flood of my narration. Did I ride? That was the undoing of the sage. When he recovered consciousness for the second time, it was to discover that the chain was missing and that the back tyre was windless. In my endeavours to find the chain I lost myself. That reminds me. I must put an advertisement in *The Times* to the effect that anyone returning a bicycle-chain to White Ladies will be assaulted. I have no desire to be reminded of today. If anybody had told me you could cover about fifty miles of open road in England without meeting anything but road-hogs, who not only failed to stop when I hailed them, but choked and blinded me with their filthy dust, I should have prayed for his soul. And not a pub open!'

He stopped to watch with a glistening eye the approach of Jill, bearing a tankard in one hand and a large jug of some beverage in the other.

'What is it?' he said.

'Shandy-gaff.'

'Heaven will reward you, darling, as I shan't.' He took a long draught. 'And yet I don't know. I've got an old pair of riding-breeches I don't want, if they're any use to you.'

There was a shriek from Agatha and Jill.

'Is anybody going to church?' said Daphne, consulting her wrist-watch.

Berry choked.

Gravely I regarded him.

'Run along and change,' said I. 'And you can return the curate his bicycle at the same time. Besides, a walk'll do you good.'

'Don't tempt me,' he replied. 'Two hours ago I registered a vow. I shall drink no water till it is accomplished.'

'Let's hear it,' said I.

'To offer no violence to a fool for six months,' said Berry, refilling his tankard. 'By the way, you'll have to be very careful when you take off my boots. They're very full of foot this evening.' He sank back and closed his eyes. 'You know I never look at the almanac, but before I was up this morning I knew that this was a blue-letter day.'

'How?' said his wife.

'I left a stud within the bath, and heard Jonah find it.'

It is now high Summer. The weather is glorious. Too glorious.

Adèle Feste, still in America, has intimated that she will return, but her date of departure has not been settled. This inevitably means that Boy can indulge in a little light dalliance with another transatlantic visitor, the beautiful Perdita Boyte.

During her stay, all has not been smooth. Due to mischance, Berry has had to endure the humiliation of having his wrists cuffed as a receiver of stolen goods; the Pleydells' dog, the Knave, has purloined a Judge's shoe; and the Jacobean refectory table they bid over a thousand pounds for turned out to have been made in 1912 (luckily they were outbid, and the set of chairs they captured for two hundred and fifty pounds proved to be worth five times that).

And now the wells at White Ladies are running dry . . .

THE ABBEY PLATE

Dusk had come into the panelled dining-room, and the radiance the candles lent to the tablecloth made bold, as the bark of a puppy, to speed the parting day. And something else it did. It showed to great advantage the beauty that graced our board. On my left, my sister, Daphne, recalled the dark perfection of Reynolds' days: on my right, my golden-haired cousin remembered those pretty princesses that live in the fairy-tales: on the other side of the table, the natural and lively sweetness of Perdita Boyte suggested a hamadryad acquainted with Vanity Fair. One other thing held the eye – and that was the pink champagne. The table was jewelled with six little rose-coloured pools, that caught the sober light and made it dance and sparkle with infinite mirth.

'I'm all disappointed,' said Perdita. 'White Ladies ought to have a ghost. I mean, if ever there was a house . . .'

'That,' said Berry, 'is what I have always said. This place would be stiff with ghosts – if there were such things.'

'But there are,' said his wife. 'Just because you don't happen to have seen one – '

'Neither have you,' said Berry. 'None of us have.'

'I know people who have,' said I.

'Who say they have,' said Berry. 'But they're always short of a witness to bear them out.'

'There's Abbess' Oak,' said Jill.

'A legend,' said Berry, 'that no one on earth can confirm.'

'I dare you,' said I, 'to stand alone under that tree for a quarter of an hour on end on a winter's night.'

My brother-in-law frowned.

'Certainly not,' he said. 'I don't believe in apparitions, but I do believe in a presence you cannot see. And that can be most disconcerting.'

'Then you do believe the legend,' said Jonah.

'No, I don't,' said Berry, 'but I'm not going to take any risks. If by chance it was true, the lady would resent my intrusion, and I don't want any spirits biting my neck.'

'Bigot,' said Daphne. 'You value your unbelief.'

'He's none to value,' said I. 'You ought to have been at Cockcrow, when they wanted to put him to sleep in the haunted room.'

Berry addressed Miss Boyte.

'Happily,' he said, 'I am proof against the darts of the ungodly. This I attribute entirely to meekness of soul – a quality more apparent to the lower animals than to certain blasphemous lepers who defile the faculty of speech. Besides, the room was hung with black arras.'

Perdita shuddered.

'That was unfair – even to a heretic. Please may I hear the legend of Abbess' Oak?'

I emptied my glass.

'Once upon a time,' said I, 'an abbey stood here – an abbey of nuns. It had the reputation of being immensely rich. It was, as were many others, suppressed by Henry the Eighth: but, in this particular case, the abbey was burned to the ground – and five years later this house was built on the site. That is all matter of fact, and now for the legend. The Abbess was warned that the King's men were on their way, so, before they came, she got all the treasure away and sent it down to the coast and over to France. Robbed of their spoil, the King's men went mad with rage, and they not only burned the abbey but they hanged the Abbess herself from a bough of the oak that stands by the mouth of the drive. And ever since then her ghost has walked of nights where the crime was done.'

Perdita took a deep breath.

'Was nothing left of the Abbey?'

'Only the cellars,' said Berry. He lifted his glass. 'This wine came out of them. They're simply gigantic. In fact, unless the nuns entertained a good deal, one is forced to the conclusion that the Abbey was justly suppressed.'

'I'd love to see them.'

'Tomorrow morning,' said I.

'The dowser,' said Daphne, 'is coming tomorrow morning.'

'For a fee of ten guineas,' said Berry. 'You know, you make me tired.'

'You won't be tired if he finds us another spring.'

With a manifest effort, Berry controlled his voice.

'There are moments,' he said, 'when I could bark with emotion. Bark . . . To hear you talk, nobody would dream we'd ever had a dowser before – and dropped two hundred quid because we believed what he said.'

There was an uneasy silence.

The remembrance was more than grievous. At the place which the wizard selected, we had dug an expensive well. At forty-two feet we found water, and at forty-three we found rock – exactly one foot of water, forty feet down. And when we had pumped it dry, the well took twelve hours to refill. . . .

'Well, we must do something,' said Daphne. 'The garden – '

'We must have water brought,' said Berry. 'Conveyed by road.'

'Hopeless,' said Jonah. 'We'd need six carts a day for the lawns alone.'

'Then,' said Berry, 'we must deepen the wells we have.'

'Out of the question,' said Jonah. 'If we are to have more water, we've got to find a new spring. And that is where the water-diviner comes in. I don't like taking his word, but we'll prove him right or wrong for a matter of thirty pounds.'

'It isn't the money,' said Berry. 'It's the knowledge that we'll have been done – for the second time . . . in the crudest possible way. You wouldn't have a child on twice, and we're not infants-in-arms.'

'*Force majeure*,' said I. 'There's nothing else to be done.'

'I'll tell you what,' said Jill. 'We can watch the Knave. He'll know if the dowser's honest. And if the Knave doesn't like him, we needn't dig.'

'Better still,' said Berry. 'We bury a bottle of whisky before he comes, and while he's walking about we watch his nose. If this begins to go red, we write home and warn his wife. And when he's gone, with his cheque – '

'I know,' said Perdita. 'Couldn't you lay a trap? Hide one of the wells, and see if he finds it out?'

There was an electric silence. Then –

'The stable well,' said Jonah. 'Ground-sheet over the flap and a flowerbed on top. You know. Like they make them for shows. Old Thorn will love to do it, but we'll have to tell him tonight. And here's a health to the lady for being so wise.'

We drank it rapturously.

'She's a paying guest,' said Berry. 'That's what she is. I feel quite different already. My gorge is falling and my spleen is fast assuming proportions less inconvenient to its distinguished company.'

Perdita smiled.

'If I'm bright tonight, you must thank your very good wine.' She touched her glass. 'Did the nuns leave this behind them? It's terribly rare.'

'The custom of the house,' said Berry. 'Tomorrow is the chatelaine's birthday. In less than twenty-four hours my hag will be sixty-nine.'

'Common man,' said Daphne. 'Last year I was twenty-seven, so now I am twenty-six. Entirely between ourselves, the Bilberry register will tell you I'm thirty-two.'

Perdita lifted her glass.

'I'm so glad to be here,' she said gently, and left it there.

★

The diviner compassed the flowerbed, rod in hand. We watched him guiltily. After a little, he set a foot on the mould. . . . And then he was full in the bed and was wiping the sweat from his face.

'There's water here,' he said shortly. 'Abundant water . . . at twenty to twenty-one feet.'

Berry took the bull by the horns.

'We congratulate you,' he said quietly. 'You're perfectly right.'

Frowning a little, the other stepped out of the bed.

'Trying me out, eh? I might have known. There's plenty of sceptics about.'

'We should like to beg your pardon,' said Berry. 'But it's fair to ourselves to tell you that two years ago we were very badly let down.'

The diviner nodded abruptly.

'Plenty of them about, too.' He pushed back his hat and tapped with his foot upon the ground. 'There's a fine spring here.' He laughed. 'Good enough for a village, but not for a place like this.'

The procession reformed, but we followed no longer as critics, but in humble respect for a talent we could not deny. So far as I was concerned, the man was a proven wizard – and that was that. The gardeners who brought up the rear were deeply impressed. Only the Knave showed indifference – or, rather, a faint surprise that we should honour a stranger whom he had rejected the moment he saw his face. The dog can hardly be blamed. The fellow was most unattractive, and so were his ways. Manners may not make magic, for all I know.

We left the walled kitchen-garden to enter the orchard beyond. . . .

Strolling by Perdita's side, I found it strange that Nature should have chosen for her prophet a practical, businessman. About the diviner there was nothing at all of the earth. That the country bored him was plain. He belonged to the town. With his precious gift, the fields should have been his office, the open sky his windows, the brooks his books. But the man was a man of business and his rod was a fountain-pen.

I murmured my feelings to Perdita.

'The shepherd's complaint,' she replied. 'You must live and let live, Lycidas – though you may have been born out of time.'

'There spoke Amaryllis,' said I. 'Supposing – '

The diviner's voice cut me short.

'There's a spring hereabouts. A good one. It mayn't be where you want it. I can't help that.'

'It's quite all right here,' said Berry. 'Isn't it, Thorn?'

'A good head of water here, sir, would do us uncommonly well.'

The diviner seemed to cast to and fro. After a little he straddled and pointed between his feet.

'Have you got a peg?' he demanded.

Thorn came forward and pressed a peg into the soil.

'At twenty-five feet,' said the other. 'Perhaps twenty-four.'

'No rock?' said Berry.

'Rock be damned. You're lucky. I've found you a master spring. It's a waste of time going on. You've got what everyone wants.'

'I'm greatly obliged,' said Berry. 'Come back to the house. I guess you can do with a drink.'

'I guess I can,' said the other, and mopped his face.

Berry and I did the honours, and that in the library. At first we had to work hard, but under the touch of liquor our guest relaxed. This to our great relief. If what he told us was true – and we had no doubt that it was – the fellow had done us a service worth very much more than his fee. We were appropriately grateful. To have our advances rejected was most discouraging.

'I notice,' said I, 'that you don't work with a twig.'

Sitting on the arm of a sofa, the diviner shook his head.

'I can, but I don't have to. If a man can really find, he can find with a bit of old iron. I've done it with wire – more than once. But some things are better than others. It all depends how you're made.' He took a soft case from his coat. 'I've three rods here. They're all of them specially built.' He slid one out of its sheath and put the others away. 'Now that's one that I use. . . .'

With his words I saw the rod move and the sentence died on his lips.

'Good Lord, more water?' said Berry.

Frowning slightly, the dowser got to his fet.

'Looks like it,' he said abruptly. 'What's beneath here?'

'Wine cellars,' said I. 'But they're as dry as a bone.'

Rod in hand, the other nodded.

'It's a long way down,' he said slowly. 'You've nothing to fear.' He put the rod away and picked up his cheque. 'And now I'll be off,' he added. 'If you've time to burn, I haven't – and that's a fact.'

His ill humour was back in full force. The slightest use of his talent seemed to lay bare his nerves.

In an awkward silence, we walked with him to his car. There we thanked him again and he asked us the way to Brooch. As his two-seater stormed down the drive –

'Well, I'm glad that's over,' said Berry. 'He may be a giddy wizard – I think he is – but of all the offensive. . . .'

'Exactly,' said I. 'But I don't believe the man's normal.'

'Yes, he is,' said Berry. 'As normal as you and I. He's a Communist – that's his trouble. One of the red-hot type . . . that wants to bring to ruin all homes like ours. And we employ and shelter twenty-two souls.'

My sister leaned out of the oriel above our heads.

'My dears, what a birthday present! A master spring. What does that mean exactly?'

'I imagine,' said I, 'that it means a very rich source.'

'And you do believe in him, Berry?'

'If I didn't, my sweet, he'd have gone twenty minutes ago – with a master flea in each ear.'

'Poor man,' said Daphne. 'Perhaps he's a master spleen.'

Three days had gone by, and the new well was nine feet deep. So much Jonah reported, measuring-tape in hand. The hour was sundown, and we had but just come home, to rush to the scene of the labour which was to confirm or deny the report the diviner had made.

'Outrageous,' said Berry. 'They haven't done three feet today.'

'It's been very hot,' said Daphne.

'It's not skilled labour,' said Berry, 'and they've got five men on the job. Any fool can dig a hole in the ground.'

Jonah looked up.

'He's perfectly right. We could dig it faster ourselves. If we put in four hours tomorrow . . .'

'I'm game,' said I.

'That's the style,' said Berry heartily. 'I only wish I could help.'

'Don't be a fool,' said Jonah. 'We must have three.'

'Why can't you help?' said Jill.

'I've got to see the dentist,' said Berry. 'Heaven knows – '

'Have you got an appointment?' said Daphne.

My brother-in-law swallowed.

'Polteney always sees me – '

In a burst of indignant derision the rest of the sentence was lost.

'All right, all right,' said Berry. 'I'll put it off. After all, what is thrush?' He took up a pick-axe and weighed it – with starting eyes. 'I think I'd better work at the top.'

'Half-hour shifts,' said Jonah. 'We shan't want very much on.'

'We'd better work barefoot,' said Berry. 'Then when we slice our feet off, we shan't have any boots to be cut away.'

'Any fool,' said I, 'can dig a hole in the ground.'

'With reasonable tools,' said Berry. 'That pick-axe – '

'It's the weight that does it,' said Jonah. 'You'll see what I mean when you've swung it for a quarter of an hour.'

As soon as Berry could speak –

'We'd better not,' he said shortly. 'We shall only offend the men. When they find we've been doing their work – Yes, Falcon?'

I turned to see the butler two paces away.

'I came to say, sir, the men went off early today. It's the foreman's silver wedding. But they're going to make it up, sir, on Saturday afternoon.'

'God bless them,' said Berry with emotion. 'God bless their simple souls.'

'They were very anxious, sir, that you shouldn't think them indifferent to your desires. They're very grateful for the beer, sir.'

'Tell them,' said Berry warmly, 'I'm more than satisfied.'

'Very good, sir. And, if you please, sir, the wine has come.'

'The wine?' said Berry. 'What wine?'

The butler moistened his lips.

'I believe it, sir, to be claret. Sixty dozen were delivered this afternoon.'

'Sixty dozen?' screamed Berry. 'But who's been being funny?'

'There you are, sir,' cried Falcon. 'I was sure there was some mistake. Again and again I insisted that you would never have ordered – '

'Seven hundred and twenty bottles?'

'And all of them loose, sir. And not a label between them. . . . It took two hours and more to get them into the bins.'

Berry put a hand to his head.

'Stand back,' he faltered. 'Stand back and give me air.'

'But where did they come from?' said Daphne.

'From some warehouse in London, madam. I'd have telephoned if I could, but they're not in the book.'

'Well, it's their look-out,' said I. 'When they render the bill, we can tell them to take it away.'

'That's all very well,' said Berry. 'Supposing I'm right, and somebody is being funny – ordering stuff in our name. . . . We shall know tomorrow morning, but I don't want five tons of guano and a hundred and fifty bedsteads in weathered oak.'

'For heaven's sake,' breathed Perdita. 'Is that sort of thing ever done?'

'I regret to say,' said Berry, 'it sometimes is. The Fairies of Castle Charing met it last year. They spent a week in Paris. When they got home they could hardly get into the drive. Four full-size billiard-tables, seventy baby-carriages, over two miles of stair-carpet, eleven kitchen-ranges and twenty tons of the very best fish manure.'

'Let's shut the gates,' said Daphne, faintly. 'If you think there's the slightest chance – '

'It's all right, my dear,' said Berry. 'They can't get very far as long as we're here. I'll give up Polteney tomorrow and spend the day on the steps.'

In fact, he was spared this penance. At seven o'clock the next morning the men returned for the wine and took it away. The lorries were laden and gone before we were down.

It was Sunday afternoon, and Perdita Boyte and I were sitting at ease on the turf at the head of the well. The others were gone to tea at a neighbouring house.

The orchard was comfortable, breathing the honest leisure of other days. So far from ruffling its calm, the sound of a distant car deposed to its possession of a peace which the world of today cannot give. The silence was rich and golden, laced with the hum of insects and, now and again, with the delicate flutter of wings.

A little shaft of sunlight was thrusting between the leaves to glorify Perdita's hair. This was uncalled for. Her beauty was vivid enough. At her feet the Knave lay couched, with his eyes on my face.

My lady opened a mouth which prose could never describe.

'Why does this spot attract you?'

'At the moment,' said I, 'I am here because you are here.'

Perdita laid herself back and regarded the sky.

'If I were out of the country, you'd be sitting beside this well.'

'I believe that,' said I, 'to be true. But I don't know why.'

'Try and think,' said Perdita, quietly.

Averting my gaze from the lady, I did as she said. After a little while –

'It's rather involved,' I said feebly. 'First, I've always had a weakness for fairy-tales. You know. There was once a youth who set out to seek his fortune. And he met a wise man by the way. And the wise man told him to dig at a certain place and that when he had dug so deep he would discover the treasure that there lay hid . . . Then, to come back to earth, the treasure itself is perfection – a lively thread of silver, a virgin source, that since the world began rolling has picked its way from the hills. . . . And then again, the well is so very old. It's figured from the beginning – in the Bible, in Aesop's fables, in Virgil and nursery rhyme. Men have always dug wells, and the simple ritual's the same as it was in Abraham's day. It is a natural labour – rendering unto Nature the things that are hers, for, once the well has been dug, it's as much a part of Nature as cockcrow itself.'

A bright, brown eye found mine.

' "Sermons in stones," ' said Perdita, sitting up. 'My dear, you're incorrigible. You're the finest costumier I know. You could dress up a fried-fish stall or an Epstein bust. And "Solomon in all his glory was not arrayed like one of these." '

'Who eggs me on?' said I. 'Who picks over the junk of ages and points to some faded relic I never found lovely before?'

'That's right. Dress me up, showman.'

'I'm afraid I shall have to undress you – to go with the well. All the best nymphs went bare-legged, with a veil draped into a tunic and one of their shoulders free.'

'Idylls while you wait,' said Perdita. 'Go on.'

'I've done,' said I. 'You've got the shape and the skin and the right-sized stars in your eyes. You've got the eager air and the mouth which the dawn gets up on purpose to see: your hair would go straight into a shepherd's song, and as for your finger-tips. . . .'

I picked them up gently enough. 'I'm afraid they're dangerous. If a god was passing when you waved your hand to a bird, I'm sure he'd come and ask for a drink. You'd have to give it him, of course. In your cupped palms, too. You know, I'm getting quite jealous.'

Perdita began to shake with laughter.

'It's all very fine to laugh,' I said severely. 'There's the poor shepherd, clean off his feed and dreaming of the lights in your hair, trying to find a rhyme for "provocative", and all the time you're giving a god a . . . drink.'

Perdita lowered her eyes.

'I daresay, if the shepherd asked nicely. . . .'

The Knave, most discreet of sentinels, lifted his lovely head – and I saw the servant coming, before he saw us.

He was plainly looking for me, so I raised my voice.

'I'm here, if you want me, William.'

The man came bustling with a salver on which was reposing a card.

Chief Inspector R. Wilson
C.I.D.
Scotland Yard.

I passed it to Perdita, frowning, and got to my feet.

'All right, William,' I said. 'Show him into the library.'

'Very good, sir.'

As he left the orchard –

'But this is thrilling,' said Perdita. 'What can he want?'

I put out my hands for hers and drew her up to her feet.

'Come and see,' said I. 'I've not the faintest idea. But I wish the others were here.'

My desire was granted forthwith.

As we left the stable-yard, I saw the flash of the Rolls at the mouth of the entrance drive.

Chief Inspector Wilson compelled respect. If his manner was masterful, his sense of duty stood out, while the way in which he stated his case would have done credit to any barrister.

He addressed himself to Berry, as being the obvious head of the eager court.

'I'm sorry to rush you like this, sir, but before I'm through you'll see that it isn't my fault.' He glanced at the six pairs of eyes which were fast on his face. 'I mean to speak openly. I'm sure that everyone here will keep what I say to themselves.'

'I promise you that,' said Berry, as a murmur of assurance went round.

The Inspector inclined his head.

'I've called to see you,' he said, 'about some wine. . . . On Thursday last, I believe, some wine was delivered here . . . several hundred bottles, whilst you were out for the day.'

'That's perfectly right,' said Berry. 'It was taken away the next morning at eight o'clock.'

'Quite so,' said the Inspector. 'Mistakes do sometimes occur. I don't know if you saw the invoice, but *Rouse and Rouse* was the name, of *Commercial Road*.'

My brother-in-law nodded.

'In fact,' said Inspector Wilson, 'there's no such firm. There *was* – five years ago, that explains the printed bill-head, but there isn't now.'

We could only stare.

'Please get hold of this,' he continued. 'The delivery of that wine was *not* a mistake. . . . And now may I see the butler?'

In a silence big with emotion, I rose and stepped to the bell. . . .

After perhaps thirty seconds, the butler entered the room.

'Falcon,' said Berry, 'Chief Inspector Wilson would like to ask you some questions about that wine.'

'Very good, sir,' said Falcon, wide-eyed.

He turned to Inspector Wilson and moistened his lips.

The other looked up from a bulging pocket-book.

'Tell me this, Mr Falcon. How many men brought the wine?'

The butler considered.

'There were five or six,' he said. 'I can't be exactly sure.'

'And how many fetched it away?'

'The same as brought it,' said Falcon. 'I think there were six, but there may have been only five.'

'Would you know them again?'

'I think so. Not all, perhaps. You see, my hands were full. The cellar's not very well lit, and what with counting the bottles and trying to – '

'Is that one?' said the Inspector, producing a photograph.

'That's right,' said Falcon, at once.

'And that?'

Another photograph passed.

'Yes, that's another,' said Falcon.

'Thank you,' said the Inspector. 'That's all I want.'

Thus abruptly dismissed, Falcon took his reluctant leave. As the door closed behind him –

'I'd like to see the cellar,' said Wilson, 'almost at once. But before you take me down, I'll tell you what we shall find. That cellar has got an air-hole.'

'That's perfectly true,' said Berry. 'There's a grating some three feet square – which gives to a slot in the ground like a miniature well.'

'I never knew that,' said Daphne.

'It's behind the lilacs,' said Berry, 'close to the stable-yard.' He returned to Inspector Wilson. 'If you're thinking of entry, that grating could never be forced. It *can* be opened – from within. But I'll swear it's never been touched for fifty years.'

'It's open now,' said the other. 'That's why I'm here.'

The sensation this statement provoked expressed itself in a silence which is commonly coupled with death. The six of us sat spellbound, not seeming to breathe.

After a little, the Inspector continued quietly.

'You remember the butler said there were five or six men. Well, there his memory's perfect. Six men delivered that wine, and five went away. Five men came for the wine, and six went away. One man was down in that cellar all Thursday night. His job was to open that grating.' He raised his eyebrows and sighed. 'It's been done before.'

'Well, I'm damned,' said Berry, and spoke for us all.

'Now, I'm not a magician,' said Wilson. 'I couldn't tell you all this, if I hadn't been told. I've been told by an informant. I hold no brief for such men, but they earn their bread. This one's sitting at Cannon Row now, afraid to go out. But that's by the way. I've been after this gang for months, and, by your leave, I'm going to get them tonight.'

'Tonight?' cried everyone.

The Inspector nodded.

'If my informant is right, they're coming tonight.'

Berry sat back in his chair and folded his arms.

'What do we do?' he said.

The Inspector smiled.

'I suppose it's asking too much that you should do nothing at all. To be honest, sir, that's what I'd like. I've five men two miles off and I'm going to bring them along as soon as it's dark. Sit up and watch, if you must – but if I'm to get home tonight, you must give that grating a miss. Try and forget about it – and all that side of the house. You see, that's the mouth of the trap. . . . My men will be down in the cellar before they come. The door, of course, will be locked, and I'd rather you kept the key.' He jerked his head at the Knave. 'You must keep that dog quiet at all costs. I'd like him shut up in some room at the other end of the house.'

'I was just going to say,' said Berry, 'it's going to be more of a matter for ears than eyes. I shall sit by the cellar door and listen in.'

My sister shuddered.

'I shall go to bed early,' she said. 'And, as the Inspector asks, I shall try to forget. What do they want, Inspector?'

'Jewels and silver, madam.' He hesitated. 'You've got some notable bracelets, I understand.'

Daphne covered her eyes.

'I believe every thief in Europe knows about them.'

The Inspector shrugged his shoulders.

'These things get round,' he said shortly, and rose to his feet. 'And now may I see the cellars? After that, the outside of the grating: and then if you'd show me a place I can park the cars – just off the road, somewhere, as near the house as you can.' He glanced at his watch. 'As I said before, I'm sorry to rush you like this, but it's only a short six hours since the news came in.'

'You've had to shift,' said Berry. 'And Sunday, too.'

The other nodded ruefully.

'I was going to the Zoo,' he said simply, 'with my little girl.'

Our visit to the cellars confirmed the informant's report. The grating had been unfastened, and its hinges were thick with grease. I swung it open myself without a sound.

Half an hour later we bade the Inspector goodbye – till the following day.

With a foot on the step of his car, he spoke his last word.

'You won't forget that dog, sir? If he were to go and give tongue . . .'

He broke off and shrugged his shoulders.

The Knave looked him full in the eyes and lifted his lip.

An hour had gone by, and Perdita, Berry and I were strolling beside the sunk fence, discussing the enterprise of the housebreaker of today.

'I confess,' said my brother-in-law, 'to a certain admiration for those about to be jugged. Sixty dozen of claret would gammon a herd of bloodhounds, let alone honest men.'

'The very three that I wanted,' said Jonah's voice. 'Daphne's too nervous, and it wouldn't be good for Jill,' and with that, he took my arm and fell into step.

'I wish to God,' said Berry, 'you wouldn't do things like that. Coming up from behind without warning. I'm ready to scream if anyone blows his nose.'

My cousin ignored the protest.

'Keep on walking, please, and listen to me. I've been on to the Assistant Commissioner – at his private house. I wanted to ask about Wilson. . . . He says he's an excellent man – *but he happens to be in Paris. No doubt at all about that. They had a talk this morning over the telephone.*'

'Good God,' said Berry, weakly, and Perdita gripped my arm.

Jonah continued firmly.

'We have just received an impostor. Be sure of that. A wolf in sheep-dog's clothing – paving his way. He's coming tonight all right, *but he and his men are the gang*.'

I put a hand to my head.

'But why – I don't understand. . . .'

'It is confusing,' said Jonah, 'but I think I can give you a lead. Wasn't it Thursday night that the Knave barked twice?'

'Of course,' I cried. 'I'd forgotten. I got up and went downstairs.'

'That's right,' said Jonah. 'I heard you. We were both of us half asleep. The Knave must have heard the fellow at work on the grating below. But, what is much more to the point, the fellow at work heard the Knave. Next day he says to his pals, "The grating's open all right, but the dog's going to give us away." So "Wilson" comes down – under orders to clear the coast. I must say he did it well. Not only the dog but *all of us* out of the way. And simply by telling a tale the truth of which we could confirm. It's "the confidence trick" once again, in a different guise.'

My cousin's brilliant deduction left me dumb.

'I give you best,' said Berry. 'How did you know?'

'I didn't,' said Jonah, frankly. 'But one thing he said made me think. *I'd rather you kept the key* – of the cellar door. To me, those words rang false. They didn't seem to belong to Scotland Yard.' He broke off there, to look at the western sky. 'It won't be dark for two hours, and I've half a plan in my head. I wish we could cut dinner out, but I don't want Jill or Daphne to get ideas. And this is where you come in. It's up to you to get them out of the way – women and children upstairs by a quarter to ten.'

'I beg your pardon,' said Perdita.

'I didn't say "maidens",' said Jonah. 'I hope you'll come in on this. I was going to ask you if you'd take charge of the Knave. And now I must go. If I'm late for dinner, don't wait. I'll tell you all I've arranged at a quarter to ten. Meanwhile please do your best to find the answer to this? What is "Wilson" after? I'd give a good deal to know.'

'Jewels and silver,' I said. 'He told us himself.'

'And warned us,' said Jonah swiftly. 'Asked us to keep the key of the cellar door. . . . I don't think that answer's right.'

'It's a ruse,' said Berry, and wiped the sweat from his face. 'They mean to come in all right, but not by the cellar at all.'

'I don't think that's right,' said my cousin. 'If they don't mean to use the grating, why did Wilson request that the dog should be put on the other side of the house?'

Perdita put in her oar.

'But if both those answers are bad, you get a third which is worse – that what they want's in the cellar.'

'Which is absurd,' said Jonah. 'I quite agree. Burglars like their liquor as much as anyone else, but they don't go lengths like these for a little Napoleon brandy and six or seven dozen of pink champagne. Never mind. Think it over. We ought to be able, between us, to do the sum.'

With that, he was gone.

We watched him reach the terrace and enter the house.

'I'm quite sorry for "Wilson",' said Berry. 'He's going to get the shock of his life. When Jonah takes off his coat it's time to go home.'

This was most true.

My cousin, Jonathan Mansel, is a man of action as swift and, if need be, as deadly as any machine-gun that ever was brought into play.

A track runs into a wood which rises beside our meadows a short three hundred yards from the orchard gate. From my perch on the bough of an oak commanding the track I could, by day, have seen the roof of the stables against the blue of the sky. But it was no longer day. Night had fallen some twenty-five minutes ago.

My orders were clear. To signal 'Wilson's' arrival: to signal the strength of his gang: to signal whether or no the cars were left unattended when 'Wilson' set out for the house. All this, of course, with my torch. If the cars were left to themselves, Perdita and the Knave would join me, to watch while I opened the bonnets and cut the high-tension leads. And then we were to join Berry, who was lying within the orchard, close to the well. As for Jonah. . . .

And there I heard the pulse of an engine.

A car – two cars had slowed down, on the road at the mouth of the track.

After, perhaps, thirty seconds, I heard them begin to back. . . .

Then I saw the glow of a tail-light – and made my report.

Two men were already afoot. Not till both cars had stopped did the others alight. Six in all I counted, and sent my news.

Things of some sort were taken out of the cars, but the lights were out now and I could not see what they were. The engines, of course, had been stopped, and since no words were spoken, the dark figures moving in the darkness were worse than sinister. I saw them cluster below me, just clear of the leading car.

And then one opened his mouth – and I nearly fell out of my tree. . . .

It was not 'Wilson' who spoke, but another, whose voice I knew.

As in a dream, I heard him issue some orders and tell off some man, called Jennet, to stay with the cars. His tone was as bitter as ever, his manner of speaking as short, and when he had done and was gone, I was not at all surprised when Jennet described him in terms which I dare not set down.

It was the diviner, indeed.

Bad masters make bad servants, and though, of course, I dared not lay hands on the cars, I was able to beat a retreat without any fuss, for Jennet, instead of patrolling, as he had been ordered to do, took his seat on one of the steps and lighted a cigarette.

I entered the meadows and followed the paling along. After perhaps forty paces, the Knave loomed out of the shadows, to put his paws on my chest.

'No luck?' breathed Perdita Boyte.

'Not at the moment,' said I, and told her my news.

'Oh, my dear,' twittered Perdita, 'what does it mean?'

'I'm damned if I know,' said I. 'Can't you work it out?'

'I can make it rather harder by telling you this. D'you remember I asked you a question this afternoon? *Why does this spot attract you?* We were sitting by the head of the well. . . . You gave me – so pretty an answer that I forgot altogether to give you mine.' I found a small hand and held it close to my heart. 'You see, Boy, it's not only you. That spot attracts us all. Ever since he told you to dig there – after all I'm only a guest, but it's never been out of my mind.'

'Well, why's that?' said I, feebly.

The small hand caught hold of my coat.

'Call me a fool, if you like, but I think it's because that man's willed us . . . been willing us ever since Monday to think of that well. That he's got one strange power we know. Well, I think he's got another. And I think he's been using that to keep our minds on that well.'

'But why should he do so, my beauty?'

The hand slipped away and up to the troubled temples which I could hardly see.

'I can't imagine,' wailed Perdita. 'And there you are. I told you I'd make it worse. But now that he's back here – in charge. . . .'

'Let's go and put it to Berry. I must get in touch with Jonah about those cars.'

Jonah and Berry were sitting on a log in the orchard, conversing in even tones.

'Come and sit down,' said the former. 'Our friends are deeply engaged. The cellar was their objective, as "Wilson" said. They seem to be taking the floor up: and as flags are not like linoleum, we've plenty of time. Then again the work would go faster if they weren't so painfully anxious to make no noise.'

'Did you recognise their leader?' said I.

' "Wilson" was the first of the string.'

'He's not in command.'

'Who then?'

'Our friend, the dowser,' said I. 'There's no mistaking his voice.'

'Go on,' said Berry, incredulously.

'I am ready,' said Jonah, quietly, 'to believe anything. Understanding's another matter. I frankly admit I'm a long way out of my depth. But very soon now we shall know. They may as well get the stuff out – whatever it is.'

'Perdita says – '

'Stop,' hissed Berry. 'Stop. I've got an idea. When he showed us rods, that wallah . . . and one of them moved. In the library, Boy, that morning. He asked what was underneath, and you said the cellars were dry.'

'Of course,' I heard myself saying. 'Of course . . . of course.'

I remembered perfectly – now. But I had forgotten the matter, as though it had never been.

Jonah was speaking.

'Tell me exactly what happened.'

Berry told him, from first to last.

'All the same,' he concluded, 'it only explains his presence – the dowser's, I mean. We want to know what he's after. And he's not come here to uncover some secret spring.'

'What does Perdita think?' said Jonah.

Perdita tried in vain to steady her voice.

'It all f-fits in,' she stammered. 'He made them forget that bit in the library. And he tried to make them forget by keeping their minds on the well – all our minds, in case they'd told us. . . .'

'I've no doubt you're right,' said Jonah. 'This dowser's no ordinary man.'

'What on earth d'you mean?' said Berry.

'This,' said Jonah. 'Water is not all that a really good dowser can find. He can detect the presence of minerals – under the earth. Gold and silver, for instance. . . .' I found myself trembling with excitement. 'When you saw his rod move that morning, you thought there was water below: but the dowser knew better: *he knew there was precious metal down in the cellars beneath* . . . he came Thursday night, to make sure – to find the exact place and the depth . . . and tonight he's come to take his findings away.'

An hour and a half crept by.

Perdita, Berry and I sat upon the log in the orchard, conversing by fits and starts but always with bated breath, while the Knave stood beside us like a statue, conscious of the presence of evil which for some strange reason he was not allowed to declare.

About his business, Jonah moved to and fro, visiting the servants he had posted, reporting progress to us or listening himself to the sounds which rose from the cellar's depths.

Jennet had been 'disposed of' and was sitting, gagged and bound, in one of the cars. These had not been disabled – my cousin had changed his plan.

An hour and a half.

Time seemed to be standing still: excitement begot an impatience which sent us half out of our minds: desire rebelled against reason again and again.

'Lifting flag-stones,' moaned Berry. 'They don't know how to work. I'd have moved a mountain by now. And I know I'd sell my soul to be doing the labour myself.'

Perdita put it in a nutshell.

'It's like when you've been given a present – and somebody else unpacks it, and you have to watch them fumbling, undoing the string.'

'I know,' said Jonah, 'I know. But when six desperate men play into your hands, it's very much better to let them. The great idea is to avoid unpleasantness.'

'I hardly think,' said Berry, 'that "The great idea" will mature. I mean, I can't help feeling that on their way back to town, no one of the six will really be at his best.'

With his words came the flash of a torch.

'They're off,' said Jonah. 'Still as death, if you please, until I come back.'

I went down on one knee. With my arm about the Knave's shoulders, I held his head to my chest. After, perhaps, two minutes I felt his ears twitch. . . .

And then I heard the men passing – two men, breathing hard as they went, as men who are anxious to hasten, while carrying weight.

Another two minutes went by.

And then, well out in the meadows, a light leaped up.

I saw figures moving against it, and one was standing still with his hands in the air. . . .

'Oh, I'm sorry for them,' said Perdita, and burst into tears.

I gave the Knave to Berry and picked her up in my arms.

'Rough justice,' I whispered. 'Not fit for a maiden's eyes. When Jonah comes back, I'm going to take you to bed.'

'Couldn't you . . . give them . . . just something? I mean . . . poor men.'

For the first time for seven days my brain seemed to leap to life.

'If they've found what I think they have, I'll give them five hundred pounds.'

'Oh, you darling,' breathed Perdita. A warm arm slid round my neck. 'What – what do you think they've found?'

'Darlings to you.' I kissed her. '*The Abbey Plate*.'

And that is very nearly the end of my tale.

A glance at the first-fruits showed that my conjecture was good: the plate had been buried, and lest it should be disinterred, the nuns had spread the report that it had been taken to France.

I took Perdita back to the house and wrote out a cheque. Then I returned to the orchard, where Berry was sitting in darkness, addressing the Knave.

'From your point of view, old fellow, it's been an utter wash-out from first to last. No hue, no cry, no dust-up, no biters bit. And what have we got to show for it? A lot of rotten utensils which we shall never use. Look at that alms-dish, for instance. No self-respecting dog would drink out of that. What if it is solid gold? You'd very much rather it was enamelled steel. . . .'

'What's happened?' I said.

'History,' said Berry, 'has just repeated itself. Two more left the cellar, laden, and were relieved of their booty in the midst of yon dewy meads. There's only the dowser left now. When the others fail to return, I suppose he'll emerge.'

'Who's in charge of the cars?'

'Fitch and Carson,' said Berry. 'They're going to deport the wicked as soon as Satan arrives. To Break Heart Heath, I believe – an appropriate spot. Jonah will follow and bring them home in the Rolls. He's really a perfect producer . . . I wish we could show a light. There's a monstrance here with a ruby as big as an eye. It can't be real, can it?'

'I'll be back in five minutes,' said I, and ran for the cars. . . .

'Chief Inspector Wilson' stared at the cheque.

Pay Mr Jennet or Order
Five hundred pounds.

'Is this a have?' he demanded.

'No,' said I, 'it's a present – from a very charming lady. You've done us extremely well, and she didn't like the idea of your going empty away.' I showed it to each of the others, then I returned to 'Wilson', folded it up and slipped it into his pocket and out of sight. 'There are five of you here,' I said, 'and, as you saw, it's made out for five hundred pounds. In a way, the inference is obvious. On the other hand, there's your leader – he'll soon be here. I haven't spoken to him, and I'll leave it to you to decide how much he should have.'

The five replied as one man. So far as I heard, each put it a different way, but each spoke straight from the heart – with a steady, blasphemous vigour that did me good. I have no wish to seem harsh, but we had done the dowser no ill, while he had abused his position with all his might.

I did not watch his translation. . . .

At three o'clock that morning we stood in the dining-room. Windows and doors were fast, and the lights were full on. The table was crowded – crammed with the Abbey plate. Chalices, platters and flagons – sacred vessels and caskets for which I can find no name . . . there was not one of silver, but all were of gold.

But the beauty was not all to the board.

On my right stood Daphne, her glorious hair unbound, turning her jade-green dressing-gown into some goddess' robe: Jill stood between Berry and Jonah on the opposite side of the oak – a King's daughter in blue and silver, with her pretty hands in her pockets, appraising her father's hoard. On my right stood Perdita Boyte, swathed to the throat in old rose, a nymph awaiting her call – to meet the dayspring upon some mountain lawn. Curious in spite of himself, the Knave moved about the table, nosing the fusty collection we seemed so much to revere.

'All these years,' murmured Daphne, 'and nobody knew.'

'What ever,' said Berry, 'what ever will Christie's say?'

'You're not going to sell it?' cried Jill.

'Yes, we are, sweetheart,' said Jonah 'In self-defence.'

Perdita breathed in my ear.

'Did they seem comforted, Boy?'

'Stopped crying at once,' I whispered. 'If their hands had been free, they'd have put their arms round my neck.'

'Oh, I didn't' – indignantly.

I tucked her arm under mine.

'I know,' said I. 'Neither did I.'

INFAMOUS RELICS

Miniature in hand, Miss Boyte regarded my brother-in-law.

'It's really fantastic,' she said. 'Shave you and cut his hair, and you would be twins. A great-great-uncle, you said?'

'That's right,' said Berry. 'Bertram. I bear his name. He was a favourite of the Prince Regent and an inveterate gambler. One night, in his cups, he staked and lost a snuff-box which had been given to him by the future King. At least, that was what was said – and an enemy told the Prince. The latter was loth to believe it, but he sent for Bertram to Brighton, and when he appeared, he asked for a pinch of snuff. When Bertram proffered the snuff *in another box*, the Prince Regent turned on his heel, and, though later he begged for an audience, he never saw him again. The fashionable world renounced Bertram, and Bertram renounced the world. As soon as he could, he took orders, and from being a Regency Buck, he spent his life in the country, preaching the gospel and doing nothing but good. But he never forgot his disgrace. Rightly or wrongly, he resented it, and he left instructions that *Put not your trust in Princes* was to be cut upon his tomb. And so it was.'

'I regret to say,' said Jonah, 'that I think he deserved what he got.'

'I quite agree,' said Berry. 'But I think he was hardly used. He would never have done as he did, if he hadn't been tight: and that being so, the fellow who won the box should have handed it back. I mean, only a skunk would have kept it.'

'I think,' said Jill, 'that it was a beastly shame. And only a cad would have gone and told the Prince.'

'It looks like a put-up job,' said Perdita Boyte. 'What became of the box? Who won it?'

'That I don't know,' said Berry. 'And I don't believe Bertram knew, because if he had, he'd have gone to the fellow who won it and bought it back. But if, as I suggest, he was blind to the world when he lost it, then, of course, he'd nothing to go on. I imagine the first he knew was when he got up the next morning and found that the box was gone.'

'It was rotten luck,' said Daphne; 'but it certainly turned a sinner into a saint. His name is still remembered at Ribbon, but his parish was wider than that.'

'That's very true,' said Berry. 'What his sermons were like I don't know, but outside his church he made a tremendous hit. Probably because of his past, he had a weakness for the lawless, and many a rogue and vagabond lost a good friend when he died. A famous highwayman, called Studd, who was finally hanged, bequeathed him the brace of pistols he always used. Bertram probably helped him once. Anyway he was most insistent that "the barkers should go to Buck Pleydell," as the clerk in holy orders was always styled.' He took his keys from his pocket and rose to his feet. 'I've got them here, in that tallboy – Daphne won't have them out.'

'They make me shudder,' said his wife. 'When all's said and done, Studd was a common robber who stuck at nothing at all. He confessed to seventeen murders before he was hanged. And most of those, I suppose, were done with these very arms. What I don't understand is how Bertram could ever have succoured a blackguard like that. I mean, he was a public enemy.'

'That,' said Berry, 'is undeniable. Still, Studd must have had some reason for making his last bequest.' He drew open a drawer. 'And at any rate here they are. Murderous record or no, they're a handsome pair.' He turned, with a fine horse-pistol in either hand. 'They were made by a gunsmith called Minty, of Bristol Town, and you'll find Studd's initials, *R.S.*, engraved upon each of the stocks.'

Perdita Boyte took one and I received the other – to examine the elegant chasing with curious gaze and think of less fortunate eyes that had seen no more than the mouth – and a ruthless finger nursing the trigger below. Honest servants these, that had kept a rogue in his saddle for fifteen years.

Jonah looked over my shoulder.

'You know,' he said, 'it's a shame to keep them in a drawer. They ought to be on the wall, in a glass-fronted case. For one thing, they're very good-looking: for another, they are a pair of historical documents. They were made by a famous gunsmith, used by a notorious highwayman, and left to a well-known priest. All that is hard fact. And if you like to draw on your fancy, they must have confronted – not killed – a good many well-known people, adorning the very world that Bertram used to adorn: for Studd used to work the home counties and, sometimes, London itself.'

My sister shook her head.

'They're infamous relics,' she said. 'I'm glad to know we've got them, but I will not have them displayed. They've a cruel and pitiless record of blood and tears. Think of the widows and orphans those things have made.'

Perdita shivered and handed her pistol back. As I made to do the same, my cousin stretched out his hand.

'One more look,' he said, 'before you hide them away.'

Between us, we bungled the business, and the weapon fell with a crash to the polished floor.

A yelp of dismay from Berry ushered the diatribe we justly deserved.

'That's an heirloom, darlings. Not a sheep's head. A sheep's head is rounder than that – you blear-eyed, banana-fingered bugbears. You're only fit to scratch a hole in a swamp. Oh, my God, you've bust it. Fallen angels, you've broken a piece right off.' He closed his eyes in distress. 'Oh, why did I take them out before you were dead? In all their service – '

'Steady,' said Jonah, stooping. 'There's nothing broken at all. There's a secret slot in the butt, and the plug that concealed it's come out.'

Feverishly examining the pistol, we found his estimate true.

A silver plug had sprung from the end of the stock, revealing a little socket sunk in the wood.

'There's a paper there,' said Berry. 'A pair of tweezers, someone. And, somebody else, a torch.'

In great excitement the operation was done.

The torch illumined the socket, to show a morsel of paper, rolled into a little tube: this clung to the walls of the socket, as though reluctant to leave, but after a little persuasion the tweezers had their way.

'And now,' said Berry, looking round.

With one consent, the five of us bade him proceed.

Carefully he smoothed out the paper. As he held it flat to the table, a child's umbrella might well have covered our heads.

The writing was ragged and dim, but still easy to read.

Bloodstock 43 Old Basing 8
15 toward O.B.
Burried thatt night.

For a moment there was dead silence.

Then Berry lifted his head.

' "Buried that night," ' he said softly. 'A pregnant phrase. I – I wonder if it's still there.'

'Where?' said Jill.

'Forty-three miles from Bloodstock, plus fifteen paces for luck. Studd buried it close to the milestone and then wrote the mileage down.'

'That's right,' said Jonah. He tapped his teeth with his pipe. 'Have we got any ordnance maps?'

'In the drawer of that table,' said I. 'But what would "it" be?'

'I imagine, a nest-egg,' said Berry. 'A hat full of guineas, or something. For all we know, "thatt night" was a bumper night, and Studd picked up a bit more than he needed for ready cash. So he "banked" the surplus against a rainy day, but before that came, he was taken. . . . It's happened before.'

Perdita let out a cry.

'That's why he left Bertram the pistols. Bertram had shown him kindness, when everyone else was waiting to do him down, so Bertram should have his money – if anyone should.'

'By Jove, she's right,' cried Berry, and smacked the arm of his chair. 'Why else leave "the barkers" to a parson – the only man of those days who never went armed?'

Now that Berry had asked it, the pertinence of the question stood out as black against white. The robber's intention was clear. He could not have had much hope that Bertram would light on the secret the pistol hid; but there was a chance that he would, and, in any event, no one but Bertram *could* find it, when once the pistols were his. Though the good might reap no reward, the wicked were certainly doomed to go empty away. At least no vile turnkey or 'red-breast' would enjoy the balance that lay in their victim's 'bank'.

As we made these points to one another, the tide of excitement rose. Daphne and Jill were at the bookcase containing guide-books and maps: Perdita and Berry examined the other pistol, to be sure that another socket was not to be found in its stock; and Jonah and I considered the ordnance sheets.

It did not take long to discover that the mileage which Studd had given was out of date. According to the milestone he quoted, the distance between the two towns was fifty-one miles. The books and maps we consulted showed it to be forty-eight. The discrepancy seemed to be fatal. It showed that the road had been shortened since Studd had buried his gold: and that, of course, meant that the milestone which he had quoted had been removed. In fact, but for Jonah's refusal so soon to admit defeat, I think that before this blow we should have thrown in our hand. It was my keen-witted cousin that picked a way for us out of this hopeless pass.

'I want you to help me to place *The Dog-Faced Man*. That's the name of an inn we once lunched at – I should say about eight years ago. I doubt if I ever knew the name of the village it served, but I think it lay west of Old Basing . . . I'll tell you why I want this. I remember *The Dog-Faced Man* – I can see it now. It was once a posting-house. Which means that the road it stands by was once a coaching road. You see what I'm getting at . . .'

The smoking flax burst into flame.

Half an hour later, perhaps, we found that the village of Coven boasted a 'Dog-Faced Man'. And Coven lay west of Old Basing by seven miles. And Bloodstock lay south-west of Coven by forty-four.

The old coach-road had fallen from its estate – at least, the twelve miles which survived were little more than a lane, while the other thirty-nine had long ago been lost in a main highway. Coven, in a word, had been by-passed, and the by-pass was shorter than the coach-road by just three miles.

All this we discovered later, for in searching for Coven, we found what we wanted to see.

My cousin, driving his Rolls, had properly taken the lead, and I was a mile behind him, expecting to join him again at *The Dog-Faced Man*. But we met before that.

At a quarter to twelve on a lovely August morning I stole round a fairy bend, to see his car at rest by the side of the way and himself and Jill and Daphne standing upon the turf which edged the road as a ribbon for half a mile.

'Oh, I can't believe it,' said Berry, and Perdita smothered a cry.

To be honest, the hopes we had harboured had been but faint. It is an age of progress, and when cars began to come in, the gentle face of England began to change. Straighten a curve of a road, and half a hundred milestones will be bearing a false report. And because that is not to be thought of, the liars are taken away. Reason forbade us to think that with all the manifold chances of modern life the milestone that Studd had quoted should not have been put in the wrong. But it was so. Leaning a little, dressed in tight, grey-green lichen – that venerable livery peculiar to 'the constant service of the antique world,' the old fellow offered his news to such as passed by. Blurred by a hundred winters, the legend could still be read:

BLOODSTOCK
43
OLD BASING
8

As we alighted, I saw Jonah pacing the turf. . . .

Before we could exchange our excitement –

'That's right,' said Berry. 'Go on. Give the whole blasted thing away before we've begun. If anyone's watching – '

'Don't be absurd,' said Daphne. 'Milestones are meant to be read.'

'They're not meant to be slobbered over,' said her husband. 'They're not meant to be leered at and – Look out. Here's somebody coming. What did I say?'

The cyclist that had been approaching passed slowly by, whilst we all did our best to dissemble and Berry loudly declared that 'the map must be wrong.' The effect was marred by a wail of laughter from Jill: it remained for the Knave to destroy it – by overtaking the stranger at thirty-five miles an hour, gaping upon him like any bull of Basan and protesting against his intrusion with a volley of malevolent barks. The hurricane of invective with which we discouraged his zeal must have convinced the cyclist that we wished to disown such behaviour with all our might, but the incident sobered us all, for it showed that the Knave had perceived that we were about some business the nature of which we had no desire to disclose.

In an uneasy silence Jonah leaned over a gate that gave to a field to peer down the back of the hedgerow before which the milestone stood, while the Knave, wide-eyed with abashment, lay down on the turf with his muzzle between his paws.

'Quite so,' said Berry, grimly. 'And now, having done enough damage, we'd better be gone. Lunch at *The Dog-Faced Man* was what we arranged. But I won't go near the place unless it is understood that a certain subject is barred. If the faintest idea gets round of what's at the back of our minds – well, we may as well leave the country. I'll lay that Jonah agrees.'

My cousin nodded.

'Can't be too careful,' he said, producing a pipe. 'But it's going to take some lifting, this box of bricks.'

'What d'you mean?' said Daphne.

Jonah shrugged his shoulders.

'As you've just seen, this road is a thoroughfare. You can't keep people at bay or order them off. And, once you've begun, you can't disguise your labour . . . You can stop, of course – if somebody rounds that bend. But unless they're feeble-minded, they'll wait until you go on. And if you don't go on, *they will*. They've just as much right as you have to, er, practise landscape-gardening by the side of the King's highway.'

There was an uneasy silence.

Then Daphne spoke for us all.

'I can wait for my lunch,' she said. 'Let's go straight home. At least, we can talk as we go.'

'All right,' said Berry. 'Only, as we're here, we may as well locate the vicarage. It's almost certainly at Coven, but we'd better make sure.'

'The vicarage?' said his wife. 'Why on earth do we want to know where the vicarage is?'

'In case we're successful,' said Berry. 'The vicar's the proper person to administer what we find.'

'But it's ours,' shrieked Daphne. 'The man meant Bertram to have it, and Bertram's right has now descended to us.'

'For shame,' said Berry. He raised his eyes to heaven and

wagged his head. 'Think of the widows and orphans to whom it never belonged. Think of the – '

'Rot,' said Daphne. 'The man – '

' – was a common robber,' said Berry. 'And I think it more than likely that when he'd sunk his, er, surplus, he went to *The Dog-Faced Man* and had a large blood and tears.'

'I was talking of – '

'Some infamous relics,' said Berry, 'if I remember aright. Which a man meant Bertram to have and have now descended to us. If we add to the grisly collection, am I to be allowed to display the ones which we have?'

My sister swallowed.

'I don't see what that's got to do with it. If – '

'Then,' said Berry, 'we'll take the vicar's advice. If he says – '

'Oh, I suppose if you want to turn the library into a Chamber of Horrors . . .'

'That's a good girl,' said Berry, and entered the nearest car. 'On the way back we'll stop at *The Case is Altered* and drink the testator's health.'

'Then you'll drink it alone,' said his wife. 'If there's anything going, we may just as well have it as anyone else. But I don't pretend I'm grateful. It wasn't the brute's to give.'

'Quite right,' said Berry, 'quite right. Besides, the question of gratitude may not arise. I mean, it mayn't be what we think. All sorts of things are b-buried. Sometimes they go so far as to bury the dead.'

I helped my sister into the other car.

Three days and a half had gone by when I brought the Rolls to rest in front of *The Dog-Faced Man*.

Outside the inn, in the shade of some whispering limes, was standing a well-worn car to which was attached a trailer, no longer smart. The two carried camping equipment of every kind – I knew: I had helped to load them five hours before.

My cousin strolled out of the inn – according to plan.

'At last,' he said. He turned to call to his sister. 'Jill, they're here. Come along.' He returned to us. 'Your advance-guard has done very well. We've found an excellent field a mile away. I fixed things up with the owner an hour ago.'

Jill and the Knave came flying out of the inn.

'Daphne darling, it's priceless. Wait till you see. He was awfully sticky at first – the owner, I mean. But Jonah talked farming with him and after a quarter of an hour he showed us a map of his land and said we could go where we liked.'

'How – how marvellous of him,' said Daphne, and meant what she said.

Ten minutes later I slowed down behind the trailer just short of the five-barred gate which gave to a field we knew. Here everyone alighted except my cousin and me. The gate was opened by Berry, and Jonah drove into the field: and then, my way being clear, I proceeded to place the Rolls. The turf by the side of the road made an excellent berth. I brought the great car to rest with her nose in line with a mile-stone some seventeen paces ahead. All this, according to plan. It was now but five o'clock and the daylight was broad, and the turf was conveniently smooth: but had it been dark and had there been a pit a yard square two paces in front of the Rolls, her head-lights, when dipped, would have illumined the hole, and what is as much to the point, if the car were advanced three paces, the petty excavation would have been lost to view. In a word, the stage was set.

That our preparations were laboured, I do not pretend to deny: but they had not been made without reason, for one cast-iron condition was ruling the enterprise. *Neither whilst it was being done nor after it had been done must we be so much as suspected of what we proposed to do.* We could not afford exposure. For one thing only, what we were going to do was against the law.

These things being so, it goes, I think, without saying that we could not make our attempt except under cover of night. Now, though we might hide our labour, we could not conceal our presence in such a neighbourhood. Hence the camping equipment. Once the two tents were up, no one would give two thoughts to the simple-minded strangers who had 'managed to get old Belcher to let them camp in his field.' So far, so good, but the work which we were to do had got to be done by the side of the King's highway. And the King's highway is open to all and sundry, by night as by day. The work would take time. Fifteen paces, Studd said. But what was the length of his paces? And had he walked perfectly straight by the edge of the road? Add to this that we could not work without light. And a light can be seen in the country a long way off. . . .

The camp would account for our presence: the Rolls, with her head-lamps dipped, would afford us a furtive light: and if the alarm was given, we had but to drive her forward to cover the hole we had dug.

As I entered the good-looking meadow –

'But we must have water,' cried Daphne. 'I'm dying to wash my hands.'

'I know,' said Berry. 'So'm I. But I'm going to tread it under and wipe them upon the grass.'

'Don't be a fool,' said his wife. 'I'm not going to go without water until we get home. Besides, we've got to wash up.'

'There's a stream,' said Jonah, pointing, 'the other side of that ridge.' He produced two canvas buckets. 'Would you rather fetch the water or put up a tent?'

'That isn't grammar,' said Berry. 'No man born of woman can put up a tent. I'll subscribe to its erection, if that's what you mean. But I'm not going to drag my nails out, clawing sail-cloth about against its will. Besides, we must spare ourselves. We didn't come here to make our abode in this field.'

'We've got to pretend that we did. So the tents have got to go up and the water has got to be fetched.'

With his eyes on the buckets –

'About this water,' said Berry, thoughtfully. 'Why don't we make a chain? A chain of people, I mean – like they do at a fire?'

'From here to the stream?' said I.

'That's right,' said Berry. 'I know we're only six, but if we spread out – '

'Which end of the chain,' said Daphne, 'are you proposing to be?'

My brother-in-law swallowed.

'Well, we ought to draw lots,' he said. 'That's the fairest way. But I don't mind. If I can walk so far, I'll – I'll take the other end.'

'All right,' said Jonah. 'You go on with the buckets. As you'll have the farthest to go, we'll give you ten minutes' start.'

'But we all start together,' cried Berry. 'That's the whole point of the thing. Then Number One falls out – at the head of this field:

Number Two at the top of the ridge: and so on. It's the only way to fetch water.'

'But what's the sense of us all going?' said Jill.

'Well, it saves time for one thing,' said Berry. 'We get the water much quicker. Number Six fills the buckets and gives them to Number Five. Number Five runs with them to Number Four. Number Four runs to Number Three. And so on.'

'But we don't get the water quicker, because when it arrives we're not here.'

'I'm not going to argue with you,' said Berry. 'If you can't see – besides, Number Six will be here. I mean, Number One.'

'No, he won't,' said Jill. 'Nobody'll be here. You said – '

'But he *must* be here,' screamed Berry. 'How can the water arrive except by his hand? Number Six arrives with the water.'

'Well, I call that silly,' said Jill. 'If Number Six – '

'I mean Number One,' snapped Berry. 'How the devil could Six be here? He's down at the stream.'

'Well, you said it,' said Jill, indignantly. 'You said – '

'What if I did?' raved Berry. 'Ignorant obstruction like this is enough to make anybody say anything. I understand you want water. God knows why, but you do. Very well. I teach you the way to get it. I lay before you the way in which water is got. In which water has been got for millions of years. It's the first labour-saving device the world ever saw. More. I – '

'But you said it saved time,' said Jill.

'So it does.'

'Well, I can't see it,' said Jill. 'There's six of us going to get it instead of one, and we shan't have it any quicker because we shan't be here when it comes.'

'But we *shall* be here,' raved Berry. 'Almost at once. And there'll be the water waiting. We'll have rushed the whole thing through in one-sixth of the time. Less than that, really: for Numbers Five and Six can wash in the stream.'

'Well, what about Number Four? He won't be able to wash for ages.'

'Yes he will. Four can take some soap with him and wash on the way. And so can Three. And so can Two and One, for the matter of that.'

'Then what's the good of getting it?' said Jill.

'There isn't any,' yelled Berry. 'There never was. Not the faintest odour of welfare. It's a waste of time and labour and an insult to common sense.'

'It is – *your* way,' said Jill. 'Fancy running about with a lot of dirty water. And I don't believe they've always done it like that. Why don't you go and get it, as Daphne said? Your way, you'd have been Number Six, so what's the difference?'

There is a naïveté which is more deadly than any wit.

So soon as he could speak –

'Show me a tent,' said Berry, violently. 'Show me some pegs and a maul.' Savagely he flung off his coat. 'Especially a maul – and I'll show you how to pretend. I'm going to *pretend* to set up a monument. You know. A thing like Stonehenge.'

'Well, don't overdo it,' said his wife. 'It's got to come down tomorrow.'

Berry laughed hysterically.

'Wait till I'm through,' he said, 'and you'll think that we're here for years.'

With a snarl, he fell upon some canvas, and, after two efforts to lift it, began to drag it incontinently towards the hedge. . . .

Perdita picked up a bucket and looked at me.

'Shall we make a chain?' she said shyly.

Two minutes later I handed her over the fence at the head of the field . . .

It was as we surmounted the ridge that Perdita caught her breath and stood suddenly still.

'I don't believe it,' she said. 'If we go any nearer, I'm sure it'll fade away.'

The scene before us might well have been painted or sung. It was like a piece of Old English – a page from The Book of Proverbs, so simple and yet as matchless as one of Shakespeare's songs.

A meadow went sloping down to the stream we sought. On the farther side of this, the rising ground was laid with a quilt of leafage, perhaps some sixty feet thick. Oak and ash and chestnut – all manner of magnificent trees, massed in inimitable disorder, made such a hanging garden as Babylon never knew, and the tops of those that stood highest were fretting with delicate green the blue of a flawless sky. Sunk like a jewel in the greenwood, set like a jewel on the silver sash of water, was an old, half-timbered mill.

Rose-red from footings to chimneys, the ancient seemed to welcome the smile of the evening sun. This laid bare a detail which filled the eye, and, even from where we stood, we could mark the good brick-nogging that was framed by the grey, old oak, the gentle sag of the roof, which is but the stoop of a man that is full of years, and the lead of the lattices keeping the aged panes. And something else we could see. Neighbouring the wall of the mill, the water-wheel hung upon its spindle over the race – a very comfortable monster, like Bottom's sucking dove. For me, it painted the lily, not only calling back Time as one having authority, but relating the business of Nature to the work of men's hands. And the wheel was running . . . the fine old fellow was at work. His felloes were dark and glistening, all the beauty of lively water flowed or dripped or leaped from his flashing fans, and the sunshine played upon the flourish, making a magic beyond the reach of art.

Perdita clasped two hands that would have added a verse to Solomon's Song.

'Oh, please may I have it? It is the very loveliest toy that I've ever seen.'

Wishing very much it was mine –

'No toy,' said I, 'but a fable – the stuff the old England was made of . . . the England that Goldsmith knew.'

Perdita nodded thoughtfully. Then she set a hand on my shoulder, keeping her eyes on the mill.

'England,' she said, 'is really a picture-book. It's old now, and some of its pages are missing and many of those that are left are torn and spoiled. But there are such a lot that are just as they always were. And this is the little vignette that goes on the title-page.' She lifted a glowing face. 'Am I lucky or not to have seen it?'

'Honours are even,' said I. 'It's seen a lot of fine ladies in all its days, but it's had to wait till now for an Eve with the way of a maid and the heart of a child.'

'I'm afraid that's not true. Don't move.' Her beautiful face approached mine. 'I'm regarding myself in your eye, and I don't think so fine a fellow would fall for a lady like me.'

'When you say "so fine a fellow" – '

'I mean the mill.'

'Never mind,' said I. 'Don't move. I'm considering the bow of your mouth. I believe – '

Perdita danced out of range and blew me a kiss.

'It's not the same,' I said sadly. 'And I needn't have given you warning of my approach.'

'I know. But that's why I like you. You – Oh, I don't know. Most men regard women as game, to be trapped or caught. But you always encourage my freedom – like a man that is glad to let live. And now let's go down to the water and be Numbers Five and Six.'

As we passed over the meadow –

'You know,' said I, 'you haven't got it quite right. I admit I'm not a satyr. But Plato's theories have never appealed to me. I'm glad to let live – as you put it, but I have a definite weakness for living myself.'

Miss Boyte took my arm and laid a cheek to my sleeve.

'You are stupid, aren't you?' she said. 'That's just what makes it so nice.'

As soon as I could speak –

'You wicked girl,' I said. I put an arm about her and held her up to my heart. 'You wicked – Now I shan't eat a carp on St Anthony's day. Oh, and put up your mouth, will you? I want to . . . straighten my tie in one of your eyes.'

With her face in my coat –

'Not before the mill,' bubbled Perdita. 'Besides, there might be somebody looking.'

'Hush,' said I. 'Number Six is waiting – to give them to Number Five.'

Seated upon a loose cushion that came from the Rolls, his back against a milestone, his right foot shoeless and resting upon a carefully folded rug, my brother-in-law greeted our appearance by raising his eyes to heaven and demanding a cigarette.

As I felt for my case –

'Lame for life,' he said shortly. 'That's what I am. I want to go home, but they say they can't spare the Rolls.'

'But how did it happen?' said Perdita.

Berry sat up.

'The history,' he said, 'will hardly go into words. You may or may not remember that I offered to erect a pavilion – a work of supererogation, which, no doubt for that reason, found favour in the sight of those I love. On my offer being accepted, I humbly desired to be furnished with the appropriate tools. You can't make ropes without sand – or whatever they use. These were not forthcoming. Instead of the maul and pegs which I had a right to expect, one was given a blacksmith's hammer, and a lot of iron nails – harsh and bestial equipment, which, if we may believe the old masters, has figured in other martyrdoms. But it is, as you know, my practice to accept without comment such trials or disabilities as a jealous Fate may appoint. I, therefore, offered up a short prayer and fell to work. Was I permitted to labour as man has always laboured, working out his own salvation in the sweat of his trunk? I was not. From the instant that I began to put into action my design, my beloved consort saw fit not only to disparage my methods – thereby exposing the running sores of ignorance with which her mind is diseased – but actually to vomit instruction the nature and quality of which would have been most justly resented by an infant of tender years. The result was inevitable. Trembling with indignation and thirsty only to bring to an end a tribulation which I in no wise deserved, I failed to invest with the requisite degree of accuracy the elegant parabola my hammer was about to describe; and the blow which had been intended not only to relieve my emotions but to blot out the bull-nosed bung which I had already missed twice, fell instead upon the toe or toe-cap of the Russia-leather "Oxford" in which this foot was enshrined.' As though the reminiscence were repugnant, he shuddered violently. 'One might have hoped, one might, without presumption, have supposed that a *contretemps* so hideous would have commanded concern, if not dismay. One would have been wrong. The act of self-immolation was greeted with yells of mirth. Like those of the early Christians, my screams were drowned in an obscene derision which, till then, I had always believed to be the prerogative of the abnormal baboon. So far from – Oh, St Vitus's Trot! Look what's escaped.'

It was with a shock that, following Berry's gaze, I perceived the approach of a pageant which justified his remark.

A small caravan, painted to resemble a doll's house in red and white, had been fitted with shafts, instead of the trailer bar: between these a mule was strolling with the nonchalance of his kind. The equipment was preceded by a man of perhaps thirty-five. He was wearing an apple-green beret, a pair of blood-red shorts and a sleeveless vest, no one of which became him in any way. A permanent grin illumined his wide-eyed face, and he looked up and down and about, as one who is pleased with life and delighted with all he sees. He was tripping, rather than walking, as though in ecstasy, and had he indeed been some prisoner, lately enlarged, he could hardly have revelled more plainly in his estate. By the side of the van was plodding another soul: but, though his attire was as wanton as that which his fellow wore, his demeanour was that of a man who would welcome death. For the most part he hung his head, but now and again he would lift it to glance at the van and the mule, after which he would cover his face as though he had seen some vision too dreadful for him to bear. Indeed, I felt sorry for him, for he plainly loathed his adventure with all his might and the relish of his companion must have inflamed his despair.

Carefully veiling our interest, we waited for the three to go by, proposing perhaps to direct them and certainly to give them good day. Of such is Life. . . . It never occurred to us that the tents which Jonah had set up were declaring a fellowship which if anyone pleased to invoke we could not deny.

The leader of the procession ripped the scales from our eyes.

Raising his headgear to Perdita, he pranced to Berry's side with an outstretched hand.

'Well met, brother,' he brayed. 'What of the pitch?'

The three of us gazed upon him, dumb with dismay. Our fond preparation, recoiling upon itself, seemed likely to bring to ruin the hopes we held. The frightening fool before us was proposing to rest by our side, to establish a post of surveillance, *to spend the night within earshot of all we did*. We were ready for interruption: the supervision, however, of such a man was something with which we were not prepared to cope.

Dazedly, Berry made answer.

'What pitch?' he said, shaking hands.

'Why, your pitch,' said the other, beaming. He pointed to the tops of the tents. 'The blithesome spot you have selected for your repose.'

There was a frightful silence.

Then –

'Oh, it's not too bad,' said Berry, faintly. 'Not – not at all what we'd hoped though. Too – too many bumble-bees.'

'Bumble-bees?' cried the other.

'Bumble-bees,' said Berry. 'Great, big, blundering brutes.' He pointed to his foot. 'I've been stung already.'

'But bumble-bees don't sting.'

'These do,' said Berry, firmly. 'That's what's so awful about it. Then again the water's too far.'

'That's all right,' said the other. 'We've got a tank.'

'Oh, is it?' said Berry. 'I mean, have you? That's, er, very convenient, isn't it?' He got to his feet and wiped the sweat from his brow. 'I hope you've plenty of carbolic. There's a terrible smell of drains.'

'Drains?' said the other, starting.

'That's right,' said Berry. 'Drains. I'm inclined to think it's a sewage-farm.' The other was snuffing the air. 'It comes and goes, you know. The stench, I mean. A moment ago it was enough to knock you down.'

'It can't be the drains,' said the stranger. 'And any way it's no odds. As long as you can smell it, it's quite all right. It's the smell you can't smell that matters.'

'That's what I'm afraid of,' said Berry; stooping to put on his shoe. 'You see, you can't smell it now.'

'Then it doesn't matter, does it?' said the other, gleefully.

'Well, you can't have it both ways,' said Berry. 'If it doesn't matter when you can, then it does matter when you can't, doesn't it?'

'Doesn't what?' said the other.

'Smell,' said Berry. 'I mean, matter.'

'Well, what if it does?' said the stranger.

In a silence big with emotion Perdita made her escape and Berry fastened his lace with all his might. As he straightened his back –

'The unprintable answer,' he said, 'is the biggest, burliest bumble-bee that ever buzzed – and many of them.'

'Now don't you worry,' said the other, clapping him on the back. 'If you don't think about them, you'll be as right as rain. And you can't move now: you've got your tents up and all.'

'Oh, no,' said Berry, shakily. 'We – we're going to stick it somehow, just for one night. But what with that and the snakes . . .'

'What snakes?'

'I don't know what make they are,' said Berry, gloomily. 'I've only seen six so far. But they're black and red, and they make a gurgling noise.'

The other shuddered. Then he turned to the caravan, which had come to rest on the opposite side of the road.

'D'you hear that, Harold? This gentleman's seen six snakes.'

From his seat on the step of the van –

'Only six?' said Harold, miserably.

His fellow returned to Berry.

'That's the best of a van,' he said. 'Once in a van, you're safe. But I'm sure you'll be all right. You must try not to think about them. Is this your first night out?'

'Oh, no,' said Berry. 'We – we're really just finishing, you know. That's what's so – so unfortunate. I mean – now take last night. Only last night we had a peach of a – of a . . . pitch. That's right. Pitch. More like a Garden of Eden than anything else.'

'Was it?' said the other excitedly.

'Oh, scrumptious,' said Berry. 'Everything you could want. Field like a bowling-green, a lovely rill of water, absolute privacy – '

'Harold, the map,' said the other. 'We'll mark this down.'

As Harold rose to his feet –

'You don't want a map,' said Berry. 'It's only just up the road.'

'Only just up the road? Then why on earth – '

'Ah, now you're asking,' said Berry. 'Because our car's broken down. There's that pearl of Arcady only ten minutes from here – just the other side of Coven, and Coven's four minutes' walk – with a farmer to do your cooking . . . and there's another thing. This fellow's a tartar – the fellow who owns this field. He wouldn't have had us, you know, if we hadn't broken down.'

'My friend,' was the genial answer, 'you have a lot to learn. "Use first and ask afterwards" is the – '

'That's just what we did,' said Berry. 'And he came down in a fury to turn us out. We – we managed to bring him round, but he's coming back in an hour to assess the damage we've done.'

'But what have you done?'

'Marked the grass,' said Berry. 'It costs us eighteen pence each time we sit down.'

'You're not going to pay it, are you?'

'He's going to seize the tents if we don't. I tell you, the man's not safe. And what with the smell of snakes – I mean, drains, and the drakes – snakes, and the bumble-bees . . .'

The other threw out his chest.

'Let Eden wait,' he declared. He found and wrung Berry's hand. 'Be of good cheer, my brother, I'm going to see you through. Come all malevolent farmers, I'll put them where they belong.' He turned to his wretched companion. 'Lead on, Harold,' he commanded. 'We spend the night with our friends.'

With that, he skipped to his van, laying hands upon it, laughing and cheering – and pushing, like a clown in some circus, before the mule itself had decided to take the strain.

As the doll's house lurched through the gateway into our field –

'Well, I'm damned,' said Berry. 'He may be a full-marks fool, but he's made me ashamed of myself. Goodwill like that must be honoured – at any cost. We must help them to settle down, and then they must come and dine. A bottle of Clicquot'll do old Harold good.'

Before five minutes had passed, the reason for Harold's depression was clear as day. A 'weaker vessel' born, it was his misfortune to find himself allied with a man who combined a distracting energy not only with the instinct of managing direction but with a blasting incompetence which had to be seen to be believed. Indeed, I shall never understand how the three had contrived to get as far as they had, for they had been twelve days on the road, yet all were alive and well.

To pitch their camp was the simplest thing in the world. They had only to choose their site, bring the mule to a standstill, let down the sprags of props which were waiting beneath the van and lead the mule from the shafts. This, however, they proved unable to do – thanks, of course, to Horace: for that was the leader's name. By his excited direction, the mule was released before the sprags were let down, and the doll's house, which had but two wheels, immediately tilted back after the manner of a tumbril which is made to discharge its load. Everything loose within it fell to the lower end, and it settled down to the crash of breaking vessels and the frantic convulsions of the water within its tank. Before we could interfere, Horace, laughing like a madman, had actually entered the van – I suppose to assess the damage which had been done: ill-advisedly moving forward, he more than restored the balance the van had lost, and, after the way of a see-saw, the doll's house flung suddenly forward, to come to rest on its shafts. By this manoeuvre, of course, its contents were rudely transferred from aft to fore and Horace was thrown against the window through which in his efforts to rise he immediately put his foot. Though we cried to him to lie still, he preferred to pick himself up and make for the door. Since this lay behind the axle, before he could gain the threshold the van once more tilted back, thereby returning its contents to their original site and, of course, pitching Horace headlong against its end. It only remained for him to make his way to the middle and balance the thing: and this he did almost at once, whereupon, because of the slope, the doll's house ran violently backwards and came to rest in a hedge some seven yards off. In no way disconcerted, Horace emerged full of orders and laughing to beat the band and forgetting in his excitement that he had seen fit to open the tap of the tank. Why he should have done so, I cannot conceive, but since no one but he was aware of what he had done, before we had salved it the doll's house was fairly awash, while the tank, of course, was as empty as when it was new. As for the mule, by Horace' insistent direction, Harold had let the beast go without removing the harness upon its back, and when we had time to look round, we saw it languidly rolling, as bare as the day it was born, while its gear was distributed about the meadow as though it had been flung away to forward some headlong flight.

I set down these curious facts, not at all in malice, but simply because they are true, and I must most frankly confess that, observing their creation, I never laughed so much in my life.

What was, perhaps, the gem of the harlequinade was the instant understanding between the mule and the Knave. That the two agreed together there can be no doubt, for, before they took any action, they nosed one another kindly and considered each other's points in evident amity. And then they began to play. To see them chase one another would have made the sternest ascetic split his sides. Even poor Harold laughed till the tears ran down his face, and when Horace, perceiving the frolic and assuming that the two were in earnest and ought to be stopped, ran violently after them both, pursuing their utmost abandon with all his might, to be himself pursued as one who had no business to interfere – then we lifted up thankful hearts that we had made the acquaintance of such a man.

If we were glad of them, at least we gave them no cause to regret their encounter with us. Had we not been there to point the way to the water and, indeed, to give them to eat, I cannot think what they would have done. Their van was untenable: proposing to live upon the country, they had no food: their bedding was drenched, their crockery broken in pieces – and Horace floundered in the ruin, shaking with laughter, dilating in all honesty upon the joys of camping and continually dispensing counsel of almost incredible futility.

With such a personality present, we had almost abandoned hope of doing that night the business we came to do, but such was the entertainment with which we had been regaled that we were more than resigned to the prospect of trying again. However, our luck was in. By trying to fob the two off, Berry had hoisted us all with his own petard: his decision to show them attention retrieved the situation beyond belief.

At eight o'clock that night the two sat down with us to a decent meal: by half past nine Horace had fallen asleep with his glass in his hand, while Harold had grown so heavy that he could hardly talk. They were by no means drunk, but since they were physically exhausted by the miles they had walked and the many tricks they had played, the wine had acted like a drug upon senses which were only too eager to take their rest.

By ten o'clock our guests were wrapped in our rugs and were lying in one of our tents. Their condition closely resembled that of the blessed dead. So far as they were concerned, the coast was clear.

More than three hours had gone by, when Berry straightened his back and wiped the sweat from his eyes.

'I give it up,' he said hoarsely. 'The stuff's not here.'

'Oh, we needn't stop yet,' said Daphne. 'It's only just one.'

'Yes, I know that bit,' said her husband. 'I know that we *can* go on till a quarter past two. If we then reverse our procedure and work like so many fiends, we'll get our hole filled up as the dawn comes in. Well, the answer is that I'd rather die in my bed. I mean, face the poisonous facts. Are you going to argue that Studd ever laboured like this? "Buried that night" were his words. D'you mean to tell me that after a spot of High Toby he rode to this place and dug a thing like a shell-hole some four feet deep?'

Looking upon our labour, I felt the force of his words. We had certainly worked like mad; but, had I not helped to make it, I never would have believed that such an excavation could have been made in three hours. Eight feet by three feet six by four, it would have swallowed a sofa of an enormous size, and Studd had buried a bag the size of his head. I found it hard to believe that our margin of error was insufficiently wide.

We had not been interrupted. The girls and the Knave, between them, were keeping watch, and were ready to flash a warning from either bend of the road. And my sister sat in the Rolls, ready to take such a signal, drive the car slowly forward and put out her lights.

'Ten minutes' rest,' said Jonah, and glanced at his watch. 'And then we'll have one more go.' He looked at my sister. 'Will you relieve Perdita, dear? It's over her time.'

As my sister sped up the road –

'Let's have the lights out,' said Berry. 'The sight of that hole makes me tired.' He laid himself down on the turf. 'Enough to make a cat laugh, isn't it? Fancy giving up a good night's rest to displace about three tons of earth and then shove it back where it was. Talk about futility. And I was laughing at Horace – three crowded hours ago.'

'Someone has said,' said Jonah, 'that unless you have sweated or shivered, you'll never meet with success. I think it was Juvenal.'

'I see,' said Berry, thoughtfully. 'In that case I've qualified for about three million pounds. I've larded the earth tonight. The wonder is the damned place isn't a swamp. Are you going to put those lights out? Or do you derive satisfaction from the almost immediate future that trough presents?'

As Perdita glided up to take her seat in the Rolls –

'I was waiting for the lady,' I said, and put out the lights.

'This is heart-breaking,' she said. 'And I'm sure it's there.'

'If it is, he was sozzled,' said Berry, 'and couldn't walk straight. We've nearly got down to the water under the earth.'

'When we start again,' said Jonah, 'we can go on for half an hour, and then we must turn and come back.'

'Oh, give me strength,' said Berry, fervently.

'The burning question is – which way do we go?'

After a little silence –

'I think it should be wider,' said I. 'We've got enough length.'

'I entirely agree,' said Jonah. 'But if we make it wider, we cannot advance the Rolls.'

'I know that,' said I. 'Let's risk it.'

'I'm terribly tempted,' said Jonah, 'I must confess. But if anyone did come along . . . I mean, you know, we should look such blasted fools. You can't explain a chasm like this.'

'You could to Horace,' said Berry. 'You'd only have to tell him you'd dropped your stud.'

'Ah, Horace – yes,' said Jonah. 'But the next to come by may be a shade less artless. We'll hardly strike two such giants in a summer's day.'

In the silence which followed I closed my eyes and tried to forget my state. My hands were raw, my back and my knees were aching as though their bones were diseased, every stitch upon me was soaked and my face was smeared and my arms were plastered with dirt. The thought that all this was for nothing was hardly bearable.

At length –

'One minute to go,' said Jonah. 'Perdita, give us some light.'

As the darkness fled, I dragged myself to my feet. Then I heard a footfall behind me and started about.

Before I could think –

'Oh, I'm so ashamed, Captain Pleydell,' said Harold's voice. 'When I found myself in your tent, I had a dreadful feeling that you would be sitting up. I turned to Horace, but . . .'

The sentence faltered and died. The sight of the yawning chasm had murdered speech.

Berry had the youth by the arm.

'It's all right, Harold. But tell me. Is Horace awake?'

'No, no. I couldn't wake him. I – '

'Thank God for that. Can we rely upon you to hold your tongue?'

'Of course, sir. I'm awfully sorry. I never dreamed – '

'Why should you?' said Berry. 'I can hardly believe it myself. Never mind. Just listen to me. By daybreak today that hole you see there will be gone. No sign of it will remain. The turf will show no traces of having been touched. May I have your solemn word that you will keep to yourself what you've seen tonight?'

'You can, indeed,' cried Harold, earnestly. 'I'm only so sorry – '

'Good enough, my lad,' said Berry. 'And now I'll tell you the truth.'

And so he did, whilst I helped Jonah to loosen another twelve inches of turf.

Harold listened – with widening eyes.

When Berry had done –

'But how – how very romantic,' he stammered. 'I mean – after all these years . . .'

'It is, isn't it?' said Berry, swallowing. 'It'd be still more romantic if we could have found the stuff: but it's nice to think that we've, er, mucked about a bit where it used to be.'

'You're not going to give up, are you? Oh, don't. Let me bear a hand.'

'By all manner of means,' said Berry. 'But it's very nearly time to start filling this cranny in.'

Harold stared at the hole, then his eyes travelled to the milestone.

'Fifteen paces,' he murmured. 'Of course, if he didn't walk straight . . . I – I wonder why he made the distance so long. I mean, it seems unnecessary, doesn't it?'

Apart from the point he had made, the way in which he spoke was suggestive of more to come, and Jonah and I stopped working to watch his face.

'As a matter of fact,' said Berry, 'Studd said "fifteen". He didn't use the word "paces", but what else can he have meant? He'd have had no measuring-line – the whole thing was improvised.'

Again Harold measured the distance from milestone to trench.

'It's such a long way,' he said slowly. 'That's what gets me. It leaves so much room for error – especially by night. Of course you're right – he'd have had no measuring-line, but' – he hesitated – 'it's great impertinence on my part . . .'

'Go on, old fellow,' said Jonah. 'We'll say if we think you're wrong.'

'Well, don't you think, perhaps – I mean, as a highwayman, he'd certainly have ridden a lot.'

'Spent his life in the saddle,' said I. 'No doubt about that.'

'That's what I mean,' said Harold, eagerly. 'So he must have been very . . . horsy. You know. Almost like a groom.'

'Go on,' said everyone.

'Well, when he said "fifteen," *d'you think he might have meant "hands"* – the measure you use when you're telling a horse's height? I mean, it would be very easy – for Studd, I mean: and fifteen by four is sixty. That makes five feet. And that's much nearer the milestone . . .'

His eyes ablaze with excitement, his voice tailed off.

Jonah was down on his knees, with one hand against the milestone and his palms side by side on the turf.

'Harold,' said Berry, with emotion, 'I give you best. You're right, of course. I know it. Whether the stuff's there or nor, we all of us know you're right.' He laid a hand on his shoulder. 'You're the *deux ex machina*, Harold – the god that rolls up in the car to put everything straight. And I have the honour to thank you for turning a hideous failure into what I'm ready to bet will be a yelling success.'

Twenty minutes later, fifteen handbreadths from the milestone, the spade I was using disclosed the remains of something that was not soil.

I do not know what it had been, for its many years of burial had corrupted it out of all knowledge and very near brought it to dust. I think, perhaps, it had been a wallet.

I gave my spade to my cousin and used my hands.

When I touched it, the stuff gave way, and my hand went into a hollow – a slight, irregular crevice, which might have been the inside of what, when first it was there, was a stout, leather bag.

At once I felt some object, and, closing my fingers upon it, I drew it out.

It was flat and small and oblong – and made of gold.

In fact, it was an exquisite snuff-box.

When Perdita had wiped it, the Royal Arms of England, beautifully done in enamel, blazed at us from the lid. And within was engraved the cipher – of the man to whom it had been given, from whom it had been stolen away.

Seven days had gone by.

The doll's house stood in our meadows, the Knave was lying down with the mule in his own domain, and Horace and Harold were standing by the library table, regarding a box and two pistols with saucer eyes.

'And there you are,' said Berry. 'Studd stopped Great-great-uncle Bertram and robbed him of all he had. The money, no doubt, he spent, but he dared not dispose of the snuff-box because of the arms on the lid. So he buried it by the wayside. He never dug it up, and when he was about to be hanged, he tried to put matters right. He left his pistols to Bertram, and hidden in one of those was a note of the place. He hoped he'd find it, of course. He never did, but, er, one of his scions did. And he went to the place and, thanks to, er, divine intervention, he found the box. So after many years, poor Bertram's honour was cleared. He'd never staked the snuff-box at all. It had been taken off him by Studd.'

'And yet he was hanged for it,' said Horace. 'You know, he ought to have spoken. Then they could have gone to the place and dug the pistols up.'

As soon as he could speak –

'I never thought of that,' said Berry, uncertainly.

Harold began to shake with laughter.

It is November, 1919. The nights have drawn in. Berry and Daphne have left for London, to open up the Cholmondeley Street residence for the Winter.

The Knave, sadly, is departed. Perdita Boyte has left these shores and Boy is, for the moment, companionless. But only for the moment . . .

THE UNKNOWN QUALITY

'Blow this out for me, Boy, there's a dear.'

The sun was streaming into the library, in a cage upon the broad hearth there was a blazing log fire, and the appointment of the breakfast table was good to look upon.

So also was Jill.

Installed behind the cups and silver, my cousin made a sweet picture. Grave eyes set wide in a smiling face, a pile of golden hair crowning her pretty head, the slenderest throat, from which the collar of a green silk coat fell gracefully on either side – so much a cunning painter might have charmed faithfully on to canvas. But the little air of importance, of dignity fresh-gathered that sat so naïvely upon her brow – this was a thing nor brush nor pencil could capture, but only a man's eye writing upon a grateful heart.

It was but three days since Daphne had left White Ladies for London, and grey-eyed Jill reigned in her stead. Berry had accompanied his wife, but Jonah and I had stayed in the country with Jill, lest we should lose a note of that echo of summer which good St Luke had this year piped so lustily.

But yesterday the strains had faltered and died. A sour east wind had risen, that set the trees shivering, and whipped the golden leaves from their galleries, to send them scudding up the cold grey roads. Worse still, by noon the sky was big with snow, so that, before the post office was closed, a telegram had fled to London warning my sister to expect us to arrive by car the following afternoon.

Jill renewed her appeal.

Above the little spirit lamp which she was holding hovered a tiny flame, seemingly so sensitive that a rough word would quench it for ever. When I had kissed my cousin, I blew steadily and fiercely from the south-west. Instantly a large tongue of fire flared half-way to where Jonah was eating his porridge and knitting his brows over *The Times*.

Jill's hand began to shake.

'You wicked child,' said I. 'You knew – '

'Oh Boy, but it's so silly. We had to leave it for you. Jonah nearly burst himself just now, trying.'

'Thing's bewitched,' said Jonah calmly. 'The more air you give it, the fiercer it burns. I'd sooner try to blow out a hurricane lamp.'

'Nonsense,' said I, taking a deep breath.

At the end of the round –

'Yes,' said Jonah. 'Do you mind blowing the other way next time? It's not my face I'm worrying about, but this is the only copy of *The Times* in the house.'

Jill was helpless with laughter, so I took the lamp away from her and advanced to the fireplace.

'I'll fix the swine,' I said savagely.

Two minutes later, with a blast that almost blew the lamp out of my hand, the flame was extinguished in a flurry that would have done credit to a whale. As I straightened my back –

'Well done, Boy,' said Jill. 'There's a letter for you from Berry. Do see what he says. Then I'll read you Daphne's.'

'Read hers first,' said I. 'Strange as it may seem, I entered this room to eat.'

'Right oh!' And in her fresh little voice my cousin began to read.

Jill Darling,

The sooner you all come up the better. Everything's ready and Berry's more than I can manage alone. His shoulder was aching last night, but when I wanted to rub him he said he was a kind of Aladdin's lamp, and wouldn't be responsible if I did. 'Supposing a genie appeared and formed fours, or the slop-pail rolled aside, disclosing a flight of steps.' Result, today in Bond Street he turned suddenly to look at a passing car, and had a seizure. He just gave a yell as if he'd been shot, and then stood stock still with his head all on one side. Of course I was horrified, but he said he was quite all right, and explained that it was muscular rheumatism. I stopped a taxi and tried to make him get in, for people were beginning to look. Do you think he would? Not a bit of it. Stood there and said it was a judgment, and that he must stay where he was till it had passed. 'That may not be for years. They'll put railings round me after a bit, and people will meet at me instead of the Tube. You will be responsible for my meals, some of which you will cook on the spot. I'll have a light lunch today about 1300 hours.' One or two people stopped, and I got into the taxi just as a man asked him if he was ill. 'Brother,' said the fool, 'my blood tests are more than satisfactory. A malignant Fate, however – ' When I asked him if he was coming, he told the man I was taunting him, so I just drove home. The Willoughbys brought him back in their car quarter of an hour later. Madge said she'd never laughed so much in her life, but I can't bear it alone. Mrs Mason is at last reconciled to the idea of an electric cooker, and your new curtains look sweet. Come along. Love to you all.

Daphne.

'Berry's version should be engaging,' said Jonah. 'Slip along with that porridge.'

'Don't hustle me. Gladstone used to masticate every mouthful he took seven million times before swallowing it. That's why he couldn't tell a lie. Or am I thinking of Lincoln?'

The hostility with which my cousins received the historical allusion was so marked that it seemed only prudent to open my brother-in-law's letter without further delay.

I did so and read the contents aloud.

Dear Brother,

Your constant derision of human suffering has satisfied me that the facts I am about to relate will afford you the utmost gratification. Natheless I consider that for form's sake my wife's brother should know that I am in failing health. This morning, whilst faring forth, as is my wont (pronounced 'wunt'), upon a mission of charity, I was seized with an agony in the neck and Old Bond Street just opposite the drinking-fountain. Believing it to be appendicitis, I demanded a chirurgeon, but nobody could spell the word. The slightest movement, however, spelt anguish without a mistake. My scruff was in the grip of Torment. Observing that I was helpless, the woman, my wife, summoned a hackney carriage and drove off, taunting and jeering at her spouse. By this time my screams had attracted the attention of a few passers-by. Some stood apparently egg-bound, others hurried away, doubtless to procure assistance. One fool asked me if I was ill. I told him that I had been dead for some days, and asked him if he knew of a good florist, as I wanted them to send no flowers. Had it not been for Madge Willoughby, I should have been there now.

Organised bodies of navvies are slowly but surely ruining the streets. No efforts are made to stop them, and the police seem powerless to interfere.

There is no room in London. I never remember when there was. But don't you come. The air is the purer for your absence, and your silk hats seem to fit me better than my own. My love for Jill is only exceeded by my hatred of you and my contempt for Jonah. I have much more to say, but I have, thank Heaven, something better to do than to communicate with a debauched connection, whose pleasure has ever been my pain, and from whom I have learned more vicious ways than I can remember. For I am by nature a little child. Just before and after rain you may still see traces of the halo which I bought at Eastbourne in '94. My gorge is rising, so I must write no more.

Berry

'What's muscular rheumatism?' said Jill, gurgling with laughter.

'Your muscles get stiff,' said Jonah, 'and you get stuck. Hurts like anything. I've had it.'

'Now you know,' said I, selecting a sausage. 'Will you be ready by half-past eleven (winter time), or must we lunch here?'

'I'm ready now,' said Jill. 'But you and Jonah said it was indecent to start earlier.'

'So it is. We shall get to Pistol comfortably in an hour and a half, and if we start again at half-past two, we shall be in London for tea.'

Jonah rose and limped to the window.

'I'll tell you one thing,' he said. 'It's going to be a devilish cold run.'

★

Jonah was right.

We sat all three upon the front seat, but even so we were hard put to it to keep warm. The prospect of a hot lunch at Pistol was pleasant indeed. Jonah was driving, and the Rolls slid through the country like a great grey bird, sailing and swooping and swerving so gracefully that it was difficult to believe the tale which the speedometer told. Yet this was true enough, for it was not a quarter to one when we swept round the last corner and into the long straight reach of tarmac, at the top of which lay the village we sought.

Pistol is embedded in a high moor, snug and warm, for all its eminence. The moor itself is girt with waving woods that stretch and toss for miles, making a deep sloping sash of foliage which Autumn will dye with such grave glory that the late loss of summer and her pretty ways seems easier to bear. Orange and purple, copper and gold, russet and crimson – these in a hundred tones tremble and glow in one giant harmony, out of which, at the release of sun, come swelling chords so deep and rich and vivid that the sweet air is quick with stifled music and every passing breeze charged to the full with silent melody.

We had left this girdle of woodland behind us and were within half a mile of the village, when some activity about the gates of a private house attracted our attention. A little knot of men stood arguing in the roadway, three cars and an old fly were berthed close to the hedge, while a good-looking landau was waiting for a furniture van to emerge from the drive.

The next moment we were near enough to learn from a large poster that 'the entire contents of Cranmer Place were to be sold by auction' this day, 'including a quantity of valuable antique furniture,' and with one accord Jill and I called upon Jonah to stop.

'What for?' said the latter, as he brought the car to a standstill. 'Don't say you want to go and watch the rector's wife bidding against her conscience and the draper for a what-not.'

'Such,' said I, 'is our intention.' I hoisted myself to my feet and, opening the door, descended stiffly into the road. As I helped Jill to follow me, 'You push on to Highlands,' I added, 'and order the lunch. We'll only stay a minute or two.'

'And you never know,' said Jill, 'we might see something priceless.'

Jonah shook his head.

'Depend upon it,' he said, 'the oleographs have gone to Christie's, same as the fumed oak. Only the dud stuff's left. However, have it your own way.' With a sigh, he let in the clutch. 'If you're not there by a quarter past one, I shall begin.'

Jill slid an arm through mine, which she squeezed excitedly.

'I'm sure we shall find something, Boy. I just feel it. It always happens like this. You see, it isn't as if we were looking for a sale. We've just run right into one. And last night I dreamed about cretonnes.'

'That settles it,' said I, as the Rolls glided out of our way and we started to cross the road. 'All the same, Jonah's probably right. But I love a sale. I'm afraid it's curiosity more than anything.'

Catalogues were handed us at the front door, and we passed into a fine square hall, where a dresser and a large gate-table, each conspicuously labelled, declared that the late occupant was a man of taste.

'Two very fine pieces, sir,' said a voice. 'Coming up this afternoon.' I turned to see a short stout man in a 1907 bowler and two overcoats, which he wore open, regarding the furniture with an appraising look. With difficulty he extracted a card from an inside pocket. 'If you're thinkin' of buyin' anythin', Captain, that's me card, an' I'll be very 'appy to ac' for you.'

'Thanks, I don't think – '

'All right, Captain, all right. Only if you should, I'm always about,' he added hastily, turning away in response to a cry which had arisen for 'Mr 'Olly.' 'Comin', comin'!' he cried, making for what I took to be the drawing-room.

I slipped his card into my pocket and we passed on . . .

The tallboy chest was standing alone in its dignity at the top of the broad staircase.

The moment I saw it I knew it was good stuff. And Jill gave a little cry and began to chatter, till I laid my hand on her arm with a warning pressure.

'Hush,' I said quickly, 'don't give it away. Of course they all know it's good, but we needn't seem over-anxious. Try and look as if you thought it might do for the harness-room if it was enamelled.'

'O-o-oh, Boy.'

Such chests may be handsome and – rarely – elegant, but this was dainty. Standing upon short cabriole legs, it was small, but of exquisite proportions, and had been built, I judged, in the reign of Queen Anne. The walnut which had gone to its making was picked wood, and its drawers were faced with oyster-shell and inlaid with box. Their handles were perfect, and, indeed, the whole chest was untouched and without blemish, shining with that clean lustre which only wax and constant elbow-grease can bring about.

When I had examined the piece as carefully as I dared, I winked at Jill and descended into the hall.

Mr Holly was awaiting us.

Casually I addressed him.

'There's a tallboy at the top of the stairs, labelled 207. I'm not crazy about it, but it's about the right size for a recess in my bedroom. If you like to buy that for me on a five per cent basis – '

'Certainly, Captain.' He wrote in a fat notebook. 'Lot 207. An' 'ow 'igh will you go?'

I hesitated.

'I'll go up to a hundred pounds. But the cheaper you get it, the better for you. Understand?'

'I'm there, Captain. Will you be comin' back?'

'No. But there's my card. You can telegraph to that address this evening, and I'll send you a cheque.'

'Very good, sir.'

A minute later we were walking along the road towards Highlands and, while Jill was talking excitedly, I was considering my own recklessness.

As we entered the grounds –

'Don't say anything about it,' I said. 'Let it be a surprise.'

The first person I saw, as I entered the lounge of the hotel, was Berry.

'Do you mind not asking me why I'm here?' he said languidly. 'I've just finished telling Jonah, and repetition always wearied me.'

'Your movements have never interested me,' said I. 'All the same, I thought you were in the grip of Torment.'

'I was and shall be. For the nonce – ' He turned to a tall dark girl who was leaning against the chimney-piece, watching us curiously. 'Let me introduce my brother-in-law. Carefully kept from me before marriage and by me ever since. Both the ablative case, I believe, but what a difference! So rich is the English tongue.'

The girl threw back her head and laughed. I observed that she had nice teeth.

'Name of Childe,' she said in a sweet voice. 'After all, we can't expect him to remember everything. Wasn't my brother in your regiment?'

'I knew I'd seen you somewhere,' said I. 'The last time you were on a towel, leaning against a bottle of hair wash. That was in Flanders in 1916.'

'That,' said Berry, 'will do. Miss Childe and I came here to lunch, not to listen to maudlin memories of the Great War. Did I ever tell you that a Spaniard once compared me to that elusive bloom to be found only upon the ungathered apricot?'

'How much did you lend him?' said I.

'Perhaps he knew more about ferns,' said Miss Childe.

'Blind from birth, I suppose,' said Jonah's voice.

My brother-in-law rose to his feet and looked about him with the expression of one who has detected an offensive odour.

'He was a man of singular insight and fine feeling,' he said. 'At the time of his outburst I was giving evidence against him for cruelty to a bullock. And now, for goodness' sake, somebody collect Jill and let's have some lunch.'

'As a matter of fact,' said Miss Childe, 'I've come down to get some butter and eggs. They're usually sent, but the housekeeper's ill, and, as I was going spare, Father suggested I should run down and pick them up.'

Her voice sounded as if she was speaking from afar, and I knew that I must call up all my reserves of willpower if I was to remain awake.

'But Berry's with you, isn't he?'

'Yes. Your sister came to lunch yesterday and happened to mention that he wanted to go to Pistol today, so I offered him a lift. He's much nicer than any chauffeur.'

'But whatever did he want to come to Pistol for?'

'Ah.' From a great distance I watched Miss Childe's brown eyes take on a look of mischief that seemed at home in its bright setting. 'He wouldn't tell you and he didn't tell Captain Mansel the truth, so I shan't give him away.' She looked at a tiny wrist-watch. 'And now I must be going. We want to start back at half-past three, and I've twenty-five miles to do before then.'

'May I come with you?'

'Certainly. But – '

I stepped to where Jill was scribbling a note.

'We needn't start before half-past three,' I said. 'Will you wait for me?'

She nodded abstractedly.

Jonah was dozing over a cigarette. Berry had disappeared.

Three minutes later I was sitting in a comfortable coupé, which Miss Childe was driving at an unlawful speed in the direction of Colt.

'You drive a lot, don't you?' flashed my companion.

'A good deal.'

'Then I expect you hate being driven by a stranger?'

'Not at all. Sometimes, of course – ' I waited for us to emerge from between two motor-lorries and a traction-engine. As we were doing over forty-five, the pause was but momentary. 'I mean – '

'That you're being frightened to death?'

'Not to death. I've still got some feeling in my right arm.' We dropped down one of the steepest hills I have ever seen, with two bends in it, at an increased speed. 'You keep your guardian angel pretty busy, don't you?'

A suspicion of a smile played for a second about my lady's lips.

'The only thing I'm really frightened of is a hansom cab,' she affirmed.

'Try and imagine that there are half a dozen round the next corner, will you?'

The smile deepened.

'Is your heart all right?' she demanded.

'It was when we started.'

'But I know this road backwards.'

'You needn't tell me that,' said I. 'We should have been killed long ago if you didn't. Seriously, I don't want to abuse your hospitality, but we're going to have kidneys for breakfast tomorrow, and I should be sorry to miss them.'

'Are you fond of kidneys?'

'Passionately. I used to go out and gather them as a child. In the morning and the meadows. Or were we talking of haddock?'

Miss Childe hesitated before replying.

'I used to, too. But I was always afraid of their being toadstools. They're poisonous, aren't they?'

'Deadly. By the way, there are six hansoms full of toadstools at the crossroads which I observe we are approaching.'

'I don't believe you.'

I was wrong. But there was a wagon full of logs and a limousine full of children, which were rather worse.

We proceeded amid faint cries of indignation.

'What do you do,' said I, 'when you come to a level-crossing with the gates shut?'

'I don't,' said Miss Childe.

I was still working this out, when my companion slowed down and brought the car to a standstill in front of a high white gate bearing the legend 'Private', and keeping a thin brown road that ran for a little way between fair meadows before plunging into a swaying beechwood.

'Anything the matter?' I asked.

Miss Childe laid a hand on my arm.

'Be an angel,' she said in a caressing voice.

'Certainly,' said I. 'With or without wings?'

'And open the gate, so that – '

'I know,' I cried, 'I know. Don't tell me. "So that the automobile may pass unobstructed between the gate-posts." Am I right?'

'How on earth did you know?'

'Instinct.' I opened the door and stepped backwards into the road. 'I'm always like this before eating kidneys,' I added.

As I re-entered the car –

'Now we can let her out,' said Miss Childe contentedly. 'It's such a relief to feel there's no speed limit,' she added, with a ravishing smile.

As soon as I could trust my voice –

'I shouldn't think your chauffeurs live very long, do they?'

'On the contrary, they grow old in our service.'

'I can believe you,' said I heartily. 'I myself have aged considerably since we left Highlands.'

By this time we had flung through and out of the beechwood, and the car was storming past stretches of gleaming bracken, all red and gold and stuck with spreading oak trees, that stood sometimes alone, sometimes in groups of two or three together, and made you think of staring cattle standing knee-deep in a golden flood.

The car tore on.

'We're coming to where I used to gather the mushrooms,' my companion announced.

'Barefoot?'

'Sometimes.'

'Because of the dew?'

She nodded.

I sighed. Then –

'Up to now I've been feeling like a large brandy and a small soda,' I said. 'Now I feel like a sonnet. What is your name, and who gave you that name?'

'I'm sure that's not necessary. I've seen a sonnet "To a lady upon her birthday." '

'As you please. Shall I post it to you or pin it to a tree in Battersea Park?'

Miss Childe nodded her head in the direction in which we were going.

'That,' she said, 'is the house.'

At the end of a long avenue of elms I could see the bold flash of windows which the afternoon sun had set afire, and a moment later we swept by the front of an old red mansion and round into a paved court that lay on its farther side.

Here was a door open, and in front of this my companion brought the car to a standstill.

I handed her out. She rang the bell and entered. I followed her in.

'Like to look round the house?' said Miss Childe. 'We've given up showing it since the Suffragettes, but if you could give me a reference – '

'Messrs Salmon and Gluckstein,' said I, 'are my solicitors.'

My lady pointed to a door at the end of the flagged passage in which we stood.

'That'll take you into the hall,' she said. 'I'll come and find you when I've seen the servants.'

I saluted and broke away in the direction she had indicated.

There was a closet that opened out of the great gallery. No door hung in the doorway, and I could see china ranged orderly against the panelling of the walls. I descended its two stairs, expecting to find it devoted to china and nothing else. But I was wrong. Facing the window and the sunshine was a facsimile of the tallboy chest which I had coveted so fiercely two hours before.

I gazed at it spellbound.

'It's very rude to stare,' said a voice.

I turned to see Miss Childe framed in the doorway.

Her gown was of apricot with the bodice cut low and the skirt gathered in loops to show her white silk petticoat, which swelled from under a flowered stomacher so monstrously, that the tiny blue-heeled slipper upon the second stair seemed smaller than ever. Deep frills of lace fell from her short sleeves, and a little lace cap was set on her thick dark hair.

I swallowed before replying. Then –

'It's a lovely chest,' I said lamely.

'Picked wood,' said Miss Childe. 'Flogged once a week for years, that tree was.'

'Flogged?'

'Certainly.'

Suddenly the air was full of music, and a jubilant chorus of voices was singing lustily –

'A woman, a spaniel and a walnut-tree,
The more you beat them, the better they be.'

As the melody faded –

'I told you so,' said Miss Childe. 'What about the butter and eggs? Will you pay for them, or shall I have them sent?'

I handed her the largest one pound note I have ever seen.

'Thanks,' she said shortly. 'Change at Earl's Court.'

A peal of boy's laughter floated in at the open window.

'Who's that?' said I.

'Love,' said Miss Childe. 'The locksmiths are here, and he's laughing at them. I think it's rather unkind myself. Besides – '

A burst of machine-gun fire interrupted her.

As the echoes died down –

'You smell of potpourri,' said I.

'Probably. I made three bags full this morning. Bead bags. Do you mind putting some coal on the fire? If there aren't any tongs, use the telephone.'

There was no fireplace and no coal-scuttle, so I took off my right boot and put it in the bottom drawer of the tallboy instead.

'Number, please,' said Miss Childe, who had entered the closet and was standing a-tiptoe before a mirror to adjust a patch beneath her left eye.

'Lot 207,' said I.

'Line's engaged,' said Miss Childe. 'Didn't you see it in *The Times*?'

By way of answer, I threw a large plate at her. She seemed more pleased than otherwise with the attention, and began to pluck the delicate flowers with which it was painted and gather them into a nosegay. In some dudgeon, I blew a small jug of great beauty on to a carved prie-dieu, to which it adhered as though made of some slimy substance.

'Cannon,' said my lady. 'Shall I put you on?'

'I wish you would. It's rather important.'

'You're through.'

'Tallboy speaking,' said a faint voice. 'Tallboy. Tallboy.'

'How d'ye do?' said I.

'Ill,' said the voice, 'so ill. All these years I've carried it, and no one knew – '

'Pardon me,' said I. 'I only put it there five minutes ago. You see, the fire was almost out and – '

'Measurements tell,' said the voice. 'But they never do that. They polish my panels and lay fair linen within me, and great folk have stood about me telling each other of my elegance, and once a baby child mirrored its little face in one of my sides. And all the time measurements tell. But they never do that.'

A sigh floated to my ears, a long, long sigh, that rose into a wail of the wind, and a casement behind me blew to with a shaking clash.

Somewhere a dog was howling.

On a sudden I felt cold. The sunshine was gone, and the chamber had become grey and dismal. Misery was in the air.

A stifled exclamation made me look round.

My lady had backed shrinking into a corner, one little hand pressed to her heart, and in her hunted eyes sat Fear dominant. The sweet face was drawn and colourless, and her breath came quickly, so that it was grievous to mark the flutter of her smooth white chest.

Mechanically I turned to seek the cause of her terror.

I saw a powerfully built man standing square in the closet's doorway. His face was coarse and red and brutal, and his small black eyes glowed with an ugly twinkle as he surveyed his quarry. Upon the thick lips there was a sinister smile, which broadened hideously as he glanced at the nosegay held betwixt his finger and thumb – the little nosegay that she had gathered so lightly from the painted plate. A wide-skirted coat of red fell nearly to his knees and hid his breeches. His short black periwig was bobbed, and a black silk tie was knotted about his neck. Stockings were rolled above his knees, and a huge tongue thrust out from each of his buckled shoes. And in his left hand was a heavy riding-whip whose handle was wrought about with gold. This he kept clapping against his leg with a smack and a ghastly relish that there was no mistaking.

Again that phantom chorus rose up and rang in my ears –

'A woman, a spaniel, and a walnut tree,
The more you beat them, the better they be.'

But the jubilant note was gone, and, though the tune was the same, the voices were harsh, and there was a dreadful mockery of woe in the stave that made me shudder.

My lady heard it, too.

'No, no, Ralph. You do me wrong. I plucked them myself. Who is there now to send me posies? And I am sick – you know it. The last time – ' The hurrying voice faltered and stumbled piteously over a sob. 'The last time I was near spent, Ralph. So near. And now – You do not know your strength. Indeed – Oh, Ralph, Ralph, what have I done that you should use me so?'

The bitter cry sank into a dull moan, and, setting a frail white arm across her eye, she bowed her head upon it, as do weeping children, and fell to sobbing with that subdued despair that spells a broken spirit.

My lord's withers were unwrung.

For a moment he stood still, leering like some foul thing that feasts on Anguish. Then he let fall the nosegay and took the whip in his right hand. . . .

And I stood there frozen and paralysed and dumb.

Posing his victim with a horrible precision, the monster raised his whip, but it struck a pendant lantern, and with an oath he turned to the gallery, where he should find room and to spare for his brutality. At this delay my lady fell upon her knees, in a wild hope, I think, to turn her respite into a reprieve, but the beast cried out upon her, struck down her outstretched hands, and, twisting his fingers in her soft dark hair, dragged her incontinently out of the closet. The little whimper she gave was awful. . . .

And I stood there paralysed.

Five minutes, perhaps, had passed, slow-treading, pregnant minutes, when my lord reappeared. He stood for a moment listening at the top of the stairs, his chin on his shoulder. Then he stepped lightly down. His vile face was pale and his eyes shifted uneasily. The devil looked out of them yet, but Fright looked with him. Two paces brought the fellow before the tallboy. He put up his hands as if to pull open a drawer, when something about the whip he was holding caught his attention. For a second he stared at it, muttering. Then, with a glance at the doorway, he thrust the thing beneath the skirt of his coat and wiped it as it had been a rapier. . . .

Again he made to open a drawer, but the spell under which I lay seemed to be lifted, and I shot out a hand and clapped him on the shoulder.

For all the notice he took, I might not have been there. The more incensed, I shook the man violently . . .

'Repose,' said Jonah, 'is one thing, gluttonish sloth another. And even if you have once again over-estimated the capacity of your stomach, why advertise your intemperance in a public place?' He lifted his hand from my shoulder to look at his watch. 'It's now ten minutes to three. Do you think you can stagger, or must you be carried, to the car?'

I sat up and looked about me. Except for Jill, who was standing a-tiptoe before a mirror, we were alone in the lounge.

'I've been dreaming,' said I. 'About – about – '

'That's all right, old chap. Tell Nanny all about it tonight, after you've had your bath. That's one of the things she's paid for.'

'Don't be a fool,' said I, putting a hand to my head. 'It's important, I tell you. For Heaven's sake, let me think. Oh, what was it?' My cousins stared at me. 'I'm not rotting. It was real – something that mattered.'

''Orse race?' said Jonah eagerly. 'Green hoops leading by twelve lengths or something?'

I waved him away.

'No, no, no. Let me think. Let me think.'

I buried my face in my hands and thought and thought . . . But to no purpose. The vision was gone.

Hastily I made ready for our journey to town, all the time racking my brain feverishly for some odd atom of incident that should remember my dream.

It was not until I was actually seated in the Rolls, with my foot upon the self-starter, that I thought about Berry.

Casually I asked what had become of him.

'That's what we want to know,' said Jill. 'He motored down here with Miss Childe, and now they've pushed off somewhere, but they wouldn't say – '

'Childe!' I shouted. 'Miss Childe! I've got it!'

'What on earth's the matter?' said Jonah, as I started the car.

'My dream,' I cried. 'I remember it all. It was about that tallboy.'

'What – the one we saw?' cried Jill.

I nodded.

'I'm going to double my bid,' I said. 'We simply must have it, whatever the price.'

Disregarding Jonah's protests that we were going the wrong way, I swung the car in the direction from which we had come, and streaked down the road to Cranmer Place.

A minute later I dashed into the hall, with Jill at my heels.

The first person I saw was Mr Holly.

'Has it come up yet?'

I flung the words at him, casting strategy to the winds.

'It 'as, Captain, an' I'm sorry to say we've lorst it. I never see such a thing. There was a gent there as meant to 'ave it. 'Cept for 'im, there wasn't a bid after twenty-five pounds. I never thort we'd 'ave to go over fifty, neither. Might 'a bin the owner 'isself, the way 'e was runnin' us up. An' when we was in the eighties, I sez to meself, I sez, "The one as calls a nundred first, 'as it. So 'ere goes." "Eighty-nine," sez 'e. "A nundred pound," sez I, bold-like. "Make it guineas," sez he, as cool as if 'e was buyin' a naporth o' figs. I tell you, Captain, it fair knocked me, it did. I come all of a tremble, an' me knees – '

'Where's the fellow who bought it?' said I.

'I'm afraid it's no good, Captain. I tell you 'e meant to 'ave them drawers.'

With an effort I mastered my impatience.

'Will you tell me where he is? Or, if he's gone, find out – '

'I don't think 'e's gorn,' said Mr Holly, looking round. 'I 'alf think – There 'e is,' he cried suddenly, nodding over my shoulder. 'That's 'im on the stairs, with the lady in blue.'

Excitedly I swung round to see my brother-in-law languidly descending the staircase, with Miss Childe by his side.

'Hullo,' he said. 'Do you mind not asking me why I'm here?'

'It's not my practice,' said I, 'to ask a question, the answer to which I already know.' I turned to Mr Holly and took out a one-pound note. 'I'm much obliged for your trouble. "Not a bid after twenty-five pounds," I think you said.' I handed him the note, which he accepted with protests of gratitude. 'You did better than you know,' I added.

'May I ask,' said Berry unsteadily, 'if this gentleman and you are in collusion?'

'We were,' said I. 'At least, I instructed him to purchase some furniture for me. Unfortunately we were outbid. But it's of no consequence.'

Berry raised his eyes to heaven and groaned.

'Subtraction,' he said, 'is not my strongest point, but I make it eighty pounds. Is that right?'

I nodded, and he turned to Miss Childe.

'That viper,' he said, 'has stung the fool who feeds him to the tune of eighty pounds. Shall I faint here or by the hat-stand? Let's be clear about it. The moment I enter the swoon – '

'Still, as long as it's in the family – ' began Jill.

'Exactly,' said I. 'The main thing is, we've got it. And when you've heard my tale – '

'Eighty paper pounds,' said Berry. 'Can you beat it?'

'That'd only be about thirty-five before the War,' said Miss Childe in a shaking voice.

'Yes,' said I. 'Look at it that way. And what's thirty-five? A bagatelle, brother, a bagatelle. Now, if we were in Russia – '

'Yes,' said Berry grimly, 'and if we were in Patagonia, I suppose I should be up on the deal. You can cut that bit.'

Miss Childe and Jill dissolved into peals of merriment.

'That's right,' said Berry. 'Deride the destitute. Mock at bereavement. As for you,' he added, turning to Jill, 'your visit to the Zoo is indefinitely postponed. Other children shall feel sick in the monkey-house and be taken to smell the bears. But you, never.' He turned to Miss Childe and laid a hand on her arm. 'Shut your eyes, my dear, and repeat one of Alfred Austin's odes. This place is full of the ungodly.'

My determination to carry the tallboy chest to London in the Rolls met with stern opposition, but in the end I prevailed, and at six o'clock that evening it was safely housed in Mayfair.

To do him justice, Berry's annoyance was considerably tempered by the strange story which I unfolded during a belated tea.

The house and park which I had seen we were unable to identify, and the Post Office guide was silent as to the whereabouts of Colt. But the excitement which Daphne's production of a tape-measure aroused was only exceeded by the depression which was created by our failure to discover anything unusual about the chest.

We measured the cornice and we measured the plinth. We measured the frame and we measured the drawers. But if the linear measurements afforded us little satisfaction, the square measurements revealed considerably less, while, since no one of us was a mathematician, the calculation of the cubic capacity proved, not only unprofitable, but provocative of such bitter arguments and insulting remarks that Daphne demanded that we should desist.

'All right,' said Berry, 'if you don't believe me, call in a consulting engineer. I've worked the blinking thing out three times. I admit the answers were entirely different, but that's not my fault. I never did like astrology. I tell you the beastly chest holds twenty-seven thousand point nine double eight recurring cubic inches of air. Some other fool can reduce that to rods, and there you are. I'm fed up with it. Thanks to the machinations of that congenital idiot with the imitation mustachios, I've paid more than four times its value, and I'm not going to burst my brains trying to work out which drawer would have had a false bottom if it had been built by a dipsomaniac who kept fowls. And that's that.'

Tearfully Miss Childe announced that it was time for her to be going, and I elected to escort her as far as the garage. As we stepped on to the pavement –

'I know a lot more about you than you think,' said I. 'I never told you all half what I dreamed.'

'What do you know?'

'Oh, nothing momentous. Just the more intimate details of your everyday life. Your partiality to mushrooms, your recognition of Love, your recklessness, pretty peculiarities of your toilet – '

'Good Heavens!' cried Miss Childe.

'But you wouldn't tell me your name.'

'False modesty. Seriously you don't mean to say – '

'But I do. Nothing was hid from me. Your little bare feet – '

A stifled scream interrupted me.

'This,' said Miss Childe, 'is awful.' We turned into the mews. 'What are you doing tomorrow?'

'Dictating. You see, there's a dream I want recorded.'

'I shall expect you at half-past one. We can start after lunch. I've a beautiful hand.'

'I know you have. Two of them. They were bare, too,' I added reflectively.

With a choking sound, Miss Childe got into the car.

'Half-past one,' she said, as she slid into the driver's seat.

'Without fail.' I raised my hat. 'By the way, who shall I ask for?'

Miss Childe flung me a dazzling smile.

'I've no sisters,' she said.

Moodily I returned to the house.

I entered the library to find that the others had retired, presumably to dress for dinner. Mechanically I crossed to the tallboy, which we had so fruitlessly surveyed, and began to finger it idly, wondering all the time whether my dream was wanton, or whether there was indeed some secret which we might discover. It did not seem possible, and yet. . . . That distant voice rang in my ears. 'Measurements tell, measurements tell. But they never do that.' *What?*

A sudden idea came to me, and I drew out the second long drawer. Then in some excitement I withdrew the first, and placed it exactly upon the top of the second, so that I might see if they were of the same size. *The second was the deeper by an inch and a half.*

I thrust my arms into the empty frame, feeling feverishly for a bolt or catch, which should be holding a panel in place at the back of where the first drawer had lain. At first I could find nothing, then my right hand encountered a round hole in the wood, just large enough to admit a man's finger. Almost immediately I came upon a similar hole on the left-hand side. Their office was plain. . . .

A moment later, and I had drawn the panel out of its standing and clear of the chest.

My hands were trembling as I thrust them into the dusty hiding-place. . . .

'Hullo! Aren't you going to dress?' said Jonah some two minutes later.

But I was still staring at a heavy riding-whip whose handle was wrought about with gold.

As is their wont, Berry and Co have settled in London for the Winter. The Gold and Silver Ball at the Albert Hall was a great success, marred only slightly by Berry getting lost in the fog. Nobby, a Sealyham, has been presented to Boy but has exhibited an unfortunate penchant for chasing the master of the house up the walls, and bathing with him. And the egregious Douglas Bladder – by no means Esq. – has been utterly routed in his attempt to escape paying out the four hundred pounds damages he inflicted upon the Pleydells' Rolls.

Now a disaster of epic – or at least epicurean – proportions has befallen the company . . .

TOO MANY COOKS

Berry laid down his knife and fork and raised his eyes to heaven.

'This,' he said, 'is the frozen edge. I'm getting used to the distemper which is brought me in lieu of soup, and, although I prefer salmon cooked to raw, you may have noticed that I consumed my portion without a word. But this. . . .' Contemptuously he indicated the severed tournedos upon his plate. 'You know, they must have been using the lime-kiln. Nobody could get such a withered effect with an electric cooker. Oh, and look at our olive. Quick, before it shuts up.'

Jill began to shake with laughter.

'I can't help it,' said Daphne desperately. 'I know it's awful, but what can we do?'

'There must be some cooks somewhere,' said I. 'The breed isn't extinct. And they can't all be irrevocably suited. I always thought the Cooks' Brigade was one of the most mobile arms of domestic service.'

'I've done everything,' said my sister, 'except advertise. Katharine Festival put me off that. She says she spent seven pounds on advertisements and never got a single answer. But I've done everything else. I've asked everybody I know, my name's on the books of every registry office I've ever heard of, and I've written and sent stamped addressed envelopes to every cook whose name I've been given. Three out of about sixty have replied, saying they were already suited. One came here, practically said she'd come, and then wrote to say she was frightened of the electric cooker. And another wanted a hundred a year and a private bathroom. It's simply hopeless.'

'If,' said Berry, 'we survive this meal, I'll write to Jonah and tell him to bring one back with him. If he can't raise one in Paris, he ought to be shot. And now let's have a sweep on the savoury. I'll bet it tastes of paraffin and looks like a pre-war divvot.'

'Let's try advertising,' said Jill. 'Katharine mayn't have had a good one.'

'I agree,' said I. 'I'll get one out tonight. A real snorter.'

In silence the traces of the course which had provoked the outburst were removed, clean plates were set before us, and the footman advanced with a dish of nauseous-looking fritters.

Daphne instinctively recoiled.

'Hullo,' said Berry. 'Another gas attack?'

With an effort my sister recovered herself and took one with a shaking hand. Loyally Jill followed her example, and, with tears running down her cheeks, induced a glutinous slab to quit the silver, to which it clung desperately.

I declined the delicacy.

With compressed lips the servant offered it to my brother-in-law.

Berry shook his head.

'Mother wouldn't like me to,' he said. 'But I can see it's very tasty.' He turned to his wife. 'What a wonderful thing perfume is! You know, the smell of burnt fat always makes me think of the Edgware Road at dusk.'

'Hush,' said I, consulting the menu. '*De mortuis*. Those were banana fritters. That slimy crust enshrined the remains of a once succulent fruit.'

'What?' said Berry. 'Like beans in amber? How very touching! I suppose undertakers are easier than cooks. Never mind. It's much cheaper. I shan't want to be reminded of food for several days now.' He looked across the table to Daphne. 'After what I've just seen, I feel I can give the savoury a miss. Do you agree, darling? Or has the fritter acted as an apéritif?'

My sister addressed herself to Jill.

'Don't eat it, dear. It's – it's not very nice.' She rose. 'Shall we go?'

Gloomily we followed her into the library, where I opened all the windows and Berry lit a huge cigar, in the hope of effacing the still pungent memory of the unsavoury sweet. Gradually it faded away. . . .

Three weeks had passed since the mistress of our kitchen, who had reigned uninterruptedly for seven years, had been knocked down by a taxi and sustained a broken leg. Simple though the fracture fortunately was, at least another nine weeks must elapse before she could attempt to resume her duties, and we were in evil case. Every day we became more painfully aware of the store which we had unconsciously set by decently-cooked food. As time went on, the physical and mental disorder, consequent upon Mrs Mason's accident, became more and more pronounced. All topics of conversation became subservient to the burning question of filling the void occasioned by her absence. Worst of all, dissatisfaction was rampant in the servants' hall, and Daphne's maid had hinted broadly that, if a cook was not shortly forthcoming, resignations would be – an intimation which made us desperate. Moreover, in another month we were due to leave town and repair to White Ladies. There, deep in the country, with no restaurants or clubs to fall back upon, we should be wholly at the mercy of whoever controlled the preparation of our food, and, unless the situation improved considerably, the prospect was far from palatable.

Moodily I extinguished my cigarette and filled and lighted a pipe in its stead. Then I remembered my threat.

Berry was writing a letter, so I extracted a sheet of notepaper from the left-hand drawer and, taking a pencil from my pocket, sat down on the sofa and set to work to compose an advertisement calculated to allure the most suspicious and *blasé* cook that ever was foaled.

Jill sat labouring with her needle upon a dainty tea-cloth, pausing now and again to hold a whispered and one-sided conversation with Nobby, who lay at inelegant ease supine between us. Perched upon the arm of a deep armchair, my sister was subjecting the space devoted by five daily papers to the announcement of 'Situations Required' to a second and more leisurely examination.

Presently she rose with a sigh and crossed to the telephone.

We knew what was coming.

Every night she and Katharine Festival communicated to one another their respective failures of the day. More often than not, these took the simple form of 'negative information'.

She was connected immediately.

'Hullo, that you, Katharine? . . . Yes, Daphne. Any luck? . . . Not much. You know, it's simply hopeless. What? . . . "Widow with two boys of seven and nine"? Thank you. I'd rather. . . . Exactly . . . Well, I don't know. I'd give it up, only it's so awful. . . . Awful.'

'If she doesn't believe it, ask her to dinner,' said Berry.

'Shut up,' said Daphne. 'It's all right, Katharine. I was speaking to Berry. . . . Oh, he's fed to the teeth.'

'I cannot congratulate you,' said her husband, 'upon your choice of metaphor.'

My sister ignored the interruption.

'Oh, rather . . . His food means a lot to him, you know.'

'This,' said her husband, 'is approaching the obscene. I dine off tepid wash and raw fish, I am tormented by the production of a once luscious fillet deliberately rendered unfit for human consumption, and I am deprived of my now ravening appetite by the nauseating reek from the shock of whose assault I am still trying to rally my olfactory nerves. All this I endure with that unfailing good – '

'Will you be quiet?' said his wife. 'How can I – '

'No, I won't,' said Berry. 'My finer feelings are outraged. And that upon an empty stomach. I shall write home and ask to be taken away. I shall – '

'Katharine,' said Daphne, 'I can't hear you because that fool Berry is talking, but Boy's getting out an advertisement, and we're going to . . . Oh, are you? I thought you said you'd given it up . . .

Another nineteen shillings' worth? Well, here's luck, anyway . . . Yes, of course. But I daren't hope . . . Goodbye.' She replaced the receiver and turned to me. 'Katharine's going to start advertising again.'

'Is she?' I grunted. 'Well, I'll bet she doesn't beat this. Listen.

'COOK, capable, experienced, is offered for three months abnormal wages, every luxury and a leisurely existence: electric cooker: constant hot water: kitchen-maid: separate bedroom: servants' hall: late breakfast: town and country: followers welcomed. – Mrs Pleydell, 7, Cholmondeley Street, Mayfair: 'Phone, Mayfair 9999.'

'That's the style,' said Berry. 'Let me know when it's going to appear, and I'll get a bedroom at the Club. When you've weeded the best out of the first hundred thousand, I'll come back and give the casting vote.'

From behind, my sister put her arms about my neck and laid her soft cheek against mine.

'My dear,' she murmured, 'I daren't. Half the cooks in England would leave their situations.'

'So much the better,' said I. 'All's fair in love and war. I don't know which this is, but we'll call it "love" and chance it. Besides,' I added cunningly, 'we must knock out Katharine.'

The light of battle leapt into my sister's eyes. Looking at it from her point of view, I realised that my judgment had been ill-considered. Plainly it was not a question of love, but of war – 'and that most deadly.' She drew her arms from my neck and stood upright.

'Couldn't you leave out my name and just put "Box So-and-so"?'

I shook my head.

'That's so intangible. Besides, I think the telephone number's a great wheeze.' Thoughtfully she crossed to the fireplace and lighted a cigarette. 'I'll send it tomorrow,' I said.

Suddenly the room was full of silvery laughter.

From Berry's side at the writing-table Jill looked up sparkling.

'Listen to this,' she said, holding up the letter which my brother-in-law had just completed.

Dear Brother,

Incompetent bungler though you are, and bitter as has been my experience of your gaucherie in the past, I am once again about to prove whether out of the dunghill of inefficiency which, with unconscious humour, you style your 'mind' there can be coaxed a shred of reliability and understanding.

It is within your knowledge that some three weeks ago this household was suddenly deprived of the services of its cook. This out of a clear sky and, if we may believe the police, in one of those uncharted purlieus which shroud in mystery the source of the Cromwell Road. After four lean days your gluttonous instincts led you precipitately to withdraw to Paris, from whence, knowing your unshakable belief in the vilest forms of profligacy, I appreciate that lack of means must ere long enforce your return.

Therefore I write.

For twenty-two unforgettable sultry days we have endured the ghastly pleasantries of charwomen, better qualified to victual the lower animals than mankind. To call the first meal 'breakfast' is sheer blasphemy: lunch is a hollow mockery: dinner, the abomination of desolation. I do what I can with grapenuts and the gas stove in the bathroom, but the result is unhappy, and last night the milk was too quick for me.

I therefore implore you to collect a cook in Paris without delay. Bring it with you when you come, or, better still, send it in advance, carriage paid. Luxury shall be heaped upon it. Its slightest whim shall be gratified, and it shall go to 'the movies' at my expense, whenever I am sent tickets. Can generosity go further? Wages no object: fare paid back to Paris as soon as Mrs Mason's leg can carry her.

Brother, I beseech you, take immediate action. The horror of our plight cannot be exaggerated. Do something – anything. Misrepresent facts, corrupt honesty, suborn the faithful, but – procure a cook.

My maw reminds me that it is the hour of grapenuts, so I must go.

Berry.

P.S. – If you can't raise one, I shouldn't come back. Just go to some high place and quietly push yourself off. It will be simpler and avoid a scene which would be painful to us both.

'That's rather worse than the advertisement,' said Daphne. 'But, as Jonah is accustomed to your interpretation of the art of letter-writing, I suppose it doesn't much matter.'

'When,' said Berry, 'you are making yourself sick upon *tête de veau en tortue* and *crêpes Suzette*, I shall remind you of those idle words.'

The advertisement appeared for the first time on Thursday morning.

As I entered the dining-room at half-past nine –

'It's in,' said Jill. 'On the front page.'

'Yes,' said Berry, 'it's most arresting. Applicants will arrive from all over the kingdom. It's inevitable. Nothing can stop them. Old and trusted retainers will become unsettled. The domestic upheaval will be unparalleled.'

I read the advertisement through. In cold print my handiwork certainly looked terribly alluring. Then I laid down the paper and strolled to the window. It had been raining, but now the sun was out, and the cool fresh air of the June morning was sweet and winsome. As I looked into the glistening street –

'It's a bit early yet,' continued Berry. 'Give 'em a chance. I should think they'll start about ten. I wonder how far the queue will reach,' he added reflectively. 'I hope the police take it past the Albert Memorial. Then they can sit on the steps.'

'Nonsense,' said I a little uneasily. 'We may get an answer or two tomorrow. I think we shall. But cooks are few and far between.'

'They won't be few and they'll be anything but far between by twelve o'clock.' He tapped the provocative paragraph with an accusing finger. 'This is a direct incitement to repair to 7, Cholmondeley Street, or as near thereto as possible – '

'I wish to goodness we hadn't put it in,' said Daphne.

'It's done now,' said her husband, 'and we'd better get ready. I'll turn them down in the library, you can stand behind the what-not in the drawing-room and fire them from there, and Boy'd better go down the queue with some oranges and a megaphone and keep on saying we're suited right up to the last.'

In silence I turned to the sideboard. It was with something of an effort that I helped myself to a thick slab of bacon which was obviously but half-cooked. From the bottom of a second dish a black-and-white egg, with a pale green yolk, eyed me with a cold stare. With a shudder I covered it up again . . . After all, we did want a cook, and if we were bombarded with applications for the post, the probability of getting a good one was the more certain.

As I took my seat –

'Is Katharine's advertisement in?' I asked.

My sister nodded.

'She's put her telephone number, too.'

'Has she? She will be mad when she sees we've had the same idea.'

'Ah,' said Berry. 'I'd forgotten the telephone. That's another vulnerable spot. I shouldn't wonder if – '

The sentence was never finished.

The hurried stammer of the telephone bell made a dramatic irruption, and Jill, who was in the act of drinking, choked with excitement.

In silence we listened, to be quite sure. A second prolonged vibration left no room for doubt.

'They're off,' said Berry.

'I – I feel quite nervous,' said Daphne.

'Let Falcon answer it.'

But Jill was already at the door . . .

Breathlessly we awaited her return.

Nobby, apparently affected by the electricity with which the air was charged, started to relieve his feelings by barking stormily. The nervous outburst of reproof which greeted his eloquence was so unexpectedly menacing that he retired precipitately beneath the table, his small white tail clapped incontinently between his legs.

The next moment Jill tore into the room.

'It's a cook!' she cried in a tempestuous whisper. 'It's a cook! She wants to speak to Daphne. It's a trunk call. She's rung up from Torquay.'

'Torquay!' I cried aghast. 'Good Heavens!'

'What did I say?' said Berry. My sister rose in some trepidation. 'Two hundred miles is nothing. Have another hunk of toast. It was only made on Sunday, so I can recommend it.'

Daphne hastened from the room, with Jill twittering at her heels, and in some dudgeon I cut myself a slice of bread.

Berry turned his attention to the Sealyham.

'Nobby, my lad, come here.'

Signifying his delight at this restoration to favour by an unusually elaborate rotatory movement of his tail, the terrier emerged from his cover and humbled himself at his patron's feet. The latter picked him up and set him upon his knee.

'My lad,' he said, 'this is going to be a momentous day. Cooks, meet to be bitten, are due to arrive in myriads. Be ruthless. Spare neither the matron nor the maid. What did Mr Henry say in 1415? –

This day is call'd the feast of Sealyham:
She that outlives this day, and comes safe home,
Will sit with caution when this day is named,
And shudder at the name of Sealyham.
She that shall live this day, and see old age,
Will yearly on the razzle feast her neighbours,
And say, "Tomorrow is Saint Sealyham":
Then will she strip her hose and show her scars,
And say, "These wounds I had on Nobby's day."
Old cooks forget; yet all shall be forgot,
But she'll remember with a flood of talk
What feats you did that day.'

Nobby licked his face enthusiastically.

Then came a swift rush across the hall, and Daphne and Jill pelted into the room.

'She's coming up for an interview tomorrow,' panted the latter. 'Six years in her last place, but the people are going abroad. If we engage her, she can come on Monday. Sixty pounds a year.'

Daphne was beaming.

'I must say I liked the sound of her. Very respectful she seemed. Her name's rather unusual, but that isn't her fault. Pauline Roper. I fancy she's by way of being an expert. She's got a certificate from some institute of cookery, and her sister's a trained nurse in Welbeck Street. That's why she wants to be in London. What's the return fare from Torquay?' she added. 'I said I'd pay it, if I took up her reference.'

'Oh, something under five pounds,' said Berry.

'What!'

'My dear,' said her husband, 'if the expenditure of that sum were to ensure me a breakfast the very sight of which did not make my gorge rise, I should regard it as a trustee investment.'

Reference to a time-table showed that the price of Pauline Roper's ticket would be two pounds nine shillings and fourpence-halfpenny.

Somewhat to our surprise and greatly to our relief, the day

passed without another application for the post of cook, personal or otherwise.

To celebrate the solitary but promising response to our SOS signal, and the prospect which it afforded of an early deliverance from our state, we dined at the Berkeley and went to the play.

On returning home we found a telegram in the hall. It had been handed in at Paris, and ran as follows:–

> *Cook called Camille François leaving for Cholmondeley Street tomorrow aaa can speak no English so must be met at Dover aaa boat due 4.15 aaa Jonah.*

The train roared through Ashford, and Berry looked at his watch. Then he sighed profoundly and began to commune with himself in a low tone.

'*Milles pardons, madame. Mais vous êtes Camille François? Non? Quel dommage! Dix milles pardons. Adieu* . . . Deuce of a lot of "milles", aren't there? I wonder if there'll be many passengers. And will she come first-class, or before the mast? You know, this is a wild mare's chest, and that's all there is to it. We shall insult several hundred women, miss the cook, and probably lose Pauline into the bargain. What did I come for?'

'Nonsense,' said Jill stoutly. 'Jonah's told her to look out for us.'

'I'll bet he never thought I should be fool enough to roll up, so she won't expect me. As a matter of fact, if he's described anyone, he's probably drawn a lifelike word-picture of Daphne.'

'It's no good worrying,' said I. 'The only thing to do is to address every woman who looks in the least like a cook as she steps off the gangway. When we do strike her, Jill can carry on.'

'It's all very well,' said Berry, 'but what does a cook look like, or look least like, or least look like? I suppose you know what you mean.' Jill began to shake with laughter. 'She'll probably be all dressed up to give us a treat, and, for all we know, she may have a child with her, and, if she's pretty, it's a hundred to one some fellow will be seeing her off the boat. You can't rule out anyone. And to accost strange women indiscriminately is simply asking for trouble. Understand this: when I've been knocked down twice, you can count me out.'

This was too much for Jill, who made no further efforts to

restrain her merriment. Fixing her with a sorrowful look, my brother-in-law sank back in his corner with a resigned air.

Jonah's telegram had certainly complicated matters.

We had received it too late to prevent the despatch of the cook whose services he had apparently enlisted. After a prolonged discussion we had decided that, while Daphne must stay and interview Pauline Roper, the rest of us had better proceed to Dover with the object of meeting the boat. It was obvious that Jill must go to deal with the immigrant when the latter had been identified, but she could not be expected to effect the identification. I was unanimously chosen for this responsible task, but I refused point-blank to make the attempt single-handed. I argued with reason that it was more than one man could do, and that the performance of what was, after all, a highly delicate operation must be shared by Berry. After a titanic struggle the latter gave in, with the result that Jill and he and I had left London by the eleven o'clock train. This was due to arrive at Dover at two minutes to one, so that we should have time for lunch and to spare before the boat came in.

But that was not all.

The coming of Jonah's *protégée* made it impossible for my sister to engage Pauline Roper out of hand. Of course the latter might prove impossible, which, in a way, would simplify the position. If, as was more probable, she seemed desirable, the only thing to do was to pay her fare and promise to let her know within twenty-four hours whether we would engage her or not. That could give us time to discover whether Camille François was the more promising of the two.

Whatever happened, it was painfully clear that our engagement of a cook was going to prove one of the most costly adventures of its kind upon which we had ever embarked.

The train steamed into Dover one minute before its scheduled time, and we immediately repaired to the Lord Warden Hotel.

Lunch was followed by a comfortable half-hour in the lounge, after which we decided to take the air until the arrival of the packet.

Perhaps the most famous of the Gates of England, Dover has always worn a warlike mien. Less formidable than renowned Gibraltar, there is a look of grim efficiency about her heights, an air of masked authority about the windy galleries hung in her cold grey chalk, something of Roman competence about the proud old gatehouse on the Castle Hill. Never in mufti, never in gaudy uniform, Dover is always clad in 'service' dress. A thousand threats have made her porterage a downright office, bluntly performed. And so those four lean years, that whipped the smile from many an English hundred, seem to have passed over the grizzled Gate like the east wind, leaving it scatheless. About herself no change was visible. As we leaned easily upon the giant parapet of the Admiralty Pier, watching the tireless waves dance to the capriccio of wind and sun, there was but little evidence to show that the portcullis, recently hoist, had for four years been down. Under the shadow of the Shakespeare Cliff the busy traffic of impatient Peace fretted as heretofore. The bristling sentinels were gone: no craft sang through the empty air: no desperate call for labour wearied tired eyes, clawed at strained nerves, hastened the scurrying feet: no longer from across the Straits came flickering the ceaseless grunt and grumble of the guns. The wondrous tales of nets, of passages of arms, of sallies made at dawn – mortal immortal exploits – seemed to be chronicles of another age. The ways and means of war, so lately paramount, were out of sight. As in the days before, the march of trade and caravan of pleasure jostled each other in the Gate's mouth. Only the soldierly aspect of the place remained – Might in a faded surcoat, her shabby scabbard hiding a loose bright blade . . .

The steamer was up to time.

When four o'clock came, she was well in sight, and at fourteen minutes past the hour the rattle of the donkey-engine came to a sudden stop, and a moment later the gangways were thrust and hauled into their respective positions.

Berry and I stood as close to the actual points of disembarkation as convenience and discretion allowed, while Jill hovered excitedly in the background.

As the passengers began to descend –

'Now for it,' said my brother-in-law, settling his hat upon his head. 'I feel extremely nervous and more ill at ease than I can ever remember. My mind is a seething blank, and I think my left sock-suspender is coming down. However . . . Of course, it is beginning to be forcibly what they call "borne in upon" me that we ought to have brought some barbed wire and a turnstile. As it is, we shall miss about two-thirds of them. Here's your chance,' he added, nodding at a stout lady with a green suit-case and a defiant glare. 'I'll take the jug and bottle department.'

I had just time to see that the object of his irreverence was an angular female with a brown paper parcel and a tumbler, when my quarry gained *terra firma* and started in the direction of the train.

I raised my hat.

'*Pardon, madame. Mais vous êtes Camille –* '

'Reeang,' was the discomfiting reply. 'Par de baggarge.'

I realised that an offer which I had not made had been rejected, and that the speaker was not of French descent.

The sting of the rebuff was greatly tempered by the reception with which Berry's advances were met.

I was too late to hear what he had said, but the resentment which his attempt had provoked was disconcertingly obvious.

After fixing my brother-in-law with a freezing stare, his addressee turned as from an offensive odour and invested the one word she thought fit to employ with an essence of loathing which was terrible to hear.

'Disgusting!'

Berry shook his head.

'The right word,' he said, 'was "monstrous." '

He turned to accost a quiet-looking girl wearing an oil-silk gaberdine and very clearly born upon the opposite side of the Channel.

With a sigh, I addressed myself to a widow with a small boy clad in a *pélérine*. To my embarrassment, she proved to be deaf, but when I had stumblingly repeated my absurd interrogation, she denied the impeachment with a charming smile. During our exchange of courtesies the child stood staring at me with a finger deep in his mouth. At their conclusion he withdrew this and pointed it directly at my chin.

'*Pourquoi s'est-il coupé, maman?*' he demanded in a piercing treble.

The question was appropriate, but unanswerable.

His mother lugged him incontinently away.

Berry was confronting one of the largest ladies I have ever seen. As he began to speak, she interrupted him.

'*Vous êtes Messtair Baxtair, n'est-ce pas? Ah, c'est bien ca. J'avais si peur de ne pas vous trouver. Mais maintenant je suis tranquille. Mon mair me suit. Ah, le voilà!*' She turned about, the better to beckon to a huge man with two bags and a hold-all.

'*Pierre! Pierre!*'

Beneath the avalanche of good-will Berry stood paralysed.

Recognising that something must be done, I sought to interfere.

'Leave me alone,' said Berry weakly. 'I've – I've got off.'

It took all my energy and most of my French to convince his *vis-à-vis* that she was mistaken.

During the interlude about fifteen 'possibles' escaped us.

I threw a despairing glance in Jill's direction, wiped the sweat from my brow, and returned to the attack.

After four more failures my nerve began to go. Miserably I turned to my brother-in-law.

He was in the act of addressing a smart-looking girl in black, bearing a brand-new valise and some wilting roses.

Before she had had time to appreciate his inquiry, there was a choking yell from the gangway, and a very dark gentleman, with an Italian cast of countenance, thrust his explosive way on to the pier.

My knowledge of his native tongue was limited to '*carissimo*' '*spaghetti*', and one or two musical directions, but from the vehemence of his tone and the violence of his dramatic gestures it was plain that the torrent which foamed from his lips was both menacing and abusive. From the shape of the case which he was clutching beneath his left arm, I judged him to be an exponent of the guitar.

Advancing his nose to within an inch and a half of Berry's chin, he blared and raved like a maniac, alternately pointing to his shrinking protégée and indicating the blue vault of heaven with frightful emphasis.

Berry regarded him unperturbed. As he paused for breath –

'In answer to your observations,' he said, 'I can only say that I am not a Mormon and have absolutely no connection with Salt Lake City. I may add that, if you are partial to garlic, it is a taste which I have never acquired. In conclusion, I hope that, before you reach the platform for which you are apparently making, you will stumble over one of the ridiculously large rings with which the quay is so generously provided, and will not only suffer the most hideous agony, but remain permanently lame as a result of your carelessness.'

The calm dignity with which he delivered this speech had an almost magical effect upon the jealous Latin. His bluster sank suddenly and died. Muttering to himself and staring at Berry as at a wizard, he seized the girl by the arm and started to move rapidly away, wide-eyed and ill at ease. . . . With suppressed excitement and the tail of my eye, I watched him bear down upon one of the stumbling-blocks to which Berry had referred. The accuracy with which he approached it was almost uncanny. I found myself standing upon one leg. . . . The screech of anguish with which he hailed the collision, no less than the precipitancy with which he dropped the guitar, sat down and began to rock himself to and fro, was irresistibly gratifying.

The muscles about Berry's mouth twitched.

'So perish all traitors,' he said. 'And now I don't know how you feel, but I've had about enough of this. My nerves aren't what they were. Something may snap any minute.'

With one accord we proceeded to rejoin Jill, who had been witnessing our humiliations from a safe distance, and was dabbing her grey eyes with a ridiculous handkerchief.

As we came up, she started forward and pointed a trembling finger in the direction of the boat. Berry and I swung on our heels.

Looking very well, Jonah was descending the gangway with a bored air.

My brother-in-law and I stared at him as at one risen from the dead. Almost at once he saw us and waved airily . . . A moment later he limped to where we were standing and kissed his sister.

'I had an idea some of you'd turn up,' he said coolly.

Berry turned to me.

'You hear?' he said grimly. 'He had an idea some of us'd turn up. An idea . . . I suppose a little bird told him. Oh, take me away, somebody, and let me die. Let me have one last imitation meal, and die. Where do they sell wild oats?'

Jonah disregarded the interruption.

'At the last moment,' he said calmly, 'I felt there might be some mix-up, so I came along too.' He turned and nodded at a nervous little man who was standing self-consciously a few paces away and, as I now observed for the first time, carrying my cousin's dressing-case. 'That,' he added, 'is Camille.'

His momentous announcement rendered us speechless. At length –

'You – you mean to say,' I gasped, 'that – that it's a man?'

Jonah shrugged his shoulders.

'Look at his trousers,' he said.

'But – but of course we expected a woman,' cried Jill in a choking voice. 'We can't have a chef.'

'Nothing,' said Jonah, 'was said about sex.'

Berry spoke in a voice shaken with emotion.

'A man,' he said. 'A he-cook, called "Camille". And it actually occurred to you that "there might be some mix-up". You know, your intuition is positively supernatural. And it is for this,' he added bitterly, 'that I have dissipated in ten crowded minutes a reputation which it has taken years to amass. It is for this that I have deliberately insulted several respectable ladies, jeopardised the *entente cordiale*, and invited personal violence of a most unpleasant character. To do this, I shall have travelled about a hundred and fifty miles, with the shade temperature at ninety, and lost what would have been an undoubtedly pleasant and possibly extremely fruitful day at Sandown Park. Don't be afraid. I wouldn't touch you for worlds. You're being reserved for some very special form of dissolution, you are. She-bears, or something. I should avoid woods, anyway. And now I'm going home. Tomorrow I shall start on a walking tour, with a spare sock and some milk chocolate, and try to forget. If that fails, I shall take the snail – I mean the veil.'

He turned on his heel and stalked haughtily in the direction of the boat train.

Gurgling with merriment, Jill laid a hand on my arm.

'Daphne will simply scream,' she said.

'If this little stunt has cost us Pauline,' said I, 'she won't leave it at that.'

We turned to follow my brother-in-law.

Jonah beckoned to Camille.

'*Venez. Restez près de moi*,' he said.

On arriving at Charing Cross we left Jonah and the cook to weather the Customs, and drove straight to Cholmondeley Street.

As we entered the hall, my sister came flying out of the library.

'Hello,' she cried, 'where's the cook?' Don't say – '

Berry uncovered.

'*Pardon, madame*,' he said, '*mais vous êtes Camille Franç* – That's your cue. Now you say "Serwine!" Just like that. "Serwine!" Put all the loathing you can into it – you'll find it can hold quite a lot – and fix me with a glassy eye. Then I blench and break out into a cold sweat. Oh, it's a great game.'

'Poor old chap,' said Daphne. 'It must have been awful. But haven't you got her?'

'It's a he!' cried Jill, squeaking with excitement. 'It's a he. Jonah's bringing him – '

'A *what*?' said my sister, taking a pace backward.

'A male,' said I. 'You know. Like Nobby. Separate legs, and shaves on Thursdays.'

'Do you mean to say that it's a chef?'

I nodded.

My sister collapsed into a convenient chair and closed her eyes. Presently she began to shake with laughter.

'It is droll, isn't it?' said Berry. 'People wouldn't believe it. Fancy travelling a hundred and fifty miles to molest a lot of strange women, and then finding that for all the good you've done you might as well have spent the day advertising for "The Lost Chord." '

My sister pulled herself together.

'Thank goodness I had the sense to engage Pauline,' she announced. 'Something told me I'd better. But I waited before taking up her reference, on the off-chance of this one being a marvel. Where is the wretched man?'

'Jonah fetched up with him. He's stayed behind because of the Customs. They ought to be here any minute.'

'Well, there's no place for him to sleep here,' said Daphne. 'Fitch will have to look after him for tonight, and tomorrow he'll have to go back.'

Berry looked at his watch.

'Five past seven,' he said. 'As the blighter's here, why not let him sub-edit the dinner tonight? It'll shorten his life, but it may save ours. You never know.'

My sister hesitated. Then –

'He'll never do it,' she said. 'I can suggest it, but, if he's anything of a cook, he'll go off the deep end at once.'

'And give notice,' said I. 'Well, that's exactly what we want. Then we shan't have to fire him. He can just push off quietly tomorrow, Pauline will roll up on Monday, and everything will be lovely in the garden.'

'That's it,' said Berry. 'If he consents, well and good. If he declines, so much the better. It's a blinkin' certainty. Whichever happens, we can't lose.'

'All right,' said Daphne. 'I shall make Jonah tell him.'

It took Jonah and M. François longer to satisfy the officers of His Majesty's Customs and Excise than we had anticipated, and I had consumed a much-needed whisky and soda and was on the way to the bathroom when I heard them arrive.

Before I had completed a leisurely toilet, it was all over.

As we waited in the lounge of the Carlton Grill for a table, which we had been too late to reserve, my sister related the circumstances which had led to the débâcle.

'The wretched little man didn't seem to take to the idea of starting in right away, but I explained that he needn't do any more than just run his eye over the menu, and that, as they were going to have the same dinner in the servants' hall, it really only amounted to looking after his own food.

'Then I sent for Falcon, explained things, and told him to look after the man this evening, and that I was making arrangements for him to stay with Fitch over the garage. Then I had Mrs Chapel up.'

'That, I take it,' said Berry, 'is the nymph lately responsible for the preparation of our food?'

Daphne nodded.

'I told her about François, and that, as he was here, he would help her with dinner tonight. I said he was very clever, and all that sort of thing, and that I wanted her to show him what she was cooking, and listen to any suggestions he had to make.'

'I suppose you added that he couldn't speak a word of English,' said her husband.

'Be quiet,' said Daphne. 'Besides, he can. Several words. Anyway, she didn't seem over-pleased, but, as Pauline's coming on Monday, that didn't worry me. So I sent her away, and rang up Fitch and told him he must fix the Frenchman up for the night.'

'Did he seem over-pleased?'

'I didn't wait to hear. I just rang off quick. Then I went up to dress. The next thing I knew was that they'd tried to murder each other, and that Camille had bitten William, and Nobby'd bitten Camille. I don't suppose we shall ever know exactly what happened.'

So far as we had been able to gather from the butler, who had immediately repaired to Daphne's room for instructions, and was labouring under great excitement, my sister's orders had been but grudgingly obeyed. Mrs Chapel had been ill-tempered and obstructive, and had made no attempt to disguise her suspicion of the chef. The latter had consequently determined to be as nasty as the circumstances allowed, had eyed her preparations for dinner with a marked contempt, and had communed visibly and audibly with himself in a manner which it was impossible to mistake. Finally he had desired to taste the soup which she was cooking. Poor as his English was, his meaning was apparent, but the charwoman had affected an utter inability to understand what he said. This had so much incensed the Frenchman that the other servants had intervened and insisted on Mrs Chapel's compliance with his request. With an ill grace she snatched the lid from the saucepan . . .

Everything was now in train for a frightful explosion. In bitterness the fuse had been laid, the charge of passion was tamped, the detonator of spleen was in position. Only a match was necessary . . .

Camille François, however, preferred to employ a torch.

After allowing the fluid to cool, the Frenchman – by this time the cynosure of sixteen vigilant eyes – introduced a teaspoonful into his mouth . . .

The most sanguine member of his audience was hardly expecting him to commend the beverage. Mrs Chapel herself must have felt instinctively that no man born of woman would in the circumstances renounce such a magnificent opportunity of 'getting back'. Nobody, however, was apparently prepared for so vigorous and dramatic an appreciation of the dainty.

For the space of two seconds the chef held it cupped in his mouth. Then with an expression of deadly loathing, intensified by a horrible squint, he expelled the liquid on to the kitchen floor. Ignoring the gasp which greeted his action, he was observed to shrug his shoulders.

'I veep my eyes,' he announced, 'for ze pore pig.'

Here the steady flood of the butler's narrative became excusably broken into the incoherence of rapids and the decent reticence of disappearing falls. Beyond the fact that Mrs Chapel had swung twice to the jaw, and that Camille had replied with an ineffectual kick before they were dragged screaming apart, few details of the state of pandemonium that ensued came to our ears. I imagine that a striking tableau vivant somewhat on the lines of Meissonier's famous painting was unconsciously improvised. That three maids hardly restrained Mrs Chapel, that the footman who sought to withhold Camille was bitten for his pains by the now ravening Frenchman, that the latter was only saved from the commission of a still more aggravated assault by the timely arrival of the butler, that Nobby, attracted by the uproar, contributed to the confusion first by barking like a demoniac and then by inflicting a punctured wound upon the calf of the alien's leg, we learned more by inference and deduction than by direct report. That our impending meal would be more than usually unappetising was never suggested. That was surmise upon our part, pure and simple. The conviction, however, was so strong that the repast was cancelled out of hand.

Mrs Chapel was dismissed and straitly charged never to return. Camille was placed in the custody of the chauffeur and escorted to the latter's rooms above the garage, to be returned to France upon the following morning. Nobby was commended for his discrimination. Jonah was reviled.

All this, however, took time. The respective dismissal and disposal of the combatants were not completed until long past eight, and it was almost nine before we sat down to dinner.

'I think,' said Daphne faintly, 'I should like some champagne.'

Berry ordered the wine.

It was abnormally hot, and the doors that were usually closed were set wide open.

From the street faint snatches of a vibrant soprano came knocking at our tired ears.

Mechanically we listened.

'*When you come to the end of a perfect day . . .*'

Berry turned to me.

'They must have seen us come in,' he said.

★

It was with a grateful heart that I telegraphed the first thing on Saturday morning to Mrs Hamilton Smythe of Fair Lawns, Torquay, asking, *pro forma*, whether Pauline Roper, now in her service, was sober, honest, and generally to be recommended to be engaged as cook.

As she had been for six years with the lady, and was only leaving because the latter was quitting England to join her husband in Ceylon, it was improbable that the reference would be unflattering. Moreover, Daphne had taken to her at once. Well-mannered, quiet, decently attired and respectful, she was obviously a long way superior to the ordinary maid. Indeed, she had admitted that her father, now dead, had been a clergyman, and that she should have endeavoured to obtain a position as governess if, as a child, she had received anything better than the rudest education. She had, she added, been receiving fifty pounds a year. Hesitatingly she had inquired whether, since the employment was only temporary, we should consider an increase of ten pounds a year unreasonable.

'Altogether,' concluded my sister, 'a thoroughly nice-feeling woman. I offered her lunch, but she said she was anxious to try and see her sister before she caught her train back, so she didn't have any. I almost forgot to give her her fare, poor girl. In fact, she had to remind me. She apologised very humbly, but said the journey to London was so terribly expensive that she simply couldn't afford to let it stand over.'

We had lunched at Ranelagh, and were sitting in a quiet corner of the pleasant grounds, taking our ease after the alarms and excursions of the day before.

Later on we made our way to the polo-ground.

Almost the first person we saw was Katharine Festival.

'Hurray,' said Daphne. 'I meant to have rung her up last night, but what with the Camille episode and dining out I forgot all about it. When I tell her we're suited, she'll be green with envy.'

Her unsuspecting victim advanced beaming. Being of the opposite sex, I felt sorry for her.

'Daphne, my dear,' she announced, 'I meant to have rung you up last night. I've got a cook.'

The pendulum of my emotions described the best part of a semicircle, and I felt sorry for Daphne.

'I am glad,' said my sister, with an audacity which took my breath away. 'How splendid! So've we.'

'Hurray,' said Katharine, with a sincerity which would have deceived a diplomat. 'Don't you feel quite strange? I can hardly believe it's really happened. Mine rejoices in the name of Pauline,' she added.

I started violently, and Berry's jaw dropped.

'*Pauline?*' cried Daphne and Jill.

'Yes,' said Katharine. 'It's a queer name for a cook, but – What's the matter?'

'But so's ours! Ours is Pauline! What's her other name?'

'Roper,' cried Katharine breathlessly.

'Not from Torquay?' – in a choking voice.

Katharine nodded and put a trembling handkerchief to her lips.

'I paid her fare,' she said faintly. 'It came to – '

'Two pounds nine and fourpence-halfpenny,' said my sister. 'I gave her two pounds ten.'

'So did I,' said Katharine. 'She was to come on – on Monday.'

'Six years in her last place?' said Daphne shakily.

'Yes. And a clergyman's daughter,' wailed Katharine.

'Did – did you take up her reference?'

'Wired last night,' was the reply.

In silence I brought two chairs, and they sat down.

'But – but,' stammered Jill, 'she spoke from Torquay on Wednesday.'

'Did she?' said Berry. 'I wonder.'

'Yes,' said Katharine. 'She did.'

'You know she did,' said Daphne and Jill.

'Who,' said I, 'answered the telephone?'

'My parlourmaid did,' said Katharine.

'And Jill answered ours,' said I. Then I turned to my cousin. 'When you took off the receiver,' I asked, 'what did you hear?'

'I remember perfectly,' said Jill. 'Exchange asked if we were Mayfair 9999 and then said, "You're through to a call-office." Then Pauline spoke.'

'Precisely,' said I. 'But not from Torquay. In that case Exchange would have said, "Torquay wants you," or "Exeter," or something. Our Pauline rang up from London. She took a risk and got away with it.'

'I feel dazed,' said Daphne, putting a hand to her head. 'There must be some mistake. I can't believe – '

' "A thoroughly nice-feeling woman," ' said Berry. 'I think I should feel nice if I could make five pounds in two hours by sitting on the edge of a chair and saying I was a clergyman's daughter. And now what are we going to do? Shall we be funny and inform the police? Or try and stop Camille at Amiens?'

'Now, don't you start,' said his wife, 'because I can't bear it. Jonah, for goodness' sake, get hold of the car, and let's go.'

'Yes,' said Berry. 'And look sharp about it. Time's getting on, and I should just hate to be late for dinner. Or shall we be reckless and take a table at Lockhart's?'

We drove home in a state of profound melancholy.

Awaiting our arrival was a 'service' communication upon a buff sheet, bluntly addressed to 'Pleydell'.

It was the official death-warrant of an unworthy trust.

Sir,

I beg leave to inform you that your telegram handed in at the Grosvenor Street Post Office at 10.2 a.m. on the 26th June addressed to Reply paid Hamilton Smythe Fair Lawns Torquay has not been delivered for the reason indicated below.

ADDRESS NOT KNOWN.

I am, Sir,

Your obedient servant,

W. B.,

Postmaster.

A TRICK OF MEMORY

'What d'you do,' said Berry, 'when you want to remember something?'

'Change my rings,' said Daphne. 'Why?'

'I only wondered. D'you find that infallible?'

My sister nodded.

'Absolutely,' she said. 'Of course, I don't always remember what I've changed them for, but it shows me there's something I've forgotten.'

'I see. Then you've only got to remember what that is, and there you are. Why don't I wear rings?'

'Change your shoes instead,' said I drowsily. 'Or wear your waistcoat next to your skin. Then, whenever you want to look at your watch, you'll have to undress. That'll make you think.'

'You go and change your face,' said Berry. 'Don't wait for something to remember. Just go and do it by deed poll. And then advertise it in *The Times*. You'll get so many letters of gratitude that you'll get tired of answering them.'

Before I could reply to this insult –

'I suppose,' said my sister, 'this means that you can't remember something which concerns me and really matters.'

In guilty silence her husband prepared a cigar for ignition with the utmost care. At length –

'I wouldn't go as far as that,' he said. 'But I confess that at the back of my mind, in, as it were, the upper reaches of my memory, there is a faint ripple of suggestion for which I cannot satisfactorily account. Now, isn't that beautifully put?'

With a look of contempt, Daphne returned to the digestion of a letter which she had that morning received from the United States. Reflectively Berry struck a match and lit his cigar. I followed the example of Jill and began to doze.

With the exception of Jonah, who was in Somerset with the Fairies, we had been to Goodwood. I had driven the car both ways and was healthily tired, but the long ride had rendered us all weary, and the prospect of a full night and a quiet morrow was good to contemplate.

On the following Tuesday we were going out of town. Of this we were all unfeignedly glad, for London was growing stale. The leaves upon her trees were blown and dingy, odd pieces of paper crept here and there into her parks, the dust was paramount. What sultry air there was seemed to be second-hand. Out of the pounding traffic the pungent reek of oil and fiery metal rose up oppressive. Paint three months old was seamed and freckled. Look where you would, the silver sheen of Spring was dull and tarnished, the very stones were shabby, and in the summer sunshine even proud buildings of the smartest streets wore but a jaded look and lost their dignity. The vanity of bricks stood out in bold relief unsightly, dressing the gentle argument of nature with such authority as set tired senses craving the airs and graces of the countryside and mourning the traditions of the children of men.

'Adèle,' said Daphne suddenly, 'is sailing next week.'

'Hurray,' said Jill, waking up.

'Liverpool or Southampton?' said I.

'She doesn't say. But I told her to come to Southampton.'

'I expect she's got to take what she can get; only, when you're making for Hampshire, it seems a pity to go round by the Mersey.'

'I like Adèle,' said Berry. 'She never seeks to withstand that feeling of respect which I inspire. When with me, she recognises that she is in the presence of a holy sage and, as it were, treading upon hallowed ground. Woman,' he added, looking sorrowfully upon his wife, 'I could wish that something of her piety were there to lessen your corruption. Poor vulgar shrew, I weep – '

'She says something about your,' said Daphne, turning over a sheet. 'Here you are. *Give Berry my love. If I'd been with you at Oxford, when he got busy, I should just have died. All the same, you must admit he's a scream. I'm longing to see Nobby. He sounds as if he were a dog of real character. . . .*'

'Thank you,' said her husband, with emotion. 'Thank you very much. "A scream," I think you said. Yes. And Nobby, "a dog of character." I can't bear it.'

'So he is,' said I. 'Exceptional character.'

'I admit,' said Berry, 'he's impartial. His worst enemy can't deny that. His offerings at the shrine of Gluttony are just as ample as those he lays before the altar of Sloth.'

'All dogs are greedy,' said Jill. 'It's natural. And you'd be tired, if you ran about like him.'

'He's useful and ornamental and diverting,' said I. 'I don't know what more you want.'

'Useful?' said Berry, with a yawn. 'Useful? Oh, you mean scavenging? But then you discourage him so. Remember that rotten fish in Brook Street the other day? Well, he was making a nice clean job of that, he was, when you stopped him.'

'That was a work of supererogation. I maintain, however, that nobody can justly describe Nobby as a useless dog. For instance – '

The sudden opening of the door at once interrupted and upheld my contention.

Into the room bustled the Sealyham, the personification of importance, with tail up, eyes sparkling, and gripped in his large mouth the letters which had just been delivered by the last post.

As the outburst of feminine approval subsided –

'Out of his own mouth,' said I, 'you stand confuted.'

Either of gallantry or because her welcome was the more compelling, the terrier made straight for my sister and pleasedly delivered his burden into her hands. Of the three letters she selected two and then, making much of the dog, returned a foolscap envelope to his jaws and instructed him to bear it to Berry. Nobby received it greedily, but it was only when he had simultaneously spun into the air, growled and, placing an emphatic paw upon the projecting end, torn the letter half-way asunder, that it became evident that he was regarding her return of the missive as a *douceur* or reward of his diligence.

With a cry my brother-in-law sprang to enlighten him; but Nobby, hailing his action as the first move in a game of great promise, darted out of his reach, tore round the room at express speed, and streaked into the hall.

By dint of an immediate rush to the library door, we were just in time to see Berry slip on the parquet and, falling heavily, miss the terrier by what was a matter of inches, and by the time we had helped one another upstairs, the medley of worrying and imprecations which emanated from Daphne's bedroom made it clear that the quarry had gone to ground.

As we drew breath in the doorway –

'Get him from the other side!' yelled Berry, who was lying flat on his face, with one arm under the bed. 'Quick! It may be unsporting, but I don't care. A-a-ah!' His voice rose to a menacing roar, as the rending of paper became distinctly audible. 'Stop it, you wicked swine! D'you hear? *Stop it!*'

From beneath the bed a further burst of mischief answered him. . . .

Once again feminine subtlety prevailed where the straightforward efforts of a man were fruitless. As I flung myself down upon the opposite side of the bed –

'Nobby,' said Jill in a stage whisper, 'chocolates!'

The terrier paused in his work of destruction. Then he dropped the mangled remains of the letter and put his head on one side.

'Chocolates!'

The next second he was scrambling towards the foot of the bed. . . .

I gathered together the débris and rose to my feet.

Nobby was sitting up in front of Jill, begging irresistibly.

'What a shame!' said the latter. 'And I haven't any for you. And if I had, I mightn't give you them.' She looked round appealingly. 'Isn't he cute?'

'Extraordinary how that word'll fetch him,' said I. 'I think his late mistress must have – '

'I'm sure she must,' said Berry, taking the ruins of his correspondence out of my hand. 'Perhaps she also taught him to collect stamps. And/or crests. And so you mean to say you've got no chocolates for him? How shameful! I'd better run round and knock up Gunter's. Shall I slip on a coat, or will the parquet do?'

'There's no vice in him,' I said shakily. 'It was a misunderstanding.'

With an awful look Berry gingerly withdrew from what remained of the envelope some three-fifths of a dilapidated dividend warrant, which looked as if it had been immersed in water and angrily disputed by a number of rats.

'It's – it's all right,' I said unsteadily. 'The company'll give you another.'

'Give me air,' said Berry weakly. 'Open the wardrobe, somebody, and give me air. You know, this is the violation of Belgium over again. The little angel must have been the mascot of a double-breasted Jaeger battalion in full blast.' With a shaking finger he indicated the cheque. 'Bearing this in mind, which would you say he was tonight – useful or ornamental?'

'Neither the one, nor the other,' said I. 'Merely diverting.'

Expectantly my brother-in-law regarded the ceiling.

'I wonder what's holding it,' he said. 'I suppose the whitewash has seized. And now, if you'll assist me downstairs and apply the usual restoratives, I'll forgive you the two pounds I owe you. There's a letter I want to write before I retire.'

Half an hour later the following letter was despatched:

Sir,

The enclosed are, as a patient scrutiny will reveal, the remains of a dividend warrant in my favour for seventy-two pounds five shillings.

Owing to its dilapidation, which you will observe includes the total loss of the date, signature, and stamp, I am forced to the reluctant conclusion that your bankers will show a marked disinclination to honour what was once a valuable security.

Its reduction to the lamentable condition in which you now see it, is due to the barbarous treatment it received at the teeth and claws of a dog or hound which, I regret to say, has recently frequented this house and is indubitably possessed of a malignant devil.

In fairness to myself I must add, first, that it was through no improvidence on my part that the domestic animal above referred to obtained possession of the document, and, secondly, that I made such desperate efforts to recover it intact as resulted in my sustaining a fall of considerable violence upon one of the least resilient floors I have ever encountered. If you do not believe me, your duly accredited representative is at liberty to inspect the many and various contusions upon my person any day between ten and eleven at the above address.

Yours faithfully,

etc.

P.S. – My cousin-german has just read this through, and says I've left out something. I think the fat-head is being funny, but I just mention it, in case.

P.P.S. – It's just occurred to me that the fool means I haven't asked you to send me another one. But you will, won't you?

A Trick of Memory

For no apparent reason I was suddenly awake.

Invariably a sound sleeper, I lay for a moment pondering the phenomenon. Then a low growl from the foot of the bed furnished one explanation only to demand another.

I put up a groping hand and felt for the dangling switch.

For a moment I fumbled. Then from above my head a deeply-shaded lamp flung a sudden restricted light on to the bed.

I raised myself on an elbow and looked at Nobby.

His body was still curled, with his small strong legs tucked out of sight, but his head was raised, and he was listening intently.

I put my head on one side and did the same. . . .

Only the hoot of a belated car faintly disturbed the silence.

I looked at my wrist-watch. This showed one minute to one. As I raised my eyes, an impatient clock somewhere confirmed its tale.

With a yawn I conjured the terrier to go to sleep and reached for the switch.

As I did so, he growled again.

With my fingers about the 'push', I hesitated, straining my ears . . .

The next moment I was out of bed and fighting my way into my dressing-gown, while Nobby, his black nose clapped to the sill of the doorway, stood tense and rigid and motionless as death.

As I picked him up, he began to quiver, and I could feel his heart thumping, but he seemed to appreciate the necessity for silence, and licked my face noiselessly.

I switched off the light and opened the door.

There was a lamp burning on the landing, and I stepped directly to the top of the stairs.

Except that there was a faint light somewhere upon the ground floor, I could see nothing, but, as I stood peering, the sound of stealthy movement, followed by the low grumble of utterance, rose unmistakably to my ears. Under my left arm Nobby stiffened notably.

For a moment I stood listening and thinking furiously. . . .

It was plain that there was more than one visitor, for burglars do not talk to themselves, and Discretion suggested that I should seek assistance before descending. Jonah was out of town, the men-servants slept in the basement, the telephone was downstairs. Only Berry remained.

The faint chink of metal meeting metal and a stifled laugh decided me.

With the utmost caution I stole to the door of my sister's room and turned the handle. As I glided into the chamber –

'Who's that?' came in a startled whisper.

Before I could answer, there was a quick rustle, a switch clicked, and there was Daphne, propped on a white arm, looking at me with wide eyes and parted lips. Her beautiful dark hair was tumbling about her breast and shoulders. Impatiently she brushed it clear of her face.

'What is it, Boy?'

I laid a finger upon my lips.

'There's somebody downstairs. Wake Berry.'

Slowly her husband rolled on to his left side and regarded me with one eye.

'What,' he said, 'is the meaning of this intrusion?'

'Don't be a fool,' I whispered. 'The house is being burgled.'

'Gurgled?'

'Burgled, you fool.'

'No such word,' said Berry. 'What you mean is "burglariously rifled". And then you're wrong. Why, there's Nobby.'

I could have stamped with vexation.

My sister took up the cudgels.

'Don't lie there,' she said. 'Get up and see.'

'What?' said her husband.

'What's going on.'

Berry swallowed before replying. Then –

'How many are there?' he demanded.

'You poisonous idiot,' I hissed, 'I tell you – '

'Naughty temper,' said Berry. 'I admit I'm in the wrong, but there you are. You see, it all comes of not wearing rings. If I did, I should have remembered that a wire came from Jonah just before dinner – it's in my dinner-jacket – saying he was coming up late tonight with Harry, and that if the latter couldn't get in at the Club, he should bring him on here. He had the decency to add "Don't sit up." '

Daphne and I exchanged glances of withering contempt.

'And where,' said my sister, 'is Harry going to sleep?'

Her husband settled himself contentedly.

'That,' he said drowsily, 'is what's worrying me.'

'Outrageous,' said Daphne. Then she turned to me. 'It's too late to do anything now. Will you go down and explain? Perhaps he can manage in the library. Unless Jonah likes to give up his bed.'

'I'll do what I can,' I said, taking a cigarette from the box by her side.

'Oh, and do ask if it's true about Evelyn.'

'Right oh. I'll tell you as I come back.'

'I forbid you,' murmured her husband, 'to re-enter this room.'

I kissed my sister, lobbed a novel on to my brother-in-law's back, and withdrew before he had time to retaliate. Then I stepped barefoot downstairs, to perform my mission.

With the collapse of the excitement, Nobby's suspicion shrank into curiosity, his muscles relaxed, and he stopped quivering. So infectious a thing is perturbation.

The door of the library was ajar, and the thin strip of light which issued was enough to guide me across the hall. The parquet was cold to the touch, and I began to regret that I had not returned for my slippers.

As I pushed the door open –

'I say, Jonah,' I said, 'that fool Berry – '

It was with something of a shock that I found myself looking directly along the barrel of a ·45 automatic pistol, which a stout gentleman, wearing a green mask, white kid gloves, and immaculate evening-dress, was pointing immediately at my nose.

'There now,' he purred. 'I was going to say, "Hands up." Just like that. "Hands up." It's so romantic. But I hadn't expected the dog. Suppose you put your right hand up.'

I shook my head.

'I want that for my cigarette,' I said.

For a moment we stood looking at one another. Then my fat *vis-à-vis* began to shake with laughter.

'You know,' he gurgled, 'this is most irregular. It's enough to make Jack Sheppard turn in his grave. It is really. However . . . As an inveterate smoker, I feel for you. So we'll have a compromise.' He nodded towards an armchair which stood by the window. 'You go and sit down in that extremely comfortable armchair – sit well back – and we won't say any more about the hands.'

As he spoke, he stepped forward. Nobby received him with a

venomous growl, and to my amazement the fellow immediately caressed him.

'Dogs always take to me,' he added. 'I'm sure I don't know why, but it's a great help.'

To my mortification, the Sealyham proved to be no exception to the rule. I could feel his tail going.

As in a dream, I crossed to the chair and sat down. As I moved, the pistol moved also.

'I hate pointing this thing at you,' said the late speaker. 'It's so suggestive. If you'd care to give me your word, you know . . . Between gentlemen . . .'

'I make no promises,' I snapped.

The other sighed.

'Perhaps you're right,' he said. 'Lean well back, please . . . That's better.'

The consummate impudence of the rogue intensified the atmosphere of unreality, which was most distracting. Doggedly my bewildered brain was labouring in the midst of a litter of fiction, which had suddenly changed into truth. The impossible had come to pass. The cracksman of the novel had come to life, and I was reluctantly witnessing, in comparative comfort and at my own expense, an actual exhibition of felony enriched with all the spices which the cupboard of sensation contains.

The monstrous audacity of the proceedings, and the business-like way in which they were conducted, were almost stupefying.

Most of the silver in the house, including a number of pieces, our possession of which I had completely forgotten, seemed to have been collected and laid in rough order upon rugs, which had been piled one upon the other to deaden noise. One man was taking it up, piece by piece, scrutinising it with an eye-glass such as watchmakers use, and dictating descriptions and particulars to a second, who was seated at the broad writing-table, entering the details, in triplicate, in a large order-book. By his side a third manipulated a pair of scales, weighing each piece with the greatest care and reporting the result to the second, who added the weight to the description. Occasionally the latter paused to draw at a cigarette, which lay smouldering in the ash-tray by his side. As each piece was weighed, the third handed it to a fourth assistant, who wrapped it in a bag of green baize and laid it gently in an open suitcase. Four other cases stood by his side, all bearing a number of labels and more or less the worse for wear.

All four men were masked and gloved, and working with a rapidity and method which were remarkable. With the exception of the packer, who wore a footman's livery, they were attired in evening-dress.

'We find it easier,' said the master, as if interpreting my thoughts, 'to do it all on the spot. Then it's over and done with. I do hope you're insured,' he added. 'I always think it's so much more satisfactory.'

'Up to the hilt,' said I cheerfully. 'We had it all re-valued only this year because of the rise in silver.'

'Splendid!' – enthusiastically. 'But I'm neglecting you.' With his left hand the rogue picked up an ash-tray and stepped to my side. Then he backed to the mantelpiece, whence he picked up and brought me a handful of cigarettes, laying them on the broad arm of my chair. 'I'm afraid the box has gone,' he said regretfully. 'May I mix you a drink?'

I shook my head.

'I've had my ration. If I'd known, I'd have saved some. You see, I don't sit up so late, as a rule.'

He shrugged his shoulders.

As he did so, my own last words rang familiarly in my ears: 'I don't sit up so late' . . . 'Don't sit up.' . . .

Jonah! He and Harry were due to arrive any moment!

Hope leaped up within me, and my heart began to beat violently. I glanced at the silver, still lying upon the rugs. Slowly it was diminishing, and the services of a second suitcase would soon be necessary. I calculated that to complete the bestowal would take the best part of an hour, and began to speculate upon the course events would take when the travellers appeared. I began to pray fervently that Harry would be unable to get in at the Club . . .

'Now, then, you three,' said a reproving voice. 'I'm surprised at you.'

Daphne!

The rogues were trained to a hair.

Before she was framed in the doorway, the cold steel of another weapon was pressing against my throat, and the master was bowing in her direction.

'Madam, I beg that you will neither move nor cry out.'

My sister stood like a statue. Only the rise and fall of her bosom showed that she was alive. Pale as death, her eyes riveted on the speaker, who was holding his right hand markedly behind him, her unbound hair streaming over her shoulders, she made a beautiful and arresting picture. A kimono of softest apricot, over which sprawled vivid embroideries, here in the guise of parti-coloured dragons, there in that of a wanton butterfly, swathed her from throat to foot. From the mouths of its gaping sleeves her shapely wrists and hands thrust out snow-white and still as sculpture.

For a moment all eyes were upon her, as she stood motionless . . . Then the man with the eye-glass screwed it back into his eye, and resumed his dictation . . .

The spell was broken.

The packer left his work and, lifting a great chair bodily with apparent ease, set it noiselessly by my side.

The master bowed again.

'I congratulate you, madam, upon your great heart. I beg that you will join that gentleman.'

With a high head, My Lady Disdain swept to the spot indicated and sank into the chair.

'Please lean right back . . . Thank you.'

The cold steel was withdrawn from my throat, and I breathed more freely.

Nobby wriggled to get to my sister, but I held him fast.

'So it was burglars,' said Daphne.

'Looks like it,' said I.

I glanced at the leader, who had taken his seat upon the club-kerb. His right hand appeared to be resting upon his knee.

'I think,' said my sister, 'I'll have a cigarette.'

I handed her one from the pile and lit it from my own. As I did so –

'*Courage*,' I whispered. '*Jonah ne tardera pas*.'

'I beg,' said the spokesman, 'that you will not whisper together. It tends to create an atmosphere of mistrust.'

My sister inclined her head with a silvery laugh.

'You have a large staff,' she said.

'That is my way. I am not a believer in the lone hand. But there you are. *Quot homines, tot sententia,*' and with that, he spread out his hands and shrugged his broad shoulders.

Daphne raised her delicate eyebrows and blew out a cloud of smoke.

' "The fewer men," ' she quoted, ' "the greater share of – *plunder*." '

The shoulders began to shake.

'*Touché*,' was the reply. 'A pretty thrust, madam. But you must read further on. "And gentlemen in Mayfair now abed Shall think themselves accursed they were not here." Shall we say that – er – honours are easy?' And the old villain fairly rocked with merriment.

Daphne laughed airily.

'Good for you,' she said. 'As a matter of fact, sitting here, several things look extremely easy.'

'So, on the whole, they are. Mind you, lookers-on see the easy side. And you, madam, are a very privileged spectator.'

'I have paid for my seat,' flashed my sister.

'Royally. Still, deadhead or not, a spectator you are, and, as such, you see the easy side. Now, one of the greatest dangers that can befall a thief is avarice.'

'I suppose you're doing this out of charity,' I blurted.

'Listen. Many a promising career of – er – appropriation has come to an abrupt and sordid end, and all because success but whetted where it should have satisfied.' He addressed my sister. 'Happily for you, you do not sleep in your pearls. Otherwise, since you are here, I might have fallen . . . Who knows? As it is, pearls, diamonds, and emerald bracelets that came from Prague – you see, madam, I know them all – will lie upstairs untouched. I came for silver, and I shall take nothing else. Some day, perhaps . . .'

The quiet sing-song of his voice faded, and only the murmur of the ceaseless dictation remained. Then that, too, faltered and died . . .

For a second master and men stood motionless. Then the former pointed to Daphne and me, and Numbers Three and Four whipped to our side.

Somebody, whistling softly, was descending the stairs . . .

Just as it became recognisable, the air slid out of a whistle into a song, and my unwitting brother-in-law invested the last two lines with all the mockery of pathos of which his inferior baritone voice was capable.

'I'm for ever b-b-blowing b-b-bub-b-bles,
B-blinkin' b-bub-b-bles in the air.'

He entered upon the last word, started ever so slightly at his reception, and then stood extremely still.

'Bubbles be blowed,' he said. 'B-b-burglars, what? Shall I moisten the lips? Or would you rather I wore a sickly smile? I should like it to be a good photograph. You know, you can't touch me, Reggibald. I'm in balk.' His eyes wandered round the room. 'Why, there's Nobby. And what's the game? Musical Chairs? I know a better one than that.' His eyes returned to the master. 'Now, don't you look and I'll hide in the hassock! Then, when I say "Cuckoo," you put down the musket and wish. Then – excuse me.'

Calmly he twitched a Paisley shawl from the back of the sofa and crossed to his wife. Tenderly he wrapped it about her feet and knees. By the time he had finished, a third chair was awaiting him, and Numbers Three and Four had returned to their work.

'Pray sit down,' drawled the master. 'And lean well back . . . That's right. You know, I'm awfully sorry you left your bed.'

'Don't mention it,' said Berry. 'I wouldn't have missed this for anything. How's Dartmoor looking?'

The fat rogue sighed.

'I have not had a holiday,' he said, 'for nearly two years. And night work tells, you know. Of course, I rest during the day, but it isn't the same.'

'How wicked! And they call this a free country. I should see your MP about it. Or wasn't he up when you called?'

The other shook his head.

'As a matter of fact,' he said, 'he was out of town. George, give the gentleman a match.' The packer picked up a matchstand and set it by Berry's side. 'I'm so sorry about the chocolates. You see, I wasn't expecting – Hullo!'

At the mention of the magical word Nobby had leapt from my unready grasp and trotted across to the fireplace. There, to my disgust and vexation, he fixed the master with an expectant stare and then sat up upon his hindquarters and begged a sweetmeat.

His favourer began to heave with merriment.

'What an engaging scrap!' he wheezed, taking a chocolate from an occasional table upon which the contents of a dessert dish had apparently been emptied. 'Here, my little apostate . . . Well caught!'

With an irrational rapidity the Sealyham disposed of the first comfit he had been given for more than six months. Then he resumed the attractive posture which he had found so profitable. Lazily his patron continued to respond . . .

Resentfully I watched the procedure, endeavouring to console myself with the reflection that in a few hours nature would assuredly administer to the backslider a more terrible and appropriate correction than any that I could devise.

Would Jonah never come?

I stole a glance at the clock. Five-and-twenty minutes to two. And when he did come, what then? Were he and Harry to blunder into the slough waist-high, as we had done? Impossible. There was probably a man outside – possibly a car, which would set them thinking. Then, even if the brutes got away, their game would be spoiled. It wouldn't be such a humiliating walk-over. Oh, why had Daphne come down? Her presence put any attempt at action out of the question. And why . . .

A taxi slowed for a distant corner and turned into the street. For a moment it seemed to falter. Then its speed was changed clumsily, and it began to grind its way in our direction. My heart began to beat violently. Again the speed was changed, and the rising snarl choked to give way to a metallic murmur, which was rapidly approaching. I could hardly breathe . . . Then the noise swelled up, hung for an instant upon the very crest of earshot, only to sink abruptly as the cab swept past, taking our hopes with it.

Two-thirds of the silver had disappeared.

Berry cleared his throat.

'You know,' he said, 'this is an education. In my innocence I thought that a burglar shoved his swag in a sack and then pushed off, and did the rest in the back parlour of a beer-house in Notting Dale. As it is, my only wonder is that you didn't bring a brazier and a couple of melting pots.'

'Not my job,' was the reply. 'I'm not a receiver. Besides, you don't think that all this beautiful silver is to be broken up?' The horror of his uplifted hands would have been more convincing if both of them had been empty. 'Why, in a very little while, particularly if you travel, you will have every opportunity of buying it back again in open market.'

'But how comic,' said Berry. 'I should think you're a favourite of Lloyd's. D'you mind if I blow my nose? Or would that be a *casus belli?*'

'Not at all' – urbanely. 'Indeed, if you would care to give me your word . . .'

Berry shook his head.

'Honour among thieves?' he said. 'Unfortunately I'm honest, so you must have no truck with me. Never mind. D'you touch cards at all? Or only at Epsom?'

Beneath the green mask the mouth tightened, and I could see that the taunt had gone home. No man likes to be whipped before his underlings.

Nobby profited by the master's silence, and had devoured two more chocolates before Berry spoke again – this time to me.

'Gentleman seems annoyed,' he remarked. 'I do hope he hasn't misconstrued anything I've said. D'you think we ought to offer him breakfast? Of course, five is rather a lot, but I dare say one of them is a vegetarian, and you can pretend you don't care for haddock. Or they may have some tripe downstairs. You never know. And afterwards we could run them back to Limehouse. By the way, I wonder if I ought to tell him about the silver which-not. It's only nickel, but I don't want to keep anything back. Oh, and what about the dividend warrant? Of course it wants riveting and –er – forging, and I don't think they'd recognise it, but he could try. If I die before he goes, ask him to leave his address; then, if he leaves anything behind, the butler can send it on. I remember I left a pair of bedsocks once at Chatsworth. The Duke never sent them on, but then they were perishable. Besides, one of them followed me as far as Leicester. Instinct, you know. I wrote to *The Field* about it.' He paused to shift uneasily in his seat. 'You know, if I have to sustain this pose much longer, I shall get railway spine or a hare lip or something.'

'Hush,' said I. 'What did Alfred Austin say in 1895?'

'I know,' said Berry. ' "Comrades, leave me here a little, while as yet 'tis early morn." Precisely. But then all his best work was admittedly done under the eiderdown.'

The clock upon the wall was chiming the hour. Two o'clock. Would Jonah never come?

I fancy the same query renewed its hammering at Berry's brain, for, after a moment's reflection, he turned to the master.

'I don't wish to presume upon your courtesy,' he said, 'but will the executive portion of your night's work finish when that remaining treasure has been bestowed?'

'So far as you are concerned.'

'Oh, another appointment! Of course, this "summer time" stunt gives you another hour, doesn't it? Well, I must wish you a warmer welcome.'

'That were impossible,' was the bland reply. 'Once or twice, I must confess, I thought you a little – er – equivocal, but let that pass. I only regret that Mrs Pleydell, particularly, should have been so much inconvenienced.'

'Don't mention it,' said Berry. 'As a matter of fact, we're all very pleased to have met you. You have interested us more than I can say, with true chivalry you have abstained from murder and mutilation, and you have suffered me to blow my nose, when a less courteous visitor would have obliged me to sniff with desperate and painful regularity for nearly half an hour. Can generosity go further?'

The rogue upon the club-kerb began to shake with laughter again.

'You're a good loser,' he crowed. 'I'll give you that. I'm quite glad you came down. Most of my hosts I never see, and that's dull, you know, dull. And those I do are so often – er – unsympathetic. Yes, I shall remember tonight.'

'Going to change his rings,' murmured Berry.

'And now the highly delicate question of our departure is, I am afraid, imminent. To avoid exciting impertinent curiosity, you will appreciate that we must take our leave as artlessly as possible, and that the order of our going must be characterised by no unusual circumstances, such, for instance, as a hue and cry. Anything so vulgar as a scene must at all costs be obviated. Excuse me. Blake!'

Confederate Number One stepped noiselessly to his side and listened in silence to certain instructions, which were to us inaudible.

I looked about me.

The last of the silver had disappeared. The packer was dismantling the scales as a preliminary to laying them in the last suitcase. The clerk was fastening together the sheets which he had detached from the flimsy order-book. Number Three had taken a light overcoat from a chair and was putting it on. And the time was six minutes past two . . .

And what of Jonah? He and Harry would probably arrive about five minutes too late. I bit my lip savagely . . .

Again the chief malefactor lifted up his voice.

'It is my experience,' he drawled, 'that temerity is born, if not of curiosity, then of ignorance. Now, if there is one vice more than another which I deplore, it is temerity – especially when it is displayed by a host at two o'clock of a morning. I am therefore going to the root of the matter. In short, I propose to satisfy your very natural curiosity regarding our method of departure, and, incidentally, to show you exactly what you are up against. You see, I believe in prevention.' His utterance of the last sentences was more silky than ever.

'The constables who have passed this house since half-past twelve will, if reasonably observant, have noticed the carpet which, upon entering, we laid upon the steps. A departure of guests, therefore, even at this advanced hour, should arouse no more suspicion than the limousine-landaulette which has now been waiting for some nine minutes.

'The lights in the hall will now be turned on, the front door will be opened wide, and the footman will place the suitcases in the car, at the open door of which he will stand, while my colleagues and I – I need hardly say by this time unmasked – emerge at our leisure, chatting in a most ordinary way.

'I shall be the last to enter the car – I beg your pardon. Tonight I shall be the last but one' – for an instant he halted, as if to emphasise the correction – 'and my entry will coincide with what is a favourable opportunity for the footman to assume the cap and overcoat which he must of necessity wear if his closing of the front door and subsequent occupation of the seat by the chauffeur are to excite no remark. . . . You see, I try to think of everything.'

He paused for a moment, regarding the tips of his fingers, as though they were ungloved. Then –

'Your presence here presents no difficulty. Major and Mrs

Pleydell will stay in this room, silent . . . and motionless . . . and detaining the dog. You' – nonchalantly he pointed an extremely ugly trench-dagger in my direction – 'will vouch with your – er – health for their observance of these conditions. Be good enough to stand up and place your hands behind you.'

With a glance at Berry, I rose. All things considered, there was nothing else to be done.

The man whom he had addressed as 'Blake' picked up Nobby and, crossing the room, laid the terrier in Berry's arms. Then he lashed my wrists together with the rapidity of an expert.

'Understand, I take no chances.' A harsh note had crept into the even tones. 'The slightest indiscretion will cost this gentleman extremely dear.'

I began to hope very much that my brother-in-law would appreciate the advisability of doing as he had been told.

'George, my coat.' The voice was as suave as ever again. 'Thank you. Is everything ready?'

Berry stifled a yawn.

'You don't mean to say,' he exclaimed, 'that you're actually going? Dear me. Well, well . . . I don't suppose you've a card on you? No. Sorry. I should have liked to remember you in my prayers. Never mind. And you don't happen to know of a good plain cook, do you? No. I thought not. Well, if you should hear of one. . . .'

'Carry on.'

Blake laid a hand on my shoulder and urged me towards the door. As I was going, I saw the master bow.

'Mrs Pleydell,' he said. 'I have the honour – Dear me! There's that ridiculous word again. Never mind – the honour to bid adieu to a most brave lady.'

With a faint sneer my sister regarded him. Then –

'*Au revoir*,' she said steadily.

'So long, old bean,' said Berry. 'See you at Vine Street.'

As I passed into the hall, the lights went up and a cap was clapped on to my head and pulled down tight over my eyes. Then I was thrust into a corner of the hall, close to the front door. Immediately this was opened, and I could hear everything happen as we had been led to expect. Only there was a hand on my shoulder. . . .

I heard the master coming with a jest on his lips.

As he passed me, he was speaking ostensibly to one of his comrades . . . ostensibly . . .

'I shouldn't wait up for Jonah,' he said.

Thanks to the fact that one of the Assistant Commissioners of Police was an old friend of mine, we were spared much of the tedious interrogation and well-meant, but in the circumstances utterly futile, attentions of the subordinate officers of the CID.

Admission to the house had been gained without breaking, and there were no fingerprints. Moreover, since our visitors had worn masks, such descriptions of them as we could give were very inadequate. However, statements were taken from my sister, Berry, and myself, and the spurious telegram was handed over. The insurance company was, of course, informed of the crime.

Despite the paucity of detail, our description of the gang and its methods aroused tremendous excitement at Scotland Yard. The master, it appeared, was a veritable Prince of Darkness. Save that he existed, and was a man of large ideas and the utmost daring, to whose charge half the great unplaced robberies of recent years were, rightly or wrongly, laid, little or nothing was known of his manners or personality.

'I tell you,' said the Assistant Commissioner, leaning back and tilting his chair, 'he's just about as hot as they make 'em. And when we do take him, if ever we do – and that might be tomorrow, or in ten years' time: we might walk straight into him next week with the stuff in his hands; you never know – well, when we do take him, as like as not, he'll prove to be a popular MP, or a recognised authority on livestock or something. You've probably seen him heaps of times in St James's, and, as like as not, he's a member of your own Club. Depend upon it, the old sinner moves in those circles which you know are above suspicion. If somebody pinched your watch at Ascot, you'd never look for the thief in the enclosure, would you? Of course not. Well, I may be wrong, but I don't think so. Meanwhile let's have some lunch.'

For my sister the ordeal had been severe, and for the thirty hours following the robbery she had kept her bed. Berry had contracted a slight cold, and I was not one penny the worse. Jill was overcome to learn what she had missed, and the reflection that she had mercifully slept upstairs, while such a drama was being enacted upon the ground floor, rendered her inconsolable. Jonah was summoned by telegram, and came pelting from Somerset, to be regaled with a picturesque account of the outrage, the more purple features of which he at first regarded as embroidery, and for some time flatly refused to believe. As was to be expected, Nobby paid for his treachery with an attack of biliousness, the closing stages of which were terrible to behold. At one time it seemed as if no constitution could survive such an upheaval; but, although the final convulsion left him subdued and listless, he was as right as ever upon the following morning.

The next Sunday we registered what was to be our last attendance of Church Parade for at least three months.

By common consent we had that morning agreed together to eschew the subject of crime. Ever since it had happened we had discussed the great adventure so unceasingly that, as Berry had remarked at breakfast, it was more than likely that, unless we were to take an immediate and firm line with ourselves, we should presently get Grand Larceny on the brain, and run into some danger of qualifying, not only for admission to Broadmoor, but for detention in that institution till His Majesty's pleasure should be known. For the first hour or two which followed our resolution we either were silent or discussed other comparatively uninteresting matters in a preoccupied way; but gradually lack of ventilation began to tell, and the consideration of the robbery grew less absorbent.

As we entered the Park at Stanhope Gate –

'Boy, aren't you glad Adèle's coming?' said Jill.

I nodded abstractedly.

'Rather.'

'You never said so the other night.'

'Didn't I?'

'I suppose, if she comes to Southampton, you'll go to meet her. May I come with you?'

'Good Heavens, yes. Why shouldn't you?'

'Oh, I don't know. I thought, perhaps, you'd rather . . .'

I whistled to Nobby, whose disregard of traffic was occasionally conducive to heart failure. As he came cantering up –

'Adèle isn't my property,' I said.

'I know, but . . .'

'But what?'

'I've never seen Nobby look so clean,' said Jill, with a daring irrelevance that took my breath away.

'I observe,' said I, 'that you are growing up. Your adolescence is at hand. You are fast emerging from the chrysalis of girlish innocence, eager to show yourself a pert and scheming butterfly.' My cousin regarded me with feigned bewilderment. 'Yes, you've got the baby stare all right, but you must learn to control that little red mouth. Watch Daphne.'

Jill made no further endeavour to restrain the guilty laughter which was trembling upon her lips.

'I b-believe you just love her,' she bubbled.

I thought very rapidly. Then –

'I think we all do,' said I. 'She's very attractive.'

'I mean it,' said Jill.

'So do I. Look at her ears. Oh, I forgot. Hides them under her hair, doesn't she? Her eyes, then.'

'I observe,' said Jill pompously, 'that you are sitting up and taking notice. Your adol – adol – er – what you said, is at hand. You are emerging from the chrysalis of ignorance – '

'This is blasphemy. You wicked girl. And what are you getting at? Matchmaking or only blackmail?'

'Well, it's time you got married, isn't it? I don't want you to, dear, but I know you've got to soon, and – and I'd like you to be happy.'

There was a little catch in her voice, and I looked down to see her eyes shining.

'Little Jill,' I said, 'if I marry six wives, I shall still be in love with my cousin – a little fair girl, with great grey eyes and the prettiest ways and a heart of the purest gold. And now shall we cry here or by the Serpentine?'

She caught at my arm, laughing.

'Boy, you're very – Oh, I say! Where's Nobby?'

We had reached the Achilles Statue, and a hurried retrospect showed me the terrier some thirty paces away, exchanging discourtesies with an Aberdeen. The two were walking round each other with a terrible deliberation, and from their respective demeanours it was transparently clear that only an immediate distraction could avert the scandal of a distressing brawl.

Regardless of my surroundings, I summoned the Sealyham in my 'parade' voice. To my relief, he started and, after a menacing look at his opponent, presumably intended to discourage an attack in rear, cautiously withdrew from his presence and, once out of range, came scampering in our direction.

My brother-in-law and Daphne, whom we had outdistanced, arrived at the same time.

As I was reproving the terrier –

'The very people,' said a familiar voice.

It was the Assistant Commissioner, labouring under excitement which he with difficulty suppressed. He had been hurrying, and was out of breath.

'I want you to cross the road and walk along by the side of the Row,' he said jerkily. 'If you see anyone you recognise, take off your hat. And, Mrs Pleydell, you lower your parasol.'

'But my dear chap,' said Berry, 'they were all masked.'

'Well, if you recognise a voice, or even – '

'A voice? My dear fellow, we're in the open air. Besides, what jury – '

'For Heaven's sake,' cried the other, 'do as I ask! I know it's a chance in a million. Think me mad, call me a fool – anything you like . . . but go.'

His earnestness was irresistible.

I whistled to Nobby – who had seized the opportunity of straying, apparently by accident, towards a bull-terrier – and started to stroll in the direction of the Row. Jill walked beside me, twittering, and a glance over my shoulder showed me my sister and Berry a horse's length behind. Behind them, again, came the Assistant Commissioner.

We crossed the road and entered the walk he had mentioned.

It was a beautiful day. The great sun flamed out of a perfect sky, and there was little or no wind. With the exception of a riding-master and two little girls, the Row was empty, but the walk was as crowded as a comfortably filled ballroom, if you except the dancers who are sitting out; for, while three could walk abreast with small inconvenience either to others or themselves, there was hardly a seat to spare.

I have seen smarter parades. It was clear that many habitués had already left town, and that a number of visitors had already arrived. But there was apparent the same quiet air of gaiety, the same good humour, which fine feathers bring, and, truth to tell, less *ennui* and more undisguised enjoyment than I can ever remember.

Idly I talked with Jill, not thinking what I said nor noticing what she answered, but my heart was pounding against my ribs, and I was glancing incessantly from side to side in a fever of fear lest I should miss the obvious.

Now and again I threw a look over my shoulder. Always Berry and Daphne were close behind. Fervently I wished that they were in front.

I began to walk more slowly.

Suddenly I realised that I was streaming with sweat.

As I felt for my handkerchief –

'Look at Nobby,' said Jill. 'Whatever's he doing?'

I glanced at my cousin to follow the direction of her eyes.

Nobby was sitting up, begging, before a large elderly gentleman who was seated, immaculately dressed, some six paces away. He was affecting not to see the terrier, but there was a queer frozen look about his broad smile that set me staring. Even as I gazed, he lowered his eyes and, lifting a hand from his knee, began to regard the tips of his fingers, as though they were ungloved . . .

For a second I stood spellbound.

Then I took off my hat.

Summer, 1920, has arrived, and with it, Adèle. The first thing she must do is meet the appalling Pleydell cousins – the other *cousins – Vandy, Emma and May, who own the family portraits but who, much to their disgust, do not own White Ladies. . . .*

A LESSON IN LATIN

'What, again?' said I, staring at the breakfast-cup which Jill was offering me, that I might pass it to Daphne. 'How many more cups is he going to drink? He's had three to my knowledge.'

'That vessel,' said Berry, 'was passed to you for information and immediate action. So, as they say in the Army, close your perishin' head and get down to it.'

'What you want,' said I, 'is a bucket. Or a private urn.'

'What's the matter with a trough?' said Jonah. 'That'd be more in keeping.'

Berry turned to Adèle.

'You see?' he said. 'Two putrid minds with but a single snort. But there you are. Don't dwell on it. Pass the marmalade instead.' He turned to his wife. 'And what's the programme for today? The glass has gone up, it's already raining, "all's right with the world." Anybody like to play ping-pong?'

'Fool,' said his wife. 'As a matter of fact, I don't think it would be a bad idea if we went over to Broken Ash for tea.' Berry made a grimace, and Jill and I groaned. Even Jonah looked down his nose at the suggestion. 'Yes,' my sister continued, 'I didn't think it'd be a popular move, but I'd like Adèle to see the pictures, and we haven't shown a sign of life since we left town.'

At Broken Ash lived the other branch of the Pleydell family, consisting of our Cousin Vandy and his two sisters. Between them and us there was little love lost. Of their jealousy of Berry, but for whose birth White Ladies would have passed into their hands, they made but an open secret; and, when he married my sister, who was his second cousin, and the Mansels – Cousins Jonah and Jill – had thrown in their lot with us, relations had become more strained than before. The conventions were, however, observed. Calendars were exchanged at Christmas, birthdays were recognised with a cold epistolary nod, and occasional calls were paid and invitations issued. Their possession of all but two of the family portraits was undoubted, and with nine points of the law in their favour they were well armed. It was an open question whether the tenth point, which was ours, was sufficiently doughty to lay the other nine by the heels. Years ago counsel had advised that the law was dead in our favour, but it was certain that Vandy and his sisters would resist any claim we made with great bitterness, and the settlement of a family quarrel in the public ring of the High Court was more than we could stomach.

Still, the pictures were worth seeing. There were a Holbein, a Van Dyck, three Gainsboroughs, and two from the brush of Reynolds among them, and, so soon as she had learned of their existence, Adèle Feste, who was on a visit from the United States, had evinced an eagerness to be shown the collection.

There was a moment's silence. Then –

'I'd hate to think you were going for my sake,' said Adèle.

'We're not, dear,' said Daphne. 'Even if you weren't here, we should have to go some day soon.'

'Yes,' said Berry. 'We hate one another like poison, but we've never declared war. Consequently, diplomatic relations are still maintained, and in due season we meet and are charmingly offensive to one another. When war broke out, they were very sticky about billeting a few Yeomanry chargers, and crawled and lied about their stabling till the authorities got fed up and commandeered all they'd got. Therefore, whenever we meet, I chivvy the conversation in the direction of horseflesh. In the same way, having regard to the burglary which we suffered last month, Vandy will spread himself on the subject of old silver. The moment they heard of it, they sent us a triumphant telegram of condolence.'

My sister laughed.

'If you say much more,' she said, 'Adèle will be afraid to come with us. I admit it's a duty call, pure and simple. All the same, there won't be any bloodshed.'

'I'm ready for anything,' said Adèle thoughtfully. 'Shall I wear a red or white rose?'

'Don't tell us you can control your cheeks,' said I. 'It's unheard of. And why are you so pensive this morning? Is it because of Ireland? Or have you trodden on your sponge?'

'I believe she's broken the soap dish,' said Berry, 'and is afraid to tell us.'

'Don't tease her,' said Jill. 'Why shouldn't she be quiet if she likes?'

But Adèle was bubbling with laughter.

'The truth is,' she announced, 'I'm trying to remember a dream I had last night.' She looked across the table to me. 'You know what it is to dream something rather vivid and interesting, and then not to be able to remember what it was?'

I nodded.

'But you can't do anything,' I said. 'It's no good trying to remember it. Either you'll think of it, or you won't.'

'Exactly,' said my brother-in-law. 'There's no other alternative. It's one of the laws of nature. I well remember dreaming that I was a disused columbarium which had been converted into a brewery and was used as a greenhouse. I was full of vats and memorial tablets and creeping geraniums. Just as they were going to pull me down to make room for a cinema, Daphne woke me up to say there was a bat in the room. I replied suitably, but, before turning over to resume my slumbers, I tried to recapture my dream. My efforts were vain. It was gone for ever.'

'Then how d'you know what it was about?' said Jill.

'I don't,' said Berry. 'What I have told you is pure surmise. And now will you pass me the toast, or shall I come and get it?'

Choking with indignation, Jill stretched out a rosy hand in the direction of the toast-rack. . . . Suddenly the light of mischief leapt into her grey eyes, and she called Nobby. In a flash the Sealyham – never so vigilant as at meal-time – was by her side. Cheerfully she gave him the last piece of toast. Then she turned to Berry with a seraphic smile.

'I'm afraid there's none left,' she said.

★

Before we had finished lunch, the rain had ceased, and by the time we were under weigh, en route for Broken Ash, the afternoon sun was turning a wet world into a sweet-smelling jewel. Diamonds dripped from her foliage, emerald plumes glistened on every bank, silver lay spilled upon her soft brown roads. No scent-bag was ever stuffed with such rare spicery. Out of the dewy soil welled up the fresh clean breath of magic spikenard, very precious.

Punctually at half-past four we swept up the avenue of poplars that led to our cousins' house.

The visit had been arranged by Daphne upon the telephone, and Vandy and his two sisters were ready and waiting. . . .

The reunion was not cordial. Ease and familiarity were not among the guests. But it was eminently correct. The most exacting Master of Ceremonies, the most severe authority upon etiquette, would have been satisfied. We were extraordinarily polite. We made engaging conversation, we begged one another's pardon, we enjoyed one another's jokes. The dispensation and acceptance of hospitality did the respective forces infinite credit.

After tea we were taken to see the pictures.

Vandy, as showman, naturally escorted Adèle. The rest of us, decently grouped about his sisters, followed like a party of sightseers in the wake of a verger.

To do our host justice, he knew his own fathers. For what it was worth, the history of the Pleydell family lay at his fingers' ends. Men, manners, and exploits – he knew them all. Indeed, years ago he had collected his knowledge and had it published in the form of a book. We had a copy somewhere.

We were half-way along the gallery, and our cousin was in full blast, when Adèle, to whom he was introducing the portraits with triumphant unction, started forward with a low cry.

'That's the very man,' she exclaimed, pointing at the picture of a middle-aged gentleman in a plum-coloured coat, which, I seemed to remember, was unsigned but attributed – without much confidence – to the brush of Gonzales Coques. 'What an extraordinary thing! I've broken my dream.'

In the twinkling of an eye Vandy's importance was snatched from him, and the prophet's mantle had fallen upon Adèle. Where, but a moment before, he had been strutting in all the pride of a proprietor, she held the stage. More. Neither our discomfited host nor his sisters could divine what was toward, and the fact that their guests crowded eagerly about Adèle, encouraging her to 'let them have it', was more disconcerting than ever.

'It was in a garden,' said Adèle, 'a quiet sort of place. I think I was walking behind him. I don't know how I got there, but he didn't see me. All the same, he kept looking round, as if he was afraid he was being watched. Presently we came to a place where there was a stone pedestal standing. It wasn't exactly a pillar – it wasn't high enough. And it was too high for a seat. Well, he stared at this for a moment; then he looked around again, very cautiously, and then – it sounds idiotic, but he began to prod the turf with his stick. At first he did it just casually, here and there: but, after a little, he started prodding at regular intervals, methodically. The ground was quite soft, and his stick seemed to go in like a skewer. Suddenly he seemed to hear something or somebody, for he listened very carefully, and then walked on tiptoe to the pedestal and leaned up against it as if he were resting. The next moment somebody – some man in ordinary clothes came out of . . .' She hesitated. 'I don't know whether it was some bushes or a wall he came out of. Some bushes, I guess. Any way, he appeared, and – don't laugh – gave him a green tomato. Then I woke up.'

'And this is the man you saw?' cried Daphne, pointing.

Adèle nodded.

'Dress and everything. He was wearing the same plumed hat and that identical coat, buttoned all down the front, with the pockets low down on either side. And I'll never forget his face. That's a wonderful picture. It's lifelike.'

'What an extraordinary thing!' said I. Then I turned to Vandy. 'Has this portrait ever been reproduced?'

He did not seem to hear me.

With dropped jaw and bulging eyes, the fellow was staring at Adèle, staring. . . .

Suddenly, as with an effort, he pulled himself together.

'Was that all you saw?' he said hoarsely.

Adèle pondered.

'I think so,' she said slowly. 'Except that there were some words carved on the pedestal. PER . . . IMP . . . PERIMP. . . . No. That wasn't it. Something like that. Not English. I can't remember.'

'Ah!'

Berry took up the running.

'You say the merchant was prodding the ground?' he said.

'That's right. It sounds silly, but – '

'Not at all,' said Berry excitedly. 'He was looking for something. It's as clear as daylight.' He turned to the picture. 'That's William Pleydell, isn't it, Vandy? Seventeenth-century bloke. The one Pepys mentions.'

My cousin nodded abstractedly. With unseeing eyes he was staring out of a window. It was patent that Adèle's recital had affected him strangely. . . .

Berry laid a hand on his arm.

'Where's the book you wrote?' he said gently. 'That may throw some light on it.'

One of our hostesses turned, as though she would fetch the volume.

'It went to be rebound yesterday,' cried Vandy in a strained, penetrating voice.

His sister stopped and stood still in her tracks. A moment later she had turned back and was murmuring a confirmation.

Jonah, who had been busy with a pencil and the back of an envelope, limped towards us from one of the windows.

'The pedestal was a sundial,' he said. Vandy looked at him sharply. He turned to Adèle. 'PER . . . IMP . . . you said. Try PEREUNT ET IMPUTANTUR. Latin. "The hours pass and are charged against us." You'll find the phrase on five sundials out of six.'

A buzz of excited applause greeted this admirable contribution.

Adèle looked at the written words.

'You are clever,' she said. 'Of course, that's it. It must be.'

Vandy's reception of Jonah's discovery convinced me that it had already occurred to him. He applauded theatrically. The fellow was playing a part, feverishly. Besides, I did not believe his rotten book was being rebound. That was a lie. There was something there which he did not want us to see. Not a doubt of it. Well, we had a copy at White Ladies. No! Our copy was in town. Hang it! What a sweep the man was!

With a horse-laugh he interrupted my reflections.

'Well, well, Miss Feste. I confess you gave me a shock. Still, if you had to meet one of our forefathers, I could have wished it had been any other than the notorious William. We enjoy his portrait, but we deplore his memory. Ha! Ha! Now, we're really proud of the next one – his cousin, James Godstow Pleydell. He it was who was responsible – '

'Forgive me,' purred Daphne, 'but I'm going to say we must fly. I'd no idea it was so late. People are coming to dinner, and we must go back by Brooch, because we've run out of ice.'

Our host protested – not very heartily – and was overruled. Mutual regret was suitably expressed. Without more ado we descended into the hall. Here at the front door the decencies of leave-taking were observed. The host and hostesses were thanked, the parting guests sped. A moment later we were sliding down the avenue to the lodge-gates. As we swung on to the road –

'Where's the book?' said Daphne. 'That man's a liar.'

'At Cholmondeley Street,' said I. 'But you're right about Vandy. He's trying to keep something back.'

'He's so excited he doesn't know what to do,' said Daphne. 'That's clear.'

'Well, what the deuce is it?' said Berry. 'I've read the blinkin' book, but I'll swear there's nothing in it about buried treasure.'

'Whatever it is,' said I, 'it's in that book. I'll get it tomorrow. D'you really want any ice?'

Daphne shook her head.

'But I couldn't stay there with that man another minute.'

Adèle lifted up her sweet voice.

'I feel very guilty,' she said. 'I've upset you all, I've given everything away to your cousin with both hands, and I've – '

'Nonsense, darling,' said Daphne. 'You did the natural thing. How could you know – '

Jonah interrupted her with a laugh.

'One thing's certain,' he said. 'I'll bet old Vandy's cursing the day he rushed into print.'

Upon reflection it seemed idle for any one of us to journey to London and back merely to fetch a volume, so the next morning one of the servants was dispatched instead, armed with a note to the housekeeper at Cholmondeley Street, telling her exactly where the book would be found.

The man returned as we were finishing dinner, and 'The History of the Pleydell Family' was brought to Berry while we sat at dessert.

Nuts and wine went by the board.

As my brother-in-law cut the string, we left our places and crowded about him . . .

Reference to the index bade us turn to page fifty-four.

As the leaves flicked, we waited breathlessly. Then –

'Here we are,' said Berry. ' "WILLIAM PLEYDELL. In 1652 Nicholas died, to be succeeded by his only child, William, of whom little is known. This is perhaps as well, for such information as is to hand, regarding his life and habits, shows him to have been addicted to no ordinarily evil ways. The lustre which his father and grandfather had added to the family name William seems to have spared no effort to tarnish. When profligacy was so fashionable, a man must have lived hard indeed to attract attention. Nevertheless, Samuel Pepys, the Diarist, refers to him more than once, each time commenting upon the vileness of his company and his offensive behaviour. Upon one occasion, we are told, at the playhouse the whole audience was scandalised by *a loose drunken frolic*, in which *Mr William Pleydell, a gentleman of Hampshire*, played a disgraceful part. What was worse, he carried his dissolute habits into the countryside, and at one time his way of living at the family seat White Ladies was so openly outrageous that the incumbent of Bilberry actually denounced the squire from the pulpit, referring to him as 'a notorious evil-liver' and an 'abandoned wretch'. If not for his good name, however, for the house and pleasure-gardens he seems to have had some respect, for it was during his tenure that the stables were rebuilt and the gardens decorated with statuary which has since disappeared. *A sundial*" ' – the sensation which the word produced was profound, and Jill cried out with excitement – ' "*a sundial, bearing the date 1663 and the cipher W.P., still stands in the garden of the old dower-house, which passed out of the hands of the family early in the nineteenth century.*" '

Berry stopped reading and laid the book down.

'The dower-house?' cried Daphne blankly.

Her husband nodded.

'But I never knew there was one. Besides – '

'Better known today as "The Lawn, Bilberry".'

'Quite right,' said Jonah. 'A hundred years ago that stood inside the park.'

'The Lawn?' cried Jill. 'Why, that's where the fire was. Years and years ago. I remember old Nanny taking me down to see it the next day. And it's never been rebuilt.'

'To my knowledge,' said I, 'it's had a board up, saying it's for sale, for the last fifteen years. Shall we go in for it? They can't want much. The house is gutted, the garden's a wilderness, and – '

A cry from Adèle interrupted me. While we were talking, she had picked up the volume.

'Listen to this,' she said. ' "William Pleydell died unmarried and intestate in 1667, and was succeeded by his cousin Anthony. Except that during the former's tenure a good deal of timber was cut, White Ladies had been well cared for. The one blot upon his stewardship was the disappearance of the greater part of the family plate, which Nicholas Pleydell's will proves to have been unusually rare and valuable. *There used to exist a legend, for which the author can trace no foundation, that William had brought it from London during the Great Plague and buried it, for want of a strong-room, at White Ladies.* A far more probable explanation is that its graceless inheritor surreptitiously disposed of the treasure for the same reason as he committed waste, viz., to spend the proceeds upon riotous living." '

Dumbly we stared at the reader . . .

The murder was out.

Berry whipped out his watch.

'Nine o'clock,' he announced. 'We can do nothing tonight. And that sweep Vandy's got a long lead. We haven't a moment to lose. Who are the agents for The Lawn?'

'It's on the board,' said I, 'and I've read it a thousand times, but I'm hanged if I can remember whether it's Miller of Brooch, or a London firm.'

'Slip over there the first thing in the morning,' said Jonah. 'If it's Miller, so much the better. You can go straight on to Brooch. If it's a London man – well, there's always the telephone.'

'I hope to heaven,' said Daphne, 'it's – it's still for sale.'

'Vandy's got Scotch blood in him,' said Berry. 'He won't lay out fifteen hundred or so without looking round.'

'More like three thousand,' said Jonah.

'It's a lot of money to risk,' said Daphne slowly.

'Yes,' said Adèle anxiously. 'I feel that. I know it's your affair, but, if it hadn't been for my dream, this would never have happened. And supposing there's nothing in it . . . I mean, it would be dreadful to think you'd thrown away all that money and gotten nothing in exchange. And they always say that dreams are contrary.'

'Let's face the facts,' said my brother-in-law. 'Taking everything into consideration doesn't it look like a vision, or second sight?'

We agreed vociferously. Only Adèle looked ill at ease.

Berry continued.

'Very well, then. Less than a month ago all our silver was taken off us by comic burglars. Doesn't it look as if we were being offered the chance of replacing it by something better?'

Again we agreed.

'Lastly, the insurance company has paid up to the tune of four thousand pounds, which amount is now standing to the credit of my deposit account at Coutts'. I tell you, if we don't have a dart, we shall be mad.'

'I agree,' said I.

'So do I,' cried Jill. 'I'm all for it.'

Only Daphne and Jonah hesitated.

I laid my hand upon the former's shoulder.

'Supposing,' I said, 'we take no action, but Vandy does. Supposing he strikes oil and lands the stuff under our noses . . . Wouldn't you cheerfully blow the four thousand just to avoid that?'

My sister's eyes flashed, and Jonah's chin went up.

'Anything,' said Daphne emphatically, 'anything would be better than that.'

So was the decision made.

We adjourned to the drawing-room and for the rest of the evening discussed the matter furiously.

The suggestion that Vandy would not wait to buy, but had already got to work at The Lawn, was summarily dismissed. Our cousin was too cautious for that. He knew that the moment we had the book, we should be as wise as he, and that, since we were at loggerheads, we should certainly not sit quietly by and permit him to enrich himself to our teeth, when a word to the owners of The Lawn would compel him to disgorge any treasure he found. No, Vandy was no fool. He would walk circumspectly, and buy first and dig afterwards.

It was Jonah who raised the question of 'treasure trove'. In some uneasiness we sought for a book of law. Investigation, however, satisfied us that, if the plate were ever unearthed, the Crown would not interfere. Evidence that an ancestor had buried it was available, and reference to the will of Nicholas would establish its identity. Whether it belonged to us or to Vandy was another matter, but reason suggested that law and equity alike would favour the party in whose land it was found.

We ordered breakfast early and the car at a quarter to nine, but, for all that, it was past midnight before we went to bed.

The next morning, for once in a way, we were up to time. Two minutes after the quarter we were all six in the car, and it was not yet nine o'clock when Jonah pulled up in the shade of a mighty oak less than a hundred paces from the tall iron gates which stood gaunt, rusty, and forbidding, to mar the beauty of the quiet by-road.

So far as we could see, there was no one about, but we were anxious not to attract attention, so Berry and I alighted and strolled casually forward.

The object of our visit was, of course, to learn from the board in whose hands the property had been placed for sale. But we had decided that, if it were possible, we must effect an entrance, to see whether the turf about the sundial had been disturbed. Moreover, if we could get Adèle inside, it would be highly interesting to see whether she recognised the place.

Wired on to the mouldering gates, a weather-beaten board glared at us.

FREEHOLD
with immediate possession
TO BE SOLD
This Very Desirable
OLD-WORLD MANSION

Standing in three acres of pleasure grounds, and only requiring certain structural repairs to be made an ideal modern residence.
F. R. MILLER, Estate Agent, High St., Brooch.

Considering that the house had been gutted nearly twenty years ago, and had stood as the fire had left it from then until now, the advertisement was euphemistic.

By dint of peering between the corrupted bars, it was possible to see for ourselves the desolation. A press of nettles crowded about the scorched and blackened walls; square gaping mouths, that had been windows, showed from the light within that there was no roof, while here and there charred timbers thrust their unsightly way from out of a riot of brambles, wild and disorderly. What we could see of the garden was a very wilderness. Tall rank grass flourished on every side, carriage-way and borders alike had been blotted into a springing waste, and the few sprawling shrubs which we could recognise hardly emerged from beneath the choking smother of luxuriant bindweed.

The gates were chained and padlocked. But they were not difficult to scale, and in a moment Berry and I were over and standing knee-deep in the long wet grass.

Stealthily we made our way to the back of the house. . . .

The sundial was just visible. The grass of what had once been a trim lawn rose up about the heavy pedestal, coarse and tumultuous. But it was untouched. No foot of man or beast had trodden it – lately, at any rate.

Simultaneously we heaved sighs of relief.

Then –

'Adèle'll never recognise this,' said Berry. 'It's hopeless. What she saw was a lawn, not a prairie.' I nodded. 'Still,' he went on, 'there used to be a door in the wall – on the east side.' As he spoke, he turned and looked sharply at the haggard building. 'Thought I heard something,' he added.

'Did you?'

I swung on my heel, and together we stared and listened. Eyes and ears alike went unrewarded. The silence of desolation hung like a ragged pall, gruesome and deathly. . . .

Without a word we passed to the east of the ruin. After a little we came to the door in the wall. Here was no lock, and with a little patience we drew the bolts and pulled the door open. It gave on to a little lane, which ran into the by-road at a point close to where the others were waiting.

I left Berry and hastened back to the car.

Exclamations of surprise greeted my issuing from the lane, and I could read the same unspoken query in four faces at once.

'We're first in the field so far,' I said. There was a gasp of relief. 'Come along. We've found a way for you.'

Adèle and Jill were already out of the car. Daphne and Jonah made haste to alight.

'Think we can leave her?' said Jonah, with a nod at the Rolls.

'Oh, yes. We shan't be a minute.'

Hurriedly we padded back the way I had come. Berry was still at the door, and in silence we followed him to where he and I had stood looking and listening a few minutes before.

'O-o-oh!' cried Jill, in an excited whisper.

'What about it, Adèle?' said Berry.

Adèle looked about her, knitting her brows. Then –

'I'm afraid to say anything,' she said. 'It may be the place I saw. I can't say it isn't. But it's so altered. I think, if the grass was cut. . . .'

'What did I say?' said my brother-in-law.

'But the pedestal was exactly that height. That I'll swear. And it stood on a step.'

'What did the words look like?' said I.

'They were carved in block letters on the side of the cornice.'

As carefully as I could, I stepped to the sundial. As I came up to it, my foot encountered a step. . . .

The column was unusually massive, and the dial must have been two feet square. Lichened and weather-beaten, an inscription upon the cornice was yet quite easy to read.

PEREUNT ET IMPUTANTUR

And the words were carved in block lettering. . . .

A buzz of excitement succeeded my report. Then Daphne turned quickly and looked searchingly at the house.

'I feel as if we were being watched,' she said, shuddering. 'Let's get back to the car.'

As Jonah followed the girls into the lane –

'What about bolting the door?' said I.

Berry shook his head.

'Doesn't matter,' he said. 'Anyway, we've trodden the grass down. Besides, there's nothing to hide.'

We dragged the door to and hastened after the others.

As we climbed into the car, Jonah started the engine.

'What are the orders?' he said. 'Is Miller the agent? You never said.'

'Yes,' said I. 'We'd better go straight to Brooch.'

Our way lay past the main entrance of The Lawn.

As we approached this, Jonah exclaimed and set his foot on the brake.

Leaning against the wall was a bicycle, and there was a man's figure busy about the gates. He appeared to be climbing over . . .

As we came up alongside, he looked at us curiously. Then he went on with his work.

A moment later he slid a pair of pliers into his pocket and, wringing the board clear of its fastenings, lowered it to the ground.

We were too late.

The Lawn was no longer for sale.

Our chagrin may be imagined more easily than it can be described.

We returned to White Ladies in a state of profound depression, alternately cursing Vandy and upbraiding ourselves for not having sent for the book upon the evening of the day of our visit to Broken Ash.

Jonah reproached himself bitterly for giving our cousin the benefit of his detective work, although both Daphne and I were positive that Vandy had identified the pedestal from Adèle's description before Jonah had volunteered the suggestion that it was a sundial.

As for Adèle, she was inconsolable.

It was after lunch – a miserable meal – when we were seated upon the terrace, that Berry cleared his throat and spoke wisely and to the point.

'The milk's spilt,' he said, 'and that's that. So we may as well dry our eyes. With that perishing motto staring us in the face, we might have had the sense to be a bit quicker off the mark. But it's always the obvious that you never see. Vandy's beaten us by a foul, but there ain't no stewards to appeal to, so we've got to stick it. All the same, he's got some digging to do before he can draw the money, and I'm ready to lay a monkey that he does it himself. What's more, the last thing he'll want is to be disturbed. In fact, any interference with his work of excavation will undoubtedly shorten his life. Properly organised innocent interference will probably affect his reason. Our course of action is therefore clear.

'Unable to procure his beastly book – our copy cannot be found – we have forgotten the incident. It comes to our ears that he has bought The Lawn and is in possession. What more natural than that some of us should repair thither, to congratulate him upon becoming our neighbour? We shall roll up quite casually – by way of the door in the wall – and, when we find him labouring, affect the utmost surprise. Of our good nature we might even offer to help him to – er – relay the lawn or tackle the drains, or whatever he's doing. In any event we shall enact the *rôle* of the village idiot, till between the respective gadflies of suspicion – which he dare not voice – and impatience – which he dare not reveal – he will be goaded into a condition of frenzy. What about it?'

The idea was heartily approved, and we became more cheerful.

Immediate arrangements were made for the entrance to The Lawn to be watched for the next twenty-four hours by reliefs of outdoor servants whom we could trust, and instructions were issued that the moment Mr Vandy Pleydell put in an appearance, whether by day or night, we were to be informed.

At eight o'clock the next morning Berry came into my room.

'They're off,' he said. 'Thirty-five minutes ago, Vandy and Emma and May arrived, unaccompanied, in a four-wheeled dogcart. He'd got the key of the gates, but the difficulty of getting them open single-handed appears to have been titanic. They seem to have stuck, or something. Altogether, according to James, a most distressing scene. However. Eventually they got inside and managed to shut the gates after them. In the dogcart there was a scythe and a whole armoury of tools.'

I got out of bed and looked at him.

'After breakfast?' I queried.

My brother-in-law nodded.

'I think so. We'll settle the premises as we go.'

As we were approaching The Lawn, I looked at my watch. It was just a quarter to ten.

The little door in the wall was still unbolted, and a very little expenditure of energy sufficed to admit my brother-in-law, Nobby, and myself into the garden.

So far as the Sealyham was concerned, 'the Wilderness was Paradise enow.' Tail up, he plunged into the welter of grass, leaping and wallowing and panting with surprise and delight at a playground which surpassed his wildest dreams. For a moment we watched him amusedly. Then we pushed the door to and started to saunter towards the house.

It was a glorious day, right at the end of August. Out of a flawless sky the sun blazed, broiling and merciless. There was nowhere a breath of wind, and in the sheltered garden – always a sun-trap –the heat was stifling.

As we drew near, the sound of voices, raised in bitterness, fell upon our ears, and we rounded the corner of the building to find Vandy waist-high in the grass about the sundial, shaking a sickle at his sisters, who were seated upon carriage cushions which had been laid upon the flags, and demanding furiously 'how the devil they expected him to reap with a sweeping motion when the godforsaken lawn was full of molehills.'

'Quite right,' said Berry. 'It can't be done.'

Emma and May screamed, and Vandy jumped as if he had been shot. Then, with a snarl, he turned to face us, crouching a little, like a beast at bay. Before he could utter a word, Berry was off.

Advancing with an air of engaging frankness, which would have beguiled the most hardened cynic, he let loose upon our cousin a voluminous flood of chatter, which drowned his protests ere they were mouthed, overwhelmed his inquiries ere they were launched, and finally swept him off his feet into the whirlpool of uncertainty, fear, and bewilderment before he knew where he was.

We had only just heard of his purchase, were delighted to think we were to be neighbours, had had no idea he was contemplating a move, had always said what a jolly little nook it was, never could understand why it had been in the market so long, thought we might find him here taking a look round, wanted to see him, so decided to kill two birds with one stone . . . What about the jolly old book? Had it come back from the binders? We couldn't find ours, thought it must be in town . . . The girls were devilling the life out of him to look it up. Was it William or Nicholas? He thought it was William. Hadn't Vandy said it was William? What was the blinking use, any old way? And what a day! He'd got a bet with Jonah that the thermometer touched ninety-seven before noon. What did Vandy think? And what on earth was he doing with the pruning-hook? And/or ploughshare on his left front? Oh, a scythe. Of course. Wouldn't he put it down? It made him tired to look at it. And was he reclaiming the lawn? Or only looking for a tennis-ball? Of course, what he really wanted was a cutter-and-binder, a steam-roller, and a gang of convicts . . .

I had been prepared to support the speaker, but, after three minutes of this, I left his side and sat down on the flags.

At last Berry paused for breath, and Emma, who had hurriedly composed and been rehearsing a plausible appreciation of the state of affairs, and was fidgeting to get it off her chest, thrust her way into the gap.

Well, the truth was, they were going to take up french gardening. There was no room at Broken Ash, and, besides, they must have a walled garden. Building nowadays was such a frightful expense, and suddenly they'd thought of The Lawn. It was sheltered, just the right size, not too far away, and all they had to do was to clear the ground. And Vandy was so impatient that nothing would satisfy him but to start at once. 'He'll get tired of it in a day or two,' she added artlessly, 'but you know what he is.'

For an improvised exposition of proceedings so extraordinary, I thought her rendering extremely creditable.

So, I think, did Vandy, for he threw an approving glance in her direction, heaved a sigh of relief, and screwed up his mouth into a sickly smile.

'Took up gardening during the war,' he announced. 'I – we all did. Any amount of money in it. Quite surprised me. But,' he added, warming to his work, 'it's the same with gardening as with everything else in this world. The most valuable asset is the personal element. If you want a thing well done, do it yourself. Ha! Ha!'

My brother-in-law looked round, regarding the howling riot of waste.

'And where,' he said, 'shall you plant the asparagus?'

Vandy started and dropped the sickle. Then he gave a forced laugh.

'You must give us a chance,' he said. 'We've got a long way to go before we get to that. All this' – he waved an unbusinesslike arm, and his voice faltered – 'all this has got to be cleared first.'

'I suppose it has,' said Berry. 'Well, don't mind us. You get on with it. Short of locusts or an earthquake, it's going to be a long job. I suppose you couldn't hire a trench-mortar and shell it for a couple of months?'

Apparently Vandy was afraid to trust his voice, for, after swallowing twice, he recovered the sickle and started to hack savagely at the grass without another word.

With the utmost deliberation, Berry seated himself upon the flagstones and, taking out his case, selected a cigarette. With an equally leisurely air I produced a pipe and tobacco, and began to make ready to smoke. Our cousins regarded these preparations with an uneasiness which they ill concealed. Clearly we were not proposing to move. The silence of awkwardness and frantically working brains settled upon the company. From time to time Emma and May shifted uncomfortably. As he bent about his labour, Vandy's eyes bulged more than ever . . .

Nobby, whom I had forgotten, suddenly reappeared, crawling pleasedly from beneath a tangled stack of foliage, of which the core appeared to have been a rhododendron. For a moment he stared at us, as if surprised at the company we kept. Then his eyes fell on Vandy.

Enshrined in the swaying grass, the latter's knickerbockers, which had been generously fashioned out of a material which had been boldly conceived, presented a back view which was most arresting. With his head on one side, the terrier gazed at them with such inquisitive astonishment that I had to set my teeth so as not to laugh outright. His cautious advance to investigate the phenomenon was still more ludicrous, and I was quite relieved when our cousin straightened his back and dissipated an illusion monstrously worthy of the pen of Mandeville.

But there was better to come.

As the unwitting Vandy, after a speechless glance in our direction, bent again to his work, Nobby cast an appraising eye over the area which had already received attention. Perceiving a molehill which had suffered an ugly gash – presumably from a scythe – he trotted up to explore, and, clapping his nose to the wound, snuffed long and thoughtfully. The next moment he was digging like one possessed.

Emma and May stiffened with a shock. With the tail of my eye I saw them exchange horror-stricken glances. Panic fear sat in their eyes. Their fingers moved convulsively. Then, with one consent, they began to cough. . . .

Their unconscious brother worked on.

So did the Sealyham, but with a difference. While the one toiled, the other was in his element. A shower of earth flew from between his legs, only ceasing for a short moment when he preferred to rend the earth with his jaws and so facilitate the excavation.

The coughing became insistent, frantic, impossible to be disregarded. . . .

As I was in the act of turning to express my concern, Vandy looked up, followed the direction of four starting eyes, and let out a screech of dismay.

'What on earth's the matter?' cried Berry, getting upon his feet. 'Been stung, or something?'

With a trembling forefinger Vandy indicated the miscreant.

'Stop him!' he yelled. 'Call him off. He'll – he'll spoil the lawn.'

'Ruin it!' shrilled Emma.

'Where?' said Berry blankly. 'What lawn?'

'*This* lawn!' roared Vandy, stamping his foot.

'But I thought – '

'I don't care what you thought. Call the brute off. It's my land, and I won't have it.'

'Nobby,' said Berry, 'come off the bowling green.'

Scrambling to my feet, I countersigned the order in a peremptory tone. Aggrievedly the terrier complied. My brother-in-law turned to Vandy with an injured air.

'I fear,' he said stiffly, 'that we are unwelcome.' Instinctively Emma and May made as though they would protest. In some dignity Berry lifted his hand. 'I may be wrong,' he said. 'I hope so. But from the first I felt that your manner was strained. Subsequent events suggest that my belief was well founded.' He turned to Vandy. 'May I ask you to let us out? I am reluctant to trouble you, but to scale those gates twice in one morning is rather more than I care about.'

Fearful lest our surprise at our reception should become crystallised into an undesirable suspicion, short of pressing us to remain, our cousins did everything to smooth our ruffled plumage.

Vandy threw down the sickle and advanced with an apologetic leer. Emma and May, wreathed in smiles, protested nervously that they had known the work was too much for Vandy, and begged us to think no more of it. As we followed the latter round to the quondam drive, they waved a cordial farewell.

The sight of the four-wheeled dogcart, standing with upturned shafts, a pickaxe, three shovels, a rake, two forks, a number of sacks, and a sieve piled anyhow by its side, was most engaging, but, after bestowing a casual glance upon the paraphernalia, Berry passed by without a word. Vandy went a rich plum colour, hesitated, and then plunged on desperately. Tethered by a halter to a tree, a partially harnessed bay mare suspended the process of mastication to fix us with a suspicious stare. Her also we passed in silence.

After a blasphemous struggle with the gates, whose objection to opening was literally rooted and based upon custom, our host succeeded in forcing them apart sufficiently to permit our egress, and we gave him 'Good day.'

In silence we strolled down the road.

When we came to the lane, Berry stopped dead.

'Brother,' he said, 'I perceive it to be my distasteful duty to return. There is an omission which I must repair.'

'You're not serious?' said I. 'The fellow'll murder you.'

'No, he won't,' said Berry. 'He'll probably burst a blood-vessel, and, with luck, he may even have a stroke. But he won't murder me. You see.' And, with that, he turned down the lane towards the door in the wall.

Nobby and I followed.

A moment later we were once more in the garden.

The scene upon which we came was big with promise.

Staggering over the frantic employment of a pickaxe, Vandy was inflicting grievous injury upon the turf about the very spot at which the terrier had been digging. Standing well out of range, his sisters were regarding the exhibition with clasped hands and looks of mingled excitement and apprehension. All three were so much engrossed that, until Berry spoke, they were not aware of our presence.

'I'm so sorry to interrupt you again' – Emma and May screamed, and Vandy endeavoured to check his implement in mid-swing, and only preserved his balance and a whole skin as by a miracle – 'but, you know, I quite forgot to ask you about the book. And, as that was really our main object in – '

The roar of a wild beast cut short the speaker.

Bellowing incoherently, trembling with passion, his mouth working, his countenance distorted with rage, Vandy shook his fist at his tormentor in a fit of ungovernable fury.

'Get out of it!' he yelled. 'Get out of it! I won't have this intrusion. It's monstrous. I won't stand it. I tell you – '

'Hush, Vandy, hush!' implored his sisters in agonised tones.

Berry raised his eyebrows.

'Really,' he said slowly, 'anybody would think that you had something to hide.'

Then he turned on his heel.

I was about to follow his example, when my cousin's bloodshot eye perceived that Nobby was once more innocently investigating the scene of Vandy's labour. With a choking cry the latter sprang forward and raised the pick. . . .

Unaware of his peril, the dog snuffed on.

One of the women screamed. . . .

Desperately I flung myself forward.

The pick was falling as I struck it aside. Viciously it jabbed its way into the earth.

For a long time Vandy and I faced one another, breathing heavily. I watched the blood fading out of the fellow's cheeks. At length –

'Be thankful,' said I, 'that I was in time. Otherwise – '

I hesitated, and Vandy took a step backwards and put a hand to his throat.

'Exactly,' I said.

Then I plucked the pick from the ground, stepped a few paces apart, and, taking the implement with both hands, spun round and threw it from me as if it had been a hammer.

It sailed over some lime trees and crashed out of sight into some foliage.

Then I called the terrier and strode past my brother-in-law in the direction of the postern.

Berry fell in behind and followed me without a word.

★

'But why,' said I, 'shouldn't you tell me the day of your birth? I'm not asking the year.'

'1895,' said Adèle.

I sighed.

'Why,' she inquired, 'do you want to know?'

'So that I can observe the festival as it deserves. Spend the day at Margate, or go to a cinema, or something. I might even wear a false nose. You never know. It's an important date in my calendar.'

'How many people have you said that to?'

I laughed bitterly.

'If I told you the truth,' I said, 'you wouldn't believe me.'

There was a museful silence.

It was three days and more since Berry and I had visited The Lawn, and Vandy and Co. were still at work. So much had been reported by an under-gardener. For ourselves, we had finished with our cousins for good and all. The brutal attack upon our favourite was something we could not forget, and for a man whom beastly rage could so much degrade we had no use. Naturally enough, his sisters went with him. Orders were given to the servants that to callers from Broken Ash Daphne was 'not at home', and we were one and all determined, so far as was possible, never to see or communicate with Vandy or his sisters again. It was natural, however, that we should be deeply interested in the success or failure of his venture. We prayed fervently, but without much hope, that it might fail . . . After all, it was always on the cards that another had stumbled long since upon the treasure, or that a thief had watched its burial and later came privily and unearthed it. We should see.

'I wonder you aren't ashamed of yourself,' said Miss Feste. 'At your age you ought to have sown all your wild oats.'

'So I have,' I said stoutly. 'And they weren't at all wild, either. I've never seen such a miserable crop. As soon as the sun rose, they all withered away.'

'The sun?'

I turned and looked at her. The steady brown eyes held mine with a searching look. I met it faithfully. After a few seconds they turned away.

'The sun?' she repeated quietly.

'The sun, Adèle. The sun that rose in America in 1895. Out of the foam of the sea. I can't tell you the date, but it must have been a beautiful day.'

There was a pause. Then –

'How interesting!' said Adèle. 'So it withered them up, did it?'

I nodded.

'You see, Adèle, they had no root.'

'None of them?'

'None.'

Adèle looked straight ahead of her into the box-hedge, which rose, stiff and punctilious, ten paces away, the counterpart of that beneath which we were sitting. For once in a way, her merry smile was missing. In its stead, Gravity sat in her eyes, hung on the warm red lips. I had known her solemn before, but not like this. The proud face looked very resolute. There was a strength about the lift of the delicate chin, a steadfast fearlessness about the poise of the well-shaped head – unworldly wonders, which I had never seen. Over the glorious temples the soft dark hair swept rich and lustrous. The exquisite column of her neck rose from her flowered silk gown with matchless elegance. Her precious hands, all rosy, lay in her lap. Crossed legs gave me six inches of black silk stocking and a satin slipper, dainty habiliments, not half so dainty as their slender charge. . . .

The stable clock struck the half-hour.

Half-past six. People had been to tea – big-wigs – and we were resting after our labours. It was the perfect evening of a true summer's day.

Nobby appeared in the foreground, strolling unconcernedly over the turf and pausing now and again to snuff the air or follow up an odd clue of scent that led him a foot or so before it died away and came to nothing.

'How,' said Adèle slowly, 'did you come by Nobby?'

Painfully distinct, the wraith of Josephine Childe rose up before me, pale and accusing. Fragments of the letter which had offered me the Sealyham re-wrote themselves upon my brain . . . *It nearly breaks my heart to say so, but I've got to part with Nobby. . . . I think you'd get on together . . . if you'd like to have him* . . . And there was nothing in it. It was a case of smoke without fire. But – I could have spared the question just then . . .

Desperately I related the truth.

'A girl called Josephine Childe gave him to me. She wanted to find a home for him, as she was going overseas.'

'Oh.'

The silence that followed this non-committal remark was most discomfiting. I had a feeling that the moments were critical, and – they were slipping away. Should I leap into the tide of explanation? That way, perhaps, lay safety. Always the quicksand of *Qui s'excuse, s'accuse*, made me draw back. I became extremely nervous. . . . Feverishly I tried to think of a remark which would be natural and more or less relevant, and would pilot us into a channel of conversation down which we could swim with confidence. Of all the legion of topics, the clemency of the weather alone occurred to me. I could have screamed. . . .

The firebrand itself came to my rescue.

Tired of amusing himself, the terrier retrieved an old ball from beneath the hedge and, trotting across the sward, laid it down at my feet.

Gratefully I picked it up and flung it for him to fetch.

It fell into a thick welter of ivy which Time had built into a bulging buttress of greenery against the old grey wall at the end of the walk.

The dog sped after it, his short legs flying. . . .

The spell was broken, and I felt better.

'You mustn't think he's a root, though,' I said cheerfully, 'because he isn't. When did you say your birthday was?'

'I didn't,' said Adèle. 'Still, if you must know, I was born on August the thirtieth.'

'Today! Oh, Adèle. And I've nothing for you. Except. . . .' I hesitated, and my heart began to beat very fast. 'But I'd be ashamed – I mean. . . .' My voice petered out helplessly. I braced myself for a supreme effort. . . .

An impatient yelp rang out.

'What's the matter with Nobby?' said Adèle in a voice I hardly recognised.

'Fed up, 'cause I've lost his ball for him,' said I, and, cowardly glad of a respite, I rose and stepped to the aged riot of ivy, where the terrier was searching for his toy.

I pulled a hole in the arras and peered through.

There was more space than I had expected. The grey wall bellied away from me.

'What's that?' said Adèle, looking over my shoulder.

'What?' said I.

'There. To the right.'

It was dark under the ivy, so I thrust in a groping arm.

Almost at once my hand encountered the smooth edge of masonry.

I took out a knife and ripped away some trails, so that we could see better.

There was nothing to show that the pedestal which my efforts revealed had ever supported a statue, but it was plain that such was the office for which it had been set up. Presumably it was one of the series which, according to Vandy's book, had displayed imaginative effigies of the Roman Emperors, and had been done away in 1710. The inscription upon the cornice upheld this conclusion.

PERTINAX IMPERATOR.

I looked at Adèle.

'PER. . . . IMP. . . .' said I. 'Does the cap fit?'

'Yes,' she said simply. 'That's right. I remember it perfectly. The other seemed likely, but I was never quite sure.' Trembling a little, she turned and looked round. 'And you came out of the break in the hedge with the tomato, and – Oh!'

She stopped, and the colour came flooding into her cheeks. . . .

Then, in a flash, she turned and sped down the alley like a wild thing. As in a dream, I watched the tall slim figure dart out of sight. . . .

A second impatient yelp reminded me that Nobby was still waiting.

The firm of silversmiths whom we employed to clean the collection, after it had been disinterred, valued it for purposes of insurance at twenty-two thousand pounds.

We saw no reason to communicate with Vandy. The exercise was probably doing him good, and he had shown a marked antipathy to interruption. A tent had been pitched at The Lawn, and the work of excavation went steadily on. Not until the twenty-eighth of September did it suddenly cease.

Three days later we had occasion to drive into Brooch. We

returned by way of The Lawn. As we approached the entrance, I slowed up. . . .

From the tall gates a brand-new board flaunted its black and white paint.

But the legend it bore was the same.

Mr Miller was evidently a Conservative.

For a moment the chronicle is taken over by another hand, as Berry and Co are seen from the outside looking in . . .

THE GYPSY'S WARNING

I saw the Pleydells arrive at the fair of horses. For a moment I hesitated, because I desired to see the 'shires' which were being shown. Then I made up my mind to make myself scarce. I do not think the Pleydells would have recognised me. In my Roman guise I have rubbed shoulders with many an acquaintance who has not dreamed of my identity. Indeed, I treasure a memory of being bundled out of my college at Oxford for a gypsy vagabond by the same under-porter who admitted me three hours later with every circumstance of respect. But the Pleydell party consisted of six good people, and – I had dined at their table only two nights before. Now twelve young eyes make no mean gauntlet to run, especially when six of them belong to ladies. I had no mind at all to have my secret exposed. If I were known for a genuine Romany Rye, my pleasant relations with Gypsies would suffer exceedingly. . . . I strode across to the tents, lifted the flap of one and passed within.

'You fly from your friends?' said Moll, looking up from her mending.

Moll is a teller of fortunes and a most handsome maid. Her features would grace any coin. Her jet black hair and the wild roses in her cheeks are things to wonder at. Her steady grey eyes suggest the blessed gift of second sight.

I laughed.

'To my friends,' I said. 'You see, I'm a lucky fellow. I can serve God and mammon too.'

Moll smiled.

'Which of the two are we?' she said.

I frowned.

'Don't press me,' I said. 'I'm loth to speak ill of the Pleydells. Besides, I have broken their bread.'

'Is it true,' said Moll, 'that they are all cousins?' I nodded.

'Major Pleydell married his second cousin – a charming woman.'

'Very beautiful,' said Moll.

'Her brother, Boy Pleydell, is betrothed to an American girl.'

'Beautiful and wise,' said Moll.

'Then there are their cousins the Mansels – Jonathan and Jill.'

'A fairy child,' said Moll. 'You ought to have married her.'

'Perhaps I shall,' said I. 'She's still in the market.'

Moll shook her head.

'Too late,' she said.

I left it there. Moll has her mystery at her fingertips. . . .

The sound of voices came through the tough sailcloth.

'Of course, if you feel you can't live unless I follow you into an airless and evil-smelling tent, there to pay half-a-crown for the doubtful privilege of being told that I'm going to "cross the water" or some equally possible, but improbable, contingency, I suppose I must go, but I warn you that, if – '

'Be quiet,' said Daphne Pleydell. 'We all know it's only a game, but it's rather fun. I believe they used to be wonderful years ago, but now any gypsy you meet will tell you a pack of nonsense, if you'll cross her palm with silver.'

'This one might be one of the old ones,' piped Jill excitedly. 'Supposing – '

'Put on Adèle's engagement ring,' grunted her brother, 'and then just see if she doesn't say you're in for a wedding.'

I felt myself blushing for shame.

Glancing at Moll, I saw a red spot of anger in either cheek.

As the voices faded, I laid a hand upon her brown arm.

'They're my friends, Moll,' I pleaded. 'They mean no ill, because they know no better.'

Moll set down her mending and rose to her feet. The movement with which she shook her fine hair into place was that of a queen. For a moment she looked at me squarely. Then –

'No man,' she said simply, 'can serve God and mammon.'

With that she lifted the flap that led to her booth and disappeared.

I stepped to the heavy canvas and set my eye to a slit. . . .

Jill Mansell came first – wearing the other girl's ring upon her third finger.

As the gypsy put out a hand, she sought to lay money in it.

'Keep your silver,' said Moll quietly, 'and give your two hands to mine.'

In silence she peered at the little white palms . . . Then she let the wrists fall.

'I see your marriage,' she said. Standing behind in the background, the others nudged one another. 'Love will come stepping under a city wall.' She beckoned to Adèle. 'Come hither, wise lady, and let me tell you the truth.'

Surprisedly Jill fell away, and Miss Feste approached. . . .

'Three water-journeys I see. You will buy that which is not for sale and lose it the self-same day. And of your own free will you will go to your doom, but you will never come there.'

Moll passed her hand across her eyes and summoned my good friend Daphne. . . .

'You shall covet, my beauty, and you shall obtain for a season, but the thing shall turn to your mischief. Those having authority in a strange land shall think you a queen – and little wonder.' She stopped and looked round the tent. 'There is a king here,' she added, and motioned to Jonathan Mansel. . . .

'King by name and nature, but not in truth, you shall find a friend beyond the snow, and he shall gladden your eyes, and you shall comfort him.'

She dismissed Jonathan with a curtsey, and Boy Pleydell stepped out. . .

'I see two ladies,' said Moll, smiling a little. There was a smothered titter, and Boy swore under his breath. 'One you will follow after: the other you will deny to her face.'

With a resigned air, Berry Pleydell approached the gypsy. Moll peered at his hands without touching them. . . .

'You will cross the water,' she said. Her victim raised his eyes to heaven, and Adèle's shoulders began to shake. Moll went on imperturbably. 'You will lose your manhood, my gentleman, and nought will avail you.'

With that she turned away. . . .

With her hand on the flap –

'Leave no silver,' she said. 'I take no payment from the friends of the Romany Rye.'

As she picked up her mending –

'Thank you, Moll,' said I. Moll never moved. 'You were very severe with the Major,' I added, smiling.

'I told him the truth,' said Moll. Then she set her work down on her knee and held up her head. 'But they should not have mocked,' she flashed. 'It was not because of you that I let them keep their silver. I could not take it, for I have given them nothing.'

I stared at her.

'But, Moll, you – '

'I told them the truth,' she said, 'but I spoke to their ears only, and not to their hearts. In a week they will not remember one word that I said.'

I left it there. Moll has her mystery at her fingertips. . . .

It is 1921. Berry and Co have decided to spend the winter abroad. Urged on by Boy and Adèle, now married, they journey to Pau in southern France, hard by the Pyrénées in two drop-head coupés, Ping and Pong.

It has been a strenuous time. Thus far, although the Pleydells and the Mansels have forgotten the circumstances, Moll the Gypsy's auguries have proved entirely accurate.

Daphne certainly 'coveted and obtained' – but only 'for a season', since what she coveted and obtained, all unwittingly, were stolen goods. And love has indeed come to Jill – in the shape of Piers, erstwhile Marquis Lecco but now, after a costly and unpleasant law-suit instigated – and lost – by one Leslie Trunk, Duke of Padua. And Jonah has been mistaken for royalty ('king by name and nature, but not in truth').

Now a fourth prophecy is about to come to pass. . .

RED VIOLETS

'You will buy that which is not for sale'
Moll, the Gypsy

'I must have a paper,' said Berry. 'I haven't read the news for fifty-five hours, and anything may have happened. Supposing the rouble and the shilling have changed over. The tie I'm wearing 'ld be worth about six hundred pounds.'

I set down my cup and picked up the receiver.

So you're really off tomorrow, are you? said an attractive voice. *Well, don't miss Fuenterrabia. It's only five miles out of your way, and it's worth seeing. They sell most lovely scent in the Calle del Puerto. Ask for their 'Red Violets'.*

With a chunk I was disconnected, and a second later a bureau clerk had promised to procure an English paper and send it up to my room.

Less than an hour ago we had arrived at San Sebastian. A very handsome run had ended becomingly enough in the drive of a palatial hotel, and, though it was growing dusk as we had slipped into the town, we had seen quite enough of our surroundings to appreciate that, where nature had succeeded so admirably, man had by no means failed.

And now we were taking tea in my sister's bedroom and discussing what Berry called 'the order of going in.'

'We'd better decide right away,' said my brother-in-law, 'to stay here a week. It's perfectly obvious that two nights are going to be no earthly.'

'All you're thinking of,' said Daphne, 'is the Casino. I knew it would be like this.'

'All right,' replied her husband; 'look at the guide-book. We haven't seen this place yet, and there are twelve excursions – all highly recommended. We can cut out Tolosa, because I see we did that this afternoon. That was where the child lobbed the jam tin into the car. I fancy I passed the cathedral when I was chasing him. Anyway, I shall say so.'

'I am told,' said I, 'that Fuenterrabia's worth seeing.'

'It's the show place about here,' said Jonah. 'Old as the hills. That'll take a morning alone.'

I yawned.

'There's a shop there,' I said, 'in the Calle del Puerto, where they sell some wonderful scent. I believe it's all good, but their "Red Violets" is simply ravishing.'

The girls pricked up their ears.

'Who told you all this?' said Adèle.

'I can't imagine,' said I truthfully. 'But she had a nice voice. You know – one of those soft, mellifluous ones, suggesting that she's bored to distraction with everything except you.' I took out a cigarette and looked about me. 'Anyone got a match?' I added.

'Blow the matches,' said my sister. 'When did all this happen?'

'This afternoon,' said I. 'I'd always heard that San Sebastian – '

'Is she staying here?' said Adèle.

'In the hotel? She didn't say.'

'But how did you come to speak to her?' demanded my wife.

'I didn't,' I said. 'She spoke to me. I tell you I've always heard that San – '

'And you communed with her?' said Berry. 'With your lawful wife working herself to death on the first floor unpacking your sponge-bag, you exchanged secrets of the toilet with a honey-toned vamp? Oh, you vicious libertine. . . . Will she be at the Casino tonight?'

'I didn't ask her.'

Berry raised his eyes to heaven.

'You don't know her name; you never asked where she's staying, and you've fixed nothing up.' He sighed heavily. 'Some people don't deserve to get on.'

'I hadn't time,' I pleaded. 'We got on to scent almost at once.'

'Why scent?' said Jonah. 'Or is that an indiscreet question?'

'Oh, that's easy,' said Berry. 'The scent was on the handkerchief he picked up. It's been done before.'

'I don't understand,' said Jill.

'I'm glad you don't, darling. One expert in the family is bad enough.' He nodded at me. 'I used to think I was useful, till I'd seen that Mormon at work. Talk about getting off. . . . Why, he'd click at the jumble sale.'

'Would he really?' said Adèle interestedly. 'I'd no idea he was so enterprising.'

Berry shrugged his shoulders.

'My dear,' he said, 'he's a blinkin' marvel. Where you and I'ld be standing outside a stage-door with a nervous grin and a bag of jujubes, he'd walk straight up to a Marchioness, say, "I feel I must tell you that you've got a mouth in a million," and get away with it. But there you are. In the present case – '

' – for once in a way,' said Adèle, 'the lady seems to have made the running.' She turned to me with a smile. 'Well, Juan me lad, tell us some more about her. Was she fair or dark?'

I nodded at Berry.

'Better ask him,' I said. 'He knows more about it than I do.'

'She was dark,' said Berry, unhesitatingly. 'A tall, willowy wench, with Continental eyes and an everlasting pout. Am I right, sir?'

'You may be,' said I. 'Not having seen the damsel. . . .'

There was an outburst of incredulous objection.

'Sorry,' I added, 'but the liaison was conducted upon the telephone. Just now. When I ordered the paper. The lady had no idea she was giving me counsel. So, you see, we're both blameless. And now may I have a match?'

'Well, I am disappointed,' announced Adèle. 'I quite thought we were off.'

'So did I,' said Daphne. 'And you never even – Oh, it's spoiled my tea.'

Even Jill protested that I had 'led them on'.

In some dudgeon, I began to wonder if I should ever understand women.

An hour and a half had slipped by.

Ready for dinner with twenty minutes to spare, I had descended to the lounge. There a large writing-table had suggested the propriety of sending a postcard to the sweetest of aunts, who, in the absence of evidence to the contrary, invariably presumed our death after fourteen days.

There being no postcards available, I started a letter.

For a page and a half my pen ran easily enough, and then, for no reason whatever, my epistolary sense faltered, laboured, and ceased to function.

I re-read what I had written, touched up the punctuation, and fingered my chin. I reviewed the past, I contemplated the future, I regarded my finger-nails – all to no effect. There was simply nothing to say. Finally I rose and went in search of a waiter. There was, I felt, a chance that a Martini might stimulate my brain. . . .

I returned to my seat to find that, while I had been gone, a heifer from another herd had come to drink at the pool.

Immediately upon the opposite side of the writing-table sat one of the prettiest women that I have ever seen. Her colouring was superb. Beneath a snow-white skin all the wild beauty of a mountain rose glowed in her cheeks; each time she moved, a flashing mystery of red and golden lights blazed from the auburn crown piled on her head; stars danced an invitation in the great grey eyes. Her small straight nose, the exquisite line of her face, her fairy mouth alone would have redeemed the meanest countenance. A plain black velvet dress, cut rather high at the throat, but leaving her lovely arms bare from the shoulder, and a complete absence of jewellery, showed that my lady knew how pictures should be framed. . . .

With an effort I bent to my letter. From being difficult, however, the composition of another two pages of coherent prose had become formidable. Turning to the past, I could remember nothing. Looking into the future, I found myself blind. As for the present, I felt instinctively that a description of the curve of my vis-à-vis' mouth would be out of place and might be misunderstood.

I observed suddenly that my lady had stopped writing.

After a moment she read over what she had written and put in two commas. Then she put a dash at the end of her last sentence. Such an addition had not occurred to me. For what it was worth I adopted it surreptitiously. When I looked up, the tips of four pointed fingers were being regarded with some severity. Finally the girl laid down her pen and, propping her chin on two ridiculous fists, stared dismally upon the neutral zone between our respective blotting pads.

'Have you dealt with the weather?' said I.

The stars, which had stopped dancing, leaped again into life.

'Fully,' she said.

'And the place?'

She nodded.

'And the people staying in the hotel?'

'I've just said they're all very dull.'

I wrote rapidly. Then –

' "The people here," ' I read, ' "are nearly all very dull." '

For a moment she looked at me. Then she picked up her pen.

'How,' she demanded, with a dazzling smile, 'do you spell "nearly"?'

'Only one "r",' I replied. 'Same as "adorable".'

'Nearly' went down – rather shakily.

I pulled up my cuffs.

' "Spanish furniture," ' I said, following my pen, ' "is like the Spanish – on the large side. Everything is too big." '

' " – too big," ' said my lady, with her head on one side. 'You see, my confidence in you is supreme.'

'One moment,' said I. 'There's only one "w" in "sweet", isn't there?'

'Yes,' she said, bubbling. 'Same as "awful".'

I cleared my throat.

' "The table, for instance," ' I continued, ' "at which we – I am writing is simply huge. If it were only half as wide, it would be much more – er – convenient." '

The two white shoulders began to shake with laughter.

I thought very swiftly. Then –

'New paragraph,' I said.

'Half a page more,' breathed my companion.

I frowned.

' "They have," ' I announced, ' "quite a good Casino here." '

Our two pens recorded the statement.

' "The great thing to do is to go there after dinner." '

The custom was reported in duplicate.

' "But I'm not going tonight," ' said the girl, ' "because –" '

'But –'

' "I've got to do my packing." '

I groaned. Then –

' "But I shan't go tonight," ' I declared, ' "because I'm going to help a friend pack." ' I looked up cheerfully. 'Yes?'

' "I shall look forward," ' she said, smiling, ' "to seeing you again – sometime." '

' "Soon." '

The pretty head went to one side.

' "With my love," ' she said quietly.

' "Your devoted servant," ' said I.

For a second my lady hesitated. Then she signed a name, crammed her letter into an envelope, and rose to her feet.

The stars in the wonderful eyes had become misty, and there was a strange wistful curve to the exquisite lips.

For an instant we looked at one another. Then –

'Just "Eulalie," ' she said.

The next moment she was gone.

I turned to see Daphne, Adèle, and Berry a dozen paces away. . . .

I advanced with what composure I could summon.

'I have been endeavouring,' I said, 'to atone for this afternoon.'

There was a frosty silence. Then –

'So I see,' said my sister icily.

Berry passed a hand across his eyes.

'Ugh!' he said, shuddering. 'I've gone all goosegogs – I mean, gooseflesh. Will she be at the Casino tonight?'

My wife set a hand upon my arm.

'I must admit,' she said, smiling, 'that she had a mouth in a million.'

By half-past ten the next morning we were again upon the road.

The almanac swore it was March, but here was a summer's day. Not a cloud was floating in the great blue sky: down to the tenderest breeze, the winds were sleeping: the sun was in all his glory. For earth herself, the strains of winter were being done away. Out of the country's coat the greys and browns, lately so prominent, were fading notably. As thick as fast, the green was coming in. As we rounded a bend and sailed down a long sweet hill towards the frontier, the road was all dappled with the shadows of youngster leaves.

Our way seemed popular. Car after car swept by, waggons and lorries went rumbling about their business, now and again two of the Guardia Civil – well-horsed, conspicuously armed and point-device in their accoutrements – sat stiff, silent, and vigilant in the mouth of an odd by-road.

Come to the skirts of Irun, we switched to the left, and five minutes later we were at Fuenterrabia.

A city with a main street some four yards wide, keeping a king's palace, if hatchments be evidence, remembering more dukes than shopkeepers, its house-walls upholding a haphazard host of balconies and overhung with monstrous eaves – a pocket stronghold, set on the lip of Spain, staring at sea and land, each sunlit road of which is fat with history – a lovely star upon the breast of fame, chosen by English poets to enrich their songs, Fuenterrabia is among the crown jewels of Europe.

We thrust up the Calle Mayor and into the Plaza de Armas. There we put the cars in the shade and alighted eagerly to view the town at close quarters.

'Look at that little boy,' cried Jill, 'eating an apple. Where's the camera? Get him to stand in the sun, Boy, against that old wall.'

'That's right,' said Berry. 'And there's a dog scratching himself. Ask him to devil his tenants beside the Post Office. If we get a good picture, we can call it *Local Affection or The Old, Old Story* and send it to *The Field*.'

To humour my cousin's whim, I approached a dirty-looking child. . . .

Despite my assurances of goodwill, however, the urchin retired as I advanced, all the time consuming his apple with a nervous energy, which suggested at once a conviction that I had my eye upon his fruit and a determination to confound my strategy. The apple was dwindling fast, and, redoubling my protests, I quickened my pace. For a second the boy hesitated. Then he took two last devastating bites, flung the core in my face, and took to his heels.

Pursuit being out of the question, I returned furiously to the others, to find them, as was to be expected, quite weak with laughter.

'It w-was good of you, Boy,' declared Jill tearfully. 'And I got such a precious picture – just as he threw it.'

'I suppose you know,' I said stiffly, 'that he hit me upon the nose.'

'There must,' said Berry, 'have been some misunderstanding. The Spaniard's courtesy is proverbial. You're sure you weren't rude to him, brother?'

'Certain,' said I grimly.

'Dear, dear,' said my brother-in-law, opening a guidebook. 'It's most mysterious. Just listen to this. *The stranger is at first apt to be carried away by the obliging tone of society, by the charming spontaneity of manner, and by the somewhat exaggerated politeness of the people he meets.* There now. Were you carried away at all? I mean, if you were – '

'I was not,' said I.

Berry returned to the book.

'*He should return these civilities in kind, but he should avoid turning the conversation on serious matters, and should, above all, refrain from expressing an opinion on religious or political questions.* I do hope you didn't. . . .'

I shook my head.

'Then,' said Berry, 'should we meet the child again, I shall cut him dead. And that's that. And now let's go and find a dairy. You'll be wanting a pick-me-up.'

For an hour and a half we went about the city.

We marked her bulwarks, we told her towers, we observed her mansions, we strolled upon her terraces, we enjoyed her prospects.

Last of all, we visited the Calle del Puerto.

Before we had taken a dozen paces along the aged alley, a faint odour of perfume began to assert itself, and a few seconds later we were standing before a tiny shop, scrupulously sweet and clean to look upon, absurdly suggestive of the patronage of marionettes. A curtain of apple-green canvas was swaying in the low doorway, while an awning of the same stuff guarded a peepshow window, which was barely three feet long and less than one foot high. Herein, ranged behind a slab of fine plate-glass, stood three plain, stoppered phials, one rose-coloured, one green, and one a faint yellow. Below, on a grey silk pillow, was set a small vellum-bound book. This was open. In capitals of gold upon the pages displayed were two words only – PARFUMS FRANÇAIS.

The effect was charming.

We gathered about the window, ejaculating surprise.

'*Urbs in rure*,' said Jonah. 'And then you're wrong. The Rue de la Paix isn't in it.'

Which is a description I cannot better.

Daphne lifted the portière, and we followed her in.

Passing suddenly out of the brilliant sunshine, we could at first see nothing. Then gradually the interior of the shop took shape.

There was no counter, but an oblong mahogany glass-topped table, standing in the centre of the polished floor, evidently was discharging that office. Upon this stood three other phials, similar to those displayed in the window, but fitted with sprays instead of stoppers. In front of each a grey gold-lettered slip of silk, laid between the glass and the mahogany, declared its contents – ROSE BLEUE . . . LYS NOIR . . . JASMIN GRIS.

The room was very low, and the walls were panelled. Upon these, except for that framing the door and window, were rows of shelves. On these, at decent intervals, stood phials of four different sizes. To judge from the colour of their glass, each wall was devoted to one of the three scents. That facing us was green, that on our left rose-coloured, that upon our right a faint yellow. A black curtain in a corner suggested a doorway leading to another part of the house. The air, naturally enough, was full of perfume.

We stared about us in silence.

After waiting perhaps five minutes, peering unsuccessfully behind the curtain, raising our voices in talk, and finally rapping upon the table without attracting attendance, we decided to return to where we had left the cars and visit the shop again on our way out of the town.

As we came to the Plaza, the clock of the great church announced the hour. A quarter to one.

'Good Heavens!' cried Daphne, checking the time by her wristwatch. 'I'd no idea it was so late. And I left word for Evelyn to ring me up at the hotel at one o'clock.' We made a rush for the cars. 'Can it be done, Jonah?'

'Only by air,' said my cousin. 'Outside a track, thirteen miles in fourteen minutes is just a shade too thick. Still, there's nothing the matter with the road after Irun, and Evelyn may be delayed getting through.'

He swung himself into Ping and started her up. My sister and Jill scrambled aboard while he was turning her round. As he headed for the Calle Mayor –

'Stop!' shrieked his sister. 'The scent, Jonah, the scent. We've got to go back.'

Jonah threw out the clutch.

'We'll get that!' cried Adèle. 'You go on, and we'll follow.'

'Right.'

The next moment Ping had dropped out of sight.

It was perhaps five minutes later that, after conjuring Berry to stay where he was and move the car for nobody, I assisted my wife on to the pavement.

When Fuenterrabia was planned, an eleven-feet-six wheel-base was not considered. To wheedle Pong to the mouth of the Calle del Puerto had been a ticklish business, and I had berthed her deliberately with an eye to our departure for the city gate, rather than to the convenience of such other vehicles as might appear. Besides, for my brother-in-law to have essayed manoeuvres in such surroundings would have been asking for trouble.

As Adèle and I hastened along the street –

'We must look sharp,' I insisted. 'She's half across the fairway. If anybody with anything broader than a mule feels they can't wait, there'll be murder done.'

We came to the shop, panting. . . .

The place was just as we had left it, and – there was no one there.

I looked round impatiently.

'What on earth,' I began, 'is the good of a – '

As I spoke, the curtain in the corner was pushed to one side, and a French girl entered the room.

Her manner was most curious.

For a moment she hesitated, as though she would turn and fly. Then, with her eyes upon Adèle, she moved slowly forward. She seemed to be making an effort to come and serve us. That she was most apprehensive was perfectly plain. . . .

Halfway between curtain and table she stopped. Then she put a hand to her throat.

'*Vous désirez, Madame. . . ?*'

'*Du parfum, s'il vous plait,*' said Adèle reassuringly.

Her cheerful tone appeared to encourage the girl. And when my wife pointed to the green phial and asked to be sprayed with its contents, I could have sworn her attitude was that of relief.

In a flash she had produced a small square of linen. This she handed to Adèle.

'*Sentez, Madame. Voyez, c'est sans parfum. Pardon.*' She sprayed it with scent. '*Voilà. C'est le "Lys Noir".*'

Adèle passed it to me. The scent was exquisite.

'*C'est délicieux,*' said Adèle.

'*Oui, Madame. C'est bon. Voulez-vous essayer les autres?*'

'*S'il vous plait.*'

French squares of linen were produced, offered for inspection, and sprayed. . . .

Each perfume seemed more ravishing than its predecessor. To test the worth of this impression, we reverted to the 'Black Lily'. One breath of this satisfied us that it was the best of the lot. To be quite sure, we smelt the 'Blue Rose', and were instantly convinced of its superiority to its fellows. A return to the 'Grey Jasmine' persuaded us that there was only one scent in the shop. It was, indeed, impossible to award the palm. Each perfume had some irresistible virtue which the others lacked.

When at last Adèle implored me to help her to a decision, I spoke to the point.

'There's only one thing to do. We can't wait now, so have a big bottle of each. Then you and Jill and Daphne can fight it out at home.'

Adèle asked the price of the scents.

'*Ils sont tous du même prix, Madame. Le grand flacon, cent pesetas – les autres, soixante-dix, cinquante et trente, selon la taille.*'

'*Eh bien. Je prendrai un grand flacon de chaque.*'

'*Merci, Madame.*'

A prolonged and vicious croak from the end of the street argued that Berry's patience was wearing thin, but to have asked the girl to make haste would have been supererogatory.

In a trice three phials had been taken down from their shelves, and three stout silk-lined cases, of the pattern of safety-match boxes, had been produced. The phial went into its tray, the tray into its sheath, the case complete into a sheet of rough grey paper, and the whole was girt with cord in next to no time.

As the last knot was being tied, Adèle touched me upon the arm.

'I almost forgot,' she said. Then she turned to the girl. '*On m'a dit de demander votre "Violettes Rouges".*'

The scissors the girl was using fell to the floor. As she recovered them –

'*Parfaitement, Madame,*' she whispered, and stepped uncertainly to the curtain.

She disappeared, to reappear almost immediately with a package in her hand precisely similar to those she had just made up. She placed it with the others.

'Oh,' said Adèle, '*mais vous n'avez pas –* '

A perfect hurricane of croaks, mingled with cries of anger, interrupted her.

'Never mind,' I cried, gathering up the parcels. 'How much is it now? Four hundred, I suppose.'

As I was counting the notes, a yell of anguish in Berry's unmistakable accents fell upon my ears.

I threw the money upon the table and bolted out of the shop with Adèle at my heels. . . .

As we came to the corner, I ran full tilt into – Eulalie. For an instant our eyes met, but she looked away pointedly, slipped to one side, and passed on. . . .

Then –

'*Obstàculos* to you, sir!' roared Berry. 'Look at my wing. . . .

Yes, I see the cabriolet. But what of that? It's perfectly happy. . . . No, it *didn't* want to get by. And if it had – Oh, go and push yourself off somewhere.' Here he caught sight of me. 'See what this greasy pantaloon's done? I told him he hadn't room, but he wouldn't wait. And now he's shoving it on to that cabriolet. . . . Oh, why can't I speak Spanish? I'd give him earache.'

I thrust our packages into the fold of the hood and ran to examine the wing. Happily the damage was slight. I announced this relievedly.

'I dare say it is,' raged Berry, as we resumed our seats. 'What I object to is the poisonous hostility of the brute. He blinkin' well meant to do it.'

'Dear, dear,' said Adèle, bubbling. 'There must have been some misunderstanding. The Spaniard's courtesy is proverbial.'

'Exactly,' said I. 'The stranger is at first apt to be carried away by the exaggerated politeness of the – '

'You may be,' said Berry, 'as blasphemous as you like, but, for the love of the home for little children, let's get out of this town.'

I let in the clutch. . . .

We were passing out of the beautiful armoried gateway, when an approaching peasant signalled to us to stop, and pointed excitedly back the way we had come. The fellow's manner suggested that we had dropped something.

I pulled up the car, opened my door, and jumped out.

As I did so, a breathless Eulalie appeared upon the other side of the car.

'I never thought I should catch you,' she said uncertainly. 'My car got mixed up with that waggon, so I chanced it and ran. And, now I'm here, I hardly know how to tell you. . . .' She addressed herself to Adèle. 'But I fancy you've got my scent – "Red Violets". It's rather – rather special. They only make it by request. And a friend of mine had ordered a bottle for me. It was put ready for me to call for, and, as far as I can make out, they've given it to you by mistake. I'm – I'm afraid I'm asking an awful lot, but might I have it? I'm leaving Spain altogether in half an hour, so I shan't have another chance.'

I never remember feeling so utterly disillusioned. Recalling the telephone conversation of the day before, I was frankly disgusted. Such sharp practice as this smacked of a bargain sale.

The scent was ours. We had bought it fairly. Besides, it had *not* been reserved. If either Adèle or Eulalie had to go empty away, law and equity alike were pronouncing in favour of my wife.

Adèle was speaking.

'Oh certainly. Boy, will you. . . ?' I stepped into the car and thrust a hand into the fold of the hood. 'I shall know which it is. The paper it's wrapped in is different. There's a line running through it, and the others were plain.' I plucked out a case and gave it to her to examine. 'That's right.' Gravely she handed it to Eulalie. 'I'm sorry you had to run so,' she added gently.

The other shrugged her shoulders.

'I caught you,' she said simply, 'and that's the great thing.' She glanced over her shoulder. 'And here comes my car. I'm really most awfully grateful. . . .'

Wish a swish the cabriolet swept alongside, skidded with locked wheels upon the pavement, and fetched up anyhow with its bonnet across our bows. It was a piece of driving for which the chauffeur ought to have been flogged.

'. . . most awfully grateful,' repeated Eulalie, swinging the case by its cord. 'You – you might have made it much harder. . . .'

The next moment she was in the cabriolet. . . .

Dazedly I watched the latter float out of sight.

'B-but she hasn't paid,' I stammered. 'She's never given us the money. Four pounds that bottle cost. . . .'

We stared at one another in dismay.

At length –

'Stung,' said Berry. 'But what a beautiful bit of work! Four pounds' worth of scent for the asking. No unpleasantness, no sleight of hand, no nothing. Just a glad eye last night and a two-minute run this morning. I don't wonder she was grateful.'

We had spent the afternoon traversing San Sebastian, and had found the place good – so good, in fact, that it was past six before we returned to the hotel.

I followed Adèle upstairs rather wearily.

'I shall never get over this morning,' I said. 'Never.' Arrived at our door, I fitted the key to the lock. 'To think that I stood there and let you hand – Oh, blast! We've left the scent in the car.'

'So we have,' said Adèle. 'What an awful nuisance! I knew we should. It's fatal to put anything in that hood. You don't see it.'

I pushed open the door.

'As soon as I've changed,' I said, switching on the light, 'I'll go and – '

The sentence was never finished.

Had I been told that a cyclone had struck our bedroom, I should not have been surprised.

Adèle and I stood staring at such a state of disorder as I had never dreamed of.

The bed had been dragged from the wall, and its clothes distributed about the room: the wardrobe and cupboards stood open: every drawer in the room was on the floor: our clothing had been flung, like soiled linen, into corners: my wife's dressing-case had been forced, and now lay open, face downward, upon the carpet, while its contents sprawled upon a mattress: a chair had fallen backwards into the empty cabin trunk, and the edge of a sheet had caught on one of its upturned legs. . . .

'Adèle! Boy!' The swish of a skirt, and there was my sister behind us. 'Our room's been – Good Heavens, yours is the same! Whatever's the meaning of it?'

Within three minutes two managers and three clerks were on the scene. To do them justice, they were genuinely perturbed. Fresh rooms – a magnificent suite – were put at our disposal: under our own eyes our belongings were gathered into sheets and carried to our new quarters: maids were summoned and placed at the girls' service: valets were sent for: the dressing-case was sent to be repaired: we were begged at our convenience to report whether there were any valuables we could not find, and over and over again we were assured that the management would not rest until the thieves were taken: jointly and severally we were offered profound apologies for so abominable an outrage.

Berry and Jonah, who had been taking the cars to the garage, arrived in the midst of the removal.

Upon the circumstances being laid before my brother-in-law, he seemed for some time to be deprived of the power of speech, and it was only upon being shown the contents of a sheet which had just been conveyed by two valets into his wife's bedroom that he at last gave tongue.

Drawing a pair of dress trousers from beneath a bath towel, a pair of brogues, and a box of chocolates, he sobbed aloud.

'You all,' he said brokenly, 'do know these trousers: I remember the first time ever I did put them on; 'twas on a summer's evening, in the Park. . . .'

With one accord and some asperity my sister and I requested him to desist.

'All right,' he said. 'But why worry? I know there's nothing valuable gone, because in that case I should have been told long ago. We've been shocked and inconvenienced, of course; but, to balance it, we've got a topping suite, a private sitting-room thrown in, and a whole fleet of bottle-washers in attendance, all stamping to wash and iron and brush our clothes as they've never been brushed before. Jonah's and Jill's rooms all right?'

'Yes.'

'Well, let them move along, any way. Then we shall all be together. And now, if we've got any sense, we shall let this sympathetic crowd straighten up everything – they're simply bursting for the word "Go!" – and gather round the fire, which I see they've lighted, and talk about something else.'

This was sound advice.

A close acquaintance with crime – the feeling that a robber has handled her personal effects, mauled her apparel, trodden her own sanctuary – is bound to jangle a sensitive woman's nerves. The less the girls thought upon the matter, the better for them. . . .

Orders were given, a sofa was drawn towards the hearth, Jonah went to seek some champagne, and I slipped on a coat and left the hotel for the garage.

When I returned some twenty minutes later, Adèle had discovered a piano and was playing 'Whispering', while the others were dancing with as much freedom from care as they might have displayed at a night-club.

When I laid the scent on the table, the dance died, and Daphne, Adèle, and Jill crowded about me.

'One for each of you,' I said. 'With my love. But wait one moment.' I turned to Adèle. 'How did you tell the "Red Violets" from the others?'

'Its paper had a line – '

I pointed to the three parcels.

'So have they all,' I said. 'It depends on the way the light strikes it. One moment you see it, and the next you can't.'

My wife examined the packages in turn.

'You're perfectly right,' she said. Then, 'Good Heavens!' she cried. 'Perhaps I gave that woman the wrong one, after all.'

I shrugged my shoulders.

'I don't suppose she cared. What's in a name? They're each of them worth four pounds.'

'That's true,' said Adèle musingly. 'Still . . .'

We opened them one by one.

The first was the Black Lily.

Then came the Grey Jasmine.

I ripped the paper off the third case and laid it upon the table.

With my fingers about the cardboard, I paused.

'And what,' said I, 'is the betting?'

'Blue Rose,' cried Jill.

'Red Violets,' said Adèle.

I opened the case.

They were both wrong.

The tray contained no perfume at all.

Crammed into the form of a scent-bottle was a dirty huddle of wash-leather.

I lifted it out between my finger and thumb.

The diamond and emerald necklace which lay beneath must have been worth a quarter of a million.

'Yes,' said the British Vice-Consul some two hours later, 'this little seaside town is a sort of Thieves' Parlour. Four-fifths of the stuff that's stolen in Spain goes out of the country this way. As in the present case, the actual thief daren't try to cross the frontier, but he's always got an accomplice waiting at San Sebastian. We know the thieves all right – at least, the police do – but the accomplices are the devil. Often enough, they go no further than Biarritz, and there are so many of the Smart Set constantly floating between the two towns that they're frightfully hard to spot. In fact, about the only chance is to trace their connection with the thief. What I mean is this. A's got the jewels, and he's got to pass them to B. That necessitates some kind of common denominator. Either they've got to meet or they've got to visit – at different times, of course – the same bureau. . . .

'Well, there you are.

'By the merest accident you stumbled upon the actual communication of the password by A to B. The voice you heard upon the telephone was that of the original thief, or of his representative. This morning you visited the actual bureau. I know the place well. My wife's bought scent there. It's always been a bit of a mystery, but I never suspected this. I've not the slightest doubt it's been used as a bureau for years. Well, in all innocence you gave the password, and in all innocence received the gems. B arrives too late, finds that you have them, and starts in pursuit. I've no doubt she really ran on to see which way you'd gone. She couldn't have hoped to catch you on foot. Of course, she couldn't understand how you'd come by the password, but the few words you'd had with her the night before made her *suspect your innocence*. Still, she wasn't sure, and that's why her chauffeur fetched up across your bows.'

'You don't mean – '

'I do indeed. If you hadn't handed them over, they'd have been taken by force. . . .

'Well, finding that either by accident or design she's been sold a pup, B communicates with the gang, and while you're out your rooms are ransacked.'

'And I walked,' I said, 'after dark from the Calle de Miracruz to this hotel with the baubles under my arm.'

The Vice-Consul laughed.

'The armour of ignorance,' he said 'will sometimes turn the keenest wits. The confidence it gives its wearer is proverbial.'

'But why,' said Adèle, 'was the shop-girl so terribly nervous? I mean, if she's used to this sort of traffic. . . .'

The Vice-Consul fingered his chin.

Then he picked up the jewels.

'Perhaps,' he said slowly, 'perhaps she knew where they came from.'

'Where was that?' said Daphne.

The Vice-Consul frowned.

'When I last saw them,' he said, 'they were in the Royal Treasury.'

At half-past ten the next morning I was walking upon the golf links of St Jean-de-Luz.

I was not there of choice.

Two very eminent detectives – one French and one Spanish – were upon either side of me.

We were close to the seventh green, when the Frenchman touched me upon the arm.

'Look, sir,' he said, pointing. 'There is a golf party coming. They are making, no doubt, for this spot. When they arrive, pray approach and look at them. If you should recognise anyone, I beg that you will take off your hat.'

He bowed, and a moment later I was alone.

I sat down on the turf and took out a cigarette. . . .

With a plop, a golf ball alighted upon the green, trickled a few feet, and stopped a yard from the hole. Presently another followed, rolled across the turf, and struggled into the rough.

I got upon my feet and strolled towards the green. . . .

It was a mixed foursome.

In a cherry-coloured jumper and a white skirt, Eulalie looked prettier than ever.

She saw me at once, of course, but she took no notice.

Her companions glanced at me curiously.

Putter in hand, Eulalie walked to her ball – the far one – and turned her back to me. After a little consideration, she holed out.

It was a match shot, and her companions applauded vigorously.

Eulalie just smiled.

'I'm always better,' she said, 'when I've something at stake.'

'And what,' said her partner, a large blue-eyed Englishman with a grey moustache, 'have you got at stake this time?'

Eulalie laughed mischievously.

'If I told you,' she said, 'you wouldn't believe me.'

Light-heartedly enough, they passed to the eighth tee.

I watched them go thoughtfully.

When the detectives came up –

'I didn't take off my hat,' I explained, 'because I wasn't sure. But I'm almost certain that somewhere before I've seen that great big fellow with the grey moustache.'

My companions were not interested.

ZERO

'Nought will avail you'
Moll, the Gypsy

'My dear,' said Berry, 'be reasonable.'

'With pleasure,' said Daphne. 'But I'm not going to let you off.'

Her husband frowned upon a roll.

'When I say,' he said, 'that I have a feeling today that my luck is in, I'm not being funny. Only once before have I had that conviction. I was at Cannes at the time – on the point of leaving for Paris. I went to Monte Carlo instead. . . That night I picked up over six hundred pounds.'

'I know,' said his wife. 'You've often told me. But I can't help it. I made you give me your word before we came here, and I'm not going to let you off.'

'I gave it without thinking,' declared her husband. 'Besides, I never dreamed I should have this feeling.'

'I did,' said Daphne shortly. 'That's why I made you promise. Have some more coffee?'

Pointedly ignoring the invitation, Berry returned to his roll and, after eyeing it with disgust which the bread in no way deserved, proceeded to disrupt and eviscerate it with every circumstance of barbarity.

Covertly, Jonah and I exchanged smiles . . .

It was the morning of our last day at San Sebastian.

During our short stay the weather had been superb, and we had been out and about the whole day long. Of an evening we had been to the Casino. . . .

For as long as I could remember, Berry had had a weakness for Roulette. For Baccarat, Petits Chevaux, and the rest he cared nothing: fifty pounds a year would have covered his racing bets; if he played Bridge, it was by request. My brother-in-law was no gambler. There was something, however, about the shining wheel, sunk in its board of green cloth, which he found irresistible.

Remembering this fascination, my sister had broached the matter so soon as we had decided to visit San Sebastian, with the happy result that, ere we left Pau, her husband had promised her three things. The first was to leave his cheque books at home; the second, to take with him no more than two hundred pounds; the third, to send for no more money.

And now the inevitable had happened.

The two hundred pounds were gone – every penny; we were not due to leave until the morrow; and – Berry was perfectly satisfied that his luck had changed. As for the promises his wife had extracted, he was repenting his rashness as heartily as she was commending her provision.

'Nothing,' said Berry, turning again to the charge, 'was said about borrowing, was it?'

'No.'

'Very well, then. Boy and Jonah'll have to lend me something. I'm not going to let a chance like this go.'

'Sorry, old chap,' said Jonah, 'but we've got to pay the hotel bill. Thanks to your activities, we're landed with – '

'How much have you got?' demanded Berry.

I cut in and threw the cards on the table.

'Brother,' I said, 'we love you. For that reason alone we won't lend you a paper franc. But then you knew that before you asked us.'

My brother-in-law groaned.

'I tell you,' he affirmed, 'you're throwing away money. With another two hundred and fifty I could do anything. I can feel it in my bones.'

'You'd lose the lot,' said Jonah. 'Besides, you've eaten your cake. If you'd limited yourself last night and played rationally, instead of buttering the board. . . .'

'I'm sure,' said Jill, 'you ought to have played on a system. If you'd put a pound on "RED" and kept on doubling each time you lost – '

'Yes,' said Berry. 'That's an exhilarating stunt, that is. Before you know where you are, you've got to put two hundred and fifty-six pounds on an even chance to get one back. With a limit of four hundred and eighty staring you in the face, that takes a shade more nerve than I can produce. I did try it once – at Madeira. Luck was with me. After three hours I'd made four shillings and lost half a stone. . . . Incidentally, when a man starts playing Roulette on a system, it's time to pray for his soul. I admit there are hundreds who do it – hundreds of intelligent, educated, thoughtful men and women. Well, you can pray for the lot. They're trying to read something which isn't written. They're studying a blank page. They're splitting their brains over a matter on which an idiot's advice would be as valuable. I knew a brilliant commercial lawyer who used to sit down at the table and solemnly write down every number that turned up for one hour. For the next sixty minutes he planked still more solemnly on the ones that had turned up least often. Conceive such a frame of mind. That wonderful brain had failed to grasp the one simple glaring point of which his case consisted – that Roulette is lawless. He failed to appreciate that he was up against Fortune herself. He couldn't realise that because "7" had turned up seven times running at a quarter past nine, that was no earthly reason why "7" shouldn't turn up eight times running at a quarter past ten. Heaven knows what fun he got out of it. For me, the whole joy of the thing is that you're flirting with Fate.' He closed his eyes suddenly and flung back his head. 'Oh,' he breathed, 'I tell you she's going to smile tonight. I can see the light in her eyes. I have a feeling that she's going to be very kind . . . very kind . . . somehow . . .'

We let him linger over the fond reflection, eyeing one another uneasily. It was, we felt, but the prelude to a more formidable attack.

We were right.

'I demand,' barked Berry, 'that I be allowed the wherewithal to prosecute my suit.'

'Not a farthing,' said Daphne. 'To think that that two hundred pounds is gone makes me feel ill.'

'That's exactly why I want to win it back – and more also.' He looked round desperately. 'Anybody want a birthright? For two hundred and fifty quid – I'd change my name.'

'It sounds idiotic, I know,' said I, 'but supposing – supposing you lost.'

'I shan't tonight,' said Berry.

'Sure?'

'Positive. I tell you, I feel – '

'And you,' said Jonah scornfully, 'you have the temerity to talk about praying for others' souls. You sit there and – '

'I tell you,' insisted Berry, 'that I have a premonition. Look here. If I don't have a dart tonight, I shall never be the same man again. . . . Boy, I implore you – '

I shook my head.

'Nothing doing,' I said. 'You'll thank us one day.'

'You don't understand,' wailed Berry. 'You've never known the feeling that you were bound to win.'

'Yes, I have – often. And it's invariably proved a most expensive sensation.'

There was a moment's silence. Then –

'Right,' said my brother-in-law. 'You're one and all determined to see me go down. You've watched me drop two hundred, and not one of you's going to give me a hand to help me pick it up. It may be high-minded, but it's hardly cordial. Some people might call it churlish. . . . Upon my soul, you are a cold-blooded crowd. Have you ever known a deal I wouldn't come in on? And now, because you are virtuous, I'm to lose my fun. . . . Ugh! What a lovely sonnet that is of Shakespeare's, "The Cakes and Ale are Over." '

Struggling with laughter, Adèle left her seat and, coming quickly behind him, set her white hands upon his shoulders.

'Dear old chap,' she said, laying her cheek against his, 'look at it this way. You're begging and praying us to let you down. Yes, you are. And if we helped you to break your word, neither you nor we would ever, at the bottom of our hearts, think quite so much of us again. And that's not good enough. Even if you won five thousand pounds it wouldn't compensate. Respect and self-respect aren't things you can buy.'

'But, sweetheart,' objected Berry, 'nothing was said about borrowing. Daphne admits it. If I can raise some money without reference to my bankers, I'm at liberty to do so.'

'Certainly,' said Adèle. 'But *we* mustn't help. If that was allowed, it 'ld knock the bottom out of your promise. You and Daphne and we are all in the same stable: and that – to mix metaphors – puts us out of court. If you ran into a fellow you knew, and he would lend you some money, or you found a hundred in the street, or a letter for you arrived – '

' – or one of the lift-boys died, leaving me sole legatee. . . . I see. Then I should be within my rights. In fact, if anything which can't happen came to pass, no one would raise any objection to my taking advantage of it. You know, you're getting too generous.'

'That's better,' said Adèle. 'A moment ago we were cold-blooded.'

Berry winced.

'I take it back,' he said humbly. 'Your central heating arrangements, at any rate, are in perfect order. Unless your heart was glowing, your soft little cheek wouldn't be half so warm.'

'I don't know about that,' said Adèle, straightening her back. 'But we try to be sporting. And that's your fault,' she added. 'You've taught us.'

The applause which greeted this remark was interrupted by the entry of a waiter bearing some letters which had been forwarded from Pau.

A registered package, for which Berry was requested to sign, set us all thinking.

'Whatever is it?' said Daphne.

'I can't imagine,' replied her husband, scrutinising the postmark. ' "Paris"? I've ordered nothing from Paris that I can remember.'

'Open it quick,' said Jonah. 'Perhaps it's some wherewithal.'

Berry hacked at the string. . . .

The next instant he leaped to his feet.

'Fate!' he shrieked. 'Fate! I told you my luck was in!' He turned to his wife breathlessly. ' 'Member those Premium Bonds you wanted me to go in for? Over a month ago I applied for twenty-five. I'd forgotten about the trash – and *here they are!*'

Two hours and a half had gone by, and we were rounding a tremendous horseshoe bend on the way to Zarauz, when my wife touched Berry upon the arm.

'Aren't you excited?' she said.

'Just a trifle,' he answered. 'But I'm trying to thread it under. It's essential that I should keep cool. When you're arm in arm with fortune, you're apt to lose your head. And then you're done. The jade'll give me my cues – I'm sure of it. But she won't shout them. I've got to keep my eyes skinned and my ears pricked, if I'm going to pick them up.'

'If I,' said Adèle, 'were in your shoes, I should be just gibbering.'

It was, indeed, a queer business.

The dramatic appearance of the funds had startled us all. Had they arrived earlier, had they come in the shape of something less easily negotiable than Bearer Bonds, had they been representing more or less than precisely the very sum which Berry had named in his appeal, we might have labelled the matter 'Coincidence', and thought no more of it. Such a label, however, refused to stick. The affair ranked with thunder out of a cloudless sky.

As for my sister, with the wind taken out of her sails, she had hauled down her flag. The thing was too hard for her.

It was Jonah who had sprung a mine in the midst of our amazement.

'Stop!' he had cried. 'Where's yesterday's paper? Those things are Premium Bonds, and, unless I'm utterly mistaken, there was a drawing two days ago. One of those little fellows may be worth a thousand pounds.'

The paper had confirmed his report. . . .

The thought that, but for his wit, we might have released such substance to clutch at such a shadow, had set us all twittering more than ever.

At once a council had been held.

Finally it had been decided to visit a bank and, before we disposed of the Bonds, to ask for and search the official bulletin in which are published the results of all Government Lottery Draws.

Inquiry, however, had revealed that the day was some sort of a holiday, and that no banks would be open. . . .

At last a financier was unearthed – a changer of money. In execrable French he had put himself at our service.

Yes, he had the bulletin. It had arrived this morning . . .

Feverishly we searched its pages.

Once we had found the column, a glance was enough. Our Bonds bore consecutive numbers, of which the first figure was 'O'. The series appeared to be unfortunate. The winning list contained not a single representative.

More reassured than disappointed, we raised the question of a loan.

Our gentleman picked at the Bonds and wrinkled his nose. After a little, he offered one hundred pounds.

This was absurd, and we said so.

The Bonds were worth two hundred and fifty pounds, and were as good as hard cash. The fellow had no office, and, when we wanted him again, as like as not he would have disappeared. His personal appearance was against him.

When we protested, his answer came pat.

He was no money-lender. In the last ten years he had not advanced ten pesetas. He was a changer of money, a broker, and nothing else.

Finally he offered one hundred and fifty pounds – at sixty per cent, a year *or part of a year*.

For one so ignorant of usury, this was not bad. We thanked him acidly, offered the Bonds for sale, and, after a little calculation, accepted two hundred and forty-three pounds in Spanish notes.

Half an hour later we had climbed into the cars, anxious to make the most of our last day in Spain . . .

If the way to Zarauz was handsome, that from Zarauz to Zumaya was fit for a king. Take us a range of mountains – bold, rugged, precipitous, and bring the sea to their foot – no ordinary sea, sirs, but ocean himself, the terrible Atlantic to wit, in all his glory. And there, upon the boundary itself, where his proud waves are stayed, build us a road, a curling shelf of a road, to follow the line of that most notable indenture, witnessing the covenant 'twixt land and sea, settled when time was born.

Above us, the ramparts of Spain – below, an echelon of rollers, ceaselessly surging to their doom – before us, a ragged wonder of coast-line, rising and falling and thrusting into the distance, till the snarling leagues shrank into murmuring inches and tumult dwindled into rest – on our right, the might, majesty, dominion and power of ocean, a limitless laughing mystery of running white and blue, shining and swaying and swelling till the eye faltered before so much magnificence and sky let fall her curtain to spare the failing sight – for over six miles we hung upon the edge of Europe. . . .

Little wonder that we sailed into Zumaya – all red roofs, white walls and royal-blue timbers – with full hearts, flushed and exulting. The twenty precious minutes which had just gone by were charged with the spirit of the Odyssey.

Arrived at the village, we stopped, to wait for the others. So soon as they came, we passed on slowly along the road to Deva. Perhaps a mile from Zumaya we ate our lunch. . . .

The comfortable hush which should succeed a hearty meal made in the open air upon a summer's day was well established. Daphne and Adèle were murmuring conversation; in a low voice Jill was addressing Berry and thinking of Piers; pipe in mouth, Jonah was blinking into a pair of field-glasses, and I was lying flat upon my back, neither smoking nor sleeping, but gradually losing consciousness with a cigarette in my hand.

I had come to the point of postponing through sheer lethargy the onerous duty of lifting the cigarette to my lips, when, with an oath that ripped the air, Jonah started to his feet.

Sleep went flying.

I sat up amazedly, propping myself on my hands. . . .

With dropped jaw, my cousin was staring through the glasses as a man who is looking upon sudden death. While I watched, he lowered them, peered into the distance, clapped them again to his eyes, let them fall, glanced swiftly to right and left, shut his mouth with a snap, and made a dash for the cars. . . .

With his hand upon Ping's door, he turned and pointed a trembling forefinger along the valley.

'There's Zed,' he cried. 'My horse. Haven't seen him since Cambrai. Leading a team, and they're flogging him.'

I fancy he knew I should join him, for he never closed Ping's door. As he changed into second, I swung myself inboard. A moment later we were flying along the dusty road. . . .

Zed had been Jonah's charger for over three years. Together, for month after month, the two had endured the rough and revelled in the smooth. They had shared misery, and they had shared ease. Together, many times, they had passed through the Valley of the Shadow of Death. And, while the animal must have loved Jonah, my cousin was devoted to the horse. At last came Cambrai. . . .

Jonah was shot through the knee and sent to England. And Zed – poor Zed disappeared.

My cousin's efforts to trace him were superhuman. Unhappily his groom had been killed when Jonah was wounded, and, though all manner of authorities, from the Director of Remounts downwards, had lent their official aid, though a most particular description had been circulated and special instructions issued to all the depots through which the horses might pass, to his lasting grief Jonah had never heard of Zed again.

And now. . . . I found myself praying that he had not been mistaken.

Jonah was driving like a man possessed.

We tore up a rise, whipped round a bend and, coming suddenly upon a road on our right, passed it with locked wheels.

The noise my cousin made, as he changed into reverse, showed that his love for Zed was overwhelming.

We shot backward, stopped, stormed to the right and streaked up a shocking road at forty-five. . . . We flashed into a hamlet, turned at right angles, missed a waggon by an inch and flung up a frightful track towards a farm. . . .

Then, before I knew what had happened, we had stopped dead, and Jonah's door was open and he was limping across the road.

In the jaws of a rude gateway stood a waggon of stones. Harnessed to this were three sorry-looking mules and, leading them, the piteous wreck of what had been a blue roan. The latter was down – and out.

For this the immediate reason was plain.

The teamster, better qualified for the treadmill, had so steered his waggon that the hub of its off fore wheel had met the gatepost. This he had not observed, but, a firm believer in the omnipotency of the lash, had determined to reduce the check, whatever might be its cause, by methods of blood and iron. Either because he was the most convenient or by virtue of his status, the leader had received the brunt of the attack. That is, of course, one way of driving . . .

The blue roan was down, and his master had just kicked him in the belly when Jonah arrived.

The Spaniard was a big fellow, but my cousin has wrists of steel. . . . He took the whip from its owner as one takes a toy from a baby. Then with the butt he hit him across the mouth. The Spaniard reeled, caught his foot on a stone and fell heavily. Jonah threw down the whip and took off his coat.

'I don't want to kill him,' he said quietly.

When the other rose, he looked extremely ugly. This was largely due to the fact that most of his front teeth were missing and that it was difficult, because of the blood, to see exactly where his face ended and his mouth began. The look in his eyes, however, was suggesting the intent to kill.

He had no idea, of course, that he was facing perhaps the one man living who could have thrashed a champion. . . .

It is not often that you will see half a dozen of the most illustrious members of the National Sporting Club attending an Assault-at-Arms held at a public school. Three years running I had that honour. The gentlemen came to see Jonah. And though no applause was allowed during the boxing, they always broke the rule . . . In due season my cousin went to Oxford. . . . In his second year, in the Inter-University contest, he knocked his opponent out in seven seconds. The latter remained unconscious for more than six hours, each crawling one of which took a year off Jonah's life. From that day my cousin never put on the gloves again . . .

All, however, that the Spaniard saw was a tall, lazy-looking man with a game leg, who by his gross interference had taken him by surprise.

He lowered his head and actually ran upon his fate. . . .

I have never seen 'punishment' at once so frightful and so punctiliously administered. Jonah worked with the swift precision of the surgeon about the operating table. He confessed afterwards that his chief concern was to keep his opponent too blind with rage to see the wisdom of capitulation. He need not have worried. . . .

When it had become obvious that the blessed gifts of sight, smell, and hearing had been almost wholly withdrawn from the gentleman, when, in fact, he had practically ceased attempting to defend himself, and merely bellowed with mortification at every stinging blow, Jonah knocked him sprawling on to the midden, and drew off his wash-leather gloves.

The next moment he was down on his knees beside the roan plucking at the rough harness with trembling fingers.

Once the horse sought to rise, but at Jonah's word he stopped and laid down his head.

Between us we got him clear. Then we stood back, and Jonah called him.

With a piteous effort the roan got upon his legs. That there was back trouble and at least one hock was sprung I saw at a glance. The horse had been broken down. He was still blowing badly, and I ran for the flask in the car. When I came back Jonah was caressing his charger with tears running down his cheeks. . . .

There is a listlessness, born of harsh treatment, sucked on dying hopes, reared on the bitter memory of happier days, which is more eloquent than tears. There is an air of frozen misery, of a despair so deep that a kind word has come to lose its meaning, which none but horses wear.

Looking upon Zed, I felt ashamed to be a man.

Gaunt, filthy, and tottering, the flies mercilessly busy about three shocking sores, the roan was presenting a terrible indictment to be filed against the Day of Judgment. '. . . And not one of them is forgotten before God. . . .' But there was worse than pain of body here. The dull, see-nothing eyes, the heavy-laden head, the awful stricken mien, told of a tragedy to make the angels weep – an English thoroughbred, not dead, but with a broken heart. We had administered the brandy, Jonah was bathing a sore, and I had made a wisp and was rubbing Zed down, when –

'Good day,' said a voice. With his arms folded upon the sill, a little grey-headed man was watching us from a window.

I looked up and nodded.

'Good day,' I said.

'Ah like boxing,' said the man. 'Ah've bin twelve years in the States, an' Ah'd rather see boxing than a bull-fight. You like baseball?'

I shook my head.

'I've never seen it,' I said.

'Haven't missed much,' was the reply. 'But Ah like boxing. You visiting Spain?'

'For a few days.'

''S a fine country. Bin to Sevilla?'

Entirely ignoring the violence which he had just witnessed, to say nothing of our trespass upon his property and our continued attention to his horse, the farmer proceeded to discuss the merits and shortcomings of Spain with as much detached composure as if we had met him in a tavern.

At length Jonah got up.

'Will you sell me this horse?'

'Yes,' said the man, 'Ah will.'

'What d'you want for him?'

'Five hundred pesetas.'

'Right,' said Jonah. 'Have you got a halter?'

The man disappeared. Presently he emerged from a door, halter in hand.

The twenty pounds passed, and Zed was ours.

Tenderly my cousin fitted the halter about the drooping head.

'One more effort, old chap,' he said gently, turning towards the gate. . . .

Out of compassion for the mules, I drew the farmer's attention to the hub which was nursing the gatepost.

He just nodded.

'Pedro could never drive,' he said.

'I should get a new carter,' I said.

He shrugged his shoulders. Then he jerked his head in the direction of the carcase upon the midden.

'He is my step-father. We do not speak,' he said simply.

We found the others in the hamlet through which we had passed. There I handed over Ping to Adèle, and thence Jonah and Zed and I walked to Zumaya.

To find a box at the station was more than we had dared hope for, but there it was – empty and waiting to be returned to San Sebastian. Beneath the influence of twenty-five pesetas, the station-master saw no good reason why it should not be returned by the evening train.

We left Jonah to accompany his horse and hurried home by car to seek a stable.

When we sat down to dinner that night at eight o'clock Jonah called for the wine-list and ordered a magnum of champagne.

When the wine was poured, he raised his glass and looked at me.

'Thank you for helping me,' he said. He glanced round with his eyes glowing. 'And all of you for being so glad.' He drank and touched Adèle upon the shoulder. 'In a loose-box, up to his knees in straw, with an armful of hay to pick over, and no congestion. . . . Have you ever felt you wanted to get up and dance?' He turned to Berry. 'Brother, your best. May you spot the winner tonight, as I did this afternoon.'

'Thank you,' said Berry, 'thank you. I must confess I'd been hoping for some sort of intuition as to what to do. But I've not had a hint so far. Perhaps, when I get to the table . . . It's silly, of course. One mustn't expect too much, but I had the feeling that I was going to be given a tip. You know. Like striking a dud egg, and then putting your shirt on a horse called "Attar of Roses". . . . Never mind. Let's talk about something else. Why did you call him "Zed"?'

'Short for "Zero",' said Jonah. 'I think my groom started it, and I – '

'Zero,' said Berry quietly. 'I'm much obliged.'

It was a quarter to eleven, and Berry had lost one hundred and seventy pounds.

Across her husband's back Daphne threw me a despairing glance. Upon the opposite side of the table, Adèle and Jill, one upon either side of Jonah, stared miserably before them. I lit my tenth cigarette and wondered what Berry had done. . . .

The table was crowded.

From their points of vantage the eight croupiers alternately did their business and regarded the assembly with a bored air.

A beautifully dressed American, who had been losing, observed the luck of her neighbour, a burly Dutchman, with envious eyes. With a remonstrance in every finger-tip, a debonair Frenchman was laughingly upbraiding his fellow for giving him bad advice. From above his horn-rimmed spectacles an old gentleman in a blue suit watched the remorseless rake jerk his five pesetas into 'the Bank' in evident annoyance. Cheek by jowl with a dainty Englishwoman, who reminded me irresistibly of a Dresden shepherdess, a Spanish Jew, who had won, was explosively disputing with the croupier the amount of his stake. Two South Americans were leaning across the table, nonchalantly 'plastering the board'. A little old lady, with an enormous bag, was thanking an elegant Spaniard for disposing her stake as she desired. Finger to lip, a tall Spanish girl in a large black hat was sizing her remaining counters with a faint frown. A very young couple, patently upon their honeymoon, were conferring excitedly . . .

'*Hagan juego, Señores.*'

The conference between the lovers became more intense.

'*Esta heco?*'

'Oh, be quick!' cried the girl. 'Between "7" and "8", Bill. Between . . .'

As the money went on –

'*No va mas,*' cried the croupier in charge.

Two pairs of eyes peered at the revolving wheel. They did not notice that the Dutchman, plunging at the last moment upon 'MANQUE', had touched their counter with his cuff and moved it to '9'.

The ball lost its momentum, poppled across the ridges, and leaped to rest.

'*Nueve.*'

Two faces fell. I wondered if a new frock had vanished into air. . . .

With the edge of his rake a croupier was tapping their counter and looking round for the claimant.

For a second the Jew peered about him. Then he pointed to himself and stretched out his hand.

I called to the croupier in French.

'No. It belongs to Monsieur and Madame. I saw what happened. That gentleman moved it with his cuff.'

'*Merci, Monsieur.*'

With a sickly leer the pretender rallied the croupier, confidentially assured the dainty Englishwoman that he did not care, and, laughing a little too heartily, waved the thirty-five pounds towards their bewildered owners.

'B-but it isn't mine,' stammered the boy.

'Yes,' I said, smiling. 'Your counter was moved. I saw the whole thing.' I hesitated. Then, 'If you'll take an old hand's advice, you'll stop now. A thing like that's invariably the end of one's luck.'

I was not 'an old hand', and I had no authority for my dictum. My interference was unpardonable. When the two stopped to thank me, as they passed from the room, I felt like a criminal. Still, they looked very charming; and, after all, a frock on the back is worth a score at the dressmaker's.

'I am going,' said Berry, 'to suspend my courtship and smoke a cigarette. Possibly I'm going too strong. If I give the lady a rest, she may think more of me.'

'I suppose,' said Daphne, 'you're bent on losing it all.'

Her husband frowned.

'Fortune favours the bold,' he said shortly. 'You see, she's just proving me. If I were to falter, she'd turn me down.'

It was impossible not to admire such confidence.

I bade my sister take heart.

'Much,' I concluded, 'may be done with forty pounds.'

'Fifty,' corrected Berry. 'And now let's change the subject. How d'you pronounce Lwow? Or would you rather tell me a fairy tale?'

I shook my head.

'My power,' I said, 'of concentration is limited.'

'Then I must,' said Berry. 'It's fatal to brood over your fortune.' He sat back in his chair and let the smoke make its own way out of his mouth. 'There was once a large king. It wasn't his fault. The girth went with the crown. All the Koppabottemburgs were enormous. Besides, it went very well with his subjects. Looking upon him, they felt they were getting their money's worth. A man of simple tastes, his favourite hobby was fowls.

'One day, just as he'd finished cleaning out the fowl-house, he found that he'd run out of maize. So he slipped on his invisible cloak and ran round to the grocer's. He always wore his invisible cloak when shopping. He found it cheaper.

'Well, the grocer was just recovering from the spectacle of two pounds of the best maize shoving themselves into a brown paper bag and pushing off down the High Street, when a witch came in. The grocer's heart sank into his boots. He hated witches. If you weren't civil, before you knew where you were, you were a three-legged toad or a dew pond or something. So you had to be civil. As for their custom – well, it wasn't worth having. They wouldn't look at bacon, unless you'd guarantee that the pig had been killed on a moonless Friday with the wind in the North, and as for pulled figs, if you couldn't swear that the box had been crossed by a one-eyed man whose father had committed arson in a pair of brown boots, you could go and bury them under the lilacs.

'This time, however, the grocer was pleasantly surprised.

' "I didn't know," said the witch, "that you were under the patronage of Royalty."

' "Oh, didn't you?" said the grocer. "Why, the Master of the Horse has got his hoof-oil here for nearly two days now."

' "Master of the Horse be snookered," said the witch. "I'm talking about the King."

' "The K-King?" stammered the grocer.

' "Oh, cut it out," said the witch, to whom an invisible cloak meant nothing. "No doubt you've been told to keep it quiet, but I don't count. And I'll bet you did the old fool over his maize."

'The grocer's brain worked very rapidly. The memory of a tin of mixed biscuits and half a Dutch cheese, which had floated out of his shop only the day before, and numerous other recollections of mysteriously animated provisions, came swarming into his mind. At length –

' "We never charge Royalty," he said loftily.

' "Oh, don't you?" snapped the witch. "Well, supposing you change this broomstick. You swore blue it was cut on a rainless Tuesday from an ash that had supported a murderer with a false nose. The very first time I used it, it broke at six thousand feet. I was over the sea at the time, and had to glide nearly four miles to make a landing. Can you b-beat it?"

'When the grocer put up his shutters two hectic hours later, he was a weary man. In the interval he had been respectively a toad, a picture postcard, and a tin of baked beans. And somebody had knocked him off the counter during his third metamorphosis, so he felt like death. All the same, before going to bed, he sat down and wrote to the Lord Chamberlain, asking for permission to display the Royal Arms. Just to make it quite clear that he wasn't relying on hoof-oil, he added that he was shortly expecting a fine consignment of maize and other commodities.

'The postscript settled it.

'The permission was granted, the king "dealt" elsewhere in future, and the witch was given three hours to leave the kingdom. So the grocer lost his two worst customers and got the advertisement of his life. Which goes to show, my children, that if only – Hullo! Here's a new shift.'

It was true.

The eight croupiers were going off duty. As they vacated their seats, eight other gentlemen in black immediately replaced them.

Berry extinguished his cigarette and handed me his last bunch of notes. In exchange for these, with the peculiar delicacy of his kind, the croupier upon my right selected, arrayed and offered me counters of the value of forty English pounds.

He might have been spared his pains.

As I was piling the money by Berry's side –

'*Zero*,' announced a nasal voice.

'We're off,' said my brother-in-law. 'Will you see that they pay me right?'

One hundred and seventy-five pounds.

Ere I had completed my calculation –

'*Zero*,' repeated the nasal voice.

'I said so,' said Berry, raising his eyebrows. 'I had the maximum that time. Will you be so good? Thank you.'

Trembling with excitement, I started to count the equivalent of four hundred and ninety pounds.

Berry was addressing the croupier.

'No. Don't touch the stake. She's not finished yet.'

'*Esta hecho?*'

'Don't leave it all,' begged Daphne. 'Take – '

'*No va mas.*'

Desperately I started to check the money again. . . .

'*Zero.*'

There was a long gasp of wonderment, immediately followed by a buzz of exclamation. The croupiers were smiling. Jill was jumping up and down in her seat. Adèle was shaking Jonah by the arm. My sister was clinging to Berry, imploring him to 'stop now'. The two Frenchmen were laughing and nodding their congratulations. The little old lady was bowing and beaming goodwill. Excepting, perhaps, the croupiers, Berry seemed less concerned than anyone present.

'No. I'm not going to stop,' he said gently, 'because that would be foolish. But I'll give it a miss this time, because it's not coming up. It's no longer a question of guessing, dear. I tell you, I *know*.'

The ball went flying.

After a moment's interval –

'*Ocho* (eight),' announced the croupier.

'You see,' said Berry. 'I should have lost my money. Now, this time my old friend Zero will come along.'

On to the white-edged rectangle went fourteen pounds.

A few seconds later I was receiving four hundred and ninety. . . .

I began to feel dazed. As for counting the money, it was out of the question. Idiotically I began to arrange the counters in little piles. . . .

'35' turned up.

'That's right,' said Berry quietly. 'And now . . . It's really very monotonous, but . . .'

With a shrug of his shoulders, he set the limit on 'Zero'.

I held my breath. . . .

The ball ceased to rattle – began to fall – ricocheted from stud to stud – tumbled into the wheel – nosed '32' – and . . . fell with a click into '0'.

Berry spread out his hands.

'I tell you,' he said, 'it's too easy. . . . And now, again.'

'Don't!' cried Daphne. 'Don't! I beg you – '

'My darling,' said Berry, 'after tonight – No. Leave the stake, please – I'll never play again. This evening – well, the money's there, and we may as well have it, mayn't we? I mean, it isn't as if I hadn't been given the tip. From the moment I woke this morning –Listen dear. Don't bother about the wheel – the lady's been hammering away. You must admit, she's done the job thoroughly. First the intuition: then the wherewithal: then what to back. I should be a bottle-nosed mug if I didn't – '

'*Zero*.'

Upon the explosion of excitement which greeted the astounding event, patrons of the baccarat table and of the other roulette wheel left their seats and came crowding open-mouthed to see what was toward. Complete strangers were chattering like old friends. Gibbering with emotion, the Spanish Jew was dramatically recounting what had occurred. The Dutchman was sitting back, laughing boisterously. The Frenchmen were waving and crying, '*Vive l'Angleterre!*' Jonah was shouting as though he had been in the hunting field. Adèle and Jill were beating upon the table.

Berry bowed his acknowledgements.

As in a dream, I watched them send for more money.

When it arrived, they gave me four hundred and ninety pounds.

'*Hagan juego, Señores*.'

Berry shook his head.

'Not this time,' he said quietly.

He was right. After a look at '0' the ball ran with a click into '15'.

A long sigh of relief followed its settlement.

'You see?' said Berry, picking up fourteen pounds. . . .

'Don't,' I said weakly. 'Don't. I can't bear it. The board's bewitched. If it turns up again, I shall collapse.'

'You mean that?' said Berry, putting the money on.

'*No va mas*.'

'I do. My heart – '

'Then say your prayers,' said my brother-in-law. 'For, as I live, that ball's going to pick out – '

'*Zero*.'

I never remember such a scene.

Everybody in the room seemed to be shouting. I know I was. Respectable Spaniards stamped upon the floor like bulls. The Frenchmen, who with Berry and several others had backed the winner, were clasping one another and singing the Marseillaise. The beautifully dressed American was wringing Adèle's hand. The old gentleman in the blue suit was on his feet and appeared to be making a speech. The Spanish girl was standing upon her chair, waving a handkerchief. . . .

In vain the smiling croupiers appealed for order. . . .

As the tumult subsided –

'Seven times in ten spins,' said Berry. 'Well, I think that'll do. We'll just run up the board on the even chances. . . .'

There was no holding him.

Before I knew where I was, he had set twelve thousand pesetas apiece on 'RED' 'ODD', and 'UNDER 19'.

Some fourteen hundred pounds on a single spin.

I covered my eyes. . . .

As the ball began to lose way, the hush was awful. . . .

'*Siete* (seven),' announced the spokesman.

With my brain whirling, I sought to garner the harvest. . . .

My brother-in-law rose to his feet.

'One last throw,' he said. ' "PASSE" for "The Poor".'

He leaned forward and put the maximum on 'OVER 18'.

A moment later, counter by counter, four hundred and seventy pounds went into the poor-box.

As I pushed back my chair, I glanced at my watch.

In exactly sixteen minutes Berry had stung 'the Bank' to the tune of – as near as I could make it – four thousand nine hundred and ninety-five pounds.

Some ten hours later we slipped out of San Sebastian and on to the famous road which leads to Biarritz. Berry, Daphne, and Jill were in one car, and Adèle and I were in the other. Jonah and Zed were to travel together by train. It was improbable that they would leave for Pau before the morrow.

As we climbed out of Béhobie, we took our last look at Spain, that realm of majestic distances and superb backgrounds. . . .

You may peer into the face of France and find it lovely; the more you magnify an English landscape, the richer it will become, but to find the whole beauty of Spain a man must stand back and lift up his eyes.

Now that we had left it behind, the pride and grandeur of the scenery beggared description. It was as though for days we had been looking upon a mighty canvas, and while we had caught something of its splendour, now for the first time had we focussed it aright. The memory we took away was that of a masterpiece.

Anxious to be home in time for luncheon, I laid hold of the wheel. . . .

We whipped through St Jean-de-Luz, sang through Bidart, and hobbled over a fearful stretch of metalling into Bayonne. . . .

As we were nearing Bidache –

'How much,' said Adèle suddenly, 'is Berry actually up?'

'Allowing for everything,' said I, 'that is, his losses, what he gave to the poor, and the various rates of exchange, about two hundred and forty thousand francs.'

'Not so dusty,' said Adèle thoughtfully. 'All the same – '

A report like that of a gun blew the sentence to blazes.

Heavily I took the car in to the side of the road. . . .

A second tyre went upon the outskirts of Pau.

Happily we had two spare wheels. . . .

As I was wearily resuming my seat, Berry, Daphne, and Jill went by with a cheer.

Slowly we followed them into the town . . .

It was not until we were stealing up our own villa's drive that at length I remembered the question which for over an hour I had been meaning to put to my wife.

As I brought the car to a standstill –

'What was it,' I demanded, 'that you had begun to say when we had the first burst near Bidache? We were talking about how much Berry was up, and you said – '

The most blood-curdling yell that I have ever heard fell upon our ears.

For a moment we stared at one another.

Then we fell out of the car by opposite doors and flew up the steps. . . .

Extended upon a chair in the hall, Berry was bellowing, clawing at his temples and drumming with his heels upon the floor.

Huddled together, Daphne and Jill were poring over a letter with starting eyes.

Dear Sir,

In case the fact has not already come to your notice, we hasten to inform you that as a result of the drawing, which took place on Monday last, one of the Premium Bonds, which we yesterday dispatched to you per registered post, has won the first prize of fr.500,000 (five hundred thousand francs).

By way of confirmation, we beg to enclose a cutting from the official Bulletin.

We should, perhaps, point out that, in all announcements of the results of drawings, the '0' or 'zero', which for some reason invariably precedes the number of a Premium Bond, is disregarded.

Awaiting the pleasure of your instructions,

We beg to remain, dear sir,

Your obedient servants.

It was perhaps five hours later that my memory again responded, and I turned to Adèle.

'The dam burst,' said I, 'at the very moment when you were going to tell me what you had been about to say when the first tyre went outside Bidache. Sounds like "The House that Jack built", doesn't it?'

'Oh, I know,' said Adèle, laughing. 'But it's no good now. I was going to say – '

The door opened, and Falcon came in with a wire.

I picked up the form and weighed it thoughtfully.

'Wonderfully quick,' I said. 'It was half-past two when I was at the Bank, and I couldn't have been at the Post Office before a quarter to three. I looked at my watch. Just under four hours.'

'The Bank?' said Adèle, staring. 'But you said you were going to the Club.'

I nodded.

'I know. I was anxious to raise no false hopes. All the same, I couldn't help feeling that half a million francs were worth a tenpenny wire. Therefore I telegraphed to Jonah. His answer will show whether that tenpenny wire was worth half a million francs.'

My wife snatched the form from my hand and tore it open.

It was very short.

Bonds repurchased. Jonah.

But my memory never recovered from the twofold slight.

To this day I cannot remember to ask Adèle what it was that she had been about to say when the first tyre burst outside Bidache.

NO THOROUGHFARE

'I confess,' said Berry, 'that the idea of having a few chairs about in which you can sit continuously for ten minutes, not so much in comfort as without fear of contracting a bed-sore or necrosis of the coccyx, appeals to me. Compared with most of the "sitzplatz" in this here villa, an ordinary church pew is almost voluptuous. The beastly things seemed designed to promote myalgia.'

'Yet they do know,' said I. 'The French, I mean. Look at their beds.'

'Exactly,' replied my brother-in-law. 'That's the maddening part of it. Every french bed is an idyll – a poem of repose. The upholsterer puts his soul into its creation. A born genius, he expresses himself in beds. The rest of the junk he turns out . . .' He broke off and glanced about the room. His eye lighted upon a couch, lozenge-shaped, hog-backed, featuring the Greek key pattern in brown upon a brick-red ground and surrounded on three sides by a white balustrade some three inches high. 'Just consider that throne. Does it or does it not suggest collusion between a private-school workshop, a bricklayer's labourer, and the Berlin branch of the YWCA?'

'If,' said Daphne, 'it was only the chairs, I wouldn't mind. But it's everything. The sideboard, for instance – '

'Ah,' said her husband, 'my favourite piece. The idea of a double cabin-washstand is very beautifully carried out. I'm always expecting Falcon to press something and a couple of basins to appear. Then we can wash directly after the asparagus.'

'The truth is,' said Adèle, 'these villas are furnished to be let. And when you've said that you've said everything.'

'I agree,' said I. 'And if we've liked Pau enough to come back next autumn, the best thing to do is to have a villa of our own. I'm quite ready to face another three winters here, and, if everyone else is, it 'ld be worth while. As for furniture, we can easily pick out enough from Cholmondeley Street and White Ladies.'

There was a moment's silence.

Then –

'I'm on,' said Jonah, who had caught three splendid salmon in the last two days. 'This place suits me.'

'And me,' said Adèle warmly.

My sister turned to her husband.

'What d'you think, old chap?'

Berry smiled beatifically. A far-away look came into his eyes.

'I shall personally superintend,' he announced, 'the removal and destruction of the geyser.'

Amid some excitement the matter was then and there decided.

The more we thought upon it, the sounder seemed the idea. The place suited us all. To have our things about us would be wholly delightful. Provided we meant for the future to winter abroad, we should save money.

Pleasedly we proceeded to lunch.

Throughout the meal we discussed what manner of house ours must be, its situation, dimensions, aspect. We argued amiably about its garden and curtilage. We determined to insist upon two bathrooms. By the time the cheese was served, we had selected most of the furniture and were bickering good-temperedly about the style of the wallpapers.

Then we rang up a house agent, to learn that he had no unfurnished villa 'to let' upon his books. He added gratuitously that, except for a ruined château upon the other side of Tarbes, he had nothing 'for sale', either.

So soon as we had recovered, we returned to the charge . . .

The third agent we addressed was not quite certain. There was, he said, a house in the town – *très solide, très serieuse, dans un quartier chic*. It would, he thought, be to our liking. It had, for instance, *une salle de fête superbe*. He was not sure, however, that it was still available. A French gentleman was much attracted, and had visited it three times.

We were greatly disgusted and said so. We did not want a house in the town. We wanted. . . .

Finally we succumbed to his entreaties and promised to view the villa, if it was still in the market. He was to ring us up in ten minutes' time. . . .

So it happened that half an hour later we were standing curiously before the great iron gates of a broad shuttered mansion in the Rue

Mazagran, Pau, while the agent was alternately pealing the bell for the caretaker and making encouraging gestures in our direction.

Viewed from without, the villa was not unpleasing. It looked extremely well-built, it stood back from the pavement, it had plenty of elbow room. The street itself was as silent as the tomb. Perhaps, if we could find nothing else . . . We began to wonder whether you could see the mountains from the second floor.

At last a caretaker appeared, I whistled to Nobby, and we passed up a short well-kept drive.

A moment later we had left the sunlight behind and had entered a huge dim hall.

'Damp,' said Berry instantly, snuffing the air. 'Damp for a monkey. I can smell the good red earth.'

Daphne sniffed thoughtfully.

'I don't think so,' she said. 'When a house has been shut up like this, it's bound to – '

'It's wonderful,' said her husband, 'what you can't smell when you don't want to. Never mind. If you want to live over water, I don't care. But don't say I didn't warn you. Besides, it'll save us money. We can grow moss on the floors instead of carpets.'

'It does smell damp,' said Adèle, 'but there's central heating. See?' She pointed to a huge radiator. 'If that works as it should, it'll make your carpets fade.'

Berry shrugged his shoulders.

'I see what it is,' he said. 'You two girls have scented cupboards. I never yet knew a woman who could resist cupboards. In a woman's eyes a superfluity of cupboards can transform the most poisonous habitation into a desirable residence. If you asked a woman what was the use of a staircase, she'd say, "To put cupboards under." '

By now the shutters had been opened, and we were able to see about us. As we were glancing round, the caretaker shuffled to a door beneath the stairs.

'*Voici une armoire magnifique*,' she announced. '*Il y en a beaucoup d'autres*.'

As we passed through the house, we proved the truth of her words. I have never seen so many cupboards to the square mile in all my life.

My wife and my sister strove to dissemble their delight. At length Cousin Jill, however, spoke frankly enough.

'They really are beautiful. Think of the room they give. You'll be able to put everything away.'

Berry turned to me.

'Isn't it enough to induce a blood-clot? "Beautiful". Evil-smelling recesses walled up with painted wood. Birthplaces of mice. Impregnable hot-beds of vermin. And who wants "to put everything away"?'

'Hush,' said I. 'They can't help it. Besides – Hullo! Here's another bathroom.'

'Without a bath,' observed my brother-in-law. 'How very convenient! Of course, you're up much quicker, aren't you? I suppose the idea is not to keep people waiting. Come along.' We passed into a bedroom. 'Oh, what a dream of a paper! "Who Won the Boat-race, or The Battle of the Blues". Fancy waking up here after a heavy night. I suppose the designer was found "guilty, but insane". That's fifty-nine. And yet another? Oh, no. The back-stairs, of course. As before, approached by a door which slides to and fro with a gentle rumbling noise, instead of swinging. The same warranted to jam if opened hastily. Can't you hear Falcon on the wrong side with a butler's tray full of glass, wondering why he was born? Oh, and the bijou spiral leads to the box-room, does it? I see. Adèle's American trunks, especially the five-foot cube, will go up there beautifully. Falcon will like this house, won't he?'

'I wish to goodness you'd be quiet,' said Daphne. 'I want to think.'

'It's not me,' said her husband. 'It's that Inter-University wallpaper. And now where's the tower? I suppose that's approached by a wire rope with knots in it?'

'What tower?' said Adèle.

'*The* tower. The feature of the house. Or was it a ballroom?'

'Ah,' I cried, 'the ballroom! I'd quite forgotten.' I turned to the agent. '*Vous n'avez pas dit qu'il y avait une salle de fête?*'

'*Mais oui, Monsieur. Au rez-de-chaussée. Je vous la montrerai tout de suite.*'

We followed him downstairs in single file, and so across the hall to where two tall oak doors were suggesting a picture gallery. For a moment the fellow fumbled at their lock. Then he pushed the two open.

I did not know that, outside a palace, there was such a chamber in all France. Of superb proportions, the room was panelled from floor to ceiling with oak – richly carved oak – and every handsome panel was outlined with gold. The ceiling was all of oak, fretted with gold. The floor was of polished oak, inlaid with ebony. At the end of the room three lovely pillars upheld a minstrels' gallery, while opposite a stately oriel yawned a tremendous fireplace, with two stone seraphim for jambs.

In answer to our bewildered inquiries, the agent explained excitedly that the villa had been built upon the remains of a much older house, and that, while the other portions of the original mansion had disappeared, this great chamber and the basement were still surviving. But that was all. Beyond that it was once a residence of note, he could tell us nothing.

Rather naturally, we devoted more time to the ballroom than to all the rest of the house. Against our saner judgment, the possession of the apartment attracted us greatly. It was too vast to be used with comfort as a sitting-room. The occasions upon which we should enjoy it as '*une salle de fête*' would be comparatively few. Four ordinary *salons* would require less service and fuel. Yet, in spite of everything, we wanted it very much.

The rest of the house was convenient. The parlours were fine and airy; there were two bathrooms; the bedrooms were good; the offices were admirable. As for the basement, we lost our way there. It was profound. It was also indubitably damp. There the dank smell upon which Berry had remarked was most compelling. In the garden stood a garage which would take both the cars.

After a final inspection of the ballroom, we tipped the caretaker, promised to let the agent know our decision, and, to the great inconvenience of other pedestrians, strolled talkatively through the streets towards the Boulevard.

'I suppose,' said Adèle, 'those were the other people.'

'Who were what other people?' I demanded.

'The two men standing in the hall as we came downstairs.'

'I never saw them,' said I. 'But if you mean that one of them was the fellow who's after the house, I fancy you're wrong, because the agent told me he'd gone to Bordeaux.'

'Well, I don't know who they were, then,' replied my wife. 'They were talking to the caretaker. I saw them through the banisters. By the time we'd got down, they'd disappeared. Any way, it doesn't matter. Only, if it was them, it looks as if they were thinking pretty seriously about it. You don't go to see a house four times out of curiosity.'

'You mean,' said Berry, 'that if we're fools enough to take it, we'd better get a move on.'

'Exactly. Let's go and have tea at Bouzom's, and thrash it out there.'

No one of us, I imagine, will ever forget that tea.

Crowded about a table intended to accommodate four, we alternately disputed and insulted one another for the better part of two hours. Not once, but twice of her agitation my sister replenished the teapot with Jill's chocolate, and twice fresh tea had to be brought. Berry burned his mouth and dropped an apricot tartlet on to his shoe. Until my disgust was excited by a nauseous taste, I continued to drink from a cup in which Jonah had extinguished a cigarette.

Finally Berry pushed back his chair and looked at his watch.

'Ladies and gentlemen,' he said, 'we came here this memorable afternoon to discuss the advisability of taking a certain messuage – to wit, the Villa Buichi – for the space of three years. As a result of that discussion I have formed certain conclusions. In the first place, I am satisfied that to dwell with you or any of you in the Villa Buichi or any other habitation for the space of three years presents a prospect so horrifying as to belittle Death itself. Secondly, while my main object in visiting the said messuage was to insure, if possible, against the future contraction of some complaint or disease of the hams, I have, I fear, already defeated that object by sitting for upwards of ninety minutes upon a chair which is rather harder than the living rock, and whose surface I have reason to believe is studded with barbs. Thirdly, whilst we are all agreed that a rent of fourteen thousand francs is grotesque, I'd rather pay twice that sum out of my own pocket than continue an argument which threatens to affect my mind. Fourthly, the house is not what we want, or where we want it. The prospect of wassailing in your own comic banqueting hall is alluring, but the French cook believes in oil, and, to us living in the town, every passing breeze will offer indisputable evidence, not only of the lengths to which this belief will go, but of the patriarchal effects which can be obtained by a fearless application of heat to rancid blubber. Fifthly, since we can get nothing else, and the thought of another winter in England is almost as soul-shaking as that of living again amid French furniture, I suppose we'd better take it, always provided they fill up the basement, put on a Mansard roof, add a few cupboards, and reduce the rent. Sixthly, I wish to heaven I'd never seen the blasted place. Lastly, I now propose to repair to the *Cercle Anglais*, or English Club, there in the privacy of the *lavabo* to remove the traces of the preserved apricot recently adhering to my right shoe, and afterwards to ascertain whether a dry Martini, cupped in the mouth, will do something to relieve the agony I am suffering as the direct result of concentrating on this rotten scheme to the exclusion of my bodily needs. But there you are. When the happiness of others is at stake, I forget that I exist.'

With that, he picked up his hat and before we could stop him, walked out of the shop.

With such an avowal ringing in our ears, it was too much to expect that he would remember that he had ordered the tea and had personally consumed seven cakes, not counting the apricot tart.

However. . . .

I followed him to the Club, rang up the agent, and offered to take the house for three years at a rent of twelve thousand francs. He promised to telephone to our villa within the hour.

He was as good as his word.

He telephoned to say that the French gentleman, who had unexpectedly returned from Bordeaux, had just submitted an offer of fourteen thousand francs. He added that, unless we were prepared to offer a higher rent, it would be his duty to accept that proposal.

After a moment's thought, I told him to do his duty and bade him adieu.

That night was so beautiful that we had the cars open.

As we approached the Casino –

'Let's just go up the Boulevard,' said Daphne. 'This is too lovely to leave.'

I slowed up, waited for Jonah to come alongside, and then communicated our intention to continue to take the air.

The Boulevard being deserted, Ping and Pong proceeded slowly abreast. . . .

A sunset which had hung the sky with rose, painted the mountain-tops and turned the west into a blazing smeltery of dreams, had slowly yielded to a night starlit, velvety, breathless, big with the gentle witchcraft of an amber moon. Nature went masked. The depths upon our left seemed bottomless; a grey flash spoke of the Gave de Pau: beyond, the random rise and fall of a high ridge argued the summit of a gigantic screen – the foothills to wit, odd twinkling points of yellow light, seemingly pendent in the air, marking the farms and villas planted about their flanks. And that is all. A row of poplars, certainly, very correct, very slight, very elegant, by the way that we take for Lourdes – the row of poplars should be recorded; the luminous stars also, and a sweet white glow in the heaven, just where the ridge of the foothills cut it across – a trick of the moonlight, no doubt. . . . Sirs, it is no such trick. That misty radiance is the driven snow resting upon the peaks of the Pyrénées. The moon is shining full on them, and, forty miles distant though they are, you see them rendering her light, as will a looking-glass, and by that humble office clothing themselves with unimaginable splendour.

As we stole into the Place Royale –

'Every minute,' announced Adèle, 'I'm more and more thankful that we're quit of the Villa Buichi. We should have been simply mad to have taken a house in the town.'

'There you are,' said Berry. 'My very words. Over and over again I insisted – '

'If you mean,' said Jonah, 'that throughout the argument you confined yourself to destructive criticism, deliberate confusion of the issues, and the recommendation of solutions which you knew to be impracticable, I entirely agree.'

'The trouble with you,' said Berry, 'is that you don't appreciate the value of controversy. I don't blame you. Considering the backlash in your spinal cord, I think you talk very well. It's only when – '

'What exactly,' said Adèle, bubbling, 'is the value of controversy?'

'Its unique ability,' said Berry, 'to produce the truth. The hotter the furnace of argument, the harder the facts which eventually emerge. That's why I never spare myself. I don't pretend it's easy, but then I'm like that. Somebody offers you a drink. The easiest way is to refuse. But I don't. I always ask myself whether my health demands it.'

There was an outraged silence.

Then –

'I have noticed,' I observed, 'that upon such occasions your brain works very fast. Also that you invariably choose the – er – harder path.'

'Nothing is easier,' said Berry, 'than to deride infirmity.' Having compassed the Place Royale, we returned to the Boulevard. 'And now, if you've quite finished maundering over the beauties of a landscape which you can't see, supposing we focussed on the subject with which we set out. I've thought out a new step I want to show you. It's called "The Slip Stitch". Every third beat you stagger and cross your legs above the knee. That shows you've been twice to the Crusades. Then you purl two and cast four off. If you're still together, you get up and repeat to the end of the row knitways, decreasing once at every turn. Then you cast off very loosely.'

Happily the speaker was in the other car, so we broke away and fled up the Rue du Lycée. . . .

The dancing-room was crowded. Every English visitor seemed to be there, but they were not all dancing, and the floor was just pleasantly full.

As we came in, I touched Adèle on the arm.

'Will you dance with me, lass?'

I was not one moment too soon.

As I spoke, two gallants arrived to lodge their claims.

'I've accepted my husband,' said Adèle, smiling.

She had to promise the next and the one after.

Whilst we were dancing, she promised the fourth and the fifth.

'I can see,' said I, 'that I'm in for my usual evening. Of course, we're too highly civilised. I feed you, I lodge you, I clothe you' – I held her off and looked at her – 'yes, with outstanding success. You've a glorious colour, your eyes are like stars, and your frock is a marvel. In fact, you're almost too good to be true. From your wonderful, sweet-smelling hair to the soles of your little pink feet, you're an exquisite production. Whoever did see such a mouth? I suppose you know I married you for your mouth? And your throat? And – but I digress. As I was saying, all this is due to me. If I fed you exclusively on farinaceous food, you'd look pale. If I locked you out of nights, you'd look tired. If I didn't clothe you, you'd look – well, you wouldn't be here, would you? I mean, I know we move pretty fast nowadays, but certain conventions are still observed. Very well, then. I am responsible for your glory. I bring you here, and everybody in the room dances with you, except myself. To complete the comedy, I have only to remind you that I love dancing, and that you are the best dancer in the room. I ask you.'

'That's just what you don't do,' said Adèle, with a maddening smile. 'If you did. . . .'

'But – '

'Certain conventions,' said Adèle, 'are still observed. Have I ever refused you?'

'You couldn't. That's why I don't ask you.'

'O-o-oh, I don't believe you,' said Adèle. 'If it was leap year – '

'Pretend it is.'

' – and I wanted to dance with you – '

'Pretend you do.'

The music stopped with a crash, and a moment later a Frenchman was bowing over my wife's hand.

'May I come for a dance later?' he asked.

'Not this evening. I've promised the next four – '

'There will, I trust, be a fifth?'

' – and after that, I've given my husband the lot. You do understand, don't you? You see, I must keep in with him. He feeds me and lodges me and clothes me and – '

The Frenchman bowed.

'If he has clothed you tonight, Madame, I can forgive him anything.'

We passed to a table at which Berry was superintending the icing of some champagne.

'Ah, there you are!' he exclaimed. 'Had your evening dance? Good. I ordered this little hopeful *pour passer le temps*. They've two more baubles in the offing, and sharp at one-thirty we start on fried eggs and beer. Judging from the contracts into which my wife has entered during the last six minutes, we shall be here till three.' Here he produced and prepared to inflate an air-cushion. 'The great wheeze about these shock-absorbers is not to – '

There was a horrified cry from Daphne and a shriek of laughter from Adèle and Jill.

'I implore you,' said my sister, 'to put that thing away.'

'What thing?' said her husband, applying the nozzle to his lips.

'That cushion thing. How could you – '

'What! Scrap my blow-me-tight?' said Berry. 'Darling, you rave. You're going to spend the next four hours afloat upon your beautiful toes, with a large spade-shaped hand supporting the small of your back. I'm not. I'm going to maintain a sitting posture, with one of the "nests for rest" provided by a malignant Casino directly intervening between the base of my trunk and the floor. Now, I know that intervention. It's of the harsh, unyielding type. Hence this air-pocket.'

With that, he stepped on to the floor, raised the air-cushion as if it were an instrument of music, and, adopting the attitude and manners of a cornet soloist, exhaled into the nozzle with all his might.

There was a roar of laughter.

Then, mercifully, the band started, and the embarrassing attention of about sixty pairs of eyes was diverted accordingly.

A moment later my brother-in-law and I had the table to ourselves.

'And now,' said Berry, 'forward with that bauble. The Rump Parliament is off.'

Perhaps, because it was a warm evening, the Casino's furnaces were in full blast. After a while the heat became oppressive. Presently I left Berry to the champagne and went for a stroll in the Palmarium.

As I was completing my second lap –

'Captain Pleydell,' said a dignified voice.

I turned to see Mrs Waterbrook, leaning upon a stick, accompanied by a remarkably pretty young lady with her hair down her back.

I came to them swiftly.

'Have you met with an accident?' I inquired.

'I have. I've ricked my ankle. Susan, this is Captain Pleydell, whose cousin is going to marry Piers. Captain Pleydell, this is Susan – my only niece. Now I'm going to sit down.' I escorted her to a chair. 'That's better, Captain Pleydell, have you seen the Château?'

'Often,' said I. 'A large grey building with a red keep, close to the scent shop.'

'One to you,' said Mrs Waterbrook. 'Now I'll begin again. Captain Pleydell, have you seen the inside of the Château?'

'I have not.'

'Then you ought,' said Mrs Waterbrook, 'to be ashamed of yourself. You've been six months in Pau, and you've never taken the trouble to go and look at one of the finest collections of tapestries in the world. What are you doing tomorrow morning?'

'Going to see the inside of the Château,' I said.

'Good. So's Susan. She'll meet you at the gate on the Boulevard at half-past ten. She only arrived yesterday, and now her mother wants her, and she's got to go back. She's wild to see the Château before she goes, and I can't take her because of this silly foot.'

'I'm awfully sorry,' said I. 'But it's an ill wind, etc.'

'Susan,' said Mrs Waterbrook, 'that's a compliment. Is it your first?'

'No,' said Susan. 'But it's the slickest.'

'The what?' cried her aunt.

'I mean, I didn't see it coming.'

I began to like Susan.

' "Slickest",' snorted Mrs Waterbrook. 'Nasty vulgar slang. If you were going to be here longer, Captain Pleydell's wife should give you lessons in English. She isn't a teacher, you know. She's an American – with a silver tongue. And there's that wretched bell.' She rose to her feet. 'If I'd remembered that *Manon* had more than three acts, I wouldn't have come.' She turned to me. 'Is Jill here tonight?'

'She is.'

'Will you tell her to come and find us in the next interval?'

'I will.'

'Good. Half-past ten tomorrow. Good night.'

On the way to the doors of the theatre she stopped to speak to someone, and Susan came running back.

'Captain Pleydell, is your wife here?'

I nodded.

'Well, then, when Jill's with Aunt Eleanor, d'you think I could – I mean, if you wouldn't mind, I'd – I'd love a lesson in English.'

I began to like Susan more than ever.

'I'll see if she's got a spare hour tomorrow,' I said. 'At half-past ten.'

Susan knitted her brows.

'No, don't upset that,' she said quickly. 'It doesn't matter. I want to be able to tell them I had you alone. But if I could say I'd met your wife, too, it'd be simply golden.'

As soon as I could speak –

'You wicked, forward child,' I said. 'You – '

'Toodle-oo,' said Susan. 'Don't be late.'

Somewhat dazedly I turned in the direction of the *salle de danse* – so dazedly, in fact, that I collided with a young Frenchman who was watching the progress of *le jeu de boule*. This was hardly exhilarating. Of the seven beings gathered about the table, six were croupiers and the seventh was reading *Le Temps*.

I collided roughly enough to knock a cigarette out of my victim's hand.

'Toodle-oo – I mean *pardon, Monsieur. Je vous demande pardon.*'

'It's quite all right,' he said, smiling. 'I shouldn't have been standing so far out.'

I drew a case from my pocket.

'At least,' I said, 'you'll allow me to replace the cigarette' – he took one with a laugh – 'and to congratulate you upon your beautiful English.'

'Thank you very much. For all that, you knew I was French.'

'In another minute,' said I, 'I shall be uncertain. And I'm sure you'd deceive a Frenchman every time.'

'I do frequently. It amuses me to death. Only the other day I had to produce my passport to a merchant at Lyons before he'd believe I was a foreigner.'

'A foreigner?' I cried, with bulging eyes. 'Then you *are* English.'

'I'm a pure-bred Spaniard,' was the reply. 'I tell you, it's most diverting. Talk about ringing the changes. I had a great time during the war. I was a perfect mine of information. It wasn't strictly accurate, but Germany didn't know that. As a double-dyed traitor, they found me extremely useful. As a desirable neutral, I cut a great deal of ice. And now I'm loafing. I used to take an interest in the prevention of crime, but I've grown lazy.'

For a moment or two we stood talking. Then I asked him to come to our table in the dancing room. He declined gracefully.

'I'm Spanish enough to dislike jazz music,' he said.

We agreed to meet at the Club on the following day, and I rejoined Berry to tell him what he had missed.

I found the fifth dance in full swing and my brother-in-law in high dudgeon.

As I sat down, he exploded.

'This blasted breath-bag is a fraud. If you blow it up tight, it's like trying to sit on a barrel. If you fill it half full, you mustn't move a muscle, or the imprisoned air keeps shifting all over the place till one feels sick of one's stomach. In either case it's as hard as petrified bog-oak. If you only leave an imperial pint in the vessel, it all goes and gathers in one corner, thus conveying to one the impression that one is sitting one's self upon a naked chair with a tennis-ball in one's hip-pocket. If one puts the swine behind one, it shoves one off the seat altogether. It was during the second phase that one dropped or let fall one's cigar into one's champagne. One hadn't thought that anything could have spoiled either, but one was wrong.'

I did what I could to soothe him, but without avail.

'I warn you,' he continued, 'there's worse to come. Misfortunes hunt in threes. First we fool and are fooled over that rotten villa. Now this balloon lets me down. You wait.'

I decided that to argue that the failure of the air-cushion could hardly be reckoned a calamity would be almost as provocative as to suggest that the immersion of the cigar should rank as the third disaster, so I moistened the lips and illustrated an indictment of our present system of education by a report of my encounter with Susan.

Berry heard me in silence, and then desired me to try the chairs at the Château, and, if they were favouring repose, to inquire whether the place would be let furnished. Stifling an inclination to assault him, I laughed pleasantly and related my meeting with the engaging Spaniard. When I had finished –

'How much did you lend him?' inquired my brother-in-law. 'Or is a pal of his taking care of your watch?'

The fox-trot came to an end, and I rose to my feet.

'The average weight,' I said, 'of the spleen is, I believe, six ounces. But spleens have been taken weighing twenty pounds.'

'Net or rod?' said Berry.

'Now you see,' I continued, 'why you're so heavy on the chairs.'

With that, I sought my wife and led her away to watch the baccarat. . . .

Before we had been in the gaming room for twenty seconds, Adèle caught me by the arm.

'D'you see that man over there, Boy? With a bangle on his wrist?'

'And a shirt behind his diamond? I do.'

'That's one of the men I saw in the Villa Buichi.'

'The devil it is,' said I. 'Then I take it he's the new lessee. Well, well. He'll go well with the ballroom, won't he?'

It was a gross-looking fellow, well-groomed and oily. His fat hands were manicured and he was overdressed. He gave the impression that money was no longer an object. As if to corroborate this, he had been winning heavily. I decided that he was a bookmaker.

While I was staring, Adèle moved to speak with a friend.

'And who,' said a quiet voice, 'is attracting such faithful attention?'

It was the Spaniard.

'You see that fat cove?' I whispered. 'He did us out of a house today. Overbid us, you know.'

My companion smiled.

'No worse than that?' he murmured. 'You must count yourself lucky.'

I raised my eyebrows.

'You know him?'

The other nodded.

'Not personally, of course,' he said. Then: 'I think he's retired now.'

'What was he?' said I.

'The biggest receiver in France.'

Ere we retired to rest, my brother-in-law's prophecy that there was 'worse to come' was distressingly fulfilled.

As the 'evening' advanced, it improved out of all knowledge. The later the hour, the hotter became the fun. Berry's ill humour fell away. Adèle and I danced furiously together. Vain things were imagined and found diverting. Hospitality was dispensed. The two spare 'baubles' were reinforced. . . .

Not until half-past two was the tambourine of gaiety suffered to tumble in its tracks.

We climbed into the cars flushed and hilarious. . . .

Late though we were, whenever we had been dancing there was one member of the household who always looked for our return and met us upon our threshold.

Nobby.

However silently the cars stole up the drive, by the time the door was opened, always the Sealyham was on parade, his small feet together, his tail up, his rough little head upon one side, waiting to greet us with an explosion of delight. In his bright eyes the rite was never stale, never laborious. It was the way of his heart.

Naturally enough, we came to look for his welcome. Had we looked in vain some night, we should have been concerned. . . .

We were concerned this night.

We opened the door to find the hall empty.

Nobby was not upon parade.

Tired as we were, we searched the whole house. Presently I found a note upon my pyjamas.

Sir

Must tell you we cannot find Nobby, the chauffeur and me looking everywhere and Fitch 'as been out in Pau all evening in quest. Hoping his whereabouts is perhaps known to you,

Yours respectfully,

J. Falcon.

I was at the Villa Buichi the following morning by a quarter to ten.

It seemed just possible that the terrier was there a captive. That he was with us before we visited the house we well remembered. Whether he had entered with us and, if so, left when we did, we could not be sure. We had had much to think about. . . .

The caretaker took an unconscionable time to answer the bell, and, when I had stated my business, stoutly refused to let me search the villa without an order. My offer of money was offensively refused. I had to content myself with standing within the hall and whistling as loud as I could. No bark replied, but I was not satisfied, and determined to seek the agent and obtain a permit the moment that Susan and I had 'done' the Château.

It was in some irritation that I made my way to the Boulevard. I had no desire to see the inside of the Château then or at any time; I particularly wished to prosecute my search for the Sealyham without delay. I had had less than four hours' sleep, and was feeling rotten. . . .

In a smart white coat and skirt and a white felt hat over one eye, Susan looked most attractive. Her fresh, pretty face was glowing, her wonderful golden hair was full of lights, and the line of her slim figure, as – hands thrust deep into her coat pockets – she leaned her small back against the balustrade, was more than dainty. Her little feet and ankles were those of a thoroughbred.

As I descended from the car –

'I say,' said Susan, 'I've got a stone in my shoe. Where can I get it out?'

I eyed her severely.

'You will have a lot to tell them,' I said, 'won't you? Go on. Get into the car.'

She climbed in, sat down and leaned back luxuriously. Then she thrust out a foot with the air of a queen. . . .

When I had replaced her shoe, she thanked me with a shy smile. Then –

'I say,' she said suddenly, 'don't let's go to the Château. I don't want to see the rotten place. Let's go for a drive instead – somewhere where you can let her out. And on the way back you can take me to get some gloves.'

'Susan,' said I, 'there's nothing doing. I know a drive in a high-powered car sounds a good deal more *chic* than being shown round a Château, but you can't have everything. Orders is orders. Besides, I've lost my dog, and I want to get a move on. But for that, you should have done the Château and had your drive into the bargain. As it is. . . .'

Susan is a good girl.

The moment she heard of my trouble, she was out of the car and haling me up to the Château as if there was a mob at our heels. . . .

I was not in the mood for sightseeing, but my annoyance went down before the tapestries as wheat before the storm.

Standing before those aged exquisites – those glorious embodiments of patience infinite, imagination high, and matchless craftsmanship, I forgot everything. The style of them was superb.

They had quality. About them was nothing mean. They were so rich, so mellow, so delicate. There was a softness to the lovely tones no brush could ever compass. Miracles of detail, marvels of stately effect, the panels were breathing the spirit of their age. Looking upon them, I stepped into another world. I heard the shouts of the huntsmen and the laughter of the handmaidens, I smelled the sweat of the chargers and the sweet scent of the grapes, I felt the cool touch of the shade upon my cheeks. Always the shouts were distant, the scent faint, the laughter low. I wandered up faery glades, loitered in lazy markets, listened to the music of fountains, sat before ample boards, bowed over lily-white hands. . . .

Here, then, was magic. Things other than silk went to the weaving of so potent a spell. The laborious needle put in the dainty threads: the hearts of those that plied it put in most precious memories – treasures of love and laughter . . . the swift brush of lips . . . the echo of a call in the forest . . . a patch of sunlight upon the slope of a hill . . . such stuff, indeed, as dreams are made on. . . .

And there is a bare truth, gentlemen, just as I have stumbled upon it. The tapestries of Pau are dreams – which you may go and share any day except Sundays.

We had almost finished our tour of the apartments, and were standing in the bedroom of Jeanne d'Albret, staring at a beautiful Gobelin, when I heard the 'flop' of something alighting upon the floor.

With one consent, the keeper, Susan, and I swung on our heels.

Advancing stiffly towards us and wagging his scrap of a tail was a small grey-brown dog. His coat was plastered with filth, upon one of his ears was a blotch of dried blood, his muzzle and paws might have been steeped in liquid soot. He stank abominably –

I put up a hand to my head.

'Nobby?' I cried, peering. And then again, '*Nobby?*'

The urchin crept to my feet, put his small dirty head one side, lowered it to the ground, and then rolled over upon his back. With his legs in the air, he regarded me fixedly, tentatively wagging his tail.

Dazedly I stooped and patted the mud upon his stomach. . . .

The bright eyes flashed. Then, with a squirm, the Sealyham was on his feet and leaping to lick my face.

'B-b-but,' shrieked Susan, shaking me by the arm, 'is this the – the dog you'd lost?'

'Yes,' I shouted, 'it is!'

Not until then did the custodian of the apartments find his tongue.

'*C'est votre chien, alors!*' he raved. '*Il nous a accompagné tout le temps et je ne l'ai pas vu. Sans laisse dans toutes ces chambres magnifiques. Mon Dieu, ce n'est pas permis aux chiens d'entrer même dans le parc. Et lui – se balader dans le Château, sale comme il est, avec une odeur de vingt boucs.*'

'Listen,' said I. 'It's my dog all right, but I never brought him. I've been looking all over Pau. What on earth – '

'*Mais vous devez l'avoir amené. C'est clair. C'est vous qui l'avez fait. Moi-même j'ai fermé toutes les chambres. Personne n'a les clefs que moi. C'est impossible.*'

I pointed to the carved bedstead.

'See for yourself,' said I. 'He's just jumped down.'

The keeper ran to the bed and peered behind the gorgeous parapet. Then he let out a scream of agony.

'*Ah, c'est vrai. Dix mille diables! Qu'un chien si dégoûtant ait souillé le lit de Jeanne d'Albret. Voyez la niche qu'il s'est faite dans les couvertures. Mon Dieu, c'est honteux. Monsieur, vous répondrez de ceci.*'

'I shall do nothing of the sort,' said I. 'But, unless you keep your mouth shut, you will. You shouldn't have let him in.'

I thought the fellow would have choked.

'*Mais je ne l'ai – A-a-ah!*' he screamed. '*Voyez il s'approche de l'écran de la reine pour l'abîmer comme il a abimé son lit.*'

'Nonsense,' I said shortly. 'He's very struck with the furniture. That's all. Anybody would be. But how the deuce. . . .'

With tears in his eyes the keeper besought me to remove my dog forthwith.

In the circumstances, it seemed best to comply, so, wishing very much that Nobby could speak for himself, I tied my handkerchief to his collar and, with Susan chattering excitedly and clinging to my arm, followed our gibbering guide to the foot of the great staircase.

'He *must* have followed him in,' cried Susan. 'He simply must. I looked at the chimney, but it's stopped up, and the man says there's no other door. And you know he unlocked each one as we came to it this morning.'

'But why's he so filthy?' I said. 'And how did he fetch up here? Let's see. He must have come with us as far as Bouzom's. That's only five minutes from here. Then we forgot all about him and left him outside. We were there for ages. I suppose he got fed up with waiting or found a pal or something, and drifted down here. All the same. . . .' I turned to the custodian and took out a fifty-franc note. 'He doesn't usually pay so much for a room, but, as this isn't a hotel and he had Jeanne d'Albret's bed. . . .'

The money passed in silence.

I fancy the keeper dared not trust himself to speak.

After all, I was very thankful that Nobby was found.

As we passed out of the gate, a sudden thought came to me, and I turned back.

'I say,' I cried, 'when last did you visit that room?'

'The Queen's room, Monsieur?'

I nodded.'

'Yesterday morning, Monsieur. At nine o'clock.'

You could have knocked me down.

I walked towards the car like a man in a dream.

The business smacked of a conjuring trick.

Having lost the terrier in the town, I had been sent to view the Château against my will, there to discover my missing chattel in a locked chamber upon the second floor.

To add to the confusion of my wits, Susan was talking furiously.

'. . . I've read of such things. You know. In case of a revolution, for the king to escape. They say there's one at Buckingham Palace.'

'One what?' said I abstractedly.

'Underground passage,' said Susan. 'Leading out into the open. The one from Buckingham Palace goes into a house. I suppose it was country once, and then the ground was built over, or, of course, it might always have led into the house, and they just had loyal people living there or someone from the Court, so that – '

'Heaven and earth!' I roared. 'The Villa Buichi!'

Susan recoiled with a cry.

I caught her white arm.

'Susan,' I yelled, 'you've got it in one! The last time we saw him was there. It's a house we saw yesterday. We thought of taking it, but, as soon as he saw us coming, another chap got in quick.'

'What a shame!' said Susan. 'If only you'd had it, you'd 've been able to go and look at the tapestries whenever you – Oh, whatever's the matter?'

I suppose my eyes were blazing. I know my brain was.

The murder was out.

'I must see my friend, the Spaniard,' I said. 'He's made a mistake. *The biggest receiver in France has not retired.*'

Susan stared at me with big eyes.

With a smile, I flung open its door and waved her into the car. . . .

I followed her in.

Then I put my arm round her waist and kissed her pink cheek.

'Now,' said I, 'you *will* have something to tell them.'

Susan gurgled delightedly.

The French are nothing if not artistic. They are also good showmen.

Five days later I had the privilege of sitting for fifty minutes upon an extremely uncomfortable chair in the Oratory of Jeanne d'Albret, listening at intervals, by means of a delicate instrument, to the biggest receiver in France and his confederates stumbling still more uncomfortably along a dank and noisome passage towards penal servitude for life.

Had he known that the Villa Buichi was surrounded, that the caretaker was already in custody, that a file of soldiers was following a quarter of a mile in his rear, and that the van which was to take him to prison was waiting in the Château's courtyard, my gentleman, who had 'lived soft', could not have been more outspoken about the condition of his path.

Not until he had quite finished and had inquired in a blasphemous whisper if all were present, was the strip of magnesium ignited and the photograph made. . . .

I have a copy before me.

The knaves are not looking their best, but the grouping is superb.

The Toilet of Venus makes a most exquisite background.

It is Spring, 1922, and Berry and Co are about to depart for England. Berry himself has certainly 'put off his manhood' by going to a fancy dress ball in the guise of 'An English Rose', although farce nearly turned to catastrophe when he was mistaken for the notorious bank robber Sycamore Tight. Now Boy, having already denied one lady to her face, is about to follow after another . . .

JOURNEY'S END

'Of your own free will you will go to your doom'
Moll, the Gypsy

My cousin showed us the letter with the artless confidence of a child.

Rome

My Darling Jill,

It's all finished now, and I can start for Paris tomorrow. I must stay there one night, to sign some papers, and then I can leave for Pau. And on next Sunday morning as ever is, we'll have breakfast together. Perhaps – No, I won't say it. Anyway, Sunday morning at latest. Everyone's been awfully kind, and – you'll never guess what's coming – Cousin Leslie's turned out a white man. He's the one, you know, who brought the suit. The day I got back from Irikli I got a note from him, saying that, while he couldn't pretend he wasn't sorry he'd lost his case, he knew how to take a beating, and, now that it was all over, couldn't we be friends, and asking me to come and dine with him and his wife at the Grand Hotel. Old Vissochi didn't want me to go, and kept quoting something out of Virgil about 'fearing the Greeks', but, of course, I insisted. And I am so glad I did. Leslie and his wife were simply splendid. Nobody could have been nicer, and considering that, if he'd won, he'd 've had the title, estates, money and everything, I think it speaks jolly well for them both. They've got two ripping little boys, and they were frightfully interested to hear about you. They'd no idea, of course, but I just had to tell them. They were so astonished at first they could hardly speak. And then Mrs Trunk picked up her glass and cried out, 'Hurray, Hurray,' and they both drank to us both, and everybody was staring, and Leslie got quite red with embarrassment at their having made such a scene. Then they made me tell them what you looked like, and I did my best, and they laughed and said I was caking it on, so I showed them your photograph. And then Mrs Trunk made me show her a letter of yours, and told your character from your handwriting, and we had a great time. Oh, Jill, I'm longing for you to see Irikli. Of course I love Rome, but I think we'll have to be at Como a lot. Father always liked it the best, and I think you will. It's so lovely, it makes you want to shout. It only wants a princess with golden hair to make it fairyland, and now it's going to have one. Oh, my darling, I'm just living to see your beautiful face again and your great grave grey eyes. Jill, have you any idea what wonderful eyes you've got? I say, we are going to be happy, aren't we? So happy, we shan't have time for anything else. But I can't wear a body-belt, dear. Not after this. I promised I would till I came back, but I'm almost melted. I don't think Jonah can be right. Anyway, I'll bet he doesn't wear one. Your very loving

Piers.

Excepting the addressee, I don't think any one of us shared the writer's enthusiasm about Mr Leslie Trunk. We quite agreed with Signor Vissochi. It was hard to believe that the man who had instituted such an iniquitous suit could so swiftly forgive the costly drubbing he had received, or, as heir-presumptive to the dukedom, honestly welcome the news of Piers' engagement. Sweetheart Jill, however, knew little of leopards and their spots. Out of respect for such unconsciousness, we held our peace. There was no hurry, and Piers could be tackled at our convenience. . . .

The conversation turned to our impending departure from France.

'I take it,' said Jonah, 'that we go as we came. If we're going to

Paris for the Grand Prix, there's not much object in stopping there now. In any event, it 'ld mean our going by train and sending the cars by sea. I'm not going to drive in Paris for anyone. I'm too old.'

After a little discussion, we decided that he was right.

'Same route?' said Adèle.

'I think so,' said Jonah. 'Except that we miss Bordeaux and go by Bergerac instead.'

'Is that shorter or longer?' said Berry. 'Not that I really care, because I wouldn't visit Bordeaux a second time for any earthly consideration. I've seen a good many poisonous places in my time, but for inducing the concentrated essence of depression, that moth-eaten spectre of bustling commerce has them, as the immortal B-B-B-Wordsworth says, beat to a b-b-b-string-bag.'

'I don't seem to remember,' said Daphne, 'that it was so awful.'

'It wasn't,' said I. 'But the circumstances in which he visited it were somewhat drab. Still, it's not an attractive town, and, as the other way's shorter and the road's about twice as good – '

'I'm glad it's shorter,' said Berry. 'I want to get to Angoulême in good time.'

'Why?' said Jill.

Berry eyed her reproachfully.

'Child,' he said, 'is your gratitude so short-lived? Have you in six slight months forgotten that at Angoulême we were given the very finest dinner that ever we ate? A meal without frills – nine tender courses long? For which we paid the equivalent of rather less than five shillings a head?'

'Oh, I remember,' said Jill. 'That was where they made us use the same knife all through dinner.'

'And what,' demanded Berry, 'of that? A conceit – a charming conceit. Thus was the glorious tradition of one court handed down to those that followed after. I tell you that for me the idea of another "crowded hour" in Angoulême goes far to ameliorate the unpleasant prospect of erupting into the middle of an English spring.'

'It's clear,' said I, 'that you should do a gastronomic tour. Every department of France had its particular dainty. With a reliable list, an almanac, and a motor ambulance, you could do wonders.'

My brother-in-law groaned.

'It wouldn't work,' he said miserably. 'It wouldn't work. They'd clash. When you were in Picardy, considering some *pâtés de Canards*, you'd get a wire from Savoy saying that the salmon trout were in the pink, and on the way there you'd get another from Gascony to say that in twenty-four hours they wouldn't answer for the flavour of the ortolans.'

'Talking of gluttony,' said Jonah, 'if they don't bring lunch pretty soon, we shall be late. It's past one now, and the meeting's the other side of Morlaas. First race, two-fifteen.'

I rose and strolled to the Club-house, to see the steward. . . .

The day was the sixteenth of April, and Summer was coming. Under our very eyes, plain, woods and foothills were putting on amain her lovely livery. We had played a full round of golf over a blowing valley we hardly knew. Billowy emerald banks masked the familiar sparkle of the hurrying Gave; a fine brown lace of rising woods had disappeared, and, in its stead, a broad hanging terrace of delicate green stood up against the sky; from being a jolly counterpane, the plain of Billère itself had become a cheerful quilt; as for the foothills, they were so monstrously tricked out with fine fresh ruffles, and unexpected equipage of greenery, with a strange epaulet upon that shoulder and a brand-new periwig upon that brow, that if high hills but hopped outside the Psalter you would have sworn the snowy Pyrénées had found new equerries.

Luncheon was served indoors.

Throughout the winter the lawn before the Club-house had made a dining-room. Today, however, we were glad of the shade.

'Does Piers know,' said Adèle, 'that's he's coming home with us?'

Jill shook her head.

'Not yet. I meant to tell him in my last letter, but I forgot.' She turned to Daphne. 'You don't think we could be married at once? I'm sure Piers wouldn't mind, and I'd be so much easier. He does want looking after, you know. Fancy his wanting to leave off that belt thing.'

'Yes, just fancy,' said Berry. 'Apart from the fact that it was a present from you, it'd be indecent.'

'It isn't that,' said Jill. 'But he might get an awful chill.'

'I know,' said Berry. 'I know. That's my second point. Keep the abdominal wall quarter of an inch deep in lamb's wool, and in the hottest weather you'll never feel cold. Never mind. If he mentions it again, we'll make its retention a term of the marriage settlement.'

Jill eyed him severely before proceeding.

'It could be quite quiet,' she continued; 'the wedding, I mean. At a registry place – '

'Mrs Hunt's, for instance,' said Berry.

' – and then we could all go down to White Ladies together, and when he has to go back to fix things up in Italy, I could go, too.'

'My darling,' said Daphne, 'don't you want to be married from home? In our own old church at Bilberry? For only one thing, if you weren't, I don't think the village would ever get over it.'

Jill sighed.

'When you talk like that,' she said, 'I don't want to be married at all. . . . Yes, I do. I want Piers. I wouldn't be happy without him. But . . . If only he hadn't got four estates of his own, we might – '

'Five,' said Berry. Jill opened her big grey eyes. 'Four now, and a share in another upon his wedding day.'

Jill knitted her brow.

'I never knew this,' she said. 'What's the one he's going to have?'

Berry raised his eyebrows.

'It's a place in Hampshire,' he said. 'Not very far from Brooch. They call it White Ladies.'

The look which Jill gave us, as we acclaimed his words, came straight out of Paradise.

'I do wish he could have heard you,' she said uncertainly. 'I'll tell him, of course. But it won't be the same. And my memory isn't short-lived really. I'd forgotten the Angoulême dinner, but I shan't forget this lunch in a hundred years.'

'In another minute,' said Berry, 'I shall imbue this omelet with tears. Then it'll be too salt.' He seized his tumbler and raised it above his head. 'I give you Monsieur Roland. May he touch the ground in spots this afternoon. Five times he's lent me an 'unter'oss out of sheer good nature; his taste in cocktails is venerable; and whenever I see him he asks when we're going to use his car.'

We drank the toast gladly.

Roland was a good sportsman, and throughout the season at Pau he had been more than friendly. He was to ride two races at the meeting this afternoon.

'And now,' said I, 'get a move on. St Jammes is ten miles off, and the road is vile. If we'd got Roland's flier, it'ld be one thing, but Ping and Pong'll take their own time.'

My brother-in-law frowned.

'Business first,' he said shortly. 'Business first. I spoke to the steward about the cutlets, and I won't have them rushed. And if that's our Brie on the sideboard – well, I, too, am in a melting mood, and it's just asking for trouble.'

There was a fresh breeze quickening the air upon the uplands beyond old Morlaas, to whip the flags into a steady flutter and now and again flick a dark tress of hair across Adèle's dear cheeks.

As we scrambled across country –

'Why, oh, why,' she wailed, 'did ever I let it grow? I'll have it cut again tomorrow. I swear I will.'

'And what about me?' said I. 'You're a joint tenant with me. You can't commit waste like that without my consent.'

'I'm sure I can abate – is that right? – a nuisance.'

'It's not a nuisance. It's a glory. When I wake up in the morning and see it rippling all over the pillow, I plume myself upon my real and personal interest in such a beautiful estate. Then I start working out how many lockets it 'ld fill, and that sends me to sleep again.'

'Does it really ripple?' said Adèle. 'Or is that a poet's licence?'

'Rather,' said I. 'Sometimes, if I'm half asleep, I feel quite seasick.'

Adèle smiled thoughtfully.

'In that case,' she announced, 'I'll reconsider my decision. But I wish to Heaven it 'ld ripple when I'm awake.'

'They're off!' cried Jonah.

A sudden rush for the bank on which we were standing confirmed his report. We had much ado to escape being thrust into the deep lane the bank was walling.

The lane was about a mile long, and so was the bank. The latter made a fair 'grand stand'. As such it was packed. Not only all the visitors to Pau, but every single peasant for twenty miles about seemed to have rallied at St Jammes to see the sport. The regular business of the race-course was conspicuously missing. Pleasure was strolling, cock of an empty walk. For sheer bonhomie, the little meeting bade fair to throw its elder brethren of the Hippodrome itself into the shadowy distance.

Roland rode a fine race and won by a neck.

We left the bank and walked up the lane to offer our congratulations. . . .

'Thank you. Thank you. But nex' year you will bring horses, eh? An' we will ride against one another. Yes? You shall keep them with me. I 'ave plenty of boxes, you know. An' on the day I will give your horse his breakfast, and he shall give me the race. That's right. An' when are you going to try my tank? I go away for a week, an' when I come back yesterday, I ask my people, "How has Captain Pleydell enjoyed the car?" "But he 'as not used it." "No? Then that is because the Major has broken her up?" "No. He has not been near." I see now it is not good enough. I tell you I am hurt. I shall not ask you again.'

'Lunch with us tomorrow instead,' laughed Daphne.

'I am sure that I will,' said Roland.

After a little we sauntered back to our bank. . . .

It was nearly a quarter to five by the time we were home. That was early enough, but the girls had grown tired of standing, and we had seen Roland win twice. Jonah we had left to come in another car. This was because he had found a brother-fisherman. When last we saw him, he had a pipe in one hand, a lighted match in the other, and was discussing casts. . . .

Falcon met us at the door with a telegram addressed to 'Miss Mansel'.

The wording was short and to the point.

Have met with accident can you come Piers Paris.

The next train to Paris left Pau in twelve minutes' time.

Adèle and a white-faced Jill caught it by the skin of their teeth.

They had their tickets, the clothes they stood up in, a brace of vanity bags, and one hundred and forty-five francs. But that was all. It was arranged feverishly upon the platform that Jonah and I should follow, with such of their effects as Daphne gave us, by the ten-thirty train.

Then a horn brayed, I kissed Adèle's fingers, poor Jill threw me a ghost of a smile, and their coach rolled slowly out of the station . . .

I returned to the car dazedly.

Thinking it over, I decided that we had done the best we could. On arrival at Bordeaux, my wife and cousin could join the Spanish express, which was due to leave that city at ten-fifteen; this, if it ran to time, would bring them to the French capital by seven o'clock the next morning. Jonah and I would arrive some five hours later. . . .

The Bank was closed, of course, so I drove to the Club forthwith to get some money. Jonah was not there, but, as he was certain to call, I left a note with the porter, telling him what had occurred. Then I purchased our tickets – a lengthy business. It was so lengthy, in fact, that when it was over I called again at the Club on the chance of picking up Jonah and bringing him home. He had not arrived.

I made my way back to the villa dismally enough.

My sister and Berry were in the drawing-room.

As I opened the door –

'Wherever have you been?' said Daphne. 'Did they catch it?'

I nodded.

'You haven't seen Jonah, I suppose?'

I shook my head.

'But where have you been, Boy?'

I spread out my hands.

'Getting money and tickets. You know their idea of haste. But there's plenty of time – worse luck,' I added bitterly. Then: 'I say, what a dreadful business!' I sank into a chair. 'What on earth can have happened?'

Berry rose and walked to a window.

'Jill's face,' he said slowly. 'Jill's face.' He swung round and flung out an arm. 'She looked old!' he cried. 'Jill – that baby looked old. She thought it was a wire to say he was on his way, and it hit her between the eyes like the kick of a horse.'

Shrunk into a corner of her chair, my sister stared dully before her.

'He must be bad,' said I. 'Unless he was bad, he 'ld never have wired like that. If Piers could have done it, I'm sure he 'ld have tempered the wind.'

' "Can you come?" ' quoted Berry, and threw up his arms.

Daphne began to cry quietly. . . .

A glance at the tea-things showed me that these were untouched.

I rang the bell, and presently fresh tea was brought. I made my sister drink, and poured some for Berry and me. The stimulant did us all good. By common consent, we thrust speculation aside and made what arrangements we could. That our plans for returning to England would now miscarry seemed highly probable.

At last my sister sighed and lay back in her chair.

'Why?' she said quietly. 'Why? What has Jill done to earn this? Oh, I know it's no good questioning Fate, but it's – it's rather hard.'

I stepped to her side and took her hand in mine.

'My darling,' I said, 'don't let's make the worst of a bad business. The going's heavy, I know, but it's idle to curse the jumps before we've seen them. Piers didn't send that wire himself. That goes without saying. He probably never worded it. I know that's as broad as it's long, but, when you come to think, there's really no reason on earth why it should be anything more than a broken leg.'

There was a dubious silence.

At length –

'Boy's perfectly right,' said Berry. 'Jill's scared stiff – naturally. As for us, we're rattled – without good reason at all. For all we know. . . .'

He broke off to listen . . . The front door closed with a crash.

'Jonah,' said I. 'He's had my note, and – '

It was not Jonah.

It was Piers, Duke of Padua, who burst into the room, looking extraordinarily healthy and very much out of breath.

We stared at him, speechless.

For a moment he stood smiling. Then he swept Daphne a bow.

'Paris to Pau by air,' he said, 'in four and a quarter hours. Think of it. Clean across France in a bit of an afternoon. You'll all *have* to do it: it's simply glorious.' He crossed to my sister's side and kissed her hand. 'Don't look so surprised,' he said, laughing. 'It really is me. I didn't dare to wire, in case we broke down on the way. And now where's Jill?'

We continued to stare at him in silence.

It was Berry – some ten minutes later – who hit the right nail on the head.

'By George!' he shouted. 'By George! I've got it in one. *The fellow who sent that wire was Leslie Trunk.*'

'*Leslie?*' cried Piers. 'But why – '

'Who knows? But your cousin's a desperate man, and Jill's in his way. So are you – more still, but, short of murder itself, to touch you won't help his case. With Jill in his hands. . . . Well, for one thing only, I take it you'd pay pretty high for her – her health.'

Piers went very white.

For myself, I strove to keep my brain steady, but the thought of Adèle – my wife, in the power of the dog – would thrust itself, grinning horribly, into the foreground of my imagination.

I heard somebody say that the hour was a quarter past seven. I had my watch in my hand, so I knew they were right. Vainly they repeated their statement, unconsciously voicing my thoughts. . . .

Only when Daphne fell on her knees by my side did I realise that I was the speaker.

Berry and Piers were at the telephone.

I heard them.

'Ask for the Bordeaux Exchange. Burn it, why can't I talk French? Do as I say, lad. Don't argue. Ask for the Bordeaux Exchange. Insist that it's urgent – a matter of life and death.'

Piers began to speak – shakily.

'*Oui. La Poste de Bordeaux. . . . C'est très urgent, Mademoiselle. . . . Il s'agit de vie et mort . . . Oui, oui. La Poste même. . . . Comment? Mon Dieu. Mais, Mademoiselle* – '

A sudden rude thresh of the bell announced that his call was over.

Berry fell upon the instrument with an oath.

'It's no good!' cried Piers. 'It's no good. She says the line to Bordeaux is out of order.'

My sister lifted her head and looked into my face.

'Can you do it by car?' she said.

I pulled myself together and thought very fast.

'We can try,' I said, rising, 'but – Oh, it's a hopeless chance. Only three hours – less *than* three hours for a hundred and fifty miles. It can't be done. We'd have to do over seventy most of the way, and you can't beat a pace like that out of Ping and Pong. On the track, perhaps . . . But on the open road – '

The soft slush of tyres upon the drive cut short my sentence.

'Jonah, at last,' breathed Daphne.

We ran to the window.

It was not Jonah. It was Roland.

So soon as he saw us, he stopped and threw out his clutch.

'I say, you know, I am mos' distress' about your lunch tomorrow. When you ask me – '

'Roland,' I cried, 'Roland, will you lend me your car?'

'But 'ave I not said – '

'Now – at once – here – to drive to Bordeaux?'

Roland looked up at my face.

The next moment he was out of his seat.

'Yes, but I am not going with you,' he said. Then: 'What is the matter? Never mind. You will tell me after. The lights are good, and she is full up with gasoline. I tell you, you will be there in three hours.'

'Make it two and three-quarters,' said I.

The day's traffic had dwindled to a handful of home-going gigs, and as we swung out of the Rue Montpensier and on to the Bordeaux road, a distant solitary tram was the only vehicle within sight.

I settled down in my seat. . . .

A moment later we had passed the *Octroi*, and Pau was behind us.

Piers crouched beside me as though he were carved of stone. Once in a while his eyes would fall from the road to the instrument-board. Except for that regular movement, he gave no sign of life. As for Berry, sunk, papoose-like, in the chauffeur's cockpit in rear, I hoped that his airman's cap would stand him in stead. . . .

The light was good, and would serve us for half an hour. The car was pulling like the mares of Diomedes. As we flung by the last of the villas, I gave her her head. . . .

Instantly the long straight road presented a bend, and I eased her up with a frown. We took the corner at fifty, the car holding the road as though this were banked for speed. As we flashed by the desolate race course and the ground on which Piers had alighted two hours before, I lifted a grateful head. It was clear that what corners we met could be counted out. With such a grip of the road and such acceleration, the time which anything short of a hairpin bend would cost us was almost negligible.

As if annoyed at my finding, the road for the next five miles ran straight as a die. For over three of those miles the lady whose lap we sat in was moving at eighty-four.

A hill appeared – a long, long hill, steep, straight, yellow – tearing towards us. . . . We climbed with the rush of a lift – too fast for our stomachs.

The road was improving now, but, as if to cancel this, a steep, winding hill fell into a sudden valley. As we were dropping, I saw its grey-brown fellow upon the opposite side, dragging his tedious way to the height we had left.

We lost time badly here, for down on the flat of the dale a giant lorry was turning, while a waggon was creeping by. For a quarter of a precious minute the road was entirely blocked. Because of the coming ascent, the check hit us hard. In a word, it made a mountain out of a molehill. What the car might have swallowed whole she had to masticate. She ate her way up the rise, snorting with indignation. . . .

A mile (or a minute, Sirs, whichever you please) was all the grace she had to find her temper. Then the deuce of a hill swerved down to the foot of another – long, blind, sinuous. The road was writhing like a serpent. We used it as serpents should be used. Maybe it bruised our heels: we bruised its head savagely. . . .

We were on the level now, and the way was straight again. A dot ahead was a waggon. I wondered which way it was going. I saw, and we passed it by in the same single moment of time. That I may not be thought inobservant, forty-five yards a second is a pace which embarrasses sight.

A car came flying towards us. At the last I remarked with a smile it was going our way. A flash of paint, a smack like the flap of a sail, and we were by.

A farm was coming. I saw the white of its walls swelling to ells from inches. I saw a hen, who had seen us, starting to cross our path. Simultaneously I lamented her death – needlessly. She missed destruction by yards. I found myself wondering whether, after all, she had held on her way. Presently I decided that she had and, anxious to retrace her steps, had probably awaited our passage in some annoyance. . . .

We swam up another hill, flicked between two waggons, slashed a village in half and tore up the open road.

The daylight was waning now, and Piers switched on the hooded light that illumined the instrument-board. With a frown I collected my lady for one last tremendous effort before the darkness fell.

She responded like the thoroughbred she was.

I dared not glance at the speedometer, but I could feel each mile as it added itself to our pace. I felt this climb from ninety to ninety-one. Thickening the spark by a fraction, I brought it to ninety-two . . . ninety-three. . . .

In a quiet, steady voice Piers began to give me the benefit of his sight.

'Something ahead on the right . . . a waggon . . . all clear . . . a cart, I think, on the right . . . no – yes. It's not moving. . . . A bicycle on the left . . . and another . . . a car coming . . . all clear . . . no – a man walking on the right . . . all clear. . . .'

So, our narrowed eyes nailed to the straight grey ribbon streaming into the distance, the sea and the waves roaring in our ears, folded in the wings of the wind, we cheated Dusk of seven breathless miles and sent Nature packing with a fork in her breech.

Sore at this treatment, the Dame, as ever, returned, with Night himself to urge her argument.

I threw in my hand with a sigh, and Piers switched on the lights as we ran into Aire-sur-l'Adour.

I heard a clock striking as we swung to the left in the town. . . .

Eight o'clock.

Two more hours and a quarter, and a hundred and nineteen miles to go.

I tried not to lose heart. . . .

We had passed Villeneuve-de-Marsan, and were nearing, I knew, crossroads, when Piers forestalled my inquiry and spoke in my ear.

'Which shall you do? Go straight? Or take the forest road?'

'I don't know the Roquefort way, except that there's pavement there. What's it like?'

'It's pretty bad,' said Piers. 'But you'll save about fifteen miles.'

'How much pavement is there? Five or six miles?'

'Thirty about,' said Piers.

'Thanks very much,' said I. 'We'll go by the forest.'

I think I was right.

I knew the forest road and I knew its surface was superb. Thirty miles of pavement, which I did not know, which was admittedly rough, presented a ghastly prospect. The 'luxury' tax of fifteen precious miles, tacked on to the way of the forest, was really frightening, but since such a little matter as a broken lamp would kill our chances, I dared not risk the rough and tumble of the pavement upon the Roquefort road.

At last the crossroads came, and we swung to the right. We had covered a third of the ground.

I glanced at the gleaming clock sunk in the dash.

Twenty-five minutes past eight.

An hour and fifty minutes – and a hundred miles to go.

With a frightful shock I realised that, *even with the daylight to help me, I had used a third of my time.*

I began to wish frantically that I had gone by Roquefort. I felt a wild inclination to stop and retrace my steps. Pavement? Pavement be burned! I must have been mad to throw away fifteen miles – fifteen golden miles. . . .

Adèle's face, pale, frightened, accusing, stared at me through the windscreen. Over her shoulder, Jill, white and shrinking, pointed a shaking finger.

With a groan, I jammed my foot on the accelerator. . . .

With a roar, the car sprang forward like a spurred horse.

Heaven knows the speed at which St Justin was passed. I was beyond caring. We missed a figure by inches and a cart by a foot. Then the cottages faded, and the long snarl of the engine sank to the stormy mutter she kept for the open road.

We were in the forest now, and I let her go.

Out of the memories of that April evening our progress through the forest stands like a chapter of a dream.

Below us, the tapering road, paler than ever – on either side an endless army of fir trees, towering shoulder to shoulder, so dark, so vast, and standing still as Death – above us, a lane of violet, all pricked with burning stars, we supped the rare old ale brewed by Hans Andersen himself.

Within this magic zone the throb of the engine, the hiss of the carburettor, the swift brush of the tyres upon the road – three rousing tones, yielding a thunderous chord, were curiously staccato. The velvet veil of silence we rent in twain; but as we tore it, the folds fell back to hang like mighty curtains about our path, stifling all echo, striking reverberation dumb. The strong, sweet smell of the woods enhanced the mystery. The cool, clean air thrashed us with perfume. . . .

The lights of the car were powerful and focussed perfectly. The steady, bright splash upon the road, one hundred yards ahead, robbed the night of its sting.

Rabbits rocketed across our bows; a bat spilled its brains upon our windscreen; a hare led us for an instant, only to flash to safety under our very wheels. As for the moths, the screen was strewn with the dead. Three times Piers had to rise and wipe it clear.

Of man and beasts, mercifully, we saw no sign.

If Houeilles knew of our passage, her ears told her. Seemingly the hamlet slept. I doubt if we took four seconds to thread its one straight street. Next day, I suppose, men swore the devil was loose. They may be forgiven. Looking back from a hazy distance, I think he was at my arm.

As we ran into Casteljaloux, a clock was striking. . . .

Nine o'clock.

We had covered the thirty-five miles in thirty-five minutes dead.

'To the left, you know,' said Piers.

'*Left?*' I cried, setting a foot on the brake. 'Straight on, surely. We turn to the left at Marmande.'

'No, no, *no*. We don't touch Marmande. We turn to the left here.' I swung round obediently. 'This is the Langon road. It's quite all right, and it saves us about ten miles.'

Ten miles.

I could have screamed for joy.

Only fifty-five miles to go – and an hour and a quarter left.

The hope which had never died lifted up its head. . . .

It was when we were nearing Auros that we sighted the van.

This was a hooded horror – a great, two-ton affair, a creature, I imagine, of Bordeaux, blinding home like a mad thing, instead of blundering.

Ah, I see a hundred fingers pointing to the beam in my eye. Bear with me, gentlemen. I am not so sightless as all that.

I could steer my car with two fingers upon the roughest road. I could bring her up, all standing, in twice her length. My lights, as you know, made darkness a thing of nought. . . . I cannot answer for its headlights, nor for its brake-control, but the backlash in the steering of that two-ton van was terrible to behold.

Hurling itself along at thirty-odd miles an hour, the vehicle rocked and swung all over the narrow surface – now lurching to the right, now plunging to the left, but, in the main, holding a wobbling course upon the crown of the road – to my distraction.

Here was trouble enough, but – what was worse – upon my sounding the horn, the driver refused to give way. He knew of my presence, of course. He heard me, he saw my headlights, and he sought to increase his pace. . . .

I sounded the horn till it failed: I yelled till my throat was sore: Piers raged and howled: behind I heard Berry bellowing like a fiend. . . . I cursed and chafed till the sweat of baffled fury ran into my eyes. . . .

For over five hideous miles I followed that bucketing van.

I tried to pass it once, but the brute who was driving swerved to the left – I believe on purpose – and only our four-wheel brakes averted a headline smash.

At that moment we might not have been on earth.

My lady stopped as a bird stops in its flight. With the sudden heave of a ship, she seemed to hang in the air. Wild as I was, I could not but marvel at her grace. . . .

Out of the check came wisdom.

It was safe, then, to keep very close.

I crept to the blackguard's heels, till our headlights made two rings upon his vile body.

With one foot on the step, Piers hung out of the car, watching the road beyond.

Suddenly the van tilted to the right. . . .

I knew a swerve must follow, if the driver would keep his balance.

As it came, I pulled out and crammed by, with my heart in my mouth. . . .

A glance at the clock made me feel sick to death.

Fifteen priceless minutes that van had stolen out of my hard-earned hoard. I had risked our lives a score of times to win each one of them. And now an ill-natured churl had flung them into the draught. . . .

I set my teeth and put the car at a hill at eighty-five. . . .

We flashed through Langon at twenty minutes to ten.

Thirty-five minutes left – and thirty miles to go.

We were on the main road now, and the surface was wide, if rough. What little traffic there was, left plenty of room.

I took the ashes of my caution and flung them to the winds. . . .

Piers told me afterwards that for the first twenty miles never once did the speedometer's needle fall below seventy-two. He may be right. I knew that the streets were coming, and the station had to be found. It was a question, in fact, of stealing time. That which we had already was not enough. Unless we could pick some out of the pocket of Providence, the game was up.

I had to slow down at last for a parcel of stones. The road was being remade, and thirty yards of rubble had to be delicately trod. As we forged through the ruck at twenty, Piers stared at the side of the road.

'BORDEAUX 16,' he quoted.

Ten more miles – and nineteen minutes to go.

The traffic was growing now with every furlong. Belated lorries rumbled about their business: cars panted and raved into the night: carts jolted out of turnings into the great main road.

When I think of the chances I took, the palms of my hands grow hot. To wait for others to grant my request for room was out of the question. I said I was coming. . . . I came – and that was that. Times out of number I overtook vehicles upon the wrong side. As for the frequent turnings, I hoped for the best. . . .

Once, where four ways met, I thought we were done.

A car was coming across – I could see its headlights' beam. I opened the throttle wide, and we raced for the closing gap. As we came to the cross of the roads, I heard an engine's roar. . . . For an instant a searchlight raked us. . . . There was a cry from Berry . . . an answering shout . . . the noise of tyres tearing at the road . . . and that was all.

A moment later I was picking my way between two labouring waggons and a trio of straggling carts.

'BORDEAUX 8,' quoted Piers.

Five more miles – and eleven minutes to go.

Piers had the plan of the city upon his knees. He conned it as best he could by the glow of the hooded light. After a moment or two he thrust the book away.

'The station's this end of the town. We can't miss it. I'll tell you when to turn.'

Three minutes more, and our road had become a street. Two parallel, glittering lines warned me of trams to come.

As if to confirm their news, a red orb in the distance was eyeing us angrily. . . .

'We turn to the right,' said Piers. 'I'll tell you when.'

I glanced at the clock.

The hour was nine minutes past ten.

My teeth began to chatter of sheer excitement. . . .

There was a turning ahead, and I glanced at Piers.

'Not yet,' he said.

With a frantic eye on the clock, I thrust up that awful road. The traffic seemed to combine to cramp my style. I swerved, I cut in, I stole an odd yard, I shouldered other drivers aside, and once, confronted with a block, I whipped on to the broad pavement and, amid scandalised shouts, left the obstruction to stay less urgent business.

All the time I could see the relentless minute-hand beating me on the post. . . .

At last Piers gave the word, and I switched to the right.

The boulevard was empty. We just swept up it like a black squall.

Left and right, then, and we entered the straight – with thirty seconds to go.

'Some way up,' breathed Piers.

I set my teeth hard and let my lady out. . . .

By the time I had sighted the station, the speedometer's needle had swung to seventy-three. . . .

I ran along the pavement, clapped on the brakes, threw out the clutch.

Piers switched off, and we flung ourselves out of the car.

Stiff as a sleepy hare, I stumbled into the hall.

'*Le train pour Paris!*' I shouted. '*Ou est le train pour Paris?*'

'This way!' cried Piers, passing me like a stag.

I continued to shout ridiculously, running behind him.

I saw him come to a barrier . . . ask and be answered . . . try to push through. . . .

The officials sought to detain him.

A whistle screamed. . . .

With a roar I flung aside the protesting arms and, carrying Piers with me, floundered on to the platform.

A train was moving.

Feeling curiously weak-kneed, I got carefully upon the step of a passing coach. Piers stepped on behind me and thrust me up to the door.

Then a conductor came and hauled us inside.

I opened my eyes to see Adèle's face six inches away.

'Better, old chap?' she said gently.

I tried to sit up, but she set a hand upon my chest.

'Don't say I fainted?' I said.

She smiled and nodded.

'But I understand,' she said, 'that you have a wonderful excuse.'

'Not for ser-wooning,' said I. 'Of course we did hurry, but. . . .'

Piers burst in excitedly.

'There isn't another driver in all – '

'Rot,' said I. 'Jonah would have done it with a quarter of an hour to spare.'

So he would.

My cousin would have walked to the train and had a drink into the bargain.

While the train thundered northward through a drowsy world, a council of five sat up in a *salon lit* and laid its plans. By far its most valuable member was Señor Don Fedriani, travelling by chance from Biarritz – a very good friend of mine and a *persona grata* with the French police. . . .

It was, indeed, in response to his telegram from Poitiers that, a few minutes before seven o'clock the next morning, two detectives boarded our train at the Gare Austerlitz.

Five minutes later we steamed into the Quai d'Orsay.

Jill, carefully primed, was the first to alight.

Except for Piers, Duke of Padua, the rest of us followed as ordinary passengers would. It was, of course, plain that we had no connection with Jill. . . .

That Mr Leslie Trunk should meet her himself was quite in order. That, having thus put his neck into the noose, he should proceed to adjust the rope about his dew-lap, argued an unexpected generosity.

Yes, he had sent the wire. He had taken that responsibility. How was Piers? Well, there was plenty of hope. He patted her delicate hand. She must be brave, of course. . . . Yes, he had just left him. He was in a nursing-home – crazy to see her. They would go there at once.

We all went 'there' at once – including Piers, Duke of Padua.

Mr Leslie Trunk, Señor Don Fedriani, and the two police-officers shared the same taxi.

'There' we were joined by Mrs Trunk.

The meeting was not cordial, neither was the house a nursing-home. I do not know what it was. A glance at the proportions of the blackamoor who opened the door suggested that it was a bastille.

It was thirty hours later that Berry pushed back his chair.

It was a glorious day, and, viewed from the verandah of the Club-house, that smiling pleasaunce, the rolling plain of Billère, was beckoning more genially than ever.

So soon as our luncheon had settled, we were to prove its promise for the last time.

'Yes,' said Berry, 'puerile as it may seem, I assumed you were coming back. My assumption was so definite that I didn't even get out. For one thing, Death seemed very near, and the close similarity which the slot I was occupying bore to a coffin, had all along been too suggestive to be ignored. Secondly, from my coign of vantage I had a most lovely view of the pavement outside the station. I never remember refuse looking so superb. . . .

'Well, I don't know how long I waited, but when it seemed certain that you were – er – detained, I emerged from my shell. I didn't like leaving the car unattended, but as there wasn't a lock, I didn't know what to do. Then I remembered that just as the beaver, when pursued, jettisons some one of its organs – I forget which – and thus evades capture, so the careful mechanic removes some vital portion of his engine to thwart the unauthorised. I had a vague idea that the part in question was of, with, or from the magneto. I had not even a vague idea that the latter was protected by a network of live wires, and that one had only to stretch out one's finger to induce a spark about a foot long and a shock from which one will never wholly recover. . . . I reeled into the station, hoping against hope that somebody *would* be fool enough to steal the swine.

'Yes, the buffet was closed. Of such is the city of Bordeaux. . . . When I recovered consciousness I sought for you two. I asked several officials if they had seen two gentlemen. Some walked away as if nettled: others adopted the soothing attitude one keeps for the inebriated. Upon reflection, I don't blame them. I had a weak case. . . .

'At last I returned to the car. Alas, it was still there. I then had recourse to what is known as "the process of exhaustion". In fact, I found it extremely useful. By means of that process I was eventually successful in starting the engine, and, in the same elementary way, I got into top gear. I drew out of that yard with a running backfire nearly blowing me out of my seat. . . .

'Well, the general idea was to find a garage. The special one was to hear what people said when I stopped to ask them the way. The fourth one I asked was a chauffeur. Under his direction, one first of all reduced the blinding stammer of the exhaust to an impressive but respectable roar, and then proceeded in his company to a dairy, a garage, another dairy and a hotel – in that order. I gave that chap a skinful and fifty francs. . . .

'Yesterday I drove home. I can prove it. All through the trams, like a two-year-old. I admit I took over six hours, but I lunched on the way. I trust that two of the poultry I met are now in paradise. Indeed, I see no reason to suspect the contrary. So far as I could observe, they looked good, upright fowls. And I look forward confidently to an opportunity of apologising to them for their untimely translation. They were running it rather fine, and out of pure courtesy I set my foot positively upon the brake. Unfortunately, it wasn't the brake, but the accelerator. . . . My recollection of the next forty seconds is more than hazy. There is, so to speak, a hiatus in my memory – some two miles long. This was partly due to the force with which the back of the front seat hit me in the small of the back. Talk about a blue streak. . . . Oh, it's a marvellous machine – very quick in the uptake. Give her an inch, and she'll take a hell of a lot of stopping. However. . . '

'Have you seen Roland?' I said.

'Yes. He dined last night. I told him you'd broken down his

beauty and that I had administered the *coup de grâce*. He quite believed it.'

'What did he say?' said Adèle.

'Since you ask me,' said Berry, 'I'll give you his very words. I think you'll value them. "I tell you," he said, "I am very proud. You say she is done. Well, then, there are other cars in the *usine*. But she has saved something which no one can buy in the world – the light in a lady's eyes." '

There are things in France, besides sunshine, which are not for sale.

Once more, another hand takes over the chronicle – on the eve of the wedding of Jill Mansel to Piers, Duke of Padua . . .

THE FAIRY CHILD

The flap of the tent was lifted, and Moll came in.

I looked up from my work.

'What are you trying to polish?' said Moll.

'A skewer,' said I: 'a fine old silver fellow, that has held together many a good roast of beef.'

'Give it to me,' said Moll, 'and I will burnish it.'

I handed over the skewer. Moll looked at it curiously.

'It is heavy and handsome,' she said: 'too good for skewering meat. See the sprays at the head upon either side: and this fair shield with the arms is finely done.'

'It was wrought by an honest smith,' said I, 'one Chawner by name, nearly a hundred and fifty years ago.'

Moll plucked a piece of stuff out of a shabby wallet and started to rub the skewer respectfully.

After a little –

'How did you come by it?' she said.

'I bought it this afternoon in open market. There was a sale of goods at Brooch, and I walked in to look at the silver. I had to show them my money,' I added, smiling, 'before they would let me pass.'

Moll breathed upon the skewer, which was beginning to gleam.

'See where the knife has scored it,' she said, pointing. 'It was a shame to use it so.'

I shrugged my shoulders.

'Silver was nothing accounted of in the days of King George the Third.'

'What will you do with it?' asked Moll, presently.

'It is to be a wedding gift,' said I.

'For the fairy child?' said Moll.

'For the same,' said I: 'the one I ought to have married.'

'She has a fine lover,' said Moll. 'The two of them came alone this afternoon.'

'Did you tell them their fortunes?' I said.

'I did that,' said Moll. 'I told them the rosy truth. And, when I had done, the child spoke very sweet. "I know you will take no money," she said, "but I'd like you to have my watch." I shook my head, but she thrust it into my palm.' Her grey eyes shining, Moll parted her dress at her breast. There, on a leather lace, a little gold wrist-watch hung by its black silk strap. With the smile of a child, Moll set the gaud to her ear, and nodded contentedly. 'And the Duke kissed my fingers,' she added, 'and bade me come to their wedding. But – '

'We'll go together,' said I.

Bilberry church was full that July day. But the ushers were watching for Moll and made room for us both.

When the wedding was over, the Duchess of Padua walked down the aged aisle over the bright brasses, seeming more than ever a fairy child. She stopped beside our pew and smiled at Moll, and I stepped out, and Moll came forward and stooped and kissed her, while the Duke shook hands with me. Then the two pretties passed on, out into the hot sunshine. . . .

Moll and I went home by the Red King Walk.

It was a summer's day, and we rested once by the way, by the side of a scuttling brook.

'Why have you always said,' I asked suddenly, 'that I ought to have married Jill Mansel, the fairy child?'

Moll stared at the cool, brown water.

'I – I don't know,' she said.

Such a confession from Moll is like an icicle in June.

'You know two things certainly,' said I. 'You know that you cannot season meat with honey, and you know that only a Roman could make me a wife.'

Moll wrinkled her beautiful brow.

'I do not know that at all,' she answered, beginning to pluck at the grass. 'If you cannot season meat with honey, neither can you season it with blackberry rob.'

'True,' said I. 'But mutton with redcurrant jelly will make a dish fit for a king.'

'Currants,' said Moll, shortly, 'do not grow amid blackberries.'

'Seldom enough,' said I; 'but it has been known. And the good red currant can grace a garden too.'

There was a long silence.

'What then?' said Moll quietly.

'This,' said I. 'You were not born a Gypsy. Will you marry a Romany Rye?'

Moll began to tremble.

'No man, nor woman either,' she said uncertainly, 'can serve God and mammon.'

'True,' said I, taking her slim brown fingers. 'But a man and maid between them might work the miracle.'

For one long minute of time, Moll stared at the emerald ferns. At length –

'I am ready to try,' she whispered, 'because – I love you so.'

Then she blushed like a little girl and hid her proud face in my coat. . . .

So, after all, I shall marry a fairy child.

Some years have passed. It is the late 1920s.

Although liveried servants of the Courts of Idleness, the Pleydells and the Mansels have never been drones. Berry presides on the bench at Brooch and Robin Hood, discriminating between neither rich nor poor ('beggars and billionaires shall get it equally in the neck'); Daphne is chatelaine of White Ladies. Jill now has two children; her brother Jonah inhabits, at times, another and more strenuous world. As for Boy, he has become a writer of thrillers . . .

LETTERS PATENT

'Oh, he mustn't die,' said Adèle. 'Don't make him die.'

'Of course he must die,' said Berry. 'In great agony. I'll help you with that bit.'

'I'm not sure I oughtn't to,' said Jonah. 'Besides, I rather fancy that chapel. Make a magnificent tomb.'

'I won't hear of it,' said my sister. 'Think of the shock to Adèle.'

'As a matter of fact,' said I, 'it's all over. I've passed the proofs.'

There was an electric silence.

In a sudden burst of ambition, I had written a book. Requiring a resourceful hero, I had looked to my cousin, Jonah, to fill the rôle. This he had so much adorned that my wife, my sister and her husband had all demanded as of right to appear in 'my next'. 'All is vanity'. When, like a fool, I consented, I cut my own throat. From that time on neither plot, nor style, nor construction – least of all my life, was my own. Berry's amendments alone may be imagined. They were, I suppose, at once the most comprehensive, devastating and utterly worthless ever conceived or expressed by any one man. Amid the sea of suggestion I began to labour and wallow, like a rudderless ship, and, when the others decided that the third chapter should be made the first and the first and second dissected and 'worked in' piecemeal towards the end of the book, I took the pages I had written and burned them before their eyes. This explosion of temper shocked them, and, before the winter evening was out, I had extracted the assurance that, if I started again, the subject should never be broached except by me. The next day I took the fair copy of the stuff I had burned, repaired to the library and strove to recover the course I had been proposing to steer.

Time passed, and the book took shape. Sometimes, when a chapter was finished, I would pull up the sluice of discussion, to see what they said; but the debate upon the last but one had proved so unsettling and provoked such a flurry of recrimination that I registered a definite vow to withstand all temptations to invite such vexation again. To this resolve I adhered, until the book had been printed and was beyond recall.

'You've *passed the proofs*?' said Berry.

Anyone would have thought from his tone that I had undertaken that he would become a monk.

'Quite right,' said I, lighting a cigarette. 'You have to do that, you know. Until you do, they can't start printing a book. You write "Press" on the top, and – '

'But I haven't seen them,' said Berry. 'They may be all wrong. Besides, I wrote most of the book. The conception burst from my brain. I supplied all the leaven. I – '

A storm of protest arose.

As it died down –

'I should certainly have seen them,' said Adèle. 'The love-affair was all my idea. Besides – '

'But I figure in it,' said Berry. 'My fragrant personality pervades the pages. The discerning reader will – '

'I play the chief part,' said Adèle. 'Jonah and I – '

'By request,' said I. 'I'm not at all certain that I should have given way. It's a question of sympathy.'

'Exactly,' said my brother-in-law. 'That's why I should have seen the proofs. I should have known in a moment. Have you said that my nose is aquiline?'

Jonah put in his oar.

'As juvenile lead and home-wrecker, I think I've a right to be told whether my *grande passion* is extinguished by the waters of death.'

'All in good time,' said I. 'In three months' time a trifling outlay of seven shillings and sixpence will – '

'Do you mean to say,' said Berry, 'that we're not to have free copies? Do you mean to stand there and – '

'I've got to live,' said I.

'No, you haven't,' said Berry. 'It's a work of supererogation.'

'Of course you must buy it,' said I. 'Why shouldn't you?'

'That's right,' said Berry. 'Bite the hand that feeds you. Savage the bosom in which you have lain. And we have allowed you to feature our dazzling personalities. But for the magic of our – Oh, you slow-belly.'

'How dare you?' said Daphne. 'You know that I will not have that disgusting phrase.'

'The occasion demands it,' said her husband. 'When I think – Did you put in that bit I gave you about the dog?'

'No, I didn't,' said I. 'I don't want the book to be banned.'

'I suppose you want it to be bought.' He shrugged his shoulders. 'Of course, where you let it right down is – '

'I know,' said I. 'By not making you the *deus ex machina*.'

My brother-in-law sighed.

'Well, it does stick out, doesn't it? Not that I care. It's the waste of good material that breaks my heart. There I am, with nothing to do. I ask you, what more natural than that I step in? The time produces the man. Is it likely that I should sit still and watch the bottom fall out for want of my outstretched hand? I mean, is that me?'

'Yes,' said everyone.

My brother-in-law frowned.

'At the critical moment,' he continued, 'I arrive at the castle, disguised as a Belgian count with boots three sizes too big and no roof to his mouth. Very good. Bewildered by my endeavours to ask my way, the villain drops an aitch. Unobserved I put my foot in it, and, while he is absorbed in his search for the missing aspirate, I step out of my boots and secrete myself in the arc-light – archway behind his back.'

'I've been writing a novel,' said I. 'Not the script of a travelling circus.'

'That's right,' said Berry. 'Be rude. Be offensive. Just because you've no sense of the dramatic – '

'Hush,' said Daphne. 'If Boy – '

'I won't hush,' said her husband. 'There was a tacit understanding that, if I consented to oblige that long-nosed fabulist . . .'

Here Falcon came in with the drinks, and the apodosis was lost.

As the butler withdrew, Adèle came behind my chair and put her arms round my neck.

'Don't leave me on the rack,' she said gently. 'Remember, I'm madly in love. If Jonah were to die . . .'

I looked up into her eyes.

'It's all right,' I said weakly. 'He – he doesn't die.'

The statement was accorded a mixed reception.

My wife and my sister applauded; Berry raised his eyes to heaven; and Jonah looked down his nose.

'Of course you've ruined it,' said Berry. 'Justice demands a victim. There's the ram all ready, caught by his corns – horns, and you ignore him. Besides, it's fantastic. He's an ounce of lead inside him and a cold on his chest. Does Adèle suck the wound?'

'Price seven and sixpence,' said I.

With an awful look, Berry returned to his glass.

Jonah fondled his pipe.

'I suppose you know best,' he said. 'But I don't see the point of the chapel, if it's not to be used.'

'Oh, no,' said my sister. 'That would have been too sad. The only thing I don't like . . .'

I left them to it, and went off to telephone.

Some two hours later, Adèle lay back on her pillows and knitted her brows.

'I do hope it goes well,' she said thoughtfully.

The profits of the book, if any, were to be spent upon the purchase of a solitaire diamond ring. There are, of course, solitaires and solitaires.

'So do I,' I said heartily.

'You don't think it would have been better to – '

'I'm sure it would,' said I. 'But it's too late now.'

Adèle sighed.

'Oh, well,' she said. 'We must hope for the best. Only, if you can't have a really big one, it's better not to have one at all. You see what I mean, don't you, Boy?'

'Let's hope they'll eat it,' said I. 'That would mean a bracelet as well.'

Three months had gone by, and the book had been on sale for nearly a week.

As I entered the dining-room –

'Two notices,' said Berry. 'One says, *Just the book for a hammock and a hot afternoon*, and the other's more cryptic. It says, *There is something about this book which formed a guard of honour. The best man was no more to be said*. I can't help feeling that – '

'It's scandalous,' said Daphne. 'Adèle and I have been right through the "Weddings", but there's nothing at all. Can't we write and complain?'

I shook my head.

'Out of the question,' I said. 'Besides, it may have been biting. After all, the hammock's bad enough. Might as well call the book a sleeping-draught and have done with it.'

'I think he means to be nice,' said Adèle. 'If I read that – By the way there's a letter the publishers have sent on.'

'From a literary agent,' said I, taking it up.

It was not from a literary agent. It was – but I will let the document speak for itself.

Sir,

I read your first book and it was alright. Now for your second. Do you for one moment imagine that your public is going to stand for this sort of thing? If so, you are very much mistaken. I am only speaking for thousands when I say that I am utterly disgusted by your fatuous glorification of a so-called love affair which must nauseate any decent-speaking man, woman or child. The whole thing is inexcusable. Thank God, I am not a writer, but, if you are so blind that you cannot realise that you cannot play fast and loose with those members of the public who in an idle moment have been so misguided as to ask for your books, then woe betide you. Some might call it impertinent of me to write thus. Far from it. I consider it my duty to expose the insult which you have gratuitously offered to the whole host of your well-

wishers who I am absolutely certain will unite with me in saying 'Never again.'

Yours faithfully,
E. D. Geoffray.

P.S. The rest of the book was quite alright, but you deliberately chose to degrade this by introducing a sordid note which will surely recoil upon your own head.

After digesting this outburst, I read it aloud.

There was a startled silence.

Then –

'There you are,' said Daphne. 'What did I say? I never wanted you to – '

'Nor did I,' said I. 'Over and over again I said it was alienating sympathy.'

Jonah and Adèle exchanged an uneasy glance.

'The man's a fool,' said Berry. He drained his cup. 'You've got to take life as you find it.'

'He's one of the public,' said I. 'And, as one of the public – '

'I don't imagine he's representative,' said Jonah. 'Personally, I think it was a very powerful bit of work. That bit where Adèle breaks down – '

'Of course,' said Berry. 'I always said that was dangerous.'

This was untrue. More. Had I adopted my brother-in-law's interpretation of 'a suitable love-interest', I should have made myself liable to arrest.

The barefaced mis-statement provoked great indignation.

'You?' said his wife. 'Why, when I wanted it out, you did nothing but rave. When Boy seemed to hesitate, you swore it would sell the book. You said it was a punch. You said – '

'Nonsense,' said Berry. 'I'm not going to argue, because I know it's no good, but, if my advice had been taken, that passage would have been excised.'

'What you mean is,' said Jonah, 'it would have been converted into a supercharged imitation of an advanced French farce. Mr Geoffray would have died of heart failure.'

'I agree with Jonah,' said Adèle. 'I don't believe he's representative. Besides, you can't please everyone.'

'If you ask me,' said Berry, 'the book's doomed. Never mind. Is anyone getting up? I want some more sole.'

I rose, passed to the sideboard, helped myself to some omelet and returned to my place.

With an awful look, Berry got to his feet. . . .

'The thing to do,' said Daphne, 'is to start a counter-attack. We must ask for it at all the bookstalls. We can begin today at Waterloo.'

'But supposing they've got it,' said Berry. 'Not that it's likely, but just supposing they have.'

'We can look first,' said my sister guardedly.

'That's right,' said Adèle. 'We can all go up separately and ask for it. Quite casually, you know. They'll be bound to have it tomorrow in self-defence.'

'And be laying for us,' said Jonah.

'Then we can say we've got it, or go down by car.'

Ascot. The weather was fine, the girls' dresses were outstanding, and Jonah had been given two very exceptional tips. We were quite expecting to enjoy ourselves to the full. Ten minutes ago our sky had been radiantly clear. It was still full of promise: only now Mr Geoffray's letter hung upon our brilliant horizon, a cloud like a man's hand.

Waterloo Station was busy. Quite a lot of people seemed to have had the idea of going to Ascot by train.

Adèle, Jonah and I had shared a taxi; my sister and Berry were coming on in the car.

Cautiously I approached the bookstall.

My book was nowhere to be seen.

Fortified by this insult, I leaned across a plateau of papers and mentioned its name.

The assistant appeared to reflect. Then he asked me when it was published and who it was by.

With a sickly smile, I gave him my pseudonym.

He turned to a colleague, frowning, and asked if they had the book.

His colleague did not even reply.

The assistant asked me to spell the author's name.

I did so miserably. Many persons were present, impatiently waiting to be served. The assistant and I were fully five feet apart.

'D'you know the publishers, sir?'

I gave him the publishers' name and wiped the sweat from my face.

The assistant glanced over my shoulder and turned to somebody else.

'Seven and sixpence, please, sir,' said a voice by my side.

I swung round to see his colleague with my book in his hand.

I paid for it dazedly.

As we passed on to the platform –

'Nothing like advertisement,' said Jonah. 'There were fourteen people behind you. If eight of them buy a copy, you'll be all square.'

Unable to think of an answer, I comforted myself with the thought that, with any luck, Berry would go the same way.

We passed down the platform leisurely.

'I think it's the best so far,' murmured Adèle. 'My dress, I mean.'

'Naturally,' said Jonah. 'America expects this day that every girl will do her duty.'

Adèle is American.

As the special drew in, Berry and Daphne appeared.

The latter was laughing, and the former had my book in his hand.

'Just the thing for Ascot,' he said, holding it up. 'I must find a quiet nook in the Enclosure and settle down. The nuisance is I've left the hammock behind. Oh, you've got one, too, have you? How exciting. Don't peep at the end, will you?' He laughed idiotically. 'Never occurred to you to stay and warn me, I suppose? No, I thought not. Perhaps you told them to keep the swine in a drawer?'

We calmed him down and took our seats in the train.

'Anyway,' said Adèle, bubbling, 'I'm sure it must have done good.'

'Nothing could have been better,' said Daphne. 'The people about were just the sort who buy books.'

'They denied themselves this morning,' said Berry. 'Not a soul in that station – '

'Only because they didn't want to have to carry them about. By the way, what shall we do with our copies? We can't leave them here.'

'Give them to the guard,' said Berry. 'Find out if he's got a hammock, and – '

'But we can't do that,' said Adèle. 'If we do, he won't buy one.'

Berry stifled an hysterical laugh.

'Nor – nor he will,' he said.

'We'd better destroy them,' said Jonah. 'Tear them to bits. If we each take two hundred pages – '

'Certainly not,' said I. 'We can't conceal the fragments, and people who find the fragments will naturally jump to the conclusion that it's a rotten book.'

'So it is,' said Berry. 'When I think – '

'We must put them in the cloakroom,' said Daphne. 'At the station, I mean.'

'That's right,' said her husband. 'Throw good money after bad. Unless you can tie them together, they'll charge you twopence each.'

'The porters 'll read them,' said Adèle.

'So much the better,' said Jonah. 'They won't have finished by five. We call for them then, and they'll have to buy a copy to see how it ends.'

'They can have mine for five shillings,' said Berry brokenly. 'When I think – '

'That'll do,' said everyone.

Berry put his hat on the rack, settled himself in a corner and closed his eyes.

After a little he appeared to be talking in his sleep.

Given a summer's day, Royal Ascot may be almost too good to be true. If it were a play, the stage-management would be hailed a miracle. But it is not a play. It is an English festival, kept by the English and their friends, with the King and Queen of England keeping it in their midst. More. It is a high festival. His Majesty is in his State.

Those who go down to the Heath in cars lose something which is of value, yet is not for sale.

A path leads out of the little country station, climbs through a hedgerow and gives to a proper hayfield, as sweet and fair and fresh as a meadow may be. Not a house, not a building is in sight. Except for the lazy hum of insects, there is no sound. Any one of those jolly haycocks might be hiding Boy Blue. And through this simple pleasance go strolling fine ladies and men. Lace and silk and satin, silver and gold: bracelets and brooches and buckles and tapestry-bags: purple and fine linen, patent leather and grey top-hats: dainty gowns out of Paris and exquisite legs: parasols and tail-coats and eye-glasses – fashion in all her glory making her way through a slice of a nursery rhyme. What stuff for old Aesop! Could he but look upon the picture, the sage would weep with delight.

Out of the peaceful meadow and into a wood, set like a pretty bulwark to save the pastoral, and so, in a moment, on to a broad highway, alive with cars and policemen and all the fuss of arrivals and settings down.

So much for the prologue. . . .

The beauty of the course and its surroundings, the rich green of the turf, the sparkle of the clean, white paintwork, the sharp shadows flung by the stands make up a setting which only some shining function could ever fill: the flowers, the fine green liveries of the servants, the brave show and promise of the Royal Box, above all, the air of expectation deck and furnish that setting to a degree of quality very seldom met with in this workaday world: and the ceaseless movement of thousands, eager, carefree, yet full-dressed and on parade, renders a Court of Honour fit for a King.

Shortly before the first race, far down the course, a glittering streak upon the green argues a cavalcade.

Very slowly the procession takes shape.

Scarlet and gold and velvet, wigs and cockades, postilions and outriders, and the magnificent greys, down the midst of the broad, green lane at a royal pace come the King's horses and the King's men. And the King and his Queen in their carriage, with equerries riding beside and their train behind. Match me that quiet progress, match me that sight in the sunshine, match me the brilliance of that moment – tradition itself ennobled by the unceremonious perfection with which it is observed.

Then the Royal Standard is broken, and the festival is begun.

Of the racing itself, I will say nothing. My pen cannot picture the finest meeting in the world. But, if a man loves horses, an hour in the paddock at Ascot will do his heart good. The parades, too, are incomparable. Enough that the *raison d'être* of Ascot is never overshadowed by the glory it has come to acquire.

I cannot pretend that we had what is called 'a good day'.

Had Adèle and I been wise, we should have lunched with Berry in the Marlboroughs' tent. But we were not wise. After the first race, we crossed the course and lunched in the tent of a Club to which I belong. As we finished our coffee, I looked at my watch.

'We ought to be going,' said I, 'or we shan't get across.'

'Have mercy,' said Adèle. 'Let me have one more cigarette.'

Ascot is Ascot. For the next three hours she would be unable to smoke.

Looking upon her, no man could have hardened his heart. Had she accompanied Moses to Pharaoh's throne, there would have been no plagues in Eygpt.

'One quick one,' said I, weakly.

Ten minutes later we were standing between two coaches about eleven paces from a gate in the rails. The coaches were three feet apart and the space between them was choked with the fashionable world. From the fact that we could not go forward I judged that the gate was shut. Because of the people behind us, we could not go back.

'Oh, Boy,' murmured my wife, 'what have I done?'

'Entirely my fault,' said I. 'I ate too much lunch.'

This was true. But for my 'repeat order' of lobster salad –

'I shouldn't read it,' said a voice. 'It doesn't come up to his last.'

The voice was feminine and came from directly behind.

Unable to move my body, I managed to screw my head round and look at Adèle. A bright, brown eye met mine expressively.

'Ah,' said another voice. 'That's often the way.'

'It begins all right,' said the first, 'but – '

'They're going up,' said the other. 'I hear the hoofs.'

We all heard them.

After a seemingly interminable interval we heard them again.

An occupant of one of the coaches was kind enough to tell us what had won the race of the day.

Ten minutes later I learned that the horse which Jonah had commended had been left at the post. Even so he ran fourth. If only . . .

When I say that, half an hour later, our second string won by a length, only to be disqualified, I think we may be forgiven for leaving before the last race.

The charm of the epilogue, however, was irresistible. The cool grove, the shadows of the elms athwart the hayfield, the pretty argument of antique toil came straight from Virgil. By the time we reached the station, I think we all felt refreshed.

Not until we were halfway to town did Adèle remember with a shock that the porters at Ascot station must still be devouring my book.

Ten o'clock that evening found us at ease in the library, licking our wounds.

Berry was writing a letter, Daphne was studying the papers, with a faint frown my wife was lining a delicate tapestry bag. Jonah and I were doing mental arithmetic of which the hypothetical problems were even more depressing than those which dealt with the truth.

'Of course they were discussing it,' said Daphne. 'Tell us again – what exactly did they say?'

'They said,' said Adèle, 'they said it began splendidly.'

Berry spoke over his shoulder.

'That doesn't sound like it,' he said. 'Mr Geoffray – '

'By the way,' said Jonah, 'you'll have to answer the wallah. What are you going to say?'

'I shall ignore him,' I said. 'I don't think he's qualified to judge. Counting the bookstall, I'm thirty-four pounds three and sixpence down on the day. Oh, and an evening paper, three and seven.'

'Ignore the man,' said my sister, 'as much as you like, but you can't ignore what he says. It's perfectly plain that he doesn't stand alone. Can't you write to the publishers and get them to stop the sale?'

'That shouldn't be difficult,' said her husband. 'And they might return the money for copies already sold. I know a man who's got one.'

'Can't you alter the next edition?' said Adèle. 'I mean, I still think it's all right, but, after that woman at Ascot . . . Did you notice her hat?'

'I hated her voice,' said I.

'Well, her hat was worse.'

She described it to Daphne with every circumstance of contempt. The two drifted into an arraignment of the hats they had seen that day.

Jonah stepped to the fireplace and knocked out his pipe.

'A revue,' he said, 'has two editions, from the second of which are omitted the less popular features of the first. Why not a book?'

'The cases are different,' said I. 'You don't print a revue. Besides, I can't possibly rewrite it.'

'Only two chapters,' said Adèle. 'Possibly three.'

'It's out of the question,' said I. 'Once a book's printed – finish. It stands or falls.'

Adèle regarded her delicate, bare right hand.

' "When unadorned, adorned the most",' I said swiftly.

My wife returned to her bag.

'That woman,' she said, 'was wearing a solitaire. It was square-cut and as big as a postage stamp.'

'But she was behind us,' I cried. 'How could you possibly – '

'D'you mean to say you didn't see it?' said Adèle.

Where other women's gems are concerned, women seem to be gifted with second sight.

Berry laid down his pen.

'I think this should do,' he said. 'Listen to this.

E. D. Geoffray, Esq.

My dear Sir,

Your kindly communication was of peculiar interest to me, and I should, indeed, be committing that most repugnant of all sins, ingratitude, were I not to render you my most heartfelt thanks for a criticism, not only suave and searching, but in itself a literary gem. In this connection allow me to say with what triumph I hail your spelling "alright". Years ago, at a kindergarten, a governess had the effrontery to correct me for the use of that written word – as you will surmise, an arrogant, flat-chested woman, totally unfitted for the high office which she sought to adorn. Besides, her teeth shook. But to the point.

For me to essay to dispute your estimate of my endeavours would be indecent. With unerring instinct you have in a sentence laid bare the nakedness of the land. But, believe me, my dear Mr Geoffray, I not only accept your masterly and, to my mind, irrefutable appreciation, but I have the honour to identify myself with every word that you write. I will go further. I regard the love affair as the crowning insult of what I can only style an obscene libel calculated to arouse the worst instincts of all who pick it up. You know. Trunk murders, etc. We are, therefore, my dear sir, at one, for I cannot help feeling that a natural leniency induced you to write encouragingly of the less offensive parts.

What, to my mind, is so distressing, is that, as you will no doubt have observed, the Press seems not only to be totally indifferent to this glaring defect, but actually to welcome a document which you so aptly describe as inexcusable. Without one dissentient voice, the public prints have seen fit to commend this apotheosis of blackguardism in the most glowing terms. I have before me a notice urging all lovers of nature and repose to lose no time in acquiring a copy of my book. Worse. The rot has set in, and I have good reason to believe that only this morning there was an unprecedented demand for my novel by persons en route for Ascot, where, I am told, there was horse-racing today.

In these circumstances it is not easy to maintain a stiff upper lip. Indeed, but for the timely arrival of your comfortable words, I might by now have bowed to the consensus of opinion, smothered the dictates of conscience and held my peace: but, now that I know that I am not alone, now that I have before me your fearless denunciation of this outrage, my fainting convictions rise up like giants refreshed and I am emboldened to look press, publishers and public in the face and cry "Quot homines, tot sententiae", *or, as they say at the Athenaeum, "One girl's scent is another girl's sewer-gas".*

Believe me, my dear Mr Geoffray,

Yours very faithfully.'

We all tried not to laugh.

At length –

'The idea's sound,' said Jonah. 'I think it should be bowdlerised and sent. You'll make a friend, and Geoffray will recommend the book.'

'Of course he won't,' said Daphne. 'And what about all the thousands that haven't written? Just because they don't write and say so, it doesn't follow they don't dislike the book.'

'Too many negatives,' said Berry. 'What you mean is – '

'I mean what I say,' said his wife. 'People won't like that love scene.'

'What does that matter?' said Berry. 'They can't get their money back. That's good old Geoffray's trouble. He's soaked in seven and sixpence, and he thinks he's been done.'

'They'll tell one another,' said Adèle. 'Think of the damage this wretched man, Geoffray, will do.'

My sister laid a hand on my arm.

'If you wrote back and said, "You're quite right, and, as soon as I can, I'm going to alter the book – " '

'And did it,' said Jonah.

'Couldn't you, darling?' said Adèle. 'Couldn't you write to the publishers and say that, as some of the book seems to be misunderstood, you propose to alter those bits before the next edition comes out?'

'I should only get a back answer.'

'Why not do it, and see what they say?'

'That's right,' said Berry. 'If they agree, all you've got to do is to rewrite the book. And, while you're about it, if you take my advice, you'll change the title. I'll answer any letters you get.'

'Be quiet,' said his wife. 'Except for the one chapter, the book's all right. Even Geoffray says so. If Boy alters that and – and just a few lines in the last . . .'

With many misgivings, I posted the following letter before I retired.

Messrs. – and Co.,
Publishers.

Dear Sirs,

To judge from the reception of my book, there seems to be a considerable consensus of opinion that the love-interest does not command sufficient sympathy. With your permission, therefore, I propose to revise this passage and to let you have the new version in time for it to appear in the second edition of the book.

Yours faithfully,

Etc.

Some eighteen hours had gone by, and the third day's racing at Ascot was nearly done. They were, in fact, going out for the seventh race.

'Don't you see it?' said Adèle. 'That woman with the blue silk scarf and the frightening hat.'

'Which hand?' said I.

'The left. There. Now you can see it. That's just about the size I should like.'

It seemed to me an admirable stone. Not too big. I estimated its value, roughly, at four hundred pounds.

With a sigh, I returned to my race-card.

'I – I don't think you'll get it,' said I.

Even without Mr Geoffray and all his works, I could not see one of my own bearing blossoms like that.

'I refuse to give up hope,' said Adèle.

I laid down my card.

'You know what got Geoffray's goat?'

'What?' said Adèle.

'Your coquetry – vampship. Scarlet is not in your line, and your wearing it stuck in his throat.'

'Ambition is always contrary. Grimaldi's one idea was to play Richard the Third.'

'But he didn't do it,' said I. 'His wife was wiser than I.'

'My great adventure,' said Adèle affectionately. 'I shan't like the second edition half so well. And you must admit, Jonah is most attractive. Any woman might be forgiven for falling for him.'

'You ought to have married him,' said I.

A distant look came into my lady's eyes.

'I don't think so,' she said slowly. 'It wouldn't have worked, because – well, it's very true that saying, "Where your treasure is, there will your heart be also".'

I returned to my card. One cannot be demonstrative in front of the Royal Box. Besides, if I was to have a bet, I must make up my mind.

Moodily, for the twentieth time, I read through the horses' names. Not one of the seventeen meant anything to me. Even Jonah had had nothing to say. The favourite would probably start at seven to four.

WARSAW
PENMANSHIP
USAGE
NEST EGG
BALADEUSE
EDGE OF FRAY . . .

For a moment I sat staring. Then, with a stifled cry, I leapt to my feet.

'For heaven's sake, Boy,' breathed Adèle.

I pointed a shaking finger.

'*Look!*'

'Edge of Fray?' she murmured. 'Well, what about it? I've never heard of the horse.'

'But, my blessed lady,' I cried, 'you've heard of the man! *E. D. Geoffray.*' Adèle caught her breath. 'Try and find the others an' . . .'

I left her frantically peering and almost ran to the ring.

I got two hundred pounds to ten pounds – and got it twice. Four hundred pounds to twenty against Edge of Fray. I could have got it ten times, if I had had the notes. As I was counting my silver to make up another pound, the race was begun.

Trying to look unconcerned, I hurried across the lawn.

'Blue and white check, blue cap.'

Of the others I could see nothing. Even Adèle had disappeared. . . .

By dint of standing a-tiptoe, I saw a ruck of horses sweep into the straight.

A blue roan was leading, with a chestnut lying second and going well. On their left a big bay – *The colours of the bay's jockey were blue and white check.*

The angle at which I viewed them grew less acute. The chestnut was gaining on the roan, and the bay on them both. The whips were out now, and I saw the roan's rider call upon his mount. The latter was holding the chestnut. If the bay had made his effort . . . People were shouting in the stands, and the woman in the frightening hat obstructed my view. As I jerked my head to one side, I saw the bay shoot forward. . . .

The papers that evening said that he won by a head.

Less than half an hour had gone by.

'I won't travel with him,' said Berry. 'I won't demean myself by – '

'Will you get in?' said his wife.

In a thunderous silence her husband entered the coach.

As the special drew out of the station –

'My first thought was for you,' I said. 'The instant I saw it, I sent Adèle to find you and put you wise.'

'I demand,' said Berry, 'I demand two hundred pounds. In my unavoidable absence, you put on ten pounds for me. I hereby ratify your action.'

'Nonsense,' said I. 'I hadn't enough for myself. If you hadn't been drinking – '

'You hear that?' said Berry excitedly. 'You hear what he says? Because I withdraw for five minutes to compose my thoughts, that venomous reptile – '

'I must say,' said Jonah, 'I think you might have seen it before.'

'You had a race-card,' said I. 'Why shouldn't you have seen it? Just because – '

'Why should we?' said Berry. 'What's E. D. Geoffray to us? But he's *your* correspondent, your critic – the only critic you've got. You've done nothing but belch his name – '

A shriek from Adèle and Daphne brought him to book. Before they could frame a protest –

'I beg your pardon,' he said. 'Regurgitate. You've done nothing but regurgitate his name for thirty-six hours; and the first time you see it printed, it takes you an afternoon to read it straight. Talk about writing books? You ought to have spelling lessons.'

'Too late now,' said Jonah mournfully. 'Just 've put me right, too. How much did you have on Usage?'

'Usage?' said I. 'I didn't have anything on.'

'I don't know why you didn't,' said Jonah. 'It was quite a good thing. Not like Edge of Fray, naturally. Still, it ran third, and I said "Only back it for a place." '

'You didn't say it to me,' said I. 'You talk about suppressing information, but – '

My cousin regarded Berry with an accusing eye.

'I gave it to you,' he said slowly. 'I gave it to you, and you promised to pass it on.'

Berry gave a start of surprise.

'You gave it to me, and I – oh, you must be dreaming,' he said. 'I have a faint recollection that you mentioned some horse, but I certainly never – '

'Oh, you liar,' said his wife. 'You rushed off to wire directly. I saw you go.'

Berry swallowed desperately.

'My dear, I – '

'So that's where you were,' said I. ' "Composing your thoughts", were you? Instead of putting me wise, you deliberately – '

'There was no time,' said Berry. 'I was down to thirty shillings. If I was to put on a tenner, I had to wire. If I'd tried to find you, I should have been too late. Surely it was better that one – '

'And you have the nerve to – '

'I acted for the best,' said Berry. 'Confronted with a painful decision, I – '

'I don't see your trouble,' said Jonah. 'You've won thirty pounds on Usage, and you couldn't have won any more on Edge of Fray. On your own confession, you'd only thirty shillings to put on.'

Berry waved him away.

'It isn't the money,' he said. 'It's the principle.'

I had telephoned to Bond Street from the course, so that, though the shop was closed, a pleasant assistant was waiting to show us some solitaire rings.

We got a very nice one for the sum of four hundred pounds.

When we re-entered the taxi, Adèle put her arms round my neck.

'Now you have made me a vampire. You've invested me with the order, the Order of the Dangerous Vampire, the ODV.'

'I'm afraid it's not so big as the woman's in the frightening hat.'

'My dear, it's miles better. Hers was quite yellow. I thought it was a topaz, at first. But this . . .' She held off her slim, white hand. 'You must admit it is a most lovely sight.'

'I've always thought so,' said I.

So we came to the house.

A letter from the publishers lay in the hall.

This was a model of courteous reassurance.

They were greatly obliged: at the same time they could not help feeling: indeed, they had every reason to anticipate: finally they begged to remain.

Reading between the lines, I was forced to the reluctant conclusion that the thought of a second edition had not so much as entered their heads.

But nothing could prick the hide of my content. That was invulnerable.

After dinner I wrote to Mr Geoffray – a cordial, grateful letter, full of goodwill.

I said it was worth writing a book, if only to receive a letter from such a man.

So it was.

SELECT BIBLIOGRAPHY

Berry and Co – Berry and Daphne Pleydell, Boy Pleydell, Jonah and Jill Mansel – appear in many of Dornford Yates's non-Berry books and stories, either as walk-on parts or as off-stage characters whose adventures and lifestyle are mentioned and commented upon – 'Berry and Co are sure to be there' (*Anthony Lyveden*, 1921); 'Repeat the (tale) about "Red Violets" and how Boy Pleydell refused to give you away. I've known him for years' (*The Stolen March*, 1926); 'This, dear, is Major Pleydell – a very old friend' ('Susan', *And Five Were Foolish*, 1924); 'Berry would never survive a winter here. He's quite all right by Lisbon' (*Ne'er-Do-Well*, 1954).

The core-Berry saga is as follows:

The Brother of Daphne, Ward Lock, 1914
The Courts of Idleness, Ward Lock, 1920 (Book II, 'How Others Left The Courts Only To Return', only)
Berry And Co, Ward Lock, 1921
Jonah And Co, Ward Lock, 1922
Adèle And Co, Hodder & Stoughton, 1931
And Berry Came Too, Ward Lock, 1936
The House That Berry Built, Ward Lock, 1945
The Berry Scene, Ward Lock, 1947
As Berry And I Were Saying, Ward Lock, 1952
B-Berry And I Look Back, Ward Lock, 1958

Most of the stories in the Berry saga were written for the *Windsor Magazine*, from 1911 to 1935, and then collected into book form. The stories in this collection originally appeared as follows:

Windsor Magazine

November 1919: Nemesis (*The Courts of Idleness*)
December 1919: A Blue Letter Day (*Berry And Co*, as 'How Will Noggin Was Fooled . . .')
March 1920: The Unknown Quality (*Berry And Co*, as 'How Daphne Wrote For Assistance . . .')

August 1920: Too Many Cooks (*Berry And Co*, as 'How Jonah Obeyed His Orders . . .')

September 1920: A Trick of Memory (*Berry And Co*, as 'How Jill Slept Undisturbed . . .')

November 1920: A Lesson In Latin (*Berry And Co*, as 'How Adèle Broke Her Dream . . .')

May 1922: Red Violets (*Jonah And Co*, as 'How Adèle Bought A Bottle Of Perfume . . .')

June 1922: Zero (*Jonah And Co*, as 'How Jonah Took Off His Coat . . .')

July 1922: No Thoroughfare (*Jonah And Co*, as 'How Berry Sought Comfort In Vain . . .')

September 1922: Journey's End (*Jonah And Co*, as 'How A Telegram Came for Jill . . .')

January 1929: Letters Patent (*Maiden Stakes*, 1929)

August 1935: The Abbey Plate, as 'Black Magic' (*And Berry Came Too*, as 'How Daphne Was Given a Present...')

October 1935: Infamous Relics, as 'Spade Work' (*And Berry Came Too*, as 'How Berry Met His Match...')

The Gypsy's Warning and The Fairy Child were written for the first edition of *Jonah And Co* as the Prologue and the Epilogue respectively. They do not appear in most subsequent editions (at least, after *ca* 1925).

ACKNOWLEDGEMENTS

My thanks go to John Jeffries and, especially, Peter Tyas (a compiler of extremely useful lists), Dornford Yates advocates both, who have each, in one way or another, expressed their enthusiasm for the Berry saga. Grateful thanks as ever to my old friend Bill Lofts, whose doughty endeavours in the British Library take much of the slog out of this kind of thing.

J.A.